Taking the Cross
by Charles Gibson

ISBN 978-1-940192-27-7

All Bible verses are from the *New American Standard Bible,*
Copyright © 1960, 1962, 1963, 1968, 1971, 1972, 1973, 1975, 1977, 1995
by The Lockman Foundation.

Occitan translations are from *Introduction to Old Occitan,*
Copyright © 1998 by William D. Paden.

Published by
◣ köehlerbooks ™

210 60th Street
Virginia Beach, VA 23451
212-574-7939
www.koehlerbooks.com

TAKING
THE CROSS

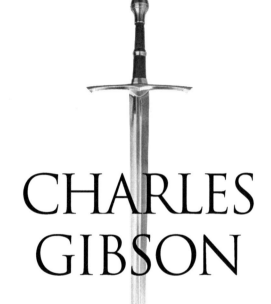

CHARLES
GIBSON

VIRGINIA BEACH
CAPE CHARLES

For Tricia, Trenton, and Logan

and

For those who seek to
bring freedom to others.

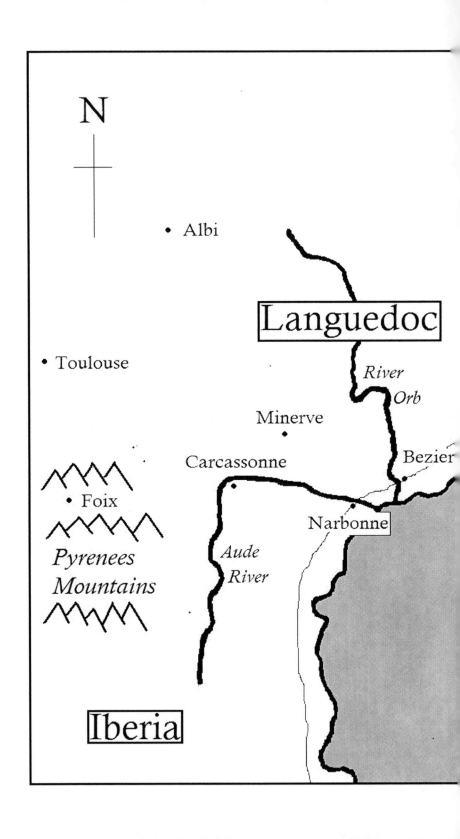

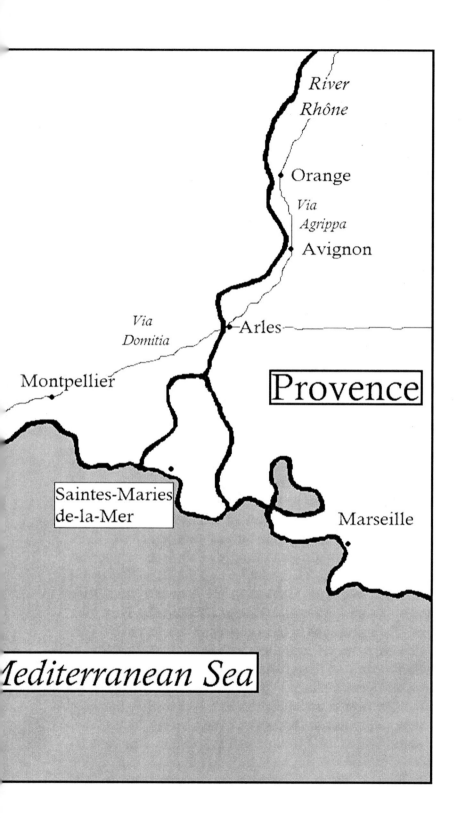

*River
Rhône*

• Orange

*Via
Agrippa*

• Avignon

*Via
Domitia*

•Arles

Provence

Montpellier
•

Saintes-Maries
de-la-Mer

Marseille
•

Mediterranean Sea

HISTORICAL NOTE

In June 1209, a crusading army assembled at Lyons, France. Its charge was to purge heretics from a Christian realm of France known as the Languedoc (Lan-gwuh-dock). It was the first crusading force raised solely to invade Christian lands. The members of the warring host bore a scarlet cross upon their garments, a symbol of the papal promise to pardon their sins. Pope Innocent III (1198-1216) desired to grow the power of the Catholic Church throughout Christendom.

The endeavor became known as the Albigensian Crusade. Two factions were its target. The primary mark was the Albigensians, or *Albigenses* as they were known in the tongue of the land. The city of Albi in the Languedoc was known for its large numbers of ascetics who called themselves *Bons Hommes* (Good Men). Those outside the Languedoc dubbed them *Albigenses*. Its adherents were not only in Albi but were spread throughout the domain. The second group that faced the sword was the Waldensians, or *Valdenses*, the Poor of Lyons. They were the outlawed followers of Vaudes (Waldo), the Poor Man of Lyons. Their presence in the Languedoc was extensive also. The *Valdenses* were lay preachers who issued proclamation of their beliefs openly on the streets. They were denied permission to preach and were declared heretical.

In the late twelfth and early thirteenth centuries, the most prominent nobles of the Languedoc gave freedom to both factions. Rome proselytized those deemed apostate. Innocent III preferred to see all the wayward in the Languedoc turn to the Catholic Church. Yet converts were few among heretics. The nobles who protected them, who dared allow religious freedom in their lands, in particular Viscount Raimon Roger Trencavel of Carcassonne, became an anathema to Rome.

In January 1208, a papal legate to the Languedoc, Pierre de Castelnau, was murdered. After the death of the pope's man, the Catholic Church dispensed with peaceful proselytizing. In March 1208, Innocent III proclaimed the Albigensian Crusade against heresy. It took a little more than a year to assemble the host for battle. After departing Lyons in June 1209, the force marched south along the River Rhône and reached the Languedoc in July.

The city of the Languedoc, foremost in the battle plan of the Crusaders, was a hilltop citadel called Beziers. Its lord was Raimon Roger Trencavel, the Viscount of Carcassonne, Albi, and Beziers. Upon hearing that the host drew near to his lands, Raimon Roger rode out with his cavaliers from the mighty stronghold of Carcassonne. The Viscount was to seek a meeting with the living papal legate, the monk Armand Amaury, commander of the crusading army.

CHAPTER 1

18 JULY 1209

The boy did not recoil at the charge of the cavaliers.

"Make way!" Andreas drove his snorting stallion toward the courageous youth. The filthy wretch trudged toward the charging cavalier, one barefoot step after the other. He was unflinchingly alone. All other refugees crowded in road ditches, leaned toward the trees, clutching them tightly.

"Make way for the Viscount!" Andreas called as a stone unleashed from a catapult. He was accustomed to having others move with speed at his commands, as if a boulder soared down upon their heads. Andreas waved his arm furiously, gesturing toward the tree line.

Still the boy plodded along the road with uncovered feet, skin on rock. A darkened mist seemed to enshroud his very soul. Since cockcrow, when their company had made departure from Beziers, Andreas had commanded all in their path to flee the road. Each traveler and refugee, whether merchant in dyed cotton or peasant in beast-colored rags, had given deference to their noble party as expected. A wide berth to fly along the road without hindrance.

Yet a little child refused to yield.

Andreas felt a strong urge to ride over the boy, to send a message to any who would dare block the way. He shook the shrill thought from his mind, searched for a spot to vacate the stone-paved road. Yet, amidst the throngs of refugees massed in the shallow, grassy ditches, pressed tight against the stands of oak and poplar and beech, there was no such place.

Space enough for a little one only, not an armed cavalcade of four and twenty.

Andreas drew rein on his muscular blackish-roan stallion. The horse reared. Its front hooves pawed with violence. Andreas slid back against the cantle of the saddle. He raised high the lance in his right hand as his left clung tightly to the reins.

"All halt!" He felt his face grow hot. The company came to an abrupt halt behind him, iron horseshoes grinding, sparking on ancient stone pavement. The barefoot wretch was a senseless intrusion. The front legs of his mount found the road once more. Andreas saw that the boy was playing no foolish game. In spite of the azure brilliance of the clear, high Languedoc sky, the close sight of the lad induced a quick, darkening chill, and Andreas shivered.

The youngster's dark, round eyes appeared sunken into his thin, sallow face. It was a countenance erratically framed by stringy, greasy black hair that hung down to his neck. His hollow gaze was fixed straight ahead at all and nothing. His undyed tunic was riven in jagged, diagonal fashion across the torso, blotted with brownish, crusty stains. A sour stench filled Andreas's nostrils, drew water from his eyes, and he turned away. The lad bore an alarming, tart odor of befouled blood and of death. But it seemed more than the smell of the unwashed. The reek seemed somehow to exude from his immortal soul itself, or even supplant it, as if the innards of the boy were being consumed by a fire unseen. A cauterized soul smoldering in a blackened cloud.

The boy continued to walk. He came within a step of the forelegs of Andreas's mount. The knight drew breath to bellow at him once more. A man, seemingly the father of the boy, emerged quickly from the compacted mass of peasants on the side of the road. He harshly clamped a sizeable, rough-hewn hand on the shoulder of the lad. Why had the fool not kept close vigil over his wretched child?

Andreas turned his hot anger on the sullied man. Tunic tattered, red hair matted and lengthy, he looked little better kempt than the boy. "Your son has detained us here and we need reach Montpellier by nightfall. Does he lack hearing?" Andreas squared his shoulders. "Your Viscount is on an urgent mission. Now yield the road."

"Many apologies, my lords, for the insolence of the boy." The man released the words in breathless gasps, turned his wary countenance and disheveled body to face Andreas. "We flee the approaching host, like all... all others in your sight." He waved his arm at the masses of refugees.

They shuffled forward and broke like a beast-colored wave around the knights, sought not to appear as if they were watching the peculiar sight of a commoner addressing his lord on the road. Andreas thought the lot of them grubby and gaunt from the journey through a sun-scorched land where dust and moisture saturated the air. Many among them had the look of fretful exhaustion, brittle terra cotta masks of fear. None seemed as the peasant lad.

The hands of the man rested on the shoulders of his little boy. "As you can see, my son stumbles around as one in a trance. If I may beg pardon, my lords, I will tell... tell of all that has befallen us." The hands of the man trembled as he gripped tight the boy. The father was clearly fear struck. The son was almost vacuous; a fleshy shell devoid of spirit.

"Continue, but speak with haste," said the rider alongside Andreas. The voice belonged to Raimon Roger Trencavel I, Viscount of Carcassonne, Albi, and Beziers. He was lord of these lands. Andreas was *châtelain* to the Viscount, nearly the equal in stature to Raimon Roger himself. Nearly, but not quite. The *châtelain* was the official given charge, among other things, for the safeguarding of the Viscount, and for the governing of the Trencavel castle, the *Chateau Comtal* in Carcassonne. The English counterpart was called a castellan. *Châtelain* was a position of rank rooted many centuries past in the time of the Frankish Merovingian kings. In those times, such an official had been called the mayor of the palace.

Andreas the *châtelain* blinked his smallish hazel eyes, rubbed his straight square nose, puckered his wide mouth, and with no small difficulty stifled a deep groan at the words of his lord. For they were words that meant their company would be stationary, at least for these few moments while the villager gave voice to his woes. Andreas removed his helmet and straightened his sweat-soaked, rumpled brown hair with a black leather gloved hand. He watched the throngs trudge by beneath him. So many flee in distress. *Why lend this one his noble ear?* Yet Raimon Roger was ever willing to hear from his subjects, to speak with them personally. It was a generosity he bestowed too liberally on his people.

Andreas placed the burnished steel helmet back upon his head. He cursed the delay under his breath. With the armies of the North drawn near, safety lay in motion. Andreas looked up and down the straight Roman road they traveled. The *Via Domitia* it was called. He saw none other than those fleeing to Beziers. Yet he was leery. Remaining still on the road was akin to surrender. Andreas could fight his way through any trap as long as he met the challenge at full battle charge.

In Iberia, seven years past, on the way to battle in Reconquista, the endeavor to reclaim Spain from the Muhammadan, their company had halted at the sound of crackling from the wood at twilight. A company of Moors twice their number had emerged from cover and attacked with disarming speed. In their light armor and atop agile mounts, thin swords hacking and slashing, the enemy retreated before the knights of the Languedoc could give chase. The Moors had charged again from another angle, and once more retreated. This was repeated thrice more until the knights were vigilant to the point of skittishness.

Andreas, only sixteen, newly dubbed a cavalier, had grown angry. "No more defenses. We attack! Who will follow?" Though he lacked the authority, most were of the same mind and followed eagerly. The rest were compelled to take up the charge or be abandoned. Andreas led the attack. Raimon Roger followed. The Moors converged on the road once more. They could not withstand the galloping force of the more heavily armored knights from the Languedoc. All the Muhammadans, though their numbers were greater, were slain in the saddle or unhorsed and trampled.

Upon hearing tell of the event, Andreas's father had told him only that he was reckless, that he should have known his place and kept formation. Yet Raimon Roger had given commendation to his impetuous knight. Andreas had admired his lord's frank acceptance of the usurpation of his authority. Since that day, Andreas had held charge over older men. Raimon Roger had eventually elevated him to *châtelain,* a position that in France was a title of heredity. He could have received no greater honor from his lord.

The fact that a little boy this day dared defy the cavalier who had risen to be *châtelain* to the Viscount of Carcassonne, Albi, and Beziers was like a mouthful of raw vinegar. It set Andreas's teeth on edge.

The boy's father continued to speak, eyes darting to and fro like a hare chased by the hounds. "Many thanks, my lord. It is a blessing to... to set eyes upon you my Viscount. My son and I have endured sorrow beyond telling. The cavaliers from the North raided our... our village two days past. They must be the *Frances* we heard of, for they spoke a... a strange tongue. They stole the chickens and beehives from the village and slay... slay all who dared oppose them."

The man's stumbling way of talk grated in a sickeningly raw way on Andreas, like the squeal of a pig at slaughter. But he kept rein on his tongue.

The boy now had head pressed against the man's belly and shook ever so slightly. The man drew the lad in closer and spoke. "His older brother, Jaufre, grabbed a staff as a weapon and struck at one. Before he could swing twice, one of the knights slashed him across the belly and ran him through the heart."

He made a cutting motion with his arm. His own chest and belly heaved as one. Tears slowly escaped the corners of the man's eyes. They traced tributaries through the gritty layer of gray dirt upon his leathery, wrinkled cheeks, slid down into his reddish beard growth. "They slashed also at little Miquel for sport and made him bleed." He clutched anew at his living son. "Now we seek refuge at Beziers."

"Like so many others." Andreas stared absently down the road at naught, felt the sting of remorse lodged as an arrow afire in his soul. The callousness of the French to slay a child in such a fashion was disturbing, a thing that exceeded the ferocity of battle. "We rode from Beziers this morn. Every hour its numbers burgeon with those who flee the scourge from the North. The road has been thick this day with others such as you."

Andreas turned to look the man in the eye, slowly drew a breath, and exhaled. "In truth, it is I who should issue apology for being so harsh. Pray accept my condolences and those of your Viscount for the most cruel death of your son. Truly we are sorry." Andreas cast a quick glance at Raimon Roger, who nodded solemnly. "We ride to Montpellier to avert war, but it seems conflict has consumed already your house."

He felt the anger rising yet again in his voice, but not toward the villager in front of him. "Had we but been there, these hell spawn, with no sense of *Paratge*, would have been slain to a man." Andreas tightened his hold of the black leather grip of his newly sharpened longsword, pressed his hand hard against the straight silver crossguard.

Andreas noticed the shifting of hooves and the snorting of nostrils. The mounts grew nervous. Was a wild boar close by, running its trampled paths through the wood?

"It was a strange thing, my lord," continued the villager, "for it is not easy to ride into our village unseen and unheard and yet these knights did so. We had no knowledge of their presence until they were upon us. Jaufre witnessed them first. We could do nothing... nothing but let him bleed and watch... watch the knights ride off with our chickens and beehives, at least those they did not smash with clubs." The man furrowed his brow. "They kept giving utterance to a word, one that was strange to my ears. Its sound was like..." The face of the man twisted and his mouth puckered. "Like *Melimarpera*."

The horses grew ever more agitated. Andreas thought he heard bees buzzing. *Melimarpera*? Andreas turned to Raimon Roger and spoke tersely. "My lord, as it is we are already desperately short of time this day. We best continue if we would make Montpellier by nightfall." For reasons he could not take hold of, Andreas felt anxious once more to abandon this dialogue. His own mount now sidestepped back and forth. It was as when they had faced the Moors. Yet he caught neither sound nor movement from the wood.

The Viscount seemed to ignore Andreas, turned to the villager. "Have you provision enough for the remainder of your trek?"

Another knight called out from their troop. "My lord, we have spare loaves of bread and full skins of water." It was Bertran. "Hunger and thirst are no friends of the traveler." Bertran rode to the front and handed down provisions to the man.

"Bless you, sir," was all he uttered.

Bertran leaned in close to the man, almost in an embrace, so near that Andreas could scarce discern his words. "We all lament your loss, for it is grave indeed. Yet tell me this, and you may think it strange, but it is in truth a matter of great import. What number of your hives did the green cavaliers thieve?"

The man looked around once more, as if for an unseen enemy on the hunt. He appeared perplexed, unsure if he should give reply. But he did, in a voice that matched the slight volume of Bertran. "They smashed so many, I am unsure... No, it was seven. By the devil, they thieved seven. They were careful about that. They stuffed seven hives into large, heavy woolen sacks, heavy enough to block a bee sting. They rode off after that in haste, the lot of them."

What did it matter the number of beehives? Bertran often issued such questions and statements with meaning unknown.

Bertran gave no perceptible response. Yet he looked again to the dense wood as he directed his white stallion back to his place in the ranks.

Andreas followed Bertran's movement with his eyes, returned his glance to the villager.

"I know the pain of death little one," said Raimon Roger, looking upon Miquel, "for my father gave up the ghost when I was but a boy." There was an emotive, bone-scraping twinge in his voice, one that gave reminder that Raimon Roger rarely spoke such things merely out of courtesy. Never had Andreas seen a lord who possessed such empathy for his lessers. Raimon Roger shifted his gaze to the boy's father. "Yet this hour grants us no time to mourn. May *Deu* spare us all in these evil days. Stay close to your living son, and make quick on your journey to sanctuary."

Turning to Andreas and the remainder of their host, Raimon Roger issued proclamation. "Onward to Montpellier!"

They rode away. Andreas looked back and saw Miquel walking along the ancient Roman road toward Beziers with his father as if his uneven, tramping steps had never known interruption. The black cloud lingered unbroken, moved like... a swarm of bees. As if the boy himself had become one of the thieved hives.

Andreas noticed also that Bertran actively scanned the forest, peered intensely into the undergrowth. But nothing gave motion there. The sound of buzzing filled his ear once more.

Bertran moved his arm that quick and his dagger flew, singing, spinning toward the wood in a brilliant circlet of silver slicing daylight. Yet no target was visible until the blade found its mark.

The penetration of flesh unleashed a staccato cry of pain followed by the release of gurgled breath. A man in a tunic of green bearing a crossbow slumped off his reddish mount and into the ditch, the dagger buried in the meat of his throat to the handle of polished silver inlaid with jewels. Andreas ordered their company to halt once more and followed close. Bertran rode out of formation, dismounted, and knelt by the man. He was sprawled on his back, arms and legs spread, his breathing coming in labored heaves. Bertran tore off the helmet of the cavalier, grasped a fistfull of curly blonde hair, and yanked his sun-starved face close.

The blood flowed down his neck evenly, spilled out like a waterfall, soaked into his tunic, turned green to hues of darkish purple. From where did the man emerge? Spirit transformed to flesh by the piercing of a knife.

Andreas dismounted.

Bertran raised his voice. "Speak your name and your city, and do it now. I may ease your passing."

The green knight simply looked at Bertran and smiled, loosed a sloshing laugh as he spew out a mist of darkest red.

Andreas kicked the knight in the ribs and he wheezed and exhaled more blood. "Hearken to him, demon. How cloak you your appearance? Are you a man or a ghoul who bleeds as one?"

Bertran had a different question. "Are you of Paris? Orleans? Chartres? Out with it!"

"I am of the light..." His eyelids drew shut eternal.

Andreas felt movement through the soles of his leather boots. The ground seemed to sway though nothing trembled within his vision. He heard resonance like the mighty roar of a thousand winds rush past, though neither leaf nor branch stirred. The

land issued a bottomless reverberation and fell away in great
chunks in a perfect circle around Andreas and the dead cavalier.
A red serpent uncoiled and surrounded Andreas, bit its tail and
formed itself around the circle. The creature shook itself violently. A swirling vortex of starless night pushed up through round
broken earth. A rumbling, like an ancient creature awakened, issued from the deep below. An axe-wielding beast the height and
breadth of an aged oak ascended from the abyss, leapt toward
Andreas, weapon raised high, poised to strike. The head of the
beast bore two horns, the body reddish and scaly, the voice was
as the sound of an inferno, and gave issuance to rasping words,
seemingly ancient. Plumes of fire descended from the heavens
with each utterance. The knight stepped back and raised high
his warsword. The axe swung down in swift descent with force
beyond comprehension.

"Andreas, focus your wits!" Bertran came into vision. Solid
ground rushed up from the void and restored itself. The serpent and the beast turned to vapor. Bertran slammed the dead
knight's head to the earth and threw his helmet into the wood.
"You see with second sight," he said to Andreas.

Bertran withdrew his dagger, wiped the thin blade in the dry
grass, and nodded toward the freshly slain knight. "He's not alone,
but a scout. We are being tracked. Andreas, I pray you circle the
company. I will fetch the man and the boy. I fear for them."

The few other times Bertran had spoken in this way, peril
had been imminent. It was he who had first warned of the Moorish assault in Iberia.

Andreas nodded silently to his friend, returned sword to
hilt, regained his mount, drew rein, and galloped back toward
Raimon Roger. The sight of the spinning chasm and of the fiend
had made his brain airy and belly tight.

"Circle the ranks!" he cried. "To haste!"

With drilled efficiency, shields were raised, and mounts
bunched in a rounded, compact formation with pikes pointed
outward beyond horses' bridles.

Anyone who dared charge their company would meet first
with the finely honed iron point of a spear. It was the only formation worthy of standing still.

There was no movement in the wood.

Bertran abandoned the body, swung himself back on his stallion, galloped toward the villager and his little boy, and unsheathed his sword. Andreas sensed danger and raised his spear, prepared to hurl it at any who made appearance in the wood.

Bertran pulled the shield from his back and held it out toward the greenwood. No sooner had he raised it then issued forth a metallic clank as an arrow bit into Bertran's stout shield, then another, and still another, stuck fast in iron-plated wood.

Bertran closed quickly the distance to the villager and his son. Reaching them, he positioned his horse between them and the forest as a wall of protection. Pulling his own crossbow from his back, he nocked an arrow and turned the windlass to tension the string.

Bertran gave a quick glance to the heavens and parted his lips slightly, as if giving release to a prayer. He then released the quarrel, which found the open mouth of a green knight in the wood.

Andreas looked to the trees and six horsed men came into view, all clad in surcoats of green, a mere fifty feet into the forest. All bore warbows, though with no arrows nocked.

Raising his shield, Andreas loosed the battle cry. "Attack, attack!" He charged across the ditch and into the wood, gripped tight his spear. Their quarry hesitated as if they did not believe at first they had been sighted. Then fled without formation.

Within seconds, the circle of cavaliers transformed to a broad line that penetrated the forest behind the *châtelain*, fanned out, and sought to flank their foemen. Branches clawed at Andreas's face and arms as he ducked under limbs, spurred his mount on, keeping his eyes fixed on their quarry.

"Be swift. Let them loose no more arrows." Gaining a clear line of sight through the trees to a cavalier, Andreas drew back his lance and let fly. Spearing leaves of oak and poplar in flight, the pike plunged itself square between the shoulder blades of the knight in green, penetrated hauberk and leather, unhorsed him.

As another of the French knights turned to face the pursuit, Andreas withdrew his mace before the knight could wield his sword and connected with a solid blow that collapsed helmet and skull. He dropped his mace and took up his shield in time to field a blow from a sword and thrust his own warsword into the shoulder of the cavalier. As the knight bent over in pain, Andreas rammed his shield into the face of the French knight, dislodging his hat-like metal helmet, and once more brought the Trencavel standard forcefully against the back of his head, forced a fatal kiss on rough oak bark.

Raimon Roger buried his warsword in the ribcage of the last of the French.

Only one member of their party sustained injury. A cavalier was slashed across the face. The wound was not serious, though staunching the blood flow was no simple task.

The knight with rent cheek trembled with eyes wide. He spoke of dark uncoiling serpents that had flashed in his sights as he battled a French cavalier.

What could draw such poison into the mind of a man?

Bertran stepped off the road into the wood. "I believe that is the sum of their numbers."

Raimon Roger drew rein and surveyed the scene of battle. "There is no time to give them burial. Leave them lie where they fell. Take the mounts, but leave the booty for others."

"Very well, my lord." Andreas readjusted his helmet. A branch had caught and twisted it sideways. "Yet what of the man and the boy?"

"I believe I know your thoughts." Raimon Roger did not turn his gaze from the fallen knights. "Do what you will."

Andreas retrieved mace and spear, rode out of the wood, halted on the opposing side of the villager and Miquel. "Are those the cavaliers that did murder to your elder son?"

The man slowly raised his eyes to meet Andreas's. When he did the connection was tentative. "Those are the knights, but only a few... few of their number. Much greater were the ranks that... that sacked our village."

Andreas narrowed his vision and sharpened his gaze and his voice. "You are coming with us to Montpellier. The strange knights in green possess a lingering interest in you. I wish to know the reason." His mount was still restless and sought to turn away. Andreas had to turn it full circle to face the villager once more. "If there truly are more, we will not abandon you to their bloodlust. For your own wellbeing, you and Miquel shall ride with us."

CHAPTER 2

18 JULY 1209

Eva was happy to see the painted wicker basket was almost cram-full. The fruit of one more tree would complete the day's bounty. The hollow rumbling in her belly gave reminder that the midday meal was swiftly approaching. She could afford to indulge her appetite with one pear at least.

Setting down the basket, she plopped herself unceremoniously on the ground. Not a soul stood within sight. Snatching the most attractive pear from the mounding pile, she bit into the fleshy fruit. A single drop of its juice dribbled lazily down her chin, clinging to her jawline. She allowed the drop to plunge to the grass below. What a blessing to have solitude this morn.

It was hot. The breeze floated lazily across the bluff, a welcome respite from the fiery white of the late morning Provençal sun. The wind gently prodded the oblong, pointed leaves of the pyramid-shaped, evenly spaced pear trees into subtle movement, swaying the flimsy tops back and forth. The leaves rubbed together in cadence, like an orderly, slow-moving chain dance in a massive open hall. Eva leaned back her uncowled head, allowed her dark brown hair to fall to the middle of her back, shut her expansive, rounded eyes of the same color, and listened to the motion of leaf and branch. The sound was restful, tranquil, like her orchard.

Her very orchard.

Eva's eyes opened, dark long lashes separated, she searched the landscape from cliffside to grassy slope. Breathing deeply, she drew the faintly sweet scent of the orchard into her slender nose, set evenly between high, rounded cheeks, and formed her unadorned red full lips into the type of contented smile that barely raises the corners of the mouth.

She finished consuming the pear, wiped her hand on her mouth, on her sleeve, raised slowly her slender, feminine frame until she stood fully upon her leather sandal-shod feet. Casting aside the uneaten core, she resumed filling the large green basket.

She moved to the next tree at the east end of the orchard, started to claim its ripe fruit with long elegant calloused fingers. Eva looked beyond the grove to the edge of the bluff, which dropped off in a vertical cliff, gave way to the valley of the River Rhône and distant lands beyond. She focused for but a moment on the far marshy bank of the broad, swift-flowing Rhône, but swiftly she looked away. The ground still appeared trampled, war-pounded, invaded.

The memory of what she had witnessed three days ago was still a raw wound, and she winced. Soldiers, knights, horses, wagons, barges, banners, overlords, *rotiers,* camp-followers, mercenaries, death.

She turned away, gaining the more pleasing view of the community of Beguines, her home. She gazed upon the city of women from the cliff's edge, thinking of when she first arrived at age ten. That marked the midpoint of her twenty-year existence.

Eva felt the mid-July sun bringing warmth to her gray robe of wool and she smiled. Truly, she was a blessed woman. She was a Beguine, a member of the guild of carpenters, and the holder of her own lands.

She was thankful for her life as a Beguine and the freedom it brought, such incomparable liberty for a woman that had redeemed her days, afforded her the opportunity to put off marriage. Without the community of Beguines, she would have felt bound to wed one of the suitors who had sought her at age fifteen. A stream of marriage seekers that had gone dry by her sixteenth summer, for word had spread among the knights of the Prince and other men of means in Orange that her beauty was exceeded only by her fire of spirit.

She smiled.

Yet a decision to spurn suitors generated no lack of detractors. Simple minds who believed a nubile woman of her age, one capable of bearing children, should be under the strict authority of husband or convent. How could women, weak-willed as they invariably were, maintain the vow of celibacy outside of the monastic enclosure? How could they live without the lordship of men apart from the Rule of St. Benedict?

Eva smiled at the oft-raised query. Her motion did not cease as she dragged her wooden stepladder clacking across exposed roots. Stopping at the next tree, she continued filling her basket with ripe fruit. Such an unwitting attitude toward women was far less common in Provence than in the North. Yet many times she had faced such rhetorical questions.

Never had she even heard the term "Beguine" until age ten, until her mother had explained that they were entering a new residence. Eva had just returned from playing *boule* in the market plaza with other children. She was wiping the grit off her carved spheres of wood.

She had returned through the arched limestone tunnels that combed the underbelly of Orange, where she encountered her mother.

Her mother, with her dark hair and eyes that burned with blackened intensity, was radiant, even in the simple clothes that ever adorned her. Lydia had been still a handsome woman, even at the age of thirty-five.

She had been waiting with that expectant look, an expression that meant she had news. "You have things to say *maire*?" Eva had always looked forward to hearing such news. The words to follow did not match her expectation.

"Eva, would you like to live in a new city with other children like you, girls and boys whose fathers were claimed also by war?" Her mother had spoken the words in a measured, soothing tone.

Eva had thought for a moment, looked heavenward, and

scrunched her nose. "I do not think so," she had replied. "I like it here in Orange, here in the house of the carpenter."

"My little *pera*." Her mother had spoken the words with a warm smile, folded Eva into her arms. "The little city is not far, only one-half league hence. We will return to Orange often. Prince Guillaume has built this new city for women and their children." Her mother had taken Eva's face in her hands and had looked her directly in the eye. Eva had looked away. "We shall have our own house."

Eva had stopped seeking to avert the gaze of her mother. "Our own house? That would be better than this little room, I do suppose." She had acknowledged the point thoughtfully and somewhat begrudgingly.

For as long as Eva had memory, she and her mother had made residence in the sparse back room of the shop of a carpenter. Her mother had run the household of the craftsman, Enric de Toulouse, while Eva, fascinated with woodworking, had sought to glean all she could about the trade.

She had even asked Enric if she could accompany him to a meet of the guild of carpenters. At first, he had simply laughed and tousled her hair, which had annoyed her. But she had been persistent and he had relented.

By the age of ten, she knew not only how to use the tools of a carpenter, to work the wood into realities that fit her imaginings, but had learned much of the economics of the trade as well, including the workings and politics of the guild.

Enric had been given the title de Toulouse in jest only because of his pompousness and not through any noble claim. He indeed hailed from Toulouse but possessed not a drop of highborn blood. Yet he could display a noble penchant for generosity. While Eva had bit her lip to hold back a smile, Enric had remarked more than once in a huff about the futility of standing between her and what she sought.

"Can I still carve wood in the new house?" she had asked of her mother with a pleading sort of hopefulness.

"That's another thing I was going to tell," her mother had replied, handing Eva a small, dull carving knife with a handle of graying ash wood.

"I have spoken with Enric, and he has agreed to give you

some of his old tools, including a lathe." Her mother had borne a triumphant smile, and Eva had known that inducing Enric to accede to such a request had been no easy thing. He would always acquiesce to help but needed persuading first, or perhaps pestering was a term more germane. "He says they need cleaning and are much in need of repair, but they are yours if you want them."

"I do want them." She had brought her hands to her face and was having difficulty giving rein to the excitement in her voice. "If it is the pole lathe, the fix will be simple. All I need do is replace the rope." Eva had picked up a piece of scrap wood and started whittling off the rough edges.

"Then we shall find you a new rope, because in the new house you'll have a room all your own for carving."

"Can we move residence this week?" she had asked with a bright smile. Her change of mind had been complete, all reluctance dissipated, like mist succumbing to encroaching sunlight. The piece of wood had been taking the rough shape of a statue.

"I thought you wanted to remain in Orange." Her mother had folded her arms across her chest and had looked at Eva with a smirk.

It had been Eva's turn to do the embracing, and she had wrapped her arms around the slender waist of her mother. "I wish to go. This day if possible?"

Her mother's look and voice tone had become matter of fact. "The house will be completed in a month and we will move in two. Yet there is a thing I must explain to you my little *pera*. Do you know what is a Beguine?"

Eva had shifted her weight and twirled a lock of hair round her finger. "A lady in the court of Prince Guillaume?"

"No, Eva," her mother had laughed. "You must rid yourself of such notions as living in the *Tor Mirmanda*." The *Tor Mirmanda* was the castle of Prince Guillaume, sovereign of the free principality of Orange. It was a *chateau* perched high on a hill, the *Pog San Eutrope,* towering over the city, the very heart of Orange.

The *Prise de Orange*, one of Eva's favorite troubadour poems, was about another Guillaume, one who had retaken Orange from the Saracens some four centuries past. Orange had been under Christian rule ever since. As consequence, the city was filled with men who bore the name Guillaume, the Prince chief among them.

"A Beguine is not a lady of the court, but a humble laywoman who goes to live in a little city with other women who seek holiness, who seek only the unfettered presence of blessed *Jhesu*. Women choose to be Beguines so they have the support of other women to live a holy life. Women who live in a community, which is what the new little city is called, take vows to be faithful to blessed *Jhesu Crist* alone. A Beguine can own property, earn an income, and even leave the community to marry if she so chooses."

Eva had shaken her head. "You speak of a nun. Nuns are not permitted to marry. I have no wish to be a nun." Eva had been unable to conceive of a woman taking such vows that were able to be broken at will. The idea of the Beguine had been a discordant one to many throughout Christendom, but it appealed to those robbed of husbands and fathers by conflict in the Holy Land, a place few of them would ever see. It provided a choice theretofore unknown.

"No my *pera*. A Beguine is not a nun. There have been nuns for hundreds of years. The first communities of Beguines were started in Flanders about twenty years past, because so many women and children had been bereaved by crusades to the Holy Land as we were. In Latin they are called *Mulieres Sanctae*, the holy women, but their common name is Beguines. It is what I will be called in this new place and what you can be called three years hence when you reach majority. That is...if you wish to be called such."

Eva had scrunched her nose. "Why would I want to be called a Beg ...

"Beguine?" Her mother had smiled again.

The name of her favorite biblical saint had entered Eva's mind at that moment. "When you say like the women who walked with *Jhesu*, you mean like Saint Maria Magdalen? She was the wife of blessed *Jhesu*. I could be like the Magdalen and have a husband!"

The smile on the face of her mother disappeared. Eva had thought for a moment she was going to get paddled. But her mother had released a long breath and sat next to Eva. Lydia had smiled that blessed smile that Eva had ever longed to see, and had oft seen. "That is but a legend of Provence. Blessed *Jhesu* does indeed have a bride, and that bride is his holy church. Maria Magdalen is the bride of *Crist* as are we my *pera*. For we will seek to be like Maria Magdalen and ardently serve the blessed *Crist*. You will experience the work of God. The Beguines believe in taking the Eucharist often. They believe in seeking to hear from God through visions and dreams and in spending time in solitude as a hermit does. They believe in studying *la Bíblia* themselves in the common tongue like the Bereans, not embracing unquestioned the words of a cleric."

Her mother went on to say that Beguines were called to study the Scriptures themselves in the common tongue, to think their own thoughts of blessed *Jhesu,* to freelance their own prayers. Nobles, including her own Prince Guillaume, funded the raising of cities of women known as beguinages to have benefit from such unscripted supplications to *Deu.*

Go to the new city they did, and they were happy for a time. Her mother was second in stature in the community beneath only the Superior. Eva enjoyed the space and the freedom of movement and of mind. She learned to pray and to scribe and to read in Occitan and Latin and ancient Greek. Over time she came to dream also in Latin, though never in Greek.

As her mind's eye returned to the present, Eva looked upon her community of Beguines with thankfulness renewed. It was a city unto itself, encompassed by limestone walls three yards in height and low towers but a yard higher, with three gates of ironbound ash wood manned by the fully armored guards of the Prince of Orange. The buildings of residence in the community were row houses of wood, brick, and stucco, built much like the *mas*, the traditional Provençal farmhouse, laid out painstakingly from Northeast to Southwest. The North ends of the buildings bore no windows in deference to the savage rage of *Mistral*. The roofs of layered terra-cotta tiles sloped gently with their low pitches to the peak, designed expressly to let the violent winds pass over rather than absorb their impact and yield shingles, as steeper pitched roofs would. Thankfully this day *Mistral* did not thunder from the North.

Through the break in the West line of houses she glimpsed the courtyard, or *common* as it was called, a flower in iris and poppy, dominated by a pear tree in the center, encompassed on two sides by churches of stone, the high church for the mass, which faced east like a *cathedral*, and the low church for prayer and the study of the Scriptures in the common tongue. The low church was joined to the infirmary, staffed always by a physician to the Prince. There was also a small stable for the packhorses, a simple hall of stone for dining built parallel to and roofed in the same fashion as the row houses, and a metal forge for the smithy. He had seen sixty-six summers and Eva thought he may not linger much more among the living. His ever present cough had worsened.

Which brought to mind her mother. Three years after they had moved to the community, but a month after Eva reached majority, her mother had taken a terrible fever one night and her soul had quit her body before cockcrow. Eva had taken up her unfinished carving once more and hewn out finely chiseled features not of the Virgin Maria but of her *maire*.

Eva had planted also a pear tree in the community of Beguines in memoriam to her. It occupied still a place of honor in the center of the common. From where she stood now, she glimpsed its elegant shape, rising above all in the common like a living spire. It was a remembrance of many things. Including the sightings.

Within a week of the passing of her mother, as Eva had felt her soul in a dizzying fall into shifting and ever-crowding darkness, the visions began. They were sightings of hazy images that blurred all bounds between corporeal and ethereal. Shapes of darkness that hovered, latched onto people around her, harassed, smothered, gave pale light, deceived, tormented, whispered words of honey sweetness. She would encounter someone in the community of Beguines, on the streets of Orange, in a cathedral, and see their home, their family, their very soul being invaded by the restless writhing and scratching of the darkness. It was all too transparent to her, a thing of which others seemed unaware. She wondered if there were more like her that saw beyond the earth and stone edges of this world. The shadows thrived all the more in the larger cities, like Orange and Avignon, but did their foul work in her little city of Beguines as well.

Still, it was not clearer glimpses of the darkness that broke her fall, but light manifest. A fortnight after the immortal soul of her mother slipped to eternity, Eva had lain awake past the hour of prime, too weary for eyes to bleed colorless sorrow.

She had rubbed her eyes as a white radiance had appeared close to the ceiling near the door, a light that only grew until it flooded the room with its warmth. The simple, powerful words were not audible, but nearly so. "I am with you Eva. I will never leave you nor forsake you."

Jhesu had touched her spirit in a way that neither answered her questions nor mollified her demands. It mattered not. The tears came fast and hot and it was all thirteen-year-old Eva had needed to hear. Though sorrow lingered even now, seven years later, in small pockets of the soul that bled slowly, despair had fled that eve, and its crushing hand had been stayed.

Stayed until three days past. What Eva had seen on the West Bank of the River Rhône as she stood at cliff's edge had brought anguish to her very soul, not only for herself but for the Languedoc; the coming of another Crusade to bring more death. Maria Magdalen had made journey from the Holy Land to Provence in a boat without sail, or so it was commonly believed. Eva's father had made pilgrimage from Provence to the Holy Land. He had fought and died on Crusade in the lands where blessed *Jhesu* once walked. But her father had battled the Muhammadan. This time, in the Languedoc, Christians would be the foemen, pitted cruelly against one another.

CHAPTER 3

18 JULY 1209

They crested a stony hill at a pace punishing to horse and rider. Andreas eased up on the reins. The stream of refugees, the long procession of souls, neared an end. The forests had parted and given way to sun-scorched meadows. Withered grass and pale-dry wildflowers flanked the road. The *châtelain* slowed the pace of their company to a trot. The horses needed rest. The villager and his son, newly plucked from the procession, looked ever more distressed and exhausted.

Their cavalcade was on course to reach Montpellier by the hour of vespers. There had been no more sign of the cavaliers in green. Even Bertran seemed at ease and kept his gaze on the road ahead.

The encounter with the little boy and his father had been disquieting. It was unsettling also to have them ride in their company, but Andreas had judged that they needed to be kept near, an opinion echoed also by Bertran. They faced a threat far exceeding that of the other refugees. The knights in green had taken the life of his eldest son, the soul of his youngest, and yet still they pursued this villager. What else did they seek? What of

Melimarpera? Andreas wished to understand. It seemed Bertran already did. The *châtelain* would question the villager once they were safely ensconced in Montpellier.

The few belongings of the man and his living son, those that could not be carried on horseback, had been distributed amongst the other villagers nearby along the road. Andreas had promised father and son they would receive more than what they had lost. The man had complied readily enough, seeming grateful to ride instead of walk, though reluctant to turn his direction back toward the French encampment.

The boy, Miquel, remained silent, almost vacant, as if his soul had indeed departed or gone into hiding. Even the swarming bees seemed to have entered their hive. That blank look made Andreas shudder each time he saw the boy, who rode with Bertran. Do the dead walk among the living? There was need to gain more knowledge of him, but not this moment.

He must clear his mind of the noise that had taken root and flourished unhindered.

The *châtelain*, utilizing the extra elevation afforded by his mount, was at last able to peer out across the Great Sea, that flat, unending sheet of pale emerald, calm at least in summer. He had been anticipating this moment since they had departed Carcassonne three days past, when the news had reached them the mighty host from the North had crossed the frontiers of the Languedoc.

From the talk of sailors and soldiers, he had heard the *Gran Mar*, the sea of *mediaterra*, was a blessed and cursed sheet of water, depending on season, bringing riches and life to some and wantonly claiming the same from others, like an arbitrary god of mythology; Neptune manifest.

He knew the Romans had called it *Mare Nostrum*, Our Sea. They had once dominated its vast expanse, claimed it as their private lake, grew rich by shipping goods across its waters. Now it was divided, battled over, pirated, and wholly possessed by no empire. It provided this day also the soft wax tablet Andreas needed on which to etch his thoughts, which were scattered randomly like the dominion of the sea.

It was not the risk of attack from the mysterious knights in green that troubled him, for he never shied away from straight-up battle and would brandish war sword against any opponent in his path. It was another thing, a thing that threatened him in a place that was not of flesh and bone, a place where no hauberk, no shield in the natural could give protection.

It was a vulnerability of spirit he had known all his days.

Mostly it had lain dormant. But at such an hour as this, when ethereal realities, things he could not see, could not explain, could not fathom, were shoved tauntingly in his face, he felt exposed, denuded of all covering, unable to rally himself to confront the challenge.

Andreas had seen six summers when the specter had first made appearance. He had sat up during first waking, woolen bedclothes muddled in sweat, utter silence in the chamber and the awful dread of the raw manifestation of an unseen but imminent presence, a pulsing evil in the dark. He had been roused from a dream in which he was being pursued through a shadowy labyrinth by a creature he could not see, yet one he knew was ever-present. He had awoken to the appearance of the thing before him. It had form but not substance. His mouth had gone dry, his tongue unable to form words. Once the thing vanished, sleep claimed him like death once more.

He had grasped at courage, but had risen again at cockcrow still trembling. He had heard his father walking the hallway, crunching the floor rushes, and had run to speak with him, to seek strong comfort.

At first his father bore a look of concern. "Andreas, what has befallen you?"

The wide-eyed six-year-old boy had spoken earnestly of the dream and of the presence in the night. As he did so, the look of the face of his father had changed. The lines grew unyielding, bright green eyes faded to hard gray. "Is my only son a coward that he shrinks from but one unpleasant dream, and now imagines it fills the air about him? If some hairy beast with fearsome claws had entered I might yield compassion, but not for a dream. There are beasts enough in the natural, do not chase shadows, Andreas." The man he had respected, the man who gave wise counsel to the father of Raimon Roger, had turned and walked briskly away.

A hairy beast with fearsome claws had indeed entered. If

only such a beast was of the natural and could be dueled with a blade of steel.

The dreams continued unabated, but he had sought to be strong and did not speak of them for a span of ten years, until the campaign in Iberia. The night after they had vanquished the Moors on the road, Andreas had roused once more at first waking, screaming in his tent, brandishing his warsword, slashing the air. Raimon Roger and Bertran had come to him. He had lowered his sword and spoken of his nightmares.

Raimon Roger had seemed to accept it as a flawed part of him. "Leave such things to the clergy," Raimon Roger had said, and then spoke again the message of Andreas's father. "Concern yourself with battling what you can slay in the natural." So Andreas had, or at least endeavored to do so. Yet this day was the first manifestation under sunlight of this bestial thing. He never discerned this adversary that periodically stole his slumber over the years.

Bertran, for his part, had seemed to understand, perhaps better than Andreas himself, for his friend seemed always to rise up in the spirit like the tall man he was and meet such challenges with vigor.

Leaning forward on his stallion, he threw his head back and felt his brown hair once again cover his shoulders. Only the men of the South let their hair grow and shaved their beards. It was a practice considered odd by the rest of Christendom, especially in Northern France, where the men sported bowl-shaped haircut and full beards. In Iberia, the French had referred to the men of the Languedoc as prissy, at least until they had engaged with the enemy. It was very hot then as it was this day. Rivulets of sweat flowed down his forehead, stung his hazel eyes, and ran down his straight nose. He experienced a curious pain in his spirit as well. A confused chorus of anguish and triumph seemed to rise from his very bowels.

His vision watery with salty perspiration, he turned his gaze to the verdant slope that visually ushered the eye down to the fine, white sand beach, and beyond to the placid water. A mere two leagues of leafy forest now separated him from the waterway to pilgrimage and blood-soaked glory.

But those two leagues were no different than two-thousand.

He would not be taking the Cross to fight against Saracen or Turk or any Muhammadan. His battles lay closer to home. Yet his eyes were drawn to the sea. He saw motion there. The surface near the shore stirred as the water in a cup swirls when a medicinal potion is stirred in with a stick, slowly at first, sluggishly resisting the will of the mixer, and then beginning to spiral downward as the level on the edges rises and the center drops precipitously, almost laying bare the bottom. The spinning increased until it became violent, causing a vertical shaft to appear in the water, and Andreas could see the bottom and it was not sandy or rocky or weedy but bleached white as if covered by the cap of a skull bone.

The bony depths cracked and split, shattered, and a head emerged like that of a leopard, yet possessed the wide mouth of a lion with teeth that glinted in the sunlight, as if made of metal. Another head rose up through the whirlpool, then still another and it continued until there were seven heads, each written upon with words unknown. One seemed to bear also a lengthy scar, as if it had been slashed by a longsword then healed.

A crowd appeared along the shore, ever burgeoning in number, spreading beyond sight, their dress strange, being not that of nobility, clergy, merchants, or peasants. They were slack-jawed and pointed at the head that bore the mark of an old wound.

The cat-like eyes of the wounded head fixed directly on Andreas, who drew back in the saddle, lost his grip on the reins, and tumbled sideways onto the stone road, a metallic clattering of chain mail and weaponry.

Raimon Roger called for the company to halt. The *châtelain* quickly regained his feet, angry and embarrassed, his hip sore, but otherwise unhurt. Bertran dismounted and helped Andreas back onto his stallion. "As I told you, you see with second sight. It is a gift you need abandon, Andreas, for it will bring no thing other than grief." The others had a look of intrigue on their faces but were not mocking.

Andreas looked toward the sea, and the whirlpool and the many-headed beast and the crowd along the shore had vanished. The surface was calm, but Andreas was not. Lifting his water skin with a trembling hand, he took a long drink and then splashed some of the liquid on his head and face. A few drops splashed on his hauberk and sizzled to steam. Though no longer cool, the water still caught the breeze and dissipated some of the day's heat.

On the road ahead, Andreas saw two figures cloaked in back. Were they but an illusion as well? The horses resumed their gait and moments later their company overtook the two men whose black robes were belted by cords of white. Both had thick brown beards and wore curious-looking wooden shoes that poked out from beneath the folds of their cowled tunics and made a rhythmic tapping on the stone road as they walked. Their heads bore no tonsure, Roman or otherwise. Like Andreas's company, they moved east against the dwindling flow of humanity. *Valdenses* they were.

"*Pax vobiscum*, my lord," stated the taller of the two, with right hand raised. He directed his eyes toward Raimon Roger. "We are but mere pilgrims who seek the Eternal City to visit the Holy Apostles."

"*Pax vobiscum* to you, friends," replied Raimon Roger, beneficently, bearing a broad smile as they moved past the robed mendicants, the horses still progressing at a trot. "I tell you your direction is true, yet beware. If you encounter the Pope's army that waits bristling for a fight on the road ahead, you may reach the Eternal City before ever you witness the gates of Rome."

Andreas smiled at the double entendre as the two pilgrims nodded and gave a sort of half-bow.

The taller gave his reply first. "Yet either is gain to us and means the completion of our pilgrimage."

Raimon Roger waved his golden ringed, jewel-studded hand in a sweeping, magnanimous gesture. "May your pilgrimage not end, my friends, before it's time."

"Many thanks, my lord, both kind and fair, and may a blessing be upon you and all your lands and all who dwell within them," called the shorter one with strong, sonorous voice. "Yet your servant cannot help but wonder, does your war party seek to battle this army of the Whore of Babylon, or join its ranks like the Count of Toulouse?"

Raimon Roger did not seem nonplussed at the boldness of the query, and raised his voice to respond. "Neither, if heaven allows. For the Count of Toulouse is my uncle, the brother of my *maire.* I mean neither to stand with the enemy nor oppose my uncle. I mean to be sure this army is relieved of all reasons for battle." Raimon Roger's frank acknowledgement of his purposes to these curious pilgrims caught Andreas unawares. It was more than his lord had revealed to him.

"Godspeed on your journey, my lord," called out the shorter of the two, who were now already several yards behind Andreas's company.

"Godspeed on your pilgrimage. A blessing be upon you," replied Raimon Roger.

So these men were not shadows. Andreas glanced furtively at his lord, who was smiling as if enjoying a private joke. Now was the time to speak, even if an audience would be privy to the exchange.

He had been searching for an opportunity to address his lord in private for a fortnight, but as of late, Raimon Roger was never unaccompanied. Now they were also surrounded not only by their company of cavaliers, but they continued yet to encounter travelers and refugees in small clumps on the road, all heading in the opposite direction toward Beziers, now mostly villagers and peasants from the countryside, like the boy and his father, looking distraught, fleeing the scourging shadow of an interloping army.

Searching for an answer to his queries, Andreas struggled to grasp the thoughts of his reeling brain. He turned his attention back to the road and studied the twin grooves sliced deep into the precise arrangement of stone, imprints of Roman chariot wheels of a millennium past. He could almost hear the rumbling and clacking of iron rolling over stone. Many legionnaires and cavaliers have traveled this road to make war, Andreas thought.

Yet now he was on horse, riding to make peace. It disturbed him. Not the seeking of peace, but the man to whom Raimon Roger would be petitioning clemency. The papal legate, a man who could bend the ear—and seemingly the will—of Pope Innocent III himself. A man who was the Abbot of the great abbey of Citeaux, the head of the Cistercian order, the very commander of the army that marched against Andreas's homeland. A monk whose very heart seemed to beat not with the peaceful rhythms of the abbey, but to pound as drums of war.

Though reticent to do so, Andreas knew he must speak with candor.

As the road descended the hill thick with oaks into an open, broad valley, carpeted by wild lavender and iris and poppy and thyme, and the sea and the mass of refugees faded from view, Andreas broke the silence.

"What case will you present to the papal legate, my lord?"

The smile vanished. "I will bow the knee and swear fealty to Armand Amaury and the Lord Pope and pledge to take the Cross."

"To slaughter heretics, my lord?" Andreas spoke out of sarcasm.

"No, Andreas, to bring peace." Raimon Roger released a heavy breath. "I shall issue passionate but empty promises to drive the heretics from my lands. Heretics like the *Valdenses* we just passed." Raimon Roger smiled once more and bore a look of relief. "I have now spoken the words aloud for all in my company to hear. I shall not betray even one of my people, regardless of their belief. If all the Languedoc takes the Cross, then who will the French have to engage in battle?"

CHAPTER 4

18 JULY 1209

Eva felt a chill slither up her spine. The peace of the day had rapidly dissipated, like the morning haze off the River Rhône yielding to the July sun. The shapeless darkness had crept into her orchard once more, a veiled presence unbidden, ever lingering on the periphery.

The fruit trees, her peaceful grove, seemed to transform once more from regal beauty to the likeness of machines of war. With all she had seen in the corporeal and ethereal but three days before, near her lands on the frontier of Provence and the Languedoc, it appeared the North was coming in force to impose its will on the South.

Metallic sounds reached her ears. It was the clashing of sword against shield, but she saw it not in the natural. It was but an echo from the nether realm ringing in her ears, or perhaps it sprung from the well of her thoughts. Distinguishing was not easy. Never was it easy. If from *Deu*, it would return over time at moments unexpected.

Something in the ethos had morphed in recent times, turned darker. The shadows had grown, like unnatural beings feeding off the living. At times, the blackness was held at bay as if by a net unseen, but then its reality would be thrust upon her once more and she was driven by the fire of her spirit to confront it. To cry out in silent prayer or with raised voice, to take up pen and scratch out her thoughts in poetry on virgin leafs of vellum. She knew she prayed against evil, but knew not of its purpose nor the effect of her prayers or scribings, if any.

As she glanced round the leafy pear trees laden with whitish yellow shapes, probing, seeking to discern the source of the ethereal shadow, the limbs appeared to be weighted with more than fruit. Every branch seemed to gnarl before her waking eyes and become as a loaded trebuchet, ready to disgorge its produce with fury at her very person if she were to give but the slightest provocation. As if all she had worked for would be thrown back against her. The very air grew darker and felt as if it were energized, crackling with the charge of impending battle. She raised quickly her hands as if to fend off the impending assault. As anger rose also within her, she lowered her hands and lifted her voice. "Halt! In the name of blessed *Jhesu*, pray take your leave from my lands."

The darkness fled and the trees were no longer machines of war.

Moving out of the shade to pick clean the remaining portion of a pear tree, Eva felt once more the heat of the sun on her gray woolen robe, but it brought no warmth to her spirit. She felt instead a stark, forceful coldness growing in the innermost of her being, like the *Mistral* spewing its icy wrath down the valley of the Rhône. The howling winds came always from the North, as had the disturbing sight to which she had borne witness.

Eva continued filling the nearly overflowing basket as her mind pondered all she had seen at midweek. Now the Sabbath approached and she had no rest from what plagued her. So absorbed was she in her thoughts, she heard not the approaching footsteps.

"I did not think *peras* grew ripe until August at least."

Eva whirled around, nearly dropped the painted basket of picked fruit. The motion caused a few pears to slide out onto the ground, bouncing and rolling along the grass toward the new arrival. "I did not hear you approach." Eva smiled at Claris, relieved it was her, heartened she had come. Briefly glancing toward the glowing heavens ever-illuminating Provence with clear light, she covered her eyes against the brilliance. "The sun has been unyielding this summer and many of the *peras* have ripened early."

Claris bent over to pick up the fallen pears. "Then you shall have to open your market stall in Orange a month early." Never one to be idle, Claris glanced at the free-standing ladder then at the still hanging fruit on the tree where Eva had been working. "Are the remainder of the *peras* on these branches in need of harvest as well?"

"Yes, and I would be pleased for your help."

"Then you shall have it." Claris grabbed an empty basket, ascended the ladder, and proceeded to pull pears from the mid-section of the tree with one hand and hold the basket with the other. Like the way she took hold of all else in life, Claris grasped the pears with a touch firm and careful before separating the fruit from branch and limb. "I hope it is agreeable to you Eva that I have come. I know this place is your sanctuary."

Eva released a heavy breath. "It is, but you are most welcome. In truth I am relieved at your presence." She looked toward the cliff. "There is no sanctuary to be found here in this hour. There has been a shadow growing in my soul and in the ethos."

Claris looked down at Eva for a moment, as if pondering something, then resumed her picking. "I have felt it too. Although I am unsure what it portends. Perhaps we can discover it together, for I know you well enough to realize you will have no rest until you gain answers."

Eva smiled. Claris indeed knew her well. "I am unsure where to start."

"Tell me of when this darkness first came upon you."

Eva did not hesitate in her response. "Three days past."

"Tell me more fully of what happened three days past." Claris spoke without looking down, continued to pick pears from the tree. "Sometimes the answers are hidden in small things, details of remembrance."

Eva hesitated. "I witnessed the approach of the army marching south."

Claris swayed and nearly fell from the ladder, clutched a limp branch that cracked in her grip yet retained strength enough so she could right herself. She dropped the pear in her hand, but managed to cling to the basket. "You saw the host? Eva that is no mere detail." The fallen pear bounced to Eva's feet. "All that has been spoken of in the community these three days past is the approach of the army. We have spoken about it. Why did you not speak of what you saw?" Claris's look changed from astonishment to concern. Her full attention upon her protege. "Did you encounter any of the cavaliers? I pray you were in nowise violated."

Eva shook her head, yet averted her eyes to the ground, picked up the wayward pear. "No. I saw them only from a distance. Yet I did feel violation. The army marched along the far bank of the river, in the Languedoc. But for the ache in my soul, they may as well have trampled my orchard, my very spirit."

"The ache in your soul...?" Claris let her voice trail off and was silent for some moments. Her mentor looked heavenward, shut her eyes, squared her body, leveled her chin, opened her eyes, and engaged Eva with a keen gaze. The delivery was coming, the query, the one that would provoke the bleeding of spirit. But it was a bloodletting that led to healing. "Have you been thinking on your *paire* Eva?" Claris smiled faintly.

Eva winced. "You poke into my spirit once more. It aches still from the time previous." Eva sighed and looked across the orchard. A pain grew in her neck and spread like a tight web over the whole of her skull. "Yet, in truth, Claris, my thoughts of late have been of my *paire*." Eva set down her basket and folded her arms across her breast and began to pace around the tree with no particular rhythm of motion. "I witnessed the great host and wondered if my *paire* had been part of such a contingent when he had trod to the coast of the Great Sea to depart for Palestine. I think I shall never have knowledge of such." Try as she might to recall any shred of him, she possessed no memory at all of her father.

Her mother had told her that Eva was less than a year old when her father had sailed from Messina to the Holy Land. She knew Anselme had been instrumental in the retaking of Acre, that great port and fortress on the coast of Outremer. Yet still she comprehended little of why he had embarked on such a journey. She did understand the citadel of Acre remained in the clutch of Latin hands.

Those hands could hold the city but not the lifeblood of her father, for his blood had been spilt leading the charge against the last, desperate Saracen defense of Acre. The assault had broken the will of the Arab garrison and the body of her father. An errant shard of stone from a mangonel had penetrated his chest, gashed his heart, and the rhythmic surge of blood could not be staunched.

"I have been told many times in the intervening years that I am blessed. Too many times. My *paire* was a victorious martyr I was told, his triumphant blood spilt in the service of the Bishop of Rome, the Lord Pope, all for the glory of Blessed *Jhesu*, and miraculously I knew the tale." After so long a time, she was surprised at the bitterness that colored her words.

Claris set down the pear in her hand and looked at Eva. "I know the sting you feel at the callousness of such remarks, yet the statements are true, Eva, though spoken not in love as blessed *Jhesu* has bidden."

Claris spoke truth. Though Eva was not blessed to have been robbed of her father, she was blessed to know of his courage in battle, his bloodletting sacrifice. When she had faced hard times, stiff challenges in her life, she had thought often, sometimes in tears, of her father pressing the assault against the defenses of Acre and chose to endure the pain and press on herself. Especially in the dark days after her mother had passed.

She was also not alone in her loss. Many in Orange, many in her own community, had lost fathers, some brothers, others husbands, and still others sons, to the recurring conflicts that erupted like an erratic volcano over that sandy spit of land known as Outremer situated on the Eastern Shore of the Great Sea. Some called it the Holy Land. To Eva it was a forsaken realm of death. Claris herself had lost her elder brother in the recapture of Jerusalem by the Saracens some twenty years past.

Of those who died on pilgrimage, most of their loved ones, Claris included, had not the story of their deaths in manuscript form, or in any form. The letter, Eva's letter, composed in Latin, scribed on sheepskin, was conveyed to her and her mother, along with some of his effects and the Beautiful Things. And this only because of the importance of her father in the reconquest of Acre, and because a compassionate priest had taken the time to know her father and learn of his family in Christendom.

But the army she saw three days past was not en route to Acre. "I believe the host was not on pilgrimage to Outremer or any other place across the sea."

Claris looked up. "What believe you, Eva?"

"I made return to bluff's edge at tierce the morn following and directed my gaze south and west. I saw the column begin a westward shift at Beaucaire. The force was turning onto the *Via Domitia* on the way to Montpellier. They were but two days march from the city.

"At that very moment I knew the great host had come to lay siege to the Languedoc. Whether to the strongholds of the Saint Gilles or the Trencavels I knew not, but both harbor heretics. The first city shielding heretics they would reach is—"

"Beziers." Claris spoke the word as a matter of settled fact. Her interruption surprised Eva. Always did Claris listen avidly, and it was uncommon for her to finish the sentence of another.

Eva stopped her pacing and looked intently at Claris. "Yes, it would be Beziers, for Montpellier expelled its heretics. I hear tell most of them took flight to Beziers."

Claris seemed to sense Eva's unspoken query. "I have a friend of old in Beziers, Catorna, who is a *Valdenses,* one of the secret friends of *Vaudes.*"

Eva smiled. "Ah, and you have concern the *Valdenses* will be targeted along with the *Bons Hommes*?"

Her mentor merely nodded.

Eva shifted her weight and clasped together her hands. "I fear, Claris, for all the people of the Languedoc, and not only those thought to be heretics."

"*Fear not* says blessed *Jhesu.*" Claris smiled and grasped the basket with both hands and looked Eva in the eye. "Be strong and courageous dear Eva, for I believe you will need to be so for what lies in front of you. The coming of this army that has taken the Cross is a sign unto you. I believe this, though I lack the knowing of what it means. Blessed *Jhesu* will reveal all you need know when the time is full."

The bells in the stone and iron cage-like tower of the high

church began to toll, low and clear. Eva had always thought it a distinctly masculine sound for a city of women.

Descending the ladder and emptying the pears from her basket into Eva's already stuffed green wicker container, Claris spoke briskly. "Forgive me for an abrupt exit, but I must take my leave. I told a penitent I would join her in prayer in the low church for the office of sext."

"At least my soul will have respite to heal from this latest prodding." Eva pretended to wince once more.

Without breaking stride, Claris threw a glance over her shoulder and smiled as she increased her pace.

Eva lingered in the orchard as Claris passed through the West Gate and returned to the community. She found places to stack pears upon pears. She finished filling the wooden basket and turned to commence the short journey home.

She looked across the orchard to the terra-cotta roofed row houses of brick rising above the walls in the distance and the women and young girls and boys busily at work, tending to the grounds, engaged in some craft, or playing *boule*. They seemed light of spirit and free of care.

At times she wished to be lightened of the unending burden of peering through the veil into the ethereal where nothing held shape for long. Often she questioned her own fortitude of mind at seeing evil at work in events or people that by all other appearances seemed innocent.

As she emerged from the grove, something registered in her peripheral vision. A shadow, but not as one should be. It formed into figures of six sides, like the honeycomb of a beehive, and then seemed to coalesce into the shape of an owl then into a circle like a *boule* or *perla*. It was from a nearby tree and she noticed that the angle seemed to have shifted though the sun had not. The shape seemed more precise, better defined than the edges of a shadow ought to be. She blinked hard, decided it was the heat and her mind playing tricks on her.

She lofted the basket onto her shoulder and walked the narrow hard packed dirt path down the grassy slope toward the east gate. Upon leaving the shade of the orchard, she could feel and smell her dark hair gathering the warmth of the sun. The knight of Prince Guillaume on guard, fully armed and in hau-

berk, opened the gate and Eva entered the community. She kept
her head low as she walked past the smithy and stables, even as
the sweet smell of hay and the tang of manure rested upon the
heated air. Eva hoped to avoid anyone else she knew well and
the resultant long dialogue that would likely follow. How many
of the women could spend hours in idle chatter, devout as they
were otherwise. The conversations with Claris rarely were idle,
but her mentor challenged her and it often left Eva tired after-
wards.

Now thoughts of her father weighed on her this day in a
fashion she had not experienced for many years. She needed to
digest the letter once more.

She reached the threshold of her home, opened the oaken
door, entered, and deposited the basket of pears on the polished
pine floor. Climbing the white tiled stairs to her bedchamber,
she entered the room and walked to the iron bound trunk of
cypress where the items were, her only physical connection to
her father

Some of the objects she knew were of exceeding value,
though she'd never had them appraised. The priest in Outremer
had made sure that her father's share of Acre's bounty was
shipped to her and her mother. Each time she opened the trunk,
she mildly chastised herself for her lax measures of safekeeping.
If the wrong soul knew what lie within—

Reaching over the gold and silver bowls and platters, and
other objects abundantly encrusted in dark colored jewels that
apparently were so prevalent in Outremer, she removed an unadorned, unvarnished, round wooden tube perhaps two-thirds
of a yard in length.

It was made of pear wood. The limb had been the perfect
thickness. The rest of the tree she had carved into use for the
choir and sacristy of the cathedral of Notre Dame de Nazare in
Orange that had been completed the year previous, in 1208.

But the limb she had kept for herself.

She had rounded it into a perfect cylinder on her pole lathe,
which was still given tension with the same strong rope her
mother had purchased ten years past, and had bored out the
center, rubbing it smooth with sandstone and pumice inside
and out, creating a fine parchment tube. It kept the letter sealed

from the dust and dampness of Provence. Removing the end of the cylinder, she carefully pulled out the lambskin parchment. Closing the trunk, she unrolled the document on top of it.

Then the remembrance jolted her.

The meeting. She had forgotten.

Her Painter said he had new carving work for her, a challenge she would relish. Carefully rolling the letter once more and returning it to the cylinder, she remembered her hunger as well.

First closing and latching the trunk, she descended the stairs and entered the pantry. Hurriedly she consumed the remainder of a loaf of bread and a wedge of cheese—she despised it when anything went to waste—and washed it down with the remainder of a flagon of wine. She snatched the piece of pear wood she had readied for the occasion, made her egress from the row house, and hastened across the common toward the East Gate and the city of Orange.

CHAPTER 5

18 JULY 1209

Their army seeking peace rode across the final expanse of the valley. Andreas felt a pang of trepidation as they abandoned the haven of such an open place. Trees once more rushed up to the road. Towers of wood to hide a foe lying in wait. He straightened his back. Without turning his head, he quickened his hearing to the sounds of the forest.

All that reached his ears was the noise of creatures in flight: the songs of sparrows, the cry of hawks circling overhead, the sound of owls in the wood, the buzzing of bees. A hive must be concealed in a nearby tree. There was enough lavender and poppies in the valley they had quitted to sustain honeybees without number. Had he indeed heard owls?

He spied more small creatures and birds than at any other point previous on their journey. The forest spilled itself onto the road. Two white rabbits hopped across the indented route of stone. Several gray squirrels leapt in front of them as a pheasant ruffled the leaves and took flight. A great wild boar with huge curved tusks rumbled through the forest, trampling the saplings in its path like tender flowers. In the periphery of his sight, Andreas saw at least three deer bounding through the underbrush. Another two, a stag and a doe, broke out of the wood and dashed across the road not ten yards in front of their company.Was it only the skittish ways of deer stirring up the wood, or another thing?

This day it would be good to be on the hunt. He was hungry. Imagining the smell and taste of venison or pork roasting on a spit was no chore.

But not only deer and boars were in motion this day.

Andreas returned his attention to the songs of birds and sensed nothing unusual, yet his apprehension remained, stubbornly lodged in his mind, like beef in one's back teeth. Wondering what Raimon Roger was thinking on, Andreas started to express his concern, then halted his speech as his lips parted and the breath filled his throat.

If there was a reason to be leery of the forest, he decided Raimon Roger already knew of it.

Andreas prided himself on knowing when to trust Raimon Roger and when to question his lord's judgment. Raimon Roger would know if anything was amiss and would have formulated a plan. Bertran also seemed unconcerned. The *châtelain* chose instead to put forth an innocent question.

"We near Montpellier, my lord. Shall we continue on to the city?"

"We reach the extent of my lands." The tone of Raimon Roger was wary. "Montpellier may be under the banner of King Pedro, even the natal city of the Viscountess, but I assure you we will receive no fair welcome there this night." He looked to the greenwood. "An inn is nearby, outside the city walls. We shall take our slumber there. The owner is a friend and remains true. He will treat us in the proper fashion. He may also have word of the French interlopers."

Bertran made a mark in the air with his finger. "Pardon my lord; has he stables for our horses?"

Raimon Roger shot him a knowing look. "Not only stables but watering troughs and feed aplenty. You yourselves will dine at table and fill your bellies and will not leave thirsty. Guilhabert will see to it."

"Ale for all!" cried Aimer, riding next to Bertran. "A man

grows parched in this accursed heat."

"I think you'll find the wine more to your liking," said Raimon Roger, feigning seriousness, knowing of Aimer's fondness for good ale. "Guilhabert is always well-stocked with barrels of Toulousain burgundy."

"Milk for the squires then. They are but babes newly weaned." Aimer looked back at the rear of the company and laughed. "At their tender age, they must not over imbibe. Or cut into the supply of our hearty wine bowls." The sturdy, red-haired knight laughed again, glanced once more at the youths, who remained impassive. Aimer ever reminded Andreas of a Norseman. He even preferred the battle axe over the warsword. The squires had no need of worry, for Aimer would be the first to make sure their flagons were filled with wine or ale.

Andreas turned to the squires and winked. He sought to give reassurance. Not that they would easily betray their angst, but he sensed it nonetheless. It was palpable. The squires knew their first engagement may soon be forthcoming. Andreas had told them as much and their response proved they had taken heed. It was one thing to prepare for battle with *pels*, the stout wooden posts imbedded in the ground that were used for training. It was another thing entirely to be locked in steely combat, bloody and imminent. Only the thrust of a sword or blow of an axe from plunging to mortality.

He had first tasted of this sickening thrill at age six and ten, seven years past.

The buzzing of bees echoed still in his ears.

Andreas looked to Raimon Roger. "My lord, I know of no inn that lies in these woods."

"There are reasons why the knowledge of its existence is elusive. It is possible to travel the Via Domitia many times and have no awareness of this inn. Its secret is jealously guarded among certain men." Raimon Roger turned his head to face the entire company of knights. "I expect it to remain so after this night."

"Have no care, my lord," said Bertran. "But tell me this I pray, where lies the graveyard of those who would speak of its setting? Surely the owners of loose lips have paid a price." He seemed to have knowledge of what he spoke.

Raimon Roger smiled grimly. "In a few days you may be able

to ask them yourself if you have want."

Andreas looked to Raimon Roger then back to Bertran.

Aimer, riding next to Bertran, pointed heavenward. "I would wonder what devil is worshipped there under a full moon in a courtyard of stone that so few have knowledge of its very existence. What infernal secret lies hidden within? What covert altar to a pagan god?"

"Perhaps it is a noble hunting lodge where the board is paid for in gold and deer hides and the souls of men." Andreas smiled but felt a flash of fear.

"You are not far from the mark, my friend, though not in the manner in which you think," said Raimon Roger softly. "Here lies the red boulder. It is time to enter the forest." He drew rein with one hand, and raised the other high. "Halt," he declared to the company as his massive chestnut mare slowed to a stop. It was a *milsoldor*, a thousand shillinger, a warhorse of exceeding value.

"We proceed single file to the right. All fall in line behind me, including you Guilhem," ordered Raimon Roger. "Lower flag and banner, we will have no more need of them this day."

The *gonfanonier* did as he was bidden and obediently moved in line behind the knights and squires.

As Andreas directed his own black stallion into place, he became aware they were at a rare spot where the road both dipped and rounded a bend all at once. Unless almost on top of them, other travelers on the road would be unable to see them. None were nearby.

A shallow streamlet that seemed to part the hill flowed alongside the extreme end of the turn in the road, vanishing in the dense wood of Lignin Oak.

Without a word, Viscount Raimon Roger Trencavel disappeared behind a triangular-shaped red monolith and plunged his horse onto a watery path. The knights and squires followed one at a time toward the unknown Inn of Guilhabert.

CHAPTER 6

18 JULY 1209

The district of the guild of painters in Orange was a warren of ancient buildings. Ochre-colored Roman stone structures barely cleaved from one another by cobblestone alleyways, which were little more than footpaths.

It was said that painters toiled there because no other merchandise was so flat as to be carried among such a tightly packed maze of stone.

Even in these compact spaces, the city was alive with the dealings of business. Customers entered and departed painters' houses; some clutched their newly purchased art or painted manuscripts.

The Painter that Eva sought had his rooms in a corner dwelling on the edge of the district, befitting his ever-rising status. He had moved from the crowded heart of the warren some thirteen years past to his ancient and elegant house.

The erupting fervor of holy building had served him well.

In an age when each burgeoning city of means wanted an imposing, inspiring cathedral to house the relics of saints and fill the coffers with the largesse of wealthy pilgrims, painters who could combine colored enamels with carved wood to match the grandeur of stained glass were greatly in favor.

The Painter was waiting for Eva when she reached his studio. She glimpsed him keeping vigil by the front window.

She tarried before making entrance, admiring the towering exterior stone wall of the city's Roman theatre. Though she had seen it countless times, it never ceased to inspire, for unlike so many Roman structures in Provence, the theatre had not dissolved to ruin. She could imagine a play by Sophocles or Euripides being performed there.

Yet she need focus on painting now and think not on dramatic stagings. She lifted her eyes from the theater and entered the Painter's triple-story villa.

Passing under the lintel, she breathed in slowly through her nostrils the startling, brain-cleansing smell of paint on wood. To Eva it was a holy odor, like the smoke of incense in Solomon's Temple lifting to the Almighty.

On a small stone table were multiple grayish clamshells filled with paints of various shades. The Painter had clearly just finished using the newly mixed paints to color the series of pear wood rosettes she had carved the month previous. They lay spread out on a canvas covered rectangular table in the center of his workspace. A few still glistened brightly, covered in bright beautiful hues of red, pink, yellow, azure, green, and purple, and still obviously wet, but she knew none would ever appear entirely dry.

Few understood the art, but the Painter was able to mix his pigments and solvents to produce an effect that seemed to bring life to the dead wood he adorned with his enamels, a way to make the paint remain glossy without rubbing or flaking off with the passage of time. The red, she knew, was produced with cinnabar obtained from Iberia, dried and crushed to a fine, bright red powder and mixed with certain oils. The azure, even more costly, came from crushed lapis lazuli from Italy, and left a luminescent, jewel-like effect that sparkled with a faint golden shimmer on parchment or wood alike. Paintings from centuries past adorned in the blue of lapis lazuli lost not a glimmer of color, ever appeared as if stroked onto the surface earlier in the day. There was no other color more costly, not even purple.

At the sight of her, the Painter deposited his sable hair-brushes in a wooden bowl filled with turpentine and removed his spattered white smock.

"Ah, my gray-robed Beguine. I thought the knowledge of our meeting may have vanished in your orchard of *peras*," said the Painter, turning his lips in a smile that did not engage his eyes. Eva took note.

"I brought the wood you requested." Eva handed him the piece.

"Ah yes. *Pera* wood," said the Painter, reaching for the rectangular object. He examined the rich brown color of the smooth-grained timber. "To simply behold such a tree, one would not know the beauty or value of its wood." His finger moved the length of the wood grain. "Do you have supply enough for the choir, sacristy, and altars? They will require perhaps forty more pieces of this size." The Painter set down the wood, turned to his stone jars.

"The ten trees nearest the valley of the Rhône have reached good size this season. They should yield twice that bounty."

"Splendid. His grace, the bishop of Avignon, will pay handsomely for the adornments. You must cut the wood now and let it dry over winter." The Painter stopped closing the stone jars with pigments, cocked his head sideways, and narrowed his eyes. "There must be no cracking as in *la cathedrale* in Arles."

Eva clucked her tongue once and let indignity fill her voice. "That was but one piece, and three years past at that."

The Painter took a step back, held up his hands in conciliation, color-etched palms outward. "I know this, and you repaired it admirably, dear Eva. I examined it anew on my recent journey to Arles and it remains whole, have no fear." He closed his right hand except for his index finger and pointed it at her. "In Avignon, there must be no such failing." He poked her thrice in the shoulder. It had ever been his way of chastening. "The city is special to Rome in ways I do not comprehend. Popes enjoy making sojourn there and celebrating mass. Success in *la cathedrale Notre Dame de Doms* will expand our good name and our business. You most certainly will earn your coinage this time."

"The one exception notwithstanding, do not I always surpass expectation?" She gave the most winsome smile she could muster, let the corners of her lips droop to a frown. "Although you receive all recognition."

Her eyes glanced casually about the room, but her mind was working like a thresher, trying to sift out what felt different about this place, this large villa occupied by only one man. Another presence was here. She could sense it. Whether corporeal or ethereal, such knowledge cluded her.

"I never reveal the name of my carver and my customers do not inquire," replied the Painter, seemingly oblivious to Eva's visual scanning of his studio.

"I never know who would approve or disapprove of a woman supplying the ornate carving of a masculine cathedral or monastery," he stated with a broad wave of his hand. He proceeded to bend over the table and blow lightly on the still drying rosettes.

"Slender fingers make the most intricate designs and latticework," replied Eva, collapsing into a black leather chair. Exhaling, she turned her full attention toward the Painter, a squat man with powerful limbs, a wild shock of black hair and penetrating, hazel-colored eyes.

Her thoughts returned to marching armies. "If the Moors again crossed the Pyrenees for Carcassonne, you would surely know it before this lowly Beguine," she said coyly, as she turned one corner of her mouth slightly upward. "You claim I was your primary informant of the armies from the North." She found herself questioning at that moment why she had told the Painter the same day of what she had seen, but had waited until this day to tell Claris. Had she somehow known Claris would ask of her father? "I may have been the first to tell you, but I doubt the singular one. Secrets give not health to the bones, nor the soul."

Raising her eyebrows, she slowly allowed her lips to form a wide grin. She loved to knock people off-balance emotionally, leaving them uncertain how to respond to her. It gave opportunity for her to supply the answer to the dilemma she had created with the right word, or phrase, or compliment.

"Unburden yourself of any dark knowledge you carry my Painter. Even as you mock me your eyes betray you."

"And your eyes bedevil me, my handsome Beguine, for I could not paint anything so beautiful if I practiced until blessed *Jhesu* returns." In past days, he would have smiled in an explosion of light like only her Painter could do and they would both laugh, even as she pretended not to be moved by the compliment. But the smile was faint, the light absent, and he averted his eyes, which was a scarce thing indeed.

Eva followed his eyes with her own and moved to meet his turning gaze. "I know that blessed *Jhesu* has called you into many business dealings with bishops, men who are not always discreet with the knowledge they possess." She shaped her slightly playful expression into one of earnestness. "I implore you, sir, do not speak in riddles. What news have you of the war against heresy? For that is what it must be."

The Painter's eyes stopped looking away and met her gaze. For a moment, he observed her determined expression. His look was as those who had studied her face, seeking knowledge of how a lady with such fair skin had dusky eyes and hair. She had been told once they were a shade of brown so rich as to be but a whisper from ebony.

Yet the Painter knew of her lineage of a pale German father and dark-haired Provençal mother. His eyes seemed to be probing beyond flesh and bone, as if to assess the tenacity of her soul. It felt as a test and was unnerving. She matched his gaze as one would return a blow in a tournament. A half smile lifted one corner of his mouth and moved his eyes. Good. "The gift of discerning is truly yours. You speak of Bishops with secrets to tell, and you are right, as always with such things." The Painter hoisted the pear wood once more and turned it in his hands and studied it as if it held a mystery beyond fathoming. After a moment, he lifted his eyes off the timber and fixed them squarely on her dark soul windows. "There is one, a *Lombart*, who has journeyed a fortnight from Siena with news. Let him unburden himself to you, Eva. He carries tales of your *paire* for your ears alone."

CHAPTER 7

18 JULY 1209

The procession advanced single file, keeping tight to the center of the stream. Andreas's leather boots were stained dark with the damp. They had long since grown sodden from the splashing of horses' hooves in the drink. He wiggled his toes in their squishy confines, longed to stop and dry them in the heat of the late afternoon sun.

There was an unspoken urgency to their watery ride through the forest of oak. It was a thing he knew in sinew and muscle yet could not translate to thought. The air hung heavy and taut with the raw, bloody smell of pursuit. Andreas sensed they were not the first company to flee this way from peril. An aroma as potent now as in ancient days.

A parade of the afflicted crossed his sight. He knew somehow they had once walked this streampath. Images translucent from a time long past. Some bore armor and weaponry as he did this day. Others wore robes, both cowled and not, others adorned in all manner of dress. Each glanced hastily back over shoulder as feet plunged footfall after footfall into the streamlet, the very same streamlet in which Andreas rode this day. They sought freedom from oppression, to worship before *Deu* and pray to Him unencumbered. How did he know this? He could see it, stark as lightning before his waking eyes. They sought liberty to speak their minds, to disagree with pope and king and do it with their heads remaining affixed in place as *Deu* intended. They saw not their hunters nor did he.

Andreas blinked and his sight was refreshed. The parade vanished. Was there no relief from such visions?

There was respite at least from the July air, for the fire of the sun did not pierce the wood.

For the third time since they veered off the road, Raimon Roger turned to their company and made a gesture imploring silence.

Andreas mouthed words questioning why. His lord looked upon him but did not respond.

Since the departure from Carcassonne, their trek had been many things, but not peaceful. Yet the mission had been purposed as one of freedom from strife. For their aim, after all, was to treat with the papal legate, not to make war. Andreas held no illusions of the outcome.

If Raimon Roger was granted the right to take the Cross, only one formidable, unyielding lord would remain in the Languedoc. Roger, Count of Foix, was himself rumored to be numbered among the *Bons Hommes*. Most certainly, this lord of the High Languedoc, fierce in battle and swift with sword and spear, would not take the Cross. Yet the majority of his redoubts were firmly entrenched near the summits of the Pyrenees. The cities of Roger of Foix, perched within sight of the Iberian frontier, would be not desirable options for the French to besiege. They could not make their statement there.

So what then of the threat looming against their own party? Andreas knew Raimon Roger was not leading them along this watery route merely to seek out a soft bed and a hot, savory meal, though he hoped both lay at trail's end. They could have reached Montpellier easily before the closing of the gates at twilight. Tomorrow, the path in front of them led still to the selfsame city.

What hostility existed this night between here and there that would be vanquished by morning? Were there more of the cavaliers in green? Advance guards of the enemy? What else did

Raimon Roger know? What else did Bertran have knowledge of?

Where would his friend have heard the word *melimarpera* before? Was it an incantation to be chanted around a fire at night in a clearing of the wood, a name of a deity to be appeased and then invoked to do one's bidding?

Tight-lipped as he was about such matters, he sensed Bertran would not easily reveal the meaning to him, if indeed he knew it.

Regardless of the *raison d'êtres* for seeking out this inn unknown and secluded, Andreas estimated they had ridden one and one-half leagues along the streambed. It was a late afternoon in July, with plenty of daylight left. Yet the dense forest allowed little of it to reach the winding liquid trail. They needed to stay alert for the stream rarely straightened itself, as if meant to cut off line of sight between hunter and the hunted.

"Why do we not ride along the bank?" Aimer mouthed the words to Andreas.

Andreas shrugged.

The birdcalls continued. They sounded from the wood to the left. Andreas saw that the streamlet divided ahead. Raimon Roger raised his hand and the war party came to a halt. He uttered not a word but told them through signals and gestures that they were to follow the water to the left and then assemble for battle. The look of Bertran's eyes had intensified. He scanned the forest but released neither dagger nor spear. Andreas saw no living forms through the trees.

They turned their direction left. A party of men dressed as stable hands emerged from the rear of a clump of oak trees. Raimon Roger motioned his company to dismount, arm themselves, and release their mounts to these folk dressed as servants. Andreas gathered all his weaponry and relinquished his stallion to a man of graying hair and imposing stature. Raimon Roger gestured for continued silence. So they were the ones to lie in wait this time. Raimon Roger took a stick, crouched down, and etched a plan of engagement into the forest floor. They were to divide, Raimon Roger taking one troop, Andreas the other. They would draw the enemy inside the point of a V formation. It was the same way Hannibal and his armies from Carthage had defeated the Romans in a battle long ago. A fight waged before even the natal day of *Jhesu*.

Andreas mouthed his words, feeling strange surprise. "So we are Carthage in this fight?"

His lord replied in kind. "And they are Rome."

It seemed right for they were indeed battling Rome.

Aimer joined Andreas's troop while Bertran went with Raimon Roger.

Andreas led his troop to the left where they were to lie in wait behind a thicket. He watched Raimon Roger's troop disappear into a shallow depression some twenty yards opposite. So they were indeed to squeeze the enemy like ripe grapes in a winepress.

Andreas had eight cavaliers and three squires with him. Looking upon the squires, their eyes intense, Andreas decided they would have eleven knights in their ranks.

It was time. They would receive the *coule*.

The *châtelain* removed the leather glove from his right hand and bid the three squires draw near. They approached him without hesitation. Andreas instructed the first one to kneel before him. The squire genuflected but kept eye contact with Andreas, who spoke in a whisper. "Your oath to safeguard the Viscount and protect the people of his realm. Do you so swear?"

"I so swear."

"So you will have always remembrance of your oath, receive the *coule*." Andreas drew back his hand and struck the squire hard in the face. The young man leaned backwards as a drop of blood slid out from his nose and water escaped his eyes, but he remained upright and silent.

Andreas administered the *coule* to the other two, and eight knights became eleven.

After a few minutes had passed, Andreas heard the voices in *Langued'oil* before he saw movement or heard footfalls. There were two distinct tones in conversation, speaking fast and low. The voices grew louder though he saw none other than those in their own troop. The unseen pursuers were now the pursued. Aimer apparently heard them as well, and nodded his head in the direction of the voices with a questioning look on his face. Andreas brought his finger to his mouth to renew the call for silence. The voices were drawn near enough for Andreas to discern each word. He heard talk of a raid upon a village and thought of Miquel and his father, who had been taken on to the Inn of Guilhabert. Of chickens and beehives and his posture stiffened. Of a slain little wretch and his hand went to the grip of his sword.

The voices told enough for him to grasp the meaning of their words. "You must have mislaid the bejeweled thing in the village and he filched it."

"We returned and searched the wretched village, tore apart house and building, razed them to earth, searched even the bloating corpse of the boy, stripped it bare. The man has it I tell you, or perhaps the boy we did not slay. But I say it is the man. The boy was too stricken with paralysis to do anything of consequence."

"Even if the fool found it, how could he wield it to our harm?"

"It is doubtful he could. But hear me now, in the hands of another, one with knowledge, it could rend the very shroud about us."

The song of the nightingale was raised. Andreas loosed the war cry and led his troop crashing through the thicket, brandishing mace and shield. Some twenty knights in green appeared in the gap, as if hastily formed up from the earth, scattered and disorganized, clearly caught off guard, as if they had not yet awoken from creation's haze, as if the malevolent demiurge of the *Bons Hommes* had newly fashioned them. But surprise quickened to hauteur as they saw they outnumbered their foe nearly two to one. Andreas charged the center, targeted the tallest knight, the one roaring out orders. Andreas brought the full force of his knobby mace against the shield of the leader, dented the standard of the knight's lord, forced his opponent back a step. Andreas blocked the counterthrust of the sword of the cavalier and broke the knees of the man with his mace. His opponent crumpled to the ground in pain. Andreas wielded his mace and brought the sum of the knight's earthly pain to an end.

The song of the thrush sounded forth. Raimon Roger and Bertran emerged from the hollows flanked by their cadre, swords drawn, shields raised. Their foemen, momentarily stricken with paralysis, looked at the charging troops then back to Andreas's company. The *châtelain* pressed the assault, drove the enemy toward Raimon Roger. When he joined with his lord, they were the point of the V. As one, the entire formation began to step backwards while compressing together.

Andreas did not hear the enemy reinforcement arrive and he saw them only after Bertran cried out to the heavens. The number of green knights had doubled. The V was widening once more. Two of Andreas's troop and three of Raimon Roger's were cut down. The enemy sought to force the *châtelain* and his lord apart. It felt as if their entire company was being stretched on the rack. Andreas commanded the newly dubbed knights into the gap. They charged in without hesitation. Even with reserves, they were outnumbered nearly two to one. Another of Andreas's cadre fell and the left side of the V was split, like tendon wrenched from bone.

Andreas struck a knight across the face and drove him back, sent three others sprawling. "To the inn, my lord."

Raimon Roger sliced though the weapon arm of his opponent and kicked him in the belly. "The inn comes to us."

"What mean you?" But Andreas did not need to wait for his lord's reply. A band in a straight line formation broke out from the trees to the rear of the green knights. In the center of the line, fully armored and commanding the men, was the stable hand who had relieved Andreas of his horse before the battle began. Guilhabert.

Guilhabert charged the rear guard of the knights in green and the V tightened once more and became a triangle. Andreas was the apex and pressed the newfound advantage. "Squeeze them!" He cut down the two in front of him. He could see frustration turn to fear in eyes of the green knights as they were pressed together inside the triangle and unable to wield their weaponry.

Within minutes the enemy was slain.

CHAPTER 8

18 JULY 1209

Eva opened the broad, iron-hinged door that led from the Painter's studio into his living rooms. The oaken planks of the door darkened with age. Ancient like the whole of her Painter's residence. A villa of white limestone raised during the reign of the Caesars, before even the natal day of blessed *Jhesu*.

The dwelling had been raised, like so many in Orange, at the behest of Caesar Augustus. Commissioned for a general of the Second Legion. One who had chosen to retire in Orange, the city in the heart of the most desirable lands of Gaul. Lands the Romans had called simply *la Provincia*, the Province. The lands Eva knew as Provence. She knew also from her reading that Pliny, the Roman statesman and historian, was captivated by Provence. He wrote of it endearingly as "another Italy."

Never had she journeyed to Italy. Yet she would make sojourn, however brief, in a place she rarely made entrance. It was the first time she had crossed the threshold of marble into the personal rooms of the home of the Painter in many years. Since the passing of her mother. But the Painter did not accompany her on this shortest of journeys. She was treading alone down a smooth gray flagstone floor. The feeling of aloneness gripped her like a vice.

What of this bishop? What 'tales' of her father did he possess?

Striding to the rear of the arched whitewashed hallway, she opened the door, another old, dark, heavy, iron-bound piece of wood. Hinges creaked and her belly rumbled. She entered the room as she had been given instruction.

Eva cast her eyes upon the presence she had felt. A man sat in a white wicker chair in a far corner of the room. The room was spacious and brightly painted. The man was not as she had expected.

The few bishops she had encountered were invariably dressed in white vestments and miter. They bore always a scepter of gold and an air of indifferent superiority. Whether their character gave merit to such authority seemed of little consequence.

Yet this cleric was relaxed, showing no shred of haughtiness. He did not purse his lips or attempt a look of piety. He was dressed in the plain, brownish tunic and sandals of a pilgrim. Much like she had imagined *Jhesu*, blessed be his name, would have been clothed. Eva found it curious that though she had been able to sense his presence in the villa, no shadows smudged the spirit air around him, quite unlike other bishops she had encountered.

At the sight of her, this bishop seemed enlivened and spoke first. His words were fluent Latin, unsurprisingly, but infused with an accent that gnawed at the rear of her mind. One she could not quite place. "*Pax vobiscum*, my lady. For many seasons I have prayed incessantly this moment would show itself before death claimed one of us. Each day I have lifted my prayers."

Eva smiled, further disarmed in spite of herself, and shifted her weight from one foot to the other. She replied in her best Latin, hoped she was not muddling the words with her Occitan dialect. "You honor me, your grace, calling me lady. Yet this robe of wool reveals your servant to be far from a noblewoman."

The bishop waved his arm dismissively. "I have seen your work in the transept of Arles' Cathedral of Saint Trophime. The table of the Eucharist is beautiful, a pure delight. A finer setting for dispensing the blood and body of our Lord I cannot fathom. I would venture to say you accomplished more with the carving of that table alone than a dozen selfish, idle noblewomen contribute to this world in the entire sum of their lifetimes. Truly it is an extraordinary gift you possess."

Eva demurred, felt the skin of her face grow warm. Likely it embraced a tinge of red. "My Painter said he never reveals the name of his carver. But apparently you know much of me already. I am at your mercy." The manner of this man put her at ease. "You seem to have been waiting a very long time to make my acquaintance," Eva continued. "I was left in suspense only as I strode the hallway." She smiled, yet her mind still held confusion about his presence here.

"Beg pardon, your grace, but what concern has a lord of the Church, one come from another land, with a Beguine of Orange? My Painter said you journeyed an entire fortnight to convene with me."

"The sum of my journeys to convene with you far exceeds a fortnight." The bishop bore a relaxed smile, but his deep green eyes looked intently upon her face. "You are the beginning and end of a mission for me." He sprang to his feet and crossed the distance between them in two strides. Grasped her shoulders and kissed her cheek. "Eva, it is indeed you my heart. You have the look of your father." Tears welled and escaped the bishop's eyes, but his expression was of purest joy. "Truly I have waited long for this moment. I have sought you Eva in the cities of Lombardy, planning official visits so that I might seek you out, in Flanders where I thought you might reside with the *mulieres sanctae*, in the lands of the Languedoc from Montpellier to Beziers to Carcassonne to Toulouse. Even Iberia, where I saw Santiago de Compostela for a second time, but you I saw not. Now *Deu* has at length led me to you in Provence. I knew not there was a city of women in Orange or any place along the Rhône."

She embraced the man and looked him in the eye, a deep gaze. The eyes of her father looked back at her. She blinked. Eva had no memory of her father. How did she see his eyes in this man? This bishop had gone to the hallowed shrine of Santiago de Compostela, the church of St. James, the brother of blessed

Jhesu, twice in search of her.

"Iberia? Why scour all of Christendom for me?" She realized she had the urge to call him father. "I am no saint. Surely, my lord, you have had matters more pressing in your bishopric to occupy your days."

The bishop leaned forward and his response was crisp. "None more vital than seeking you." He looked toward the window once more. "Even now I fear that day fades and night draws nigh."

Eva smiled even as a pang rippled through her gut. "You speak as a troubadour. Were you once a jongleur as was the bishop of Toulouse? Pray tell the meaning of your words poetic. Are they part of a song?"

The bishop shook his head. "I am no troubadour. It has been not a lively or celebratory quest seeking you Eva, nor a safe one." He grasped her hand. "Call me Pietro, my heart. We may dispense with formality. Let us also dispense with ignorance, for there is much you do not know. You have lived with a potent danger concealed these many years." Pietro released her hand, continued to look out the window. "The darkness gathers in power in these lands. Even now I feel it as a spiky oppression. It is strong here in Orange, but was at floodtide in Avignon."

The tingling began at the back of her neck and spread quickly across her body, raised the gooseflesh. The sensation closed over her like an unexpected bath in a January river. Her hands clenched, neck muscles tightened. The fear. Somehow she knew, she had always known. He spoke her thoughts.

"Do you... do you truly sense such things, Pietro? Do you see... the shadows?" It was as if she was airborne and looking over Orange and Avignon and the lands between. Beautiful lands inhabited by light and dark. Many shadows moved about each city and made journey between them. In Avignon there was a place near the River that was devoid of all light.

The bishop stood and walked toward the window and pulled the draperies completely closed. "At times, dear Eva, though not at will." He paused and turned toward her. "If you ask, you must see such things also. Is it true?"

Eva felt tired. "It is true. I have seen into the nether world for the seven years past."

"I lack surprise at this. Your father seemed to peer through the veil at will." The bishop regained his chair, exhaled slowly, leaned his head back, and turned his eyes once more to the window, where a remaining crack in the flaxen draperies opened a view to the alleyway of brick and stone. At the mention of her father, Eva was seized with the urge to ask more of him, but she stifled the impulse, sensed the bishop had more timely words to speak. His grace appeared to be looking somewhere much farther away than the narrow street outside.

It was rare to find another made weary by the same quest.

He turned his face to her. "My dear, Eva, I need look upon the letter once more. You have been the keeper of knowledge of which I believe even you lacked awareness. The treasure of your *paire*, his share of the spoils, is it still in your possession?"

Eva merely nodded.

The bishop smiled. "I assume it is still because you spoke of it. Believe me my daughter, it is of the uttermost need or I would not trouble you to revisit the loss of your parentage." The cleric noticed Eva's gaze was cast on his ecclesiastical ring and he shook his head. "You need not kiss the blessed ring, my lady." He gestured toward a few chairs that were placed opposite of him. "I pray you would find a comfortable chair, for our visit may consume some time. If you wish, you can show honor by indulging my many queries."

Eva stepped slowly back and settled hesitatingly into another wicker chair with a soft, red velvet cushion. The chair creaked slightly as it absorbed her weight. She was glad it issued not a loud complaint. Wicker was not kind to those with generously rounded bellies or hips, groaning loudly and complaining of the burden foisted upon it. She was glad the chair did not protest her presence in such a way.

The bishop shifted in his chair and the painted wicker responded agreeably. A vigorous looking man of purpose, he bore not the pale, drawn look of an ascetic. His hair, gray but full, his frame thin but not gaunt. With the many rotund clerics she had known, she would have feared for the wholeness of the chair if one had settled his bulk into it.

Her eyes returned swiftly to the bishop's ring. Drawn there by the force of many years of waiting, questioning.

"Your grace, at the risk of sounding far too bold, may I gain a closer look at your ring?" Eva's eyes remained fixed on the thick golden band with engraved marks on the bishop's right hand. She squinted but could not decipher the symbols from where she sat.

"Please, dear one, call me Pietro. I come to you not as a bishop this day, but as a man seeking the daughter of his dearest friend, for I knew your father in Outremer. Knew him soul and spirit." His voice grew soft. "A good man he was." He averted his gaze then engaged her again. The enthusiasm reformed in his voice. "How long have I sought you, and now my travels and dead ends beyond counting have at last yielded fruit! It is a joy to lay eyes on you after these long years. I consider you as my daughter."

A smile broke across her face as she leaned forward and folded her hands in her lap. She believed him, and could sense he was that rare amalgamation of a kind and holy lord of the Church. Eva looked at him for a moment, unsure of her emotion and at a loss for words.

The cleric had already exceeded his calling many years past by penning the letter Eva had preserved, and by arranging for shipment of the worldly possessions of her father back to Provence.

He had paid the captain of the Italian galley, a Venetian merchant, a substantial sum for security and secrecy during transport. Her mother had told her thus.

Now it seemed he had come from Outremer *via* Siena to give the presence of her father back to her, at least a shard of his soul. Is that why she could sense him? Was that true? How was this possible? After so long a time, why was her past thrust to the fore this day?

He removed the ring, walked over, and gently placed it in her outstretched palm.

At first she simply stared at the band, made no effort to clasp it or remove it from her palm for inspection. It was a heavy ring, one that bore evidence of a long and vigorous history. The gold was scratched and pitted in places, the band no longer perfectly round, but compressed into the shape of an uneven oval.

Slowly she clasped the ring with the fingers of her other

hand. Drew it near to her face for inspection. She ran a finger over the engraved images on the flat apex of the ring. Pressed the finger onto the ring. Left a short-lived relief of an eagle soaring above a raging, consuming fire.

She could have felt it with her eyes closed and recognized the signet. Perhaps the edges of the golden symbols had faded. Yet the outlines of the raised symbol in the letter's wax seal had softened as well.

Eva's first memory as a child was breaking the varnished wax seal and rolling out the cream-colored lambskin parchment. It was during her third summer. Her natal day was the autumn equinox.

Even as a newly received letter, it had appeared old to her young mind. Her mother had hovered over her. Admonished her to be careful. For it was a letter about her father. One last occasion to bid him farewell. She had cried then. The tears had left watermarks the letter bore still. Miraculously, the varnished halves of the red beeswax seal still clung to the manuscript as well.

The seal had cleaved neatly in half when she opened the letter, leaving the eagle flying high at the top and the flames burning far below. Her mother had told her that it was a promise from blessed *Jhesu*. That her father was now soaring with the angels in heaven, free of the cares of this world, far removed from the flaming brimstone of the lake of fire.

"So you still possess it then, the letter?" asked the bishop as Eva simply nodded. "You appear very well acquainted with my signet." His hand went to the side of his neck. Rubbed it as if to relieve the soreness of ever craning it in search of something. "It is from the words of the Hebrew prophet Isaiah: *Those who wait upon the Lord shall mount up with wings as eagles*."

Eva fingered the ring. She did not look up. "I possess still both the letter and the treasure."

"That heartens me, for though they have proved a bane they may also be our deliverance. That is the soul of the reason I have searched for you these last five and ten years. Long years since I returned to Siena from Outremer." Pietro spoke in a deliberate tone. "I was not able to return and weep with you as I had promised in the letter. For I had no knowledge that your mother had brought you here from Lombardy—"

"What say you?" interrupted Eva. She rose to her feet, clutched tight the ring. "Did my *paire* not tell you he was of Provence? I am no *Lombarta*. I am a *Provençaux*." Her voice sounded defiant, angry, but she felt also exposed, vulnerable, as if her garments had been rent through on a cold day.

"No, Eva," replied Pietro steadily, but softly, as if he sensed the delicate ground upon which he tread. "You are not of Provence but of Siena in Lombardy. That is your natal city."

Eva folded her arms across her breast. "No, I am of Provence. My *maire* told me thus." Her lips trembled slightly as she felt the itch of a tear on her cheek. She realized she also felt betrayed, although she was unsure by whom. Unable to stay still, she strode about the room.

"Did she tell you, or simply allow you to believe such a story? I daresay she would have done so for your own safekeeping. You would have been only two or three when you left Lombardy. Your mother had reasons for moving you, reasons for wanting not you or any other soul to know you were of Siena."

She stopped and looked at him. "The treasure?"

"Yes, but it is more than that. There is much to tell."

Eva scrunched her nose and added confusion to her expression. "What need you with the letter and golden objects? I do have them all, save one, a golden bowl, studded with jewels. I sold it to raise funds for my purchase of land."

"You are a possessor of lands? Splendid," said the bishop clasping his hands, his eyes reflecting the passion of his voice. "I should like to see these lands, and the community of Beguines, and the things I spoke of. I am also relieved, because I do not think your golden bowl is what I seek."

"What do you seek Pietro?" Eva sat down once more. It was an easy thing to address this bishop by his given name.

"In truth, I was hoping you would know, dear Eva, at least possess some clue, some inkling where to begin. I seek the circle and triangle within, that is all I know."

Eva furrowed her brow. "The triangle and circle within...? Within what? What is the meaning?"

The bishop looked disappointed. "You've had the letter and the golden objects for many years. I hoped you would possess some intimate knowledge of them. I hoped you would know of the triangle and circle. "There is a message in that language we must discern. It was spoken by many in Outremer, though I never was compelled to learn it. You are fluent in the language of *Oc*, or Occitan as some call it?"

"*Oc*," she said, smiling.

It was Pietro's turn to bear a look of perplexion.

"In Occitan, *oc* means yes," she continued, reverting to Latin.

"So then, Langue d'oc is the language of yes?"

"*Oc*," she said again, laughing.

CHAPTER 9

18 JULY 1209

Quickly they gathered their own dead and wounded, abandoned the bodies of the knights in green. Andreas's only thought to glean answers from the man he had taken pity on this morn. In silence they returned to horse and continued to follow the streamlet. The bejeweled thing unknown was a fabricator of death. His compassion toward the villager turned to anger. They rounded another bend and witnessed their watery trail vanish beneath a ragged arch of red stone.

Raimon Roger issued proclamation. "We follow the streamlet below ground. The passage inside arches to such a height we may remain on horse." None other spoke. The faces of all were sober.

They passed under the arch single file, made entrance to the hill. The path grew darker. The light was only behind them, not in front. The tunnel did not traverse the whole of the hill. The underground passage sprouted fanciful, milky columns on either side, stalactites and stalagmites that lined the way, a subterranean portico. In the damp of the cave, the smell of pursuit no longer tarried. Andreas saw the parade of the afflicted find safe haven and succor within. Their company melded into the long train of those persecuted in times past.

Andreas saw motion in the periphery of his vision. The very wall of the cavern made movement. In truth it rolled aside. A giant round stone on a level groove of limestone slowly made revolution. The massive thing had fused perfectly with the remainder of the cave wall, at least as far as sight could tell. The space it vacated was a breach large enough for a mounted knight to ride through with head held high. A place of dignity. Raimon Roger turned his *milsoldor* and rode into the Inn of Guilhabert. Andreas, Aimer, Bertran, three new knights, and the remainder of the cavalcade followed.

The massive round stone was anchored on the inside by four short stout cemented rods of iron connected to a series of wooden and iron gears. The whole apparatus was driven by a large steel hand crank that could be worked by one person. The turning apparatus was on a track as well and moved along with the stone. Notches in floor and ceiling, evenly spaced and perfectly aligned, allowed the teeth of a lower gear to use the floor for leverage and the teeth of an upper gear the ceiling. The notches and gears transformed the power of one man into force enough to move a massive stone that possessed a diameter of at least ten feet, was over a foot thick, and clearly weighed many a ton.

The stables were on the same level as the rolling stone, down a wide arched tunnel and to the left. The stalls for the horses, individually hewn from solid limestone, were clean and sweet smelling, piled with new hay. The arrival of their troop had been expected.

Chiseled stairs of stone led to the upper level of the inn.

Andreas found the villager sitting alone on a bench in the main hall. He made entrance to the hall and sat next to him. "Why do these knights pursue you?"

The man flinched but spoke nothing. His eyes locked upon the smooth limestone floor. Unmoving was his head, as if affixed in place by an iron stanchion unseen.

Andreas arose from the bench adjoining the wooden trestle

table. His anger surged once more at the thought of three of his friends slaughtered in the woods. He walked round behind the seated man, made his steps heard on the stone floor. He bent over, his mouth but inches from the ear of the villager, his voice a whisper. "Hear me now. One of your sons is dead in body, the other in spirit." He gave increase to the volume of his speech. "Three of my men, skilled fighters, friends whom I have known since I was a child, are now slain as well." The *châtelain* stepped in front of the man and faced him square. "In the wood, before he was slain, one of the knights in green spoke of a charmed thing he had mislaid in your village. He believed truly you possessed it." Andreas, his nose nearly touching that of the villager, roared in fury. "The whole of his troop met their death in pursuit of its return." Head cocked to one side, Andreas looked into the man's eyes and was uncertain whom he saw. His voice grew low. "Why would they risk such an end?"

The man was silent.

Andreas slowly unsheathed his sword. He allowed the villager to look upon the blade that glinted even in the dim light thrown off by votive candles burning on wall sconces of bronze. The tip cleared the hilt. Andreas brought the weapon quick against the throat of the man, who twitched, but otherwise remained without motion.

"Do you know of what they seek?"

The mouth of the man opened, but no words emerged. The twitch became a tremor. Senseless blubbering issued forth from trembling lips as the man became as a puddle of dew. Truly a puddle, as the tang of warm urine stung Andreas's nose. The villager wet himself in no small volume. The tremor grew violent. Reaching under a fold of his tunic with a shaking hand, the incontinent fool pulled out an ornamental silver dagger. The blade was thin and appeared wickedly sharp. Andreas thought the man might slit his throat himself, so unwieldy was his grip on the slender weapon.

Andreas snatched the dagger with his left hand, continued to press sword against the gullet of the man with his right. The handle of the mysterious weapon was ringed by embedded dark jewels with six sides that seemed to hold the light as much as reflect it. The bejeweled thing. There were seven of the hexagonal precious stones that formed a spiral rising from the blade. A helix of four emeralds, punctuated by two rubies and a sapphire that sat at the center of the grip. Colored steps ascended a circular tower: Emerald, ruby, emerald, sapphire, emerald, ruby, emerald.

He had seen its likeness this very morn. It was a match to the one Bertran had hurled at the green knight. Andreas's brain felt airy once more.

Perchance he interrogated the wrong man.

"They mislaid this at your doorstep?" The *châtelain* had moved not his longsword. The blade bit slightly into the quivering neck flesh of the man. It drew forth a viscous trickle of blood that appeared black in the yellowish light. The eyes of the man strained against the confinement of his eye pits. A drop of blood slid beneath his tunic.

Andreas withdrew his warsword. The man gulped air and bawled like a child with a gash.

"You already lost one son to their bloodlust. Why pilfer such a thing? Did you not think they would search for it?" Andreas exhaled and looked toward the rough-hewn ceiling. "I would kill you now and think no more of it, for such is the merit of your deeds. You have endangered many more than yourself and your son." He sheathed his sword. "Yet little Miquel has seen enough of death this week, or of any week." Andreas raised the dagger and held it inches from the face of the villager. "This weapon is what they seek?"

The man only nodded and mumbled something, his eyes wild and bewildered, like the storms of lightning and thunder and wind that laid siege each summer to the Languedoc.

Andreas set the dagger slowly and deliberately on the bench.

"Do you believe it to be true?" Andreas pulled back his arm and smashed a gloved fist into the edge of the trestle table, tipping the oaken top unbalanced, nearly knocking it to ground. "Say the words so I can hear them man!"

The stammering response was soon forthcoming. "I... I believe that... that is all... all they seek."

"You speak like an idiot." Andreas exhaled. "Yet you have paid a dear cost. I shall take you at your word." Andreas snatched up the dagger once more. "If you bear false witness, may death find you quickly. May your son be borne into better hands." The tremoring villager doubled over in breathless sobs. Andreas placed the weapon in his satchel and strode from the room.

The *châtelain* negotiated the stone hallways of the underground Inn of Guilhabert. The design of the place was curious. Intrigue dueled anger. Intrigue overcame. It was as if the Inn of Guilhabert itself was an answer to the riddle that was this day. Andreas explored as if his questions about the dagger could find resolution here. Most passages were ramrod straight. Yet one was curved. All had been hand-hewn many years past out of solid limestone. Two of the straight hallways were equal in length and juxtaposed at right angles like beams of a cross. The curved passage was shaped like a horseshoe with both ends of the shoe terminating at right angles against a third straight hallway. That passage in turn bisected the cross. Some rooms were triangular while others were square. A few were circular, as if the ancients that did the carving had cordoned off a section of a stone-lined well deep below ground.

Andreas found the boy in a round chamber off the curved hallway. Gone were the shredded garments that reeked of death. The boy was washed clean and clothed in a spotless white robe of Egyptian cotton. Probably the only finery he has ever known, Andreas thought. The countenance of the boy was brightened merely by his face being scrubbed. Bertran sat with Miquel, tenderly spoke kind words to dull ears.

"There is a matter of which we must talk. A matter not for his hearing." The *châtelain* nodded toward the child.

Bertran stroked the clean hair of Miquel and squeezed lightly his shoulder, left the boy under the watchful eye of his squire. He rose and followed Andreas down the hall, the curve of the horseshoe, which was lined with wooden arch top doors of lignin oak, darkened with age, likely cut from the wood just beyond the cave. Sconces of burnished bronze lined the walls at eye level. Holders of light evenly positioned in the space spanning from one door to the next. The votive candles gave a dim but peaceful light to the corridor.

The curve straightened out. Reaching the end of the hallway, Andreas found a wall that was cut not from the limestone, but constructed of quarried blocks of it and built around a lintel of stone and a rectangular door of wooden planks with large iron strap hinges, a door that seemed older than the rest.

Pulling on the handle, Andreas realized it was locked and possessed an ornate keyhole, ornamented in bronze. "It seems we go no further."

Bertran grasped Andreas by the forearm. "Stand aside, for we do indeed go further." He produced a key that was ornamented in like fashion to the lock. "I obtained this from Guilhabert." Clamping a hand on Andreas's shoulder, he said, "Let us speak where not even friendly ears can hear."

Andreas looked upon the key and the lock and the face of his friend, but spoke nothing. He was aware of every movement of Bertran, every expression of countenance.

Inserting the bronze key deftly into the lock, a key topped in relief with what appeared to be the letter P struck through with an X, Bertran turned it and the door opened easily with nary a groan or protest. "Guilhabert is meticulous in his upkeep. Even the doors make no sound."

They entered the stairwell. Bertran softly closed and bolted the door behind them. Andreas flinched. They descended a faintly lit, roughly chiseled stairwell. It curved to the right perhaps twelve steps down then descended in a straight line another twenty steps or so. The whole of the stairs widened and opened into a broad chamber. The walls lining the stair were coarse as well, as if all was hewn by the fiery fingers of God and not those of man.

The air was laden with the pungency of mildew and mist. Andreas could hear the sound of rushing water, a sound that seemed to grow with each passing moment. Two cressets upon the walls, small iron buckets filled with oil that fed a burning wick, cast a pale light on the roughhewn walls, gave only the faintest illumination to the cavern.

Andreas started to walk toward the sound of water, but his advance was blocked by the outstretched arm of Bertran. "Guilhabert requested we go no further than the bottom of the stair." Bertran smiled. "What you hear is an underground river whose level can rise without warning. We could be swept out to sea unawares. Many a soul fleeing martyrdom has made journey down this waterway."

Andreas waited until Bertran looked to the side. He grabbed the right arm of Bertran with both hands, twisted the wrist, and pushed Bertran to ground. He placed his knee on the back of Bertran, just below the neck and held up the arm at a right angle to the prone body, the wrist bent forward at a right angle to the arm.

Bertran laughed. "I yield. You caught me unawares Andreas. Always at battle you are. This is no moment for training."

Andreas became all the more angry. It seethed in his voice. "Am I to be made such a martyr? Who are you? I do not believe I truly know you."

Bertran, his cheek pressed against cold limestone, looked for the first time dismayed. He slowly drew a breath of the pungent air and released it. "You have questioned the villager about why he is pursued." Silence for a long moment. "What knowledge did you gain?"

"I learnt the dagger you hurled this morn is the selfsame kind as this." Andreas held the wrist of Bertran with one arm and removed the dagger from the satchel with the other. "This jeweled dagger is the reason the knights in green pursue the villager. They mislaid it in his village and he picked it up, utter fool that he is. It has sliced to pieces already many lives."

Andreas readjusted his grasp on the wrist of Bertran, who turned his hand, his arm, his body, threw off Andreas, swung his leg around, kicked Andreas in the gut, and knocked him backwards. Bertran sprang to his feet, withdrew his own silver dagger, his blue eyes alight. "You speak of this weapon. Did ever you think to query me first, my *châtelain*? Do your thoughts ever rise above the fire in your belly?"

Andreas arose and held his ground. Confusion roiled his mind. He withdrew his sword and thrust it toward the dagger of Bertran. "Speak of how you obtained that."

Bertran lowered his dagger. "Sheathe your warsword and I will tell, but only if we can speak as friends, as brothers. You must have trust of me soul and spirit, Andreas. I am not your foeman."

Andreas looked back at his friend, searched his face, his eyes for some esoteric clue. In the eyes he saw only Bertran. To his surprise, he noticed a faint, though long scar on Bertran's left cheek, running from mouth corner to earlobe.

Something about the dim light revealed the mark, highlighted the path. Why had he not recognized its presence before? Bertran had endured a thing of which Andreas was unaware.

Andreas returned sword to hilt. "I do have trust of your soul my friend, my brother. It is my own in which I lack trust. Forgive me. I am sorely tried by the events of this day." He pointed toward the face of Bertran. "Tell me of the scar on your cheek."

As if by instinct, Bertran ran his finger down the line on his face. "One cannot battle evil without being marked by the struggle. I have taken my leave from *l'orde* and lived to tell."

Andreas felt an icy chill, much colder than the cavern about him. "Taken your leave from *l'orde*?" There was a malevolent presence, rage upon the air. The beast unseen was among them. "You speak as if it were a guild of craftsmen from which one could simply renounce membership. I know of no one who has made egress from *l'orde* with both mind and body still whole. One or the other are ever claimed."

Bertran raised his eyes heavenward, his voice quiet. "You know of me. They have no claim on me."

"You... How...?"

"Guilhabert. Strong is his discernment, skilled his wielding of the weapons of the Spirit. I came under his protection. Many of his men were once as I was. That is why they are so well equipped to battle the knights in green. Yet even here, I dare not speak more of *l'orde*. Only to say that they would pursue to no end a man they thought had taken a ritual dagger such as this, or any item they called sacred."

Andreas took more mildewed air into his lungs and sighed. The moisture around them brought cool sweat to his brow. "What are we to do with such a weapon? Have done with it then?"

Bertran's response was crisp and blunt. "Some of us have stood against *l'orde*, some of us will make such a stand." Bertran looked Andreas in the eye. "Yet I see not the villager ever being able to make such a stand. He cannot have protection every hour of every day for the whole of his life. And it is the life of father and son that is forfeit lest the power of this accursed object be broken."

Andreas rubbed his eyes. Tiredness washed over him like an unwelcome bath of saltwater. "How does one accomplish such a feat?"

The voice of Bertran became quiet, as if listening ears strained even in this place. "Leave that to me."

CHAPTER 10

18 JULY 1209

va noticed the Painter standing quietly in the doorway. His head and shoulder casually leaned against the jamb. He bore a smile. She ceased her laughter. She had not heard the door open. It was because of the laughter. It felt good to laugh after such a day of heavy burdens.

Pietro turned his head, noticed the other man for the first time. The Painter took a step into the room. "Pardon the interruption, your grace. If you wish to remain unknown in Orange, now is the hour to make journey to the community of Beguines." The Painter glanced over at Eva and winked. She smiled upon the realization that Pietro would make sojourn in her little city. "It is the time of *siesta*, when all seek shelter from the sun. Do you have such in Siena?"

The bishop nodded.

"Eva will accompany you then. The way to the community will be desolate, devoid of all others." The Painter shot her a serious look, a knowing look. It was his signal to take action.

She arose from her chair. "I will show you my home and the other things we spoke of Pietro."

At the use of the Christian name of the bishop, the Painter shot Eva a quizzical look. But it transformed to a smile that moved greatly both his eyes. He clasped his hands together. "You have found her at last your grace. Is she not as I have told you? Does she not possess the spirit of her father?" The Painter's Latin was impeccable. His words released a wave of sadness and joy that broke over her soul.

The bishop bore a look of tenderness, one that made Eva long for her father. "None of the travails I have endured in the seeking of her are in vain. They were but light and momentary trials. She is a worthy heir of the man I buried in the sands of Outremer. For I see I covered over only his body in Acre. The legacy of Anselme is undimmed." He rose to his feet. "Blessed *Iesu* be praised."

Eva smiled. The lower rim of her eyes was an inadequate well for the tears. The Painter walked up and put his arm around her. Quickly she turned and embraced him, buried her head in his shoulder. "I never knew him before, but now I have belief I do. Many thanks to you both for bringing him near to me."

The Painter released her from the embrace. She wiped her eyes and left the room. Pietro and the Painter followed. Eva's walk to the alley door of the villa, down the hallway of flagstone and whitewash had not the feel of isolation. It was not simply the accompanying presence of the Painter and Pietro, with his lithe frame, piercing, deep green eyes, and graying hair.

It was the sense of reunion with her father, of finally experiencing something of the man whose example of courage and sacrifice had always motivated her, and yet made her restless at times. This *Lombart* could not bring her father to her. Yet perhaps he could help her find peace in all that troubled her about the man who had begat her. He had seen her as an infant. Never had she known him. The Beautiful Things ever felt as a curse. Even the letter at certain moments had seemed to her more curse than blessing.

It was difficult to identify the source of her foreboding. The treasure was beautiful and crafted exquisitely. Yet she found it troubling to even examine it for any length of time. It was the reason for her lack of care. Even now, after so many years, she doubted she could recite even half of the contents in her iron-bound cypress trunk from memory.

She treasured things most that were living or at the very least had once held life. Even when sawn from a tree, wood still breathed somehow and brought warmth to cold stone places. Most thought gold and silver and jewels to possess far greater splendor than even the finest carved woods. But she was not among them.

Perhaps she was odd in that respect. Still she lacked understanding about why blessed *Jhesu* wished her to have such cold, dead, Beautiful Things. The answer seemed to lie in learning more of her father. Claris had proved right in asking about her father. Eva realized she had been more troubled by thoughts of him than the reality of the marching host from the North making incursion into the Languedoc.

Eva knew what the Painter had in mind.

"I understand your reluctance to be recognized in Orange. Yet another day I should like to show you our handiwork, your grace. I thought we should begin with the Cathedral of *Notre Dame de Nazare?*"

"Truly I should wish to lay eyes upon it. Many of the cathedrals in Lombardy would lift the spirits even closer to heaven if they were adorned with such painted carvings as I have already witnessed."

Coming from any other cleric, Eva would have viewed such words as flattery.

"There is a new cathedral in fact being raised in Siena," continued Pietro, "near the main square, the Piazza de Campo, on a site where a temple to the Roman goddess Minerva once sat. It is a magnificent structure of black and white marble, and truly fitting that blessed *Iesu* and his wisdom will be worshipped there now..."

They reached the rear of the villa. Eva passed under the lintel and into the alley. She did not look back to see if the bishop followed.

Eva reached the end of the alleyway, came within sight of the columned wall of the theater and waited. The theater seemed always to reverberate with the many echoes past that lingered richly throughout this vibrant *polis*. Though they lived centuries removed from the time of Empire, Orange was still thoroughly a Roman city. The curtain walls, anchored by strong, square towers, were built still upon the same foundations as the original Roman enceinte. The grid of streets was unchanged.

Eva noticed a man walking toward the street of the jewelers. She had seen him before, but where? The guild. He was a member also of the guild of carpenters. She knew not his name. It was difficult to make out his features. Dark shapes smudged the air around him. Never had she noticed such before, but perhaps she had lacked attention. The shadows, once seen, swirled violently about him, as if to obfuscate. One hand seemed to bear a hammer while another held three long spikes. Oft times she could see the purpose of a foul spirit, as if each bore a sign that named it, yet the dark cloud that festered around this carpenter was uncertain. She shivered and the back of her head and neck felt as if dipped in ice water.

She lifted silent prayers, asked for the names of the black imps revolving about him. She saw no names but a doorway that led underground, down many steps of chiseled stone. The end of the stair was shrouded, beyond her sighting. Journey would need to be made to the bottom to see the truth about this man, know the names of the spirits. Eva sensed she was not yet ready, pursued not the man in the natural or any more in the spirit.

He disappeared from sighting as the bishop emerged from the rear of the villa and into the shaded alley. Pietro reached her and they trod past the theater The multi-columned structure still towered over the north half of the city, eclipsed in height only by the spires of the Cathedral of Notre Dame de Nazare. It seemed fitting for only with the building of cathedrals had the architecture of her time began to surpass that of the Romans. Yet they still waged the same ethereal battles as in Roman times. St. Augustine, who had lived under the waning years of the Caesars, had written of the warfare of the spirit. Some things did not change.

Yet in the midst of battles of spirit she had fought for years, a thing had changed this day. She had found a partner in war. She spoke in low tones with a smile. "So I, a humble Beguine, shall become friends with Pietro, the bishop of Siena, lord of the Church?"

He looked up at the columns of the theater. "That is a thing that has already occurred."

CHAPTER 11

19 JULY 1209

SABBATH

T he road to Montpellier was deserted. The reason lay sprawled out in the distance. A great mass of canvas tents; the encampment of the crusading army. The tents for the knights and soldiers curled around the northeast of the city. Their number was difficult to discern. An expanse of counts and earls and dukes lay on the far side of the city.

The sky was clear and high and blue. The air was hot and wet. Andreas removed his helmet and wiped his brow. The camp was quiet. In cases where a forced march was not required, commanders at times allowed the ranks additional hours of sleep in the days before battle. The slumbering state was confirmation to Andreas that the North had indeed come to fight.

The honey-colored walls of Montpellier, raised only a decade earlier, were a contrast standing at attention. The strong clear lines on the merlons and parapets were not yet worn by wind or rain. The guards at the west gate stood at attention and welcomed them as a noble party.

The streets within the walls were sparsely trod. Doors were closed and windows shuttered, as if the looming presence of the Northern host had driven even those granted safe haven indoors.

Encamped armies rarely kept their manners or the promises of their leaders or left even friendly burgs entirely unmolested. However glad the citizens of Montpellier may have been to witness an army avowed to hunt down heretics, they did not personally offer the welcome cup.

Raimon Roger ordered the company to stay mounted and alert in the plaza, which was deserted as well. Raimon Roger and Andreas dismounted and entered the church. Guilhabert had said the papal legate would be here this hour in prayer.

A canon appeared in a black cowled robe and inquired of their business. He looked them over, his eyes focused upon their swords, the crest of *seme fleurs de lis* upon their surcoats, and the many rings on the hands of Raimon Roger.

Andreas spoke to announce his liege. "My lord, Raimon Roger Trencavel I, the Viscount of Carcassonne, Albi, and Beziers, seeks an audience with his grace, the Abbot of Citeaux, legate of our Lord Pope Innocent III." While giving a show of reverence, Andreas inwardly choked down the urge to loose phlegm along with the words.

The canon gave a deferential nod and led them into the nave of the church. The head of Armand Amaury was bowed before the altar, eyes closed, lips moving. He recited the final line of the *Paternoster*, "*Libera nos a malo.*" Deliver us from evil.

The leader of the crusading army raised his head and looked toward the sound of footsteps. The canon cleared his throat and spoke out in a voice of proclamation. "Your grace, I give you Raimon Roger Trencavel I, Viscount of Carcassonne, Albi, and Beziers." Andreas recognized the canon as one who had made journey across the Languedoc for many years with Armand Amaury, who sought to convert the *Bons Hommes*.

The papal legate himself, in his gilded white vestments and miter, beamed beatifically as he turned to face them. The personal representative of Innocent III appeared as if the pope himself, stood next to the carved and painted altar of wood, allowed the start of a frown to frame his lips. He quickly subdued it with a smirk.

Amaury spoke in Latin. "Viscount Trencavel, it appears you

have caught me at end of prayer. Nothing brings peace to the soul like the chanting of the *Paternoster*. Would you not agree?"

Raimon Roger gave a quick, respectful bow, and replied in the same tongue. "How could the prayer of blessed *Iesu* not bring comfort, your grace?"

The legate studied Raimon Roger for a moment. "Your presence here is most unexpected lord Trencavel. I believed you would be occupied with preparing in vain the defenses of your rogue cities. What is your business here in this house? Surely you have not come to pray to the Christian God." The abbot of Citeaux furrowed his brow.

Raimon Roger strode briskly toward the papal legate. "My purpose is singular, your grace, and I will not delay in speaking it. I have come to swear my allegiance to the Bishop of Rome. I am prepared to take the Cross against the enemies of the Holy Church."

Raimon Roger genuflected in front of Armand Amaury and bowed low his head. Andreas felt his jaw constrict.

A shrewd gleam appeared in the eyes of the wily churchman. "In its short history, this church of San Peire of Montpellier has witnessed already many confessions. Will you yourself be next? What say you? Arise and speak plainly. I know your father died when you were but a boy. Tell me forthwith, and truly, after his passing, who was your tutor, my fair Viscount?"

"Bertran du Saissac, your grace," Raimon Roger replied evenly, without hesitation, rising to his feet and looking Armand Amaury square in the eye. "Yet you have lived and traveled in the Languedoc for some years and are likely aware already of my parentage. I do not wish to bore you with things of which you already have knowledge."

Armand Amaury took a few steps toward Raimon Roger, hands clasped behind his back. "Have no care, Viscount Trencavel; nothing could stir me to greater interest. I am sure you are aware that children tend to follow the ways of their parents and pupils of their teachers. Are you prepared to tell me you were all those years under the tutelage of Bertran du Saissac, only to remain free of the deep stain of his heresy?" Amaury issued the query thoughtfully, as if probing a deep topic.

In spite of the legate's well-practiced air of piety, Andreas could not help but think of the man as merely a little pope.

"I am free of such a stain, my lord," said Raimon Roger solemnly. Andreas, standing to the right of Raimon Roger, winced. His lord seemed to have no knowledge of the trap he had just sprung.

"Well, truly I am delighted then." The mouth of Amaury broke into an even wider smile. "So you acknowledge that Bertran du Saissac is a heretic."

"No, your grace," sputtered Raimon Roger. "I mean only to say that I am Catholic and loyal to the Bishop of Rome."

"So you say Bertran du Saissac is not a heretic then?" The brow furrowed again. Amaury had mastered the look of thoughtful puzzlement. "He who believes, as the *Albigenses* do, that the earth and everything in it was created by the devil, including the very wafers and wine that become the body and blood of blessed *Iesu* in Holy Eucharist. Who believes that the other sacraments of the Church, such as marriage or the baptizing of infants are an evil, or frivolous at best. Who believes it is not appointed unto a man once to die and then the judgment, but teaches that souls migrate from one body to the next until they become perfect, whether those bodies be animal or human." Reaching beneath a fold of his vestments, he produced a manuscript of honey-colored parchment.

"I have here a list of two-hundred twenty-two names of the people of Beziers, heretics all. If Bertran du Saissac and his ilk truly are heretics, release them to the Church for chastisement. Then perhaps your lands will know the peace you have no doubt come here to seek. If you claim they are not heretics they shall regardless be taken by force from your midst. Then whomever will perish, *will* perish. If you are truly untainted by the insane belief of the *Albigenses*, then all you need do is make sure these residents of Beziers, these profligate subjects of yours, are surrendered to Bishop Rainaud when he makes his final appeal to the *Bitterois* this very night. The bishop himself carries also the identical list. You may have this selfsame copy."

Armand Amaury nodded to the canon. The cleric retrieved the letter from the legate's hand and delivered it to Raimon Roger. The lines on the face of the legate that made him appear thoughtful now seemed to harden, giving the appearance of winter's onset. "If these heretics are not surrendered before the feast day of the Magdalen, then God's mercy will genuflect to his wrath."

As the pope's personal representative spoke, Andreas noticed that the morning sun had now risen high enough above the rim of the world to give full illumination to the simple stained glass window behind the altar. The light seemed to gather and grow in brilliance around the center object imbedded in the window, a deep crimson cross, which seemed to glow of its own until radiance issued forth, projecting a red Latin cross onto the left breast of Raimon Roger. The lines of the image were sharp, not smudged in the least.

"Grant me my right to take the cross, your grace, and I will see that justice is dispensed in my lands to all who threaten the Holy Roman Church."

Andreas searched for any lingering sarcasm amongst the last three words. His lord spoke firmly and convincingly.

"I have seen many such promises rent asunder in these deceitful days." Amaury looked and sounded sad. If he noticed the illumined cross now borne by Raimon Roger, the abbot betrayed no sign of it. He spoke toward the timber beams of the ceiling. "I fear I may not trust you to mete out punishment." The little pope, with sober voice, turned his countenance sharp upon Raimon Roger. "Truly Viscount Trencavel you are a heresiarch. From what I hear, you barely hold sway over the *Bitterois* rabble. Let the people of Beziers decide their own fate."

The color in the face of Raimon Roger rose to meet that of the luminescent cross on his surcoat. "Those in Beziers are my people. I am their Viscount, your grace." The sarcasm welled up and inhabited the last two words. "Their lives are not yours for the taking." His voice, strong and voluble, filled the church. "I will not surrender even one soul to your keeping. It is not for you to determine who lives and dies, who is a heretic and who is not. The *Valdenses* merely differ in practice, wish to preach and read the Bible in the common tongue. Yet you call them heretical, apostate. Was the Bible first written in Latin? Was not Latin once a common tongue of the people the way Occitan is in the present age? As for the *Bons Hommes*—the *Albigenses* you name them—cannot mighty Rome withstand a challenge from those who merely wish to perfect and purify themselves?" Raimon Roger crossed his arms, took a step forward, and looked upon the papal legate without blinking.

All was silent.

The little pope flinched.

Raimon Roger uncrossed his arms and pointed a finger at Armand Amaury. "You..."

Armand Amaury took a small step backward.

Raimon Roger leaned forward. "You, your grace, are a petulant lord of a corrupt church. A church whose unlettered priests keep concubines and sire whoresons and care not for the souls of their flocks. A church that auctions off its offices to those who have the fattest purses or curry the greatest favor with kings. A church without torchlight, wandering in the dark. Yet you accuse the *Valdenses* of being blasphemous in their practice?" Trencavel looked at the letter. "You have listed *Valdenses* among the numbers here, your grace." Raimon Roger loudly crumpled the manuscript and hurled it at the papal legate. The balled-up parchment struck Amaury on the chest and bounced back to Andreas who quietly retrieved it.

The legate's air of piety dissipated, replaced by a darkened scowl. "You would call me petulant? In these lands I am as the pope himself." His voice rose in crescendo. "We will keep no faith with those who keep faith with heretics! Away with you!" The papal legate gave a dismissive sweep of his hand, pivoted sharply on the ball of his right foot, and strode away.

Before the words finished reverberating off the stone and timber and glass of the church, one half-dozen knights, in burgundy surcoats all, emerged from the shadows. Raimon Roger and Andreas walked out of the church and back into the daylight before they could be forcibly removed. In the periphery of his vision, the *châtelain* thought he saw the crimson cross linger upon the breast of his lord for a few moments after Raimon Roger turned away from the window.

❧ ☙

The rest of their party was found at the ready in the plaza. Andreas's soul was a cauldron of emotion.

He fumed about his lord being treated without consideration by the arrogant legate, but he was more enthused about the cross that had appeared on the surcoat of Raimon Roger. Was this the very reason they had made sojourn, however brief, in Montpellier? Did his liege fight for a holy cause? Was it a sign *Deu* would favor them and grant victory over their enemies?

It had gone badly with the little pope, Armand Amaury, as Andreas had expected, but perhaps their journey was not in vain. The *châtelain* glanced up at little Miquel, motionless, expressionless, sitting behind Bertran, clinging to him atop his *destrier*. The boy would yet find health of soul again. Their journey was not in vain.

The *châtelain* exhaled and glanced round the plaza. "Look to your mounts. We must fly to Beziers at once!" Andreas gained his *destrier* and drew rein. "Godspeed!"

"I fear their armies march on Beziers this very day," Trencavel, the color drained from his face, looked tired, bewildered. Andreas's lord clearly had not anticipated such a complete rebuff.

"What of the knights emerging from the shadows, from invisibility?" asked Andreas. "Perchance the knights in green are his as well by some foul craft. Surely the papal legate wishes you slain, my lord."

"He may soon have his wish," was Raimon Roger's curt reply.

As all the knights and squires reined their steeds to action and the company rode out of Montpellier, Andreas moved next to Raimon Roger.

"My lord," he spoke low in a voice only Raimon Roger could hear. "Amaury could not deny you the cross. It was there upon your breast. Did you not see it? The radiance from the window left its mark. Two crimson bands of light crossing each other. *Deu* himself has granted you favor. You made journey across your lands to receive the cross and it has been granted you by the Almighty himself."

Raimon Roger bore a look of pained skepticism and his mouth puckered. "I saw the Latin cross in the window illumined as the sun rose. I glimpsed no such thing upon my person. As to the matter of whether *Deu* has granted me favor, we shall see."

"*Deu* is with us, my lord. He will grant us victory." Andreas sounded far more assured than even he felt.

~❧ ❧~

Spurring on their mounts, stopping but twice to rest and water the *cavales*, the company reached Beziers by vespers. The road was clear of refugees and travelers and plundering bands. There was a dearth of bird calls or of forest life overflowing onto the *Via Domitia*.

They arrived at Beziers as the bells of the cathedral pealed in strong, clear tones announcing the evening office. Andreas looked to the citadel that seemed an extension of the hillside, ochre stone rising from ochre ground, giving the walls an even higher appearance than they possessed.

Beziers was truly a hillside city. No part of the ground was flat inside the walls; the entire city sloped downward from east to west. Indeed, it was said that if a man dropped a round object near the east wall, it would roll the distance through the city, out the west gate if open, down the steep slope and across the bridge spanning the River Orb.

The city looked well-fortified, prepared for a siege of forty days and nights. Ballista and small mangonels sat atop the thick curtain walls between rounded *tors*. At the base of the ramparts were mounds of hay, likely prepared to take flame and scorch those who would scale the walls. The River Orb to the west of the city was broad. Archers were already in position. Andreas, for the first time in many days, felt somewhat at ease.

The hillside suburb outside the walls was known as the *Faubourg*. It was built on the steeply angled ground that lay between the elevated ramparts and the plain below. It curled round the city to the River Orb and teemed with activity this day. Andreas knew that if Raimon Roger indeed gave him charge as they had discussed during the ride, one of his first endeavors would be to order the hill dwellers inside the broad walls of the city, abandon the suburbs entirely, and, if necessary, destroy the settlement in order to deny the French cover so near the citadel walls.

Reaching the final ascent to the east gate up the hill at a full gallop, pennons, and gonfanons caught high in the hot, stale

breeze, the east gate of the city swung open at the approach of
Viscount Raimon Roger Trencavel I and his knights.

⚘

Leaving Bertran to show their company to quarters for the
night, a monastery near the cathedral, Andreas walked the narrow streets toward the walls. He wanted to see the lay of the city
and the lands beyond as they appeared at night in case the fight
to come ever lingered past sunset.

It was quiet.

The *Bitterois* had been generous in taking the refugees into
their homes. He sensed the city was tired and hoped it was an
exhaustion that could be remedied by a good night's sleep, or
perhaps two.

They would have at most three cycles of the sun before the
French host invaded the plain below Beziers.

Ascending a stair on the inner side of the ramparts, Andreas
stood atop the walls as the gate opened and a small group of *Bitterois* made their egress with Bishop Rainaud from the city to
join the Northern host.

They walked quickly down the hill, journeying to the East on
the *Via Domitia*.

It was a treacherous act, a betrayal of their city. Yet what
were a few hundred souls out of a city of thousands?

The *châtelain* wondered if there were two-hundred and
twenty-two that left with Rainaud after all.

It was reassuring to hear the clanking of metal as the iron-
bound east gate was swung shut and bolted once more.

He made count of the watchmen he could see stationed atop
the towers and patrolling the allure on the walls. He was unsure
they had full visual command of the field. They would need increase in their numbers.

It was fully dark now as Andreas descended the rampart
stair. He turned onto an empty street and noticed that the darkness around him seemed to grow ever blacker. A shadow, long
and wispy passed over him and he shivered. Another shadow
appeared, a circle that seemed to unroll itself and then slither
off.

Unsheathing his sword, he raised it high, prepared to wield it against any who might spring from the shadows.

He saw no one, but the chill lingered.

Looking to the end of the street he saw the silhouette of a church and was drawn there. All he could see was a distinct outline of the structure, as if the interior had been carved out and abandoned to utter blackness. Indeed, it seemed filled not with mere darkness but with the utter absence of light.

Yet as he drew near to the church he now recognized as that of Saint Maria Magdalen, the lack of radiance gave way to the shapes of windows and blocks of stone. The frigid aura only grew.

A shadow moved across *la plasa* as though floating in the form of a darkened robe. Or was it the absence of light in the form of a man? He reached the church of the Magdalen and saw no one. In his mind's eye he saw a picture of an assailant wielding a dagger, but no one was there.

It was decided that Raimon Roger would journey on to Carcassonne, taking with him the Jews of Beziers, some of whom held positions of authority in the city. Though not specifically the targets of the Crusade, the sons and daughters of Israel were ever in danger in such situations. The Jewish Quarter was often the first part of a captured city that was plundered and pillaged.

The villager and Miquel departed for Carcassonne also.

Andreas would command the defense of Beziers until Trencavel could raise a relief force to break the siege the city would soon fall under.

Raimon Roger departed at midnight with a pledge to go through dark and on unceasing until he reached Carcassonne. Andreas and the remainder of the cavalcade set to work hardening the defenses of Beziers the *Bitterois* had already put in place.

CHAPTER 12

The long, rectangular, gray stone and timber dining hall functioned as both supper chamber and secular gathering place for the community of Beguines. It was the newest edifice to be raised around the common, and as such, the ceiling beams of pine still infused the air with their scent. Occasionally, a drop of newly fallen, amber-colored resin was found splayed on the limestone slab floor or on a trestle table top.

Eva loved distinctive, earthy smells, and would often go to the hall when it was devoid of others to wrestle in prayer and breathe in the odor of the building as it aged. She felt closer to God when his creation tingled her nostrils.

The hall itself possessed a singular feature, unintended by its builders. It captured and held onto its sound in a withering embrace. When inside, she could hear others speak readily enough. But when she took even a step outside all echoes of the hall abandoned the ears, and not on the North side only, which lacked windows.

Perhaps the noise simply bounced around the timbers that supported the terra-cotta roof, or was absorbed by the stone walls, but those walls were common limestone only, found in abundance in Provence.

Yet there was another thing about the structure, one that had become apparent only this hour at first light. There were no shadows in the hall. No darkness from the nether realm. She would see at times the charcoal tinged air in her orchard, in the common, in even her own residence, even her very bedchamber, but not here. It was a puzzling thing. There was only peace. It was good air to breathe.

It was cockcrow. Excepting her and Pietro, the hall was barren of people once more, as often it was outside of meals and other gatherings. Eva and her Painter had funded and overseen its construction, though only the Superior of the community and Claris had knowledge of this.

The old dining area, now divided into receiving and hospitality rooms for visitors to the Superior, had grown cramped as the community continued to enlarge. Making use of their extensive connections amongst the guilds of carpenters and stonemasons, woodcarver and Painter had called in many favors. The hall had been raised at a price that was little above the cost of the limestone and timber and roof tiles. Many of the tradesmen had been eager to work upon the structure for a time, if only to have their immortal souls and those of their families prayed over by the Beguines. Two years later, families still made journey from as far away as Marseille to tell of miraculous answers to prayers raised by the women in the community on their behalf.

The other Beguines were told only that benefactors unknown from Orange had made payment for the structure. With all she had benefitted from the adornment of holy buildings, not to mention all she had received from the Holy Land itself, Eva had felt obliged to help fund such a hall.

Since the community had already possessed an ornate high church and a simple chapel, and she had reaped benefit from her carving work on both, she had chosen to build a spacious place of meeting for the Beguines to sup together at the board. It was a simple, if solid, building, not adorned with carvings or pear wood in any form.

It also was an idyllic place for a public tête-à-tête with private utterances.

Though she had trust of him personally, Eva was chary of the appearance of allowing the bishop into her home. As the first shards of light streamed over the walls of the community dispelling darkness, she had asked Pietro to go ahead to the dining hall, while she retrieved the letter and met him there. He had made request they wait until this day, the feast of the Magdalen, before looking upon the parchment together. They had been waiting upon the breaking of this day for three cycles of the sun.

She entered clutching in both arms the wooden tube that housed the precious document. The bishop had a curious look on his face at beholding the protective container. "Did you fashion that tube for the letter?"

"From the limb of a pear tree." She sat down across from him at a trestle table. Eva placed the protective container upon the tabletop between them

"Eva." Pietro paused, as if searching for the precise words to convey a difficult truth. He shifted in his chair. "Now we come to it, Eva. I have reason to believe that letter in the tube, the one I sent you of your father, is a palimpsest."

Silence. Eva, expecting him to speak of the Beautiful Things, scrunched her nose. "A palim... what?"

Pietro laughed at her reaction. "You amuse with your expressions." The bishop smiled. "A palimpsest is a manuscript that was once written upon. But then the old scribing was scraped off, cleansed if you will, and written over once more. It comes from the Greek *palimpsestos*, which means 'scraped again.'"

"Palimpsest." Eva let the word roll off her tongue, lingering on the last syllable. She saw her father in the desert with bleeding heart. He looked up at her as he lay on the hot sand. Stones hurled with violence had done far more than scrape his body. His very rib cage was shattered. Somehow, in a bloodless way, he tore his heart from his chest and presented it to her. She took it in her hands and it seemed to melt into her palms as warmth coursed through her, reached her toes and the crown of her head.

She shook her head, blinked hard, and returned her eyes to the Bishop. Palimpsest. "Did not you realize it was such when you penned it?"

"No." Pietro beheld her with curiosity. "For the script is not my own. I dictated it to a Greek Orthodox clerk, a scribe for the Sovereign Order of Saint John of Jerusalem. You know of them as the Knights Hospitaller. The scribe wrote it in an ornate script far beyond my skill."

Eva frowned. "Why would the scribe make use of a manuscript that already possessed writ?"

Pietro looked round the hall, eyes probing. "It is not uncommon. Lambskin is durable and pliable as you know, and especially scarce and precious in the Holy Land, as you likely do not know." He settled his gaze on Eva. "If a scribe considers the contents of a manuscript of no value, he will not hesitate to put it to better employ. The question more crucial is what of the writ he erased? I have also reason to believe I am not alone in the seeking of this manuscript."

Eva sat up straight in her chair. "How came you to know this?"

"After I spoke the letter to the scribe, I did not lay eyes on him again for over a dozen years, until five summers past. He came to me in secret, in the early morn, before prime, not many days after I had been ordained bishop of Siena. He was trembling, agitated, persisted in looking around, as if he was the prey of the hunt.

"He revealed that the letter he had scribed for me, that very letter you possess in that cylinder, was written over a much older document, one with ancient script. He said he took the sheepskin out of ignorance, thinking it a practice parchment used to put newly sharpened quills to the test, believing it was filled only with the nonsensical writings and doodlings that scribes often etch in the readying of their writing materials for serious work. He washed it with the juice of a lemon and scraped it with a pumice stone. Upon it he penned the letter I bid him write."

Eva scrunched her nose. "I have had possession of the letter for over seven and ten years. Never have I witnessed any underlying script. Have you belief of this scribe?"

Pietro looked directly at Eva and his words were crisp. "I have no reason to doubt him, for he delivered his message to me at great cost. Less than a week after I spoke with him, one of my canons discovered him slain—it had been a ritual slaying. The scribe had been pierced through the heart with a thin dagger. It is a wound characteristic of ritual. I recall it clearly for it was 22 July, the feast day of Maria Magdalen, precisely five years past this day. That is why I wished to look upon it this 22 July of the year 1209. There is a thing about the feast day of Maria Magdalen I do not comprehend. The corpse of the scribe was a ghastly sight for much of his body had been burnt, though not charred in its entirety, for the heart and the face were both whole. The scribe was found slain on the spot in the piazza that was undergoing preparation for a gleaming new cathedral, the one I made mention of at the villa of the Painter."

A silhouette of an owl gliding through moonlit trees crossed through her mind. "The cathedral that is being raised over a site once dedicated to the goddess Minerva?"

Pietro nodded. "You give attention to detail and have strong recollection. Such skills will serve you well." The bishop looked her directly in the eye unwavering. "Eva, these are people with cold souls whose very bloodstream is the venom of the serpent. There was a note on the body—I viewed it with mine own eyes, fixed in place by an iron stake driven through his right wrist. It put me in the mind of the spikes used to nail our Lord to the cross. The note, itself stuck on the stake, read 'a sacrifice to Minerva'."

Eva fidgeted. "So what of Minerva? Who is she?"

"She is a goddess of the Roman pantheon. Along with Jupiter and Juno, she formed what was known as the Capitoline Triad."

"Like Father, Son, and Holy Ghost. The Roman trinity."

"Yes, the Roman trinity." Pietro looked toward the ceiling and furrowed his brow. "I had not thought of that."

"What else do you know of her?" Eva was intrigued, if still shaken. She noticed the goose flesh upon her arms.

"She was their goddess of war, that is all else I know. Yet there was another thing spoken by the scribe. I know not if it has to do with Minerva. He said 'look for the circle and triangle within.' He would not elaborate."

"You said it before but I know not the meaning." Yet she thought of the geometric shadows of the day past; owl, circle, and triangle. Is the owl within the circle?

The look of the bishop was both disappointed and pleading.

He leaned back in his chair, shoulders slumped. "Truly I was hoping you would have knowledge, dear Eva."

She shifted uncomfortably, kept her gaze fixed on the bishop. "I am afraid I have only ignorance. You expressed a desire when first we met to dispense with ignorance. Let us begin with danger. You mentioned danger before. How could I lie in the way of danger? Others seek the letter, but do they have knowledge that I possess it? Knowledge I am in Provence, in Orange?"

"I know not my daughter, but that is my gravest concern. If I thought there was any profit in secreting you away, I would have done so already. But our foe is too clever." He grasped her hands and looked her in the eye. It was a strong, comforting gaze. "If they know you are here, you are already under their watch, and it is a close watch, cruel and overbearing. If not by human eyes, than by those of the ethereal fiends, of demons of hell. I have not the answers, Eva. You need trust the hand of *Deu* to draw you through this peril. But if we can ascertain what lies underneath the words about your father, then I may find the answers to those selfsame questions."

Eva's eyes went to the letter. She exhaled and drew new breath slowly. "I have ever known I was watched. I knew it but had not the words for it." She looked upon the tube containing the letter that lay between them. She spoke the word aloud. "Palimpsest." So much bound up in one word. One Greek word. It almost seemed as if it held life, and yet it held death also. "Did you peruse the manuscript before you placed your seal?"

"I did. I read it and it said what I meant it to say. I did not notice a solitary thing about it that gave me pause. I rolled it up and applied the wax and seal and varnish with my own hand. Now, after so many years, I wish to look upon the letter once more, perhaps with vision afresh, and finally ascertain if indeed there is any veracity to the scribe's tale."

"Then let us do so." Eva grasped the parchment tube and removed the lid. Slowly, carefully she fingered an edge of the document and gingerly slid it from its housing.

The bishop showed such a strong emotional reaction on his face at seeing the letter once more, his mouth opening as he clasped his hands together, that Eva was unsure if he would weep or cry out in joy. But he did neither and waited with a look of excitement and anticipation, much like a well-behaved child about to receive a long expected toy. "It was inside of a fortnight of the recapture of Acre I had it penned. I gave no thought at the time of ever seeing it once more."

Placing it on the table, Eva unrolled the cream colored lambskin, slightly mottled with age and the tear stains of a three-year old little girl, and held it flat so they both could read it. She loved the sound of the parchment, the way it crinkled. "Here is the same message I have read hundreds of times, dear though it is. I see no other words."

"The scribe said the ancient script and symbols can only be seen in dim light and when perceived at an angle."

"I have viewed it in flickering light many an eve."

"Yes." Pietro smiled at her. "But how often do you read something from a sloping angle?" Picking up the letter, he lifted it and tilted it. "How often do you hold a manuscript like this? I have thought about this. It is not intuitive. Wait," his voice was taut with excitement, "I see... I see nothing."

Eva smiled, stifled a laugh. "Let us take it into the corner. That one," she said pointing past the bishop to the most distant end of the hall.

Before Eva had withdrawn her finger, Pietro had already grasped the manuscript and was on his feet, striding with purpose toward the corner, the most isolated, and dimly lit, realm of the building. Eva watched him for a moment before rising herself.

She had always admired people of action, those who were willing to put steps to their belief, to risk all for what they held dear. This lord of the Church was exposing much to risk even by journeying to meet with her, risking still more by sharing his heart with her and regarding her as a daughter.

By the time she walked to the corner herself, the bishop had issued a shout of excitement, a cry that bespoke clearer vision of the underlying script.

Eva squinted and cocked her head sideways in an attempt to be enlightened, but she saw nothing other than the message about her father in Latin. "I see nothing beyond the letter itself." She kept adjusting her neck and changing the angle of her view, but to no avail.

"It must be viewed from about a thirty degree angle, like this."

She attempted to mimic Pietro's stance from the other side of the manuscript. Turning her head slowly, and by degrees, she thought caught a brief glimpse of faint script, but it could be simply the grain of the parchment. She brought her face slowly toward the letter, seeking to maintain the same angle. Simultaneously, the bishop also moved closer until their cheeks nearly touched.

In the periphery of her vision, as they huddled together in the corner, Eva spied Claris gaining entrance to the hall and turning her gaze upon them.

"I did not expect a Beguine to be sharing such an intimate corner with a lord of the church." Claris burst out laughing.

Eva, disarmed to the full, clasped her hands together by her waist and could only smile.

So much for seeking to avoid any appearance of impropriety.

CHAPTER 13

22 JULY 1209
THE FEAST DAY OF
SAN MARIA MAGDALEN

The elegantly robed merchant in blue-dyed cotton tunic stood in front of Andreas, silently holding his ground, glaring, unmoving.

The *châtelain* fingered the pommel of his sheathed war sword. "You must depart now. All must take their leave from the *Faubourg*. These homes are to be razed. You were given notice two days past to vacate." He grasped the handle. "We cannot protect you here, and we cannot allow the *Frances* cover so near the city. You must go behind the walls."

"If we refuse?" The man clutched in one hand a long-handled axe with a sharpened edge that reflected the first sun of daybreak, but the head of the weapon remained on the steep, hardpan street. In the other hand he held a square object that reflected also in abundance the brilliance of the day's first light. It did not appear to be a weapon. He tightened his grip on the handle of the axe.

"Have you a wish for your soul to quit the body?" Andreas nodded toward Bertran. "If you refuse to leave my sergeant can separate the axe from your grip before you can raise it to your waist, and drive it deep into your belly before you can raise your arms to ward off the blow. Release it now or know his skill."

Bertran took a step forward and the man in blue loosed his grip on the wooden handle and for a moment the axe was vertical, balanced on its head. The handle slowly pitched sideways and met the street with a crack as the man began striding up the hill, square object still clutched in the other hand, out of the *Faubourg* towards the West Gate. The others behind him lingered for a moment in the bleary-eyed paralysis of dawn before hastily following in fashion.

Andreas watched them take their leave and retrieved the axe from ground. Its handle was of ash wood and the whole of the intricately etched weapon was weighted and balanced perfectly, as if the slightest motion would cause it to seek out a place to imbed its blade. It felt but an extension of his hands. If only the affairs of faith and earthly dominion were so aligned. "Why are the *Bitterois* so obstinate?"

Bertran looked at Andreas with mild surprise. "Would you have them yield all stubbornness and capitulate to the pope? Do not be too harsh with them, Andreas. Would you wish to surrender your home to fire?"

"I would rather surrender my home than my life, would rather watch it burn to cinders than to put the whole of my city at risk." Andreas raised his voice to the knights and soldiers around him. "Douse these buildings in pitch and oil. Bring more hay about the ramparts and soak it in pitch and oil as well."

If the French sought to take the settlements as cover, they would have life and shelter burnt away.

As Andreas was directing the saturation of the last of the houses and mounds of hay in incendiary liquid, the cry came from the sentries. "The *Frances* approach!" Andreas and Bertran scrambled up the hill, through the West Gate, and onto the thick, high, ramparts of Beziers itself. Reaching the southernmost tower, Andreas took in the sight. Waves of color melding together, rippling slowly over the plain, bobbing low and high in unyielding rhythm, making an appearing in the distance, seeming to stretch to the haze of land and sky, to the very margin of the world, as an unbroken, multi-hued cloud floating at grass tip. Indeed a wide fantastical beast splashed in color, one that had head and tail separated by many miles.

Wishing to believe the sight a chimera rising from the steamy heat of the morning, Andreas witnessed the vibrant shroud slowly sharpen into a multitude of banners and flags caught high on lengthy staffs. Blots of color separating into scores of crests of every imaginable shade from green to scarlet to blue to gold.

Those bearing the insignia paraded over the fold of a hill into view. Had they weapons, the multiple *gonfanoniers* holding aloft the crests of their lords would have themselves comprised a sizeable siege army, especially if banner and flagpoles were as lances. Yet these *gonfanoniers* were but heralds of a force far more immense.

The number of noble banners being paraded across the field south of Beziers toward the River Orb pointed to an army not of thousands but tens of thousands. More soldiers than anyone in the South had imagined. Indeed, he did not know the French army held so many men. Was this truly a Christian army hell-bent on besieging Christian lands? Such an urge must rise up as a poisonous vapor from the lake of fire, inhaled and spat out like acid from the mouths of fiends.

"Bertran, they are upon us." Andreas spoke the obvious, a thing for which he possessed a gift, his tongue loosened at last. "Raise the alarum in full. Tell the people to cease their feasting at once and make ready for battle. Inform the soldiers to spread word amongst all the *Bitterois*. Pull all forces out of the *Fau-bourg*, and above all, make certain the gates are secure. Once the hillside is emptied, the West Gate is not to be opened again under any circumstances, unless I personally give allowance."

He turned to look at Bertran, who already hastened toward the West Gate to discharge the task.

As the Northern army continued its march to the River Orb, Andreas began to recognize some of the banners raised high. Some were of dukes and counts around the Ile de France, from Normandy, Brittany, Burgundy, even Aquitaine and Gascony, one of the last realms in France still under English sovereignty. In their midst, he saw the banner of the Earl of Leicester of Eng-land. Soon he glimpsed other crests of lords English and Scot-tish and those of nobles Frankish, Flemish, Saxon, Breton, and

Bohemian.

"All of the North of Christendom has come," said Andreas quietly. "Aimer," said the *châtelain*, raising his voice, "Did you set eyes upon any of those banners in Iberia?"

"Yes, of lords Frankish, English, and German. Have they mistaken us for the infidel? Are we now as Moors and Turks and Saracens also?"

"It appears they see little difference between us and the Muhammadans, my friend." Andreas smiled. "Indeed, they may despise us the more. Innocent himself proclaimed heretics to be more evil than Saracens. Some believe us all to be heretics by association. Truly, they have come united against us." Andreas resumed his work on the *ballista*.

Though all amongst the approaching army would have taken the Cross and pledged quarantine in exchange for the promise of absolution, the underlying motives of many joining such an army would have variance as wide as the host itself. Some likely believed they were saving their immortal souls, while others believed the temporal riches of conquest awaited. Some would have come to slay heretics, others to receive the pay of mercenaries, others to satiate their bloodlust by slaying any foe.

Andreas moved onto the next ballista. "How do we prevail in battle against the whole of Christendom?"

"It is they who must bring the battle to us, and we shall be waiting." Aimer issued a broad smile as he grasped the handle of his double-bladed axe and wielded it, slicing the air in bursts of wind. "They still must scale these walls. If they do, we shall be at the ready. Even with tens of thousands, they will not breach the city in forty days."

Andreas looked to the host and back to the ramparts. "Nonetheless, be certain the siege engines are at the ready. Circle the walls, especially those facing the river, and check our readiness."

Aimer nodded and hastened off to carry out the command.

The French crossed the River Orb about one-half mile south of Beziers, well out of range of crossbow or catapult. A rearguard of French knights provided cover for the fording. Andreas could see they intended to circle back north and west and position themselves between Beziers and any relief that may arrive from Carcassonne to break the siege. It took some three hours for the whole of the giant beast to cross the Orb.

The vast field to the Southwest across the River, vacant but a few short hours ago, was now awash with activity. The industry of a great host making preparation for a long siege.

Tents were being raised, fires lit, food prepared, horses fed and watered, siege engines rolled into place and aim calibrated, latrines dug, trees on the edge of the plain felled for more fuel.

Andreas thought also he heard singing. Did his ears traffic in deceit? The sound was of the chanting of monks in Latin. *Veni, Creator Spiritus*, an ancient hymn of the faith. Though he could not see the source of the music, Beziers was downwind of the French. The sound of the voices was drifting on the breeze. It was beautiful, but also haunting. As they sang the words *Hostem repellas longius*, which mean, "drive from us the foe we dread," Andreas took hearty agreement and prayed for the French to be driven far from this place.

The music intermingled with the noise of the splashing of water. The warmth of the early afternoon, the time of siesta, was severe, and a number of the *rotiers*, mercenaries who fought for pay or plunder, along with some kitchen boys and muleteers, had scurried down to the river to dispel the heat from their raga-muffin bodies in the drink.

Bertran returned from checking the defenses. "The gates are properly barred and secure, the West Gate most of all. I bid them double the cross-planking and the guard. No one should be able to gain entrance or exit. I reminded them of your ad-monishment that under no circumstances are the gates to be swung open, excepting on your direct orders."

Andreas nodded and resumed his watch of the preparations. He rested his hands on the stone crenellation of the wall and slowly released his breath. "It is the feast day of Saint Maria Magdalen," he said, looking still off in the distance. "Something about being in Beziers on this day provokes an angst that settles into my bones, though I am unsure the reason."

Bertran strode up and stood next to Andreas, watching also the activity of the enemy. "As his life breath was being snuffed out by a mob of *Bitterois*, the grandfather of our lord Trencavel probably wished he had not come to Beziers either on the feast day of the Magdalen."

Andreas looked at Bertran with surprise. "You speak truth. It was 1167."

Bertran nodded. "Yes, two and forty years past. Then our lord Trencavel's *paire*, Roger II, avenged his own father by slaughtering the *Bitterois* by the hundreds, two years later, again on the feast day of the Magdalen, 1169. As I know you have heard tell, all men in the city were put to the sword, only the women and children were spared."

Andreas winced. "After the deeds of his *paire*, it is a miracle our Lord Trencavel is received by the *Bitterois*."

Bertran shook his head. "Raimon Roger is decisively unlike his *paire* or grandfather. He would not commit the atrocities of the past and the *Bitterois* know it."

"Forty years past. The number forty is an evil. A massacre took place within these very walls forty years past and now we must hold off an invading horde, replete with *rotiers*, for as many days."

Those two days of killing had indeed cast a specter over 22 July, the feast day of Maria Magdalen, given her a bloody name in the Languedoc. Andreas felt the same dread that had crept over him a few days ago while traveling to Montpellier. A thing darker than siege warfare. In spite of clear, scintillating sunshine, the day felt shadowed and the ethos muddled.

"Bertran, what think you of San Maria Magdalen? Is she the source of evil and not the number forty? Or is such too perilous a question?

Bertran turned down his eyes and studied his broad hands as if they held the answer. "Too perilous a question? No. But I do not believe you are prepared for the true answer." He raised his head and looked Andreas in the eye. "That is where the peril lies. Do not peel the orange if you are not prepared to eat it."

Andreas looked upon Bertran for a moment with impatient irritation but did not retort, instead he returned his attention to the *rotiers*. They likely cared nothing of the Magdalen. Although unlike their knighted counterparts, the followers of the camp, on the east bank, downwind of the city, would have been close

enough to smell the aroma of the feast food made in honor of
Maria Magdalen. It was a scent sweet and savory that filled the
city, overpowered even the sweaty stench of the refugees and
their animals.

Yet to Andreas, the vagrants and mercenaries and camp servants, as they shamelessly splashed about in the River Orb, in
range of the crossbows, seemed quite ignorant of their vulnerable position. He was tempted to pull out his bow and take target practice. What a wretched horde.

Yet if the walls were breached, they would find their way into
the city.

He shuddered visibly at the thought. They are like little scorpions that inflict a brutish, painful sting and then flee. Yet the
jab of the *rotier* was often fatal. He had seen the aftermath of
a Moorish village in Iberia that *rotiers* and camp followers had
hacked and slashed to pieces. All inhabitants were slain and few
bodies left whole.

Andreas watched as one of the vagabonds, a gangly, scrawny
youth with spindly legs and ragged black hair, scampered onto
the main bridge spanning the wide river, the one whose road led
to the main city gate. Without weapons or a tunic, and clad only
in a soaked, brownish undergarment, the *rotier* dashed halfway
across the bridge.

As the youth looked around, Andreas thought he saw the
chest of the *rotier* swell with pride as the wretch began to taunt
the *châtelain* and his cavaliers upon the wall.

From his post, Andreas could hear the young man shouting,
but could not discern the words. It mattered not. Let him yell
himself hoarse, thought Andreas.

This city is not Jericho. These walls will not be felled by
raised voices alone.

"The idiot," said Bertran, motioning to the gesturing *rotier*
on the stone bridge. "He is in easy range of the crossbow. Shall
I send a message to his ilk?"

"Not yet," cautioned Andreas. "Let them expend their energy
and discharge their folly. Save your aim and your bolts for when
the hour of need is truly visited upon us."

In the edge of his vision, Andreas saw the thick doors of the
West Gate of Beziers thrown open. He turned in confirmation

as a group of *Bitterois*, dressed for battle, but armed solely with a few spears, rocks, and axes, and emitting what sounded like ridiculous, ignorant, almost comic war cries, rushed the short distance down the hill and charged onto the bridge inchoate, unable to hold formation, even when unopposed.

A few among them were waving what looked to be flags of cloth, like small pennons, but the triangular banners lacked any sort of regalia, as if they had sliced fabric and tied it to staffs themselves.

"What are those fools doing, playing at war?" Andreas growled to Bertran, "I commanded them to keep the gate closed under all circumstances unless I personally gave allowance, as did you. Trencavel gave warning as well."

"It is a harmless sally, Andreas. The *Bitterois* are but head-strong. They'll simply kill the miserable little *rotier*," replied Bertran, "and then retreat up the hill like the cowardly *Bitterois* they are. Nothing will come of it."

"I pray you utter truth, Bertran, but I fear you overreach your grace for them. This day, the feast day of the Magdalen, has filled me with dread. But look!" Andreas pointed toward the bridge. "Our own *Bitterois* rabble is indeed dispatching the wretch *de Fransa*."

So consumed was he with giving insult to the wall guard and all others in the city, the vagabond somehow failed to take heed of the approaching horde from Beziers until it was upon him.

The group of *Bitterois* surrounded the knave, mocking him, striking and kicking him until he collapsed. They dumped his limp body head first into the river, the first casualty of the siege, and raised arms and voices as if they had won the day.

"Now you have tasted war, fools, and drawn first blood," Andreas said under his breath, unsheathing his sword. "Scamper back up the hill so the watchmen will shutter the gates." He raised high the weapon. "Let there be no doubt. I will make sure they are shuttered."

"Andreas, the *Bitterois* are under attack!" Bertran shouted, pointing toward the river. "Someone is rallying the *rotiers* to charge the bridge."

Bertran nocked a bolt in his crossbow and tightened the windlass with deft finger work. The *châtelain* looked to see mercenaries and also kitchen boys, muleteers, and other servants and vagrants running toward the bridge from every direction, coming from out of the river, half-naked from their swim, from nearby tents, and from locales across the plain, halting all they were engaged in and grabbing knives, clubs, anything they could wield in assault.

Bertran groaned. "This is no harmless little sally outside the walls. They place us all at risk." He took aim with the crossbow and pulled the trigger. The arrow seemed to vanish and reappear in the chest of one of the *rotiers* who was almost upon the *Bitterois* sortie. The force of the impact knocked the vagabond back into his charging comrades, halting their momentum but briefly, until the ones behind trampled the one who had fallen.

They gathered on the west end of the bridge as if every city in Christendom had emptied its alleys and cleared its cobbles of all walking filth. Their numbers stacked up on the opposing side of the bridge, appearing a gelatinous, oily mass overflowing its bounds, rapidly growing from dozens to hundreds as their ranks continued to swell.

The *Bitterois* were now fighting for their very lives as they attempted to fend off the dirty, soaked, ever-enlarging mass of humanity that was hurling itself at them.

"*Deu* help us, they will not hold the bridge." Andreas was wide eyed, checking his distance from the gate.

Up the hill from the river, Andreas saw that the West Gate of the city remained open. On the west bank, more and more of the *rotiers* were running onto the span of arched stone, makeshift weapons in hand. Each volley of arrows loosed from atop the walls checked their advance, but only for a moment.

Andreas growled. "Why do they not shutter the gate? Let those *sebencs* stand on their own. Close it at all costs!"

Andreas and Bertran, seeing the increasing vulnerability of the city, started sprinting north along the allure, behind the crenellated wall, shouting orders that the guards at the gate seemingly could not hear. "Close the gates, let the fools perish!" they roared. "Save the city! Shut the gates!" Though he felt the words leave his mouth, the sound of his voice seemed to emanate from a far off place.

As increasing numbers of the club and knife bearing followers of the Crusader camp joined the frenzied melee on the stone bridge, the *Bitterois* commenced an erratic retreat toward the city. Yet it was obvious they lacked even the most rudimentary battle training, for they knew not how to set up a line of retreat or to fend off even so ragged a foe.

Two more of the *Bitterois* were slashed by knives across the gut, while another three were bludgeoned to death.

Screaming still at full volume and sprinting at full bore, Andreas watched as at least a dozen of the *rotiers* penetrated the dissolving ranks of the *Bitterois*, hacking and slashing all the while.

The gate was still open. It did not even quiver. Someone was holding it open, refusing to close it. Why that was, God alone had knowledge.

Perhaps the keepers thought it could be swung shut in the space between *Bitterois* and *rotier*, but from his view atop the ramparts, Andreas could see that such a gap was all but vanished. As the camp vagrants ascended the hill on the offensive and the *Bitterois* in retreat there was soon no separation between the two mobs.

They reached the open gate and as one stumbled into the city.

Andreas turned on his heel to order the archers to loose their arrows, but there was no need. Volley after volley was already raining down on the pathetic mass that was streaming across the bridge and up the steep slope. Lacking armor, the followers of the camp were easy targets for the archers, but more numerous than their arrows.

For every one cut down on the bridge or the sloping approach to the West Gate, two or three more barged into the city, swinging and slashing with impunity.

Stepping over, around, and on top of their fallen members, in an unbroken line that kept the deep stone arch of Bezier's West Gate forced ajar, the *rotiers* flowed into the city like rancid liquid death.

Andreas saw a familiar figure on the far bank of the River. It was Armand Amaury, in miter and vestments of white, bearing a gilded, bejeweled scepter, consulting with someone who appeared a baron of some minor stature. The papal legate nodded approvingly as he looked upon the *rotiers* in the breach and spoke in booming tones and used forceful gestures Andreas did not comprehend. Nonetheless, the *châtelain* shivered once more.

CHAPTER 14

22 JULY 1209
THE FEAST DAY OF
SAN MARIA MAGDALEN

The Bishop of Siena was flushed blood-red in his face, his innocence splashed across his features. There seemed no guile in his soul. As if he never had given even a moment's thought to the appearance of being huddled together cheek to cheek in the corner of a building with a young woman lacking a husband.

Claris could not stop laughing. Eva, with half-smile, stood with her hands clasped in front of her, waiting for her mentor to expel more sharpened wit from her tongue. Instead, Claris calmed herself, efficiently erased her smirk, and spoke plainly. "Eva informed me of your presence here, your grace." She spoke also in Latin. "She also told me all she has learnt of you in so short a time. It was why I felt I could be informal with you. I feel I am making acquaintance not with the bishop of Siena but with Eva's father."

The bishop stretched out the fingers on his hands and looked toward the ceiling of timber. "Perhaps you are. My life is not my own. That much has become plain to me. I play the role *Deu* gives to me." Handing the letter to Eva, the bishop walked over to Claris, the crimson now drained from his complexion. "To be spoken of in the selfsame breath as Eva's father, gives me great pleasure. He was a great man. I believed never would I find a soul who was his equal. But I may have found such in his daughter." He looked at Eva. "She is a remarkable young woman, and you must be strong in your gifts of mentoring."

Eva could feel her cheeks flush even as the look on Claris's face turned sober, expressionless, and the daughter of Anselme knew a question would be forthcoming. "Are you always as effusive with your praise?"

Without hesitation, the bishop responded. "Whenever honesty compels I am so."

Eva fought the urge to cringe, for she knew Claris would use the words of Pietro as a foundation on which to place a more burdensome question, like a cornerstone of granite wrenched into place to set the course of all conversing. "Well then, my lord, how does honesty compel you to answer my next query: Why are Christian armies marching at behest of pope and king into Christian lands, into the Languedoc. Lands whose people themselves have taken the Cross in great numbers and bled heavily in the taking of Jerusalem, the retaking of Acre, and have bled on pilgrimage ever since?" Her voice choked and was momentarily captive in her throat. "My very brother, my only brother, fell atop the hallowed walls of Jerusalem fighting the Muhummadan hordes. Are such battles worth the cost? You know well of what befell Eva's father Anselme."

The bishop showed no impatience or irritation with what Eva considered to be the impertinence of her mentor. Not that the question itself was not worthy of the asking. But to raise it so quickly, in so startling a fashion, like throwing down the gauntlet, lacked the proper measure of respect.

But Pietro did not appear slighted in the least. After looking out a window for a moment, he made soft reply. "I am truly sorry about your brother. He did not die in vain. Know in your heart. He died so that many could live." Pietro turned, looked directly at Claris, and spoke plainly. "As for this pilgrimage against the *Albigenses* and the *Valdenses*, it was not my decision, and I abhor it. I held council with Innocent summer last and pleaded with him to ignore the warmongering of Armand Amaury and give more time for proselytizing. I told him to absolve the *Valdenses* and make use of their capable speechmaking to preach to the *Albigenses*, the so-called *Bons Hommes*. To give the *Valdenses* leave to proselytize as they would, for already they do such with great effectiveness. Innocent considered my words, he did not simply brush them aside, thought on them for several hours, but ambition took the better of him and he heeded instead the council of Amaury. Now I fear the *Valdenses* will be targeted as well."

Pietro's voice rose along with the color in his face. "I begged him to reform the very problems within the Church that have allowed the *Bons Hommes* to flourish in the Languedoc. Innocent himself has spoken repeatedly of the corruption and ignorance of the clergy and is enraged by it." Pietro was pacing about and raising his arms as he spoke. "The people of the Languedoc, though targeted they are by those who have taken the Cross, are not as the rulers of the Muhammadans, those who would invade Christendom once more on the slightest pretext or opportunity. The *Bons Hommes* are a threat to the Church only to the extent she makes herself vulnerable."

There was only silence. Claris's expression was unchanging for a time. Slowly her features took on the look of astonishment, a rare expression for her, and never had Eva seen her lacking speech. "Forgive me, your grace," she finally stammered. "Truly I am sorry. You have risked much, perhaps life and limb, speaking so boldly before Innocent himself." She looked upon him square, her face softened by a look of wonder. "Have you not been threatened with the loss of your bishopric?"

Pietro shook his head. "I believe Innocent is no tyrant, though many would vehemently say otherwise. Yet his ambition is to see all of Christendom come under the hegemony of the Church in his lifetime. His true zealousness for Christ and his Holy Church renders him impatient at times and able to be manipulated by those who are tyrants such as Armand Amaury, who wish merely to extend their own power."

The bishop walked over and retrieved the letter from Eva, who was hovering near the corner, feeling still as if a bystander.

Viewing the parchment from an angle for a minute, as if to study it and refresh his memory, he approached Claris once more. "The answer to why this darkness comes may be found on this document." Pietro bid her to look at the letter from an angle, to peer from that view at the center of the manuscript. He asked her what sight uncovered.

"It appears to be washed-out script in Occitan, underneath the Latin text." Claris halted her examining and glanced at the bishop. "Have you a reading stone, your grace? For I think that would be more effectual than examining this writing at odd angles."

The bishop appeared impressed by the idea. "Perhaps you are correct, though I do not usually carry such an object on my person." Pietro loosed a smile.

"What is a reading stone?" Eva abandoned her role as bystander.

"It is a piece of glass or polished rock crystal," replied the bishop in a gently instructive tone. "Typically it is rounded in shape and is used to magnify the script of a parchment, a hemisphere of glass, if you will, that makes things appear larger than their true size."

Rock crystal. Something tugged with persistence at the back of her mind, and Eva wrestled to pull it into conscious thought. The objects in her trunk. At least one was perhaps a rounded piece of the precious crystal. She started for the door, even before giving utterance. Without looking back, she called out "Wait here. I shall rejoin your company in a moment."

Running across the courtyard, she entered her home and bounded up the steps to her bedchamber. Throwing open the lid of her heavy trunk, a crystalline sparkle almost immediately flashed her eye. The depths of the case, where rarely even she peered, much less probed with her hand, did contain such a piece of rock crystal and a large one at that, perhaps three inches in diameter. It appeared to her as a glass *boule* cut in two, half of a sphere with a flat bottom. Rather carelessly removing the objects above it, including an alabaster reliquary, she snatched it out of the trunk, tucked it in a fold of her robe, left everything else as it was, strewn haphazardly on the floor, and ran back across the common to the dining hall.

As she made entrance, the bishop eyed the object in Eva's hand. "You do possess a reading stone. Splendid."

Eva smiled. "It lay at the bottom of my trunk. I knew not that it was there."

"With the addition of Claris, I think we can all reconvene inside your home Eva with nary a hint of scandal. What say you?"

Both Pietro and Claris looked at her with expectation. "To my home it is," she smiled, and then thought of the objects she had left scattered on the floor. "And we need examine more than the letter."

Long had she been troubled by the spoils of war that had come to her, and she yearned for resolution.

Eva unrolled the palimpsest on the board in her kitchen, placing wooden blocks on the corners to keep them from curling. Her nose caught a faint whiff of burning, but not so pungent as to compel her to seek out the source. She placed her fingers on the reading stone to lift it on the parchment and she heard a sound as the sizzling of bacon on an iron skillet. She recoiled her arm as the pain spiked in her fingers. "*Ai!*" The tips of the fingers on her right hand were all red nearly to the point of glowing and each bore a large round blister. In the moment she looked, each blister dried and cracked and blood oozed out, trickling in a thin line down each of her fingers. Movement of her hand or arm was beyond her.

Claris came beside her. "What is it Eva?"

"Pain... searing, as if my shoulders were stung by a swarm of bees aflame and the hot poison of the entire hive flowed through my fingers. That stone is afire."

Claris ran to the pantry and returned with a small loaf of bread. Tearing off the crust, she thrust it in front of Eva. "Place your fingers here."

Eva did so. Bread was effective at removing the sting from burns, but not now. The only effect was her hand leaving five lines of blood upon the bread. The pain only grew and coursed through her hand and up her arm. Her eyes watered and her body trembled.

Pietro put his hand on her shoulder. "You are as one aflame, even through your robe. The fires of hell. They scorch the very air around us. Do you not feel it?"

Eva nodded slowly looking around. There were shadows unseen circling about with fury unbridled. She could feel their dreadful, putrid, gaseous presence upon her. A wreath of white hot rage encircled the room. For but a second she glimpsed what appeared to be the faint outlines of a large, horrid face upon the plastered whitewashed wall. It felt as if the path they were about to trod was blocked by the entire host of hell.

Claris rubbed Eva's arm vigorously even as Pietro clutched her hand, "We must petition first the Sovereign Lord to cover us, arm us for battle. For to battle we go as surely as if we had sword and hauberk." He prayed in Latin. "*Deu* be as a salve for her, take this pain and wounding from Eva. Remove the sting from this clear stone. Banish the evil charm from all such things owned by Eva that are cursed. Shield us all, blessed *Iesu*. We give you thanks; you go before us and are our rearguard."

Claris grasped Eva by the shoulder and hand.

Eva stretched out her right hand. "It is gone. The hurt fades and the blisters are vanished. The hounds of hell are driven back." The tips of her fingers were entirely undamaged and all pain was dissipated. So complete was the reversal, she began to doubt she had experienced any pain or wounding from the reading stone. Yet the lines of her blood remained upon the bread.

She straightened her arm, wiggled her fingers, and went to grasp the reading stone once more. "I will not be driven back. We must look upon the palimpsest." Eva took the reading stone without pain and placed it on the center of the manuscript, and knew that doing so was indeed an unvarnished declaration of war. "You are as one who prays in the common tongue." She smiled at Pietro.

Eva squinted and slowly slid the stone over parchment. There was evidence of careful knife scrapes and faded script, a straight uniform script. "I see a word in Occitan, *soldada*." She paused for a few seconds. "There are several rows of writing— perhaps twenty rows, and each row appears to be made of several words of Occitan mashed together as one. The whole is as a square. The remaining words in the first row are *flamier, folpidor, mostier,* and *mercadan,* though they are written as one."

Claris leaned over. "I do not like the whole of those words, Eva."

Pietro leaned forward. "What is the meaning?"

Eva positioned the reading stone over the first row, to be sure she saw correctly. "*Soldada* means recompense or to repay, perhaps to seek vengeance, *flamier* means blaze, or fire, *folpidor* is best rendered a place for discarded victory, a *mostier* is a church, and *mercadan* is a merchant."

Claris took up the stone. "The line that follows reads *valensa, issartz, ifernaus, saumier, sembelin* which is worth, a cleared field, infernal, packhorse, and sable."

Eva frowned. "The second line, I know not what it means. The first line could speak to something such as a battle victory abandoned to fire as payback, as vengeance, but I know not about the merchant or the church."

CHAPTER 15

22 JULY 1209
FEAST DAY OF
SAN MARIA MAGDALEN

Bertran, Aimer, take thirty knights and make for the West Gate." Andreas loosed an arrow and pierced a *rotier* on the slope below the open gate. "Push them out of the city. If we shutter the accursed gate, we can force them back across the river."

Bertran fidgeted. "If I depart your presence, how then will I give you safeguarding?"

Andreas stopped as he was nocking the next quarrel and looked at Bertran, who appeared strangely awkward and unsure in his stance. "Safeguarding? Since when have I been in need of protection? My own *paire* did not give protection, and I proved my lack of need for such. Now away with you." Andreas gave Bertran a shove in the direction of the gate. Reluctantly his friend joined Aimer in the task of rounding up a troop, which they did with efficiency and made quickly for the West Gate.

Andreas sought to direct the archers. "Target not the wretches near the gate, but aim for the bridge. Stack up the bridge with their dead so they cannot cross." The hundreds of *rotiers* that had been arrow slain on the slope had become as a fleshy, bloody carpet for the other vagabonds who ran over the backs of their dying comrades. Still they kept coming. Throwing their arrowed dead off the bridge into the River Orb, still they kept coming.

And they were not alone. The entire Crusader camp was astir. The Northern cavaliers and foot soldiers had gained awareness of events, of the open gate. Now the plain below seemed to flow as many tributaries toward the River. Knights were saddling their mounts in haste, some were already horsed and riding toward the Orb, some on bareback. A few had reached the river and were already in skiffs paddling across the Orb, carrying ladders. Soldiers grabbed their weapons and ran toward the city, many lacked helmets or even armor.

The garrison need quickly close the gate and give staunch defense of the walls.

Before the decision was formed in his brain, Andreas was descending the nearest stair into the erupting cauldron of Beziers. He would fight his way to Bertran and Aimer and they would carve a path to the gate and shutter it themselves. That was of the uttermost need.

The street of the cobblers, that ran along the southwest section of the wall, was quiet. But it was not merely silent, it was hushed in a way that the noise of the crowd is muffled by a coming storm.

Then he saw them. The stragglers who had breached the defenses. Three *rotiers*, their tunics, bare feet, and arms carelessly stained with a liquid that looked of red wine, though clearly bore not the selfsame odor.

One of the mercenaries, possessing curly blonde hair himself, had the long, beaded black hair of a woman matted onto his feet and ankles by a brownish, caked substance.

They were emerging from a triple-story house of wood and stone that was owned by a wealthy merchant family. Or was before this day.

All the *rotiers* bore clubs in one hand and improvised cloth sacks of cotton or linen that bulged sharply and clinked with metal objects in the other. All wore new leather shoes, taken from cobbler's shops.

Their backs to Andreas, the vagabonds were about twenty yards up the street.

It was a visceral reaction. No strategy floated through Andreas's mind, though he had extensive training in battling multiple foes at once. No thought at which wretched human being he was going to slay first.

His thoughts were of the woman whose strands of hair now clung to a *rotier's* feet, of the children whose blood most certainly stained the mercenaries' foul garments and skin. The hellspawn would breathe their last this day.

Racing ahead at full battle charge, he had closed the gap to less than five yards when he turned his head to look though the open door of the merchant house.

The image of wanton slaughter seared itself into his brain.

He saw in an instant seven bodies, three adults and four small children, all prone on the floor, clothing shredded, limbs severed, skulls misshapen and sheathed in a mask of fresh blood.

The floor of the front room apparently slanted slightly toward the door, because the pools of still-liquid blood had merged into one on the wooden floor and followed an easy path out the front door and onto the stone steps leading to the narrow street.

His cheek muscles tensed to the point of twitching. He turned his head toward those who had done murder, sauntering casually up the street ahead of him. They were laughing and shaking their bags to see which clanked the loudest, oblivious to the cavalier rushing toward them, the metallic swish of chain mail.

He closed the distance in three strides.

Unsheathing his sword, Andreas thrust it upward through the right kidney and out the breastbone of the curly haired one, who crumpled silently into eternity. Before the slain *rotier's* sack of gold had struck the ground, Andreas had withdrawn his sword and beheaded the second vagabond.

The last of the three remaining among the living, still clutching his sack of plundered wealth, watched the severed, greasy head of his companion bouncing and rolling back toward the trickle of blood that had just reached the sidewalk from the bourgeois house, flinging its own erratic trail of red death.

The hesitation proved deadly as Andreas severed the youth's club-wielding hand at the wrist and slashed him across the belly, his entrails pushing out into the sunlight. As the follower of the camp plunged forward, clutching his burgeoning belly with his one remaining hand, Andreas kicked him in the head and abandoned him, knowing it would take several minutes for the blood loss to bring on death.

Let him writhe in pain like those he had butchered.

More of the wretches emerged from the houses lining the street. Despite their slain compatriots lying nearby, they closed round Andreas, ten of them, circling him, mocking him, growling like feral dogs.

One turned up his mouth in a wicked smile. "We will have our way with this city. We own it now. We will claim all we desire and more. You shall be next." His face and hands were coated in wet blood, as if dipped in a cauldron of purplish-brown gravy. Indeed, it dripped from his fingers in a steady flow onto the cobblestones.

He winked at his companion on the opposite side of the circle behind Andreas and they both raised clubs and charged. There was a flash of light and crunch of bone and the first *rotier's* lower right arm, hand still locked around the club, went sliding across the pavement.

Without breaking his motion or turning around, Andreas thrust his sword back under his own left armpit and ran the blade through the heart of the other charging *rotier*. Whirling around, Andreas put his foot on the vagabond's chest and kicked off with his boot, freeing his sword. The *rotier* flew backward against the cobblestones, coughing and wheezing as his lifeblood pulsed from his chest.

The remaining eight charged as one.

Andreas stepped toward the nearest three and, as he raised his sword, he grabbed his mace from his belt and unleashed a blow that crushed the skull of one, who tumbled into a second one, knocking him down. Andreas slit that one's throat before he could get up and kicked out the legs of the third one and cracked his skull open with a single blow from the mace.

Andreas then whirled around, swinging mace and sword as he did. He felled two more. The remaining three flinched for the first time, and took a step backward. "Are you a ghoul?" asked one, almost hissing at Andreas. "No one of flesh and bone moves like that. Not in armor."

"Whatever you believe me to be, I am that, and worse." Charging with sword raised high, Andreas lowered it at the last second and sliced off the leg of one below the knees, and ran the next one through at the neck. The remaining *rotier* managed to swing his club at Andreas who blocked the blow with his sword then crushed the rib cage of the vagabond with a swift blow from the mace. Unable to breathe, the *rotier* suffocated in the street, eyes wide, pleading for breath.

Ten *rotiers* were now dead around Andreas while three writhed in pain, their lifeblood ebbing away. He walked up to the one whose arm he had severed at the elbow, the one who had taunted him, placing his boot on the chest of the *rotier*.

"Have your way with the city now, wretch. Enjoy your booty, in hell."

With a quick stroke, Andreas slit his throat.

"Why did I not see this coming? I should have known." The pain and confusion on the face of Bertran jabbed at Andreas's soul. Somehow, in the midst of a growing slaughter, he ached for his friend. Andreas had found Bertran but two streets from the city gate, slowly falling back, having pushed the *rotiers* as far back as he could compress their numbers. Even now if the gate would be shuttered, they could stand their ground.

Ringing church bells reached his ears, pounding in the cadence of a funeral dirge, slow and solemn. The church of Saint Maria Magdalen! Andreas recognized the clear sound of its tolling, ringing barren truth into his brain. There would be no closing of the West Gate. Too many *rotiers* had already passed through the open portal.

Herd the people to sanctuary.

Aimer rushed up to Andreas. "The city is being butchered. Families, women, children slaughtered on the street, in their homes, dismembered even in death. They show no mercy. Never shall we repel them now. A few slipped through our perimeter and are at large in the city. Their numbers are too many. We yield ground and cavaliers and soldiers *Frances* scale the walls on all sides." He paused. "What orders?"

Andreas grasped Aimer by the shoulder. "We must save as many as God allows. We are already cut off from *la cathedrale*.

We need preserve safe passage to the Church of Saint Maria Magdalen." He straightened his helmet. "I think I just slay the *rotiers* who have penetrated the farthest into Beziers." Andreas raised his sword and his voice. "Call the *Bitterois* to church!"

Leaving a rearguard led by Aimer to defend their retreat, Andreas, Bertran and a cadre of knights and soldiers banged sword flat against shield and called out to the people. "Sanctuary! You must seek sanctuary in the Church of the Magdalen!"

Slowly at first, and then as a river bursting a dam, the *Bitterois* and the refugees began spilling out of homes and moving toward the Church of the Magdalen. They knew where to go. The faces, by and large, showed fear, and the lack of belongings most carried showed they at last grasped the desperation of the hour. One who finally seemed prepared to flee was the merchant in blue Andreas had ordered out of the *Faubourg* that morn. He emerged from a house on the street of the jewelers, grasping still the brilliant square object in his hand. Yet the merchant sought to go against the tide and Andreas stopped him. "You must seek refuge in the church of the Magdalen, else I will not protect you. Now go!" Andreas shoved the man forward toward the building of refuge. Still he strove to turn away and other cavaliers pushed him toward sanctuary. Andreas kept vigil until the merchant made entrance into the church.

As the people were making egress from their homes, the first *rotiers*, in small, straggly bunches, reached the streets of that quarter of the city. As one family was clubbed to death, panic ensued amongst the *Bitterois* until Andreas and Bertran slaughtered the perpetrators, and all vagabonds that had penetrated that far into the city, and some sense of order returned as the cavaliers maintained a wall of protection around those seeking sanctuary.

Within a quarter-hour, with the knights slaying any *rotier* that entered the Northwest quarter of Beziers, the crowd of *Bitterois* descended on *la plasa* and into the Church of the Magdalen, perhaps three-thousand in all, stuffing the interior of the ancient building cram-full.

Andreas went among them and noticed that the merchant in blue, still clutching the mother of pearl box, went to the choir and probed the floor, as if searching for a lost thing.

CHAPTER 16

22 JULY 1209
FEAST DAY OF
SAN MARIA MAGDALEN

E va removed her axes and saws from the wooden rack over her workbench and loaded them into her handcart. The pear trees needed felling and her restless hands needed industry. After consuming the three hours past peering through the looking glass, squinting at a faint square of Occitan text, her mind could think of many meanings hidden within the palimpsest. Yet it was all mere speculation. A rising source of frustration. The honey sweetness of the coming of the bishop and the revealing of words unknown had soured quickly to a taste bitter as unwatered vinegar. An axe biting into the trunk of a tree was authentic. The wood chips from her labors could be seen and smelt. It was a good scent.

She would go to cliff's edge alone. Never mind the pain in her soul. The Bishop had returned to his quarters and Claris had gone to Orange for reasons she did not reveal. Eva took her leave from her workshop through the wide double doors she had constructed for the purpose of hauling her handcart in and out. The West Gate of the community fixed in her view, no other persons in her sighting. She moved quickly toward the gate. The ash wood barriers swung open with smart timing and she passed through and started up the hill toward her orchard, left the lands of the community and trod upon her own.

"The ten trees nearest the valley of the Rhône." These trees had grown well but their harvest was ever scarce. They served more as a wind block for the rest of the orchard, as their pears were often blown off the branches before becoming ripe. As she had made mention to the Painter, their trunks and limbs would more than suffice for the extensive carvings needed for *la cathedrale Notre Dame de Doms* in Avignon. It would be by far the largest such project ever she had undertaken.

Anxiety and sorrow rose within her as she approached the row at cliff's edge. Her breath grew shallow. Leather boots upon her soul. Soldiers on the march, knights on horseback, trampling all in their path. She stopped, grabbed an axe, and set her stance. The first blow bit cleanly into the trunk of the pear tree, and the second, and the third. With each strike of the axe, she called out to the valley of the Rhône below. "You would trample my lands!" Crack. "My very spirit!" Crack. "Steal the lifeblood of my *paire!*" Crack. "Slay heretics!" Crack. "Well curse you all!" Crack. "May you know hellfire!" Crack. "You shall not trample me!" Crack. "Do you hear?" Crack. "Can you not hear me?"

A small pile of woodchips at her feet, a horizontal "v" deeply cut into the trunk, Eva flung down the axe, embedded the blade in dry earth, raised her foot and kicked the tree with the heel of her sandal-shod foot. The fifteen-foot high pear tree toppled over with little resistance revealing an audience heretofore hidden. The Painter, Claris, and Pietro stood watching her. She looked upon them for a moment, irritated and grateful for their appearing, but spoke nothing. She shook her head and they smiled. She reclaimed the axe and approached the next tree. They spoke nothing, nodded, and walked toward her handcart. Pietro grabbed the other axe while Claris and the Painter took up the handsaws.

Eva moved silently to the next tree and pointed at the row that was to be felled. Pietro walked to the other end of the row and unleashed his first blow with the axe. Claris wielded the saw and cut through the last strip of wood and bark connecting the fallen tree to its stump. She then joined the Painter in separating limb from trunk. The smaller branches were then cut from the limbs. Pietro felled his first tree and Eva her second.

It was the feast day of the Magdalen, normally a day of great celebration in the community. It would be such this day, but it felt not as a celebration to her. There would be lamb, sweetmeats like honeyed almonds, and pears of course. Always she gave at least a bushel to the feast, depending on the abundance of early harvest. Later she would retreat to the silence of hermitage to pray.

Yet this moment she could not remain silent.

"Do you not share my frustrations?" She spoke to all and none. "How do we know that the palimpsest is not merely the whimsical lettering of a practicing scribe?"

The Painter stopped sawing halfway through a limb. "What palimpsest do you speak of?"

Claris separated branches from another limb. "Painter, that is why I asked you to come here. Eva's letter about the death of her *paire* has proven to be a palimpsest. It appears to contain a cipher of some sort, a troubling message we comprehend not. That is why also Pietro has come."

The Painter began stacking limbs. He shot Pietro a look of surprise.

Pietro released another blow from the axe. Thud. "It is not the sole reason." Thud. "I would have sought the daughter of Anselme regardless." Thud. "It but heightened the immediacy of my quest."

Eva pushed over her third tree. "The palimpsest has words in Occitan grouped together without rhyme or reason in the shape of a square. Pietro says the scribe who penned the letter in the Holy Land for him was slain in Siena, had murder done to him five years past on this very feast day. This underlying script was the reason."

Claris moved to another limb. "Does it speak of Saint Maria Magdalen in some way?"

Pietro felled his second tree. "The scribe was slain as a sacrifice to the Roman goddess Minerva. Slain on the day of the Magdalen. Why do such a thing?"

The Painter raised himself to his feet, straightened his back. "It is not the first time the feast of the blessed Magdalen was a day of unholy slaughter. Not the first time. Some forty years past, on the feast day of the Magdalen, the first Viscount of Carcassonne, Albi, and Beziers had murder done to him in his own city of Beziers. In the church of Saint Maria Magdalen. Sacrifice. The new Viscount, the son, Raimon Roger's *paire*, unleashed a hellish retaliation upon the *Bitterois* a few years later on the very same feast day. Sacrifice."

There was a scraping of metal, the clashing of warswords, the screams of wounded men, the shouts of battle charge. Eva looked round the orchard. There was no one excepting Pietro, Claris, and the Painter within earshot. She saw the back of a knight in a mustard colored surcoat, fully armored in double ring hauberk, his hair spilling out the back of his helmet, wielding a sword and mace with speed and ferocity. He stood ankle deep in a substance like gravy, cut down many savage foes and sought to protect the innocent. Somehow she knew this. The prayer for his safekeeping was released from her spirit before thought escaped her mind. Why did she see such things?

The Painter stopped and looked her in the eye. "What is it, Eva?"

She looked toward cliff's edge. "I heard swordplay and saw a knight in battle. He fought on city streets the most ragged of men ever I have seen."

Pietro spoke, his voice swollen with excitement. "You saw a vision. Truly you are a mystic. I knew it to be true. Your father was gifted in such a way." The Bishop looked thoughtful for a moment. "Do you believe the vision occurs in times past or days future?"

"I know not. Perhaps I imagine such things. How do I know it to be a vision?" She felled the fourth tree.

The reply confirmed a belief she had long held close.

"If it be from *Deu* it will return at times unexpected and in ways unsought."

The labor of her friends upon tasks that were her own was unexpected and unsought. The Painter and Claris had stripped two tree trunks and the limbs bare of branches and stacked and now moved to a third tree. She had not expected to finish until tomorrow, but the work would be finished this day before the supper bell rang out, before the commencing of the feast. Perhaps together they could make similarly short work of the palimpsest. Perhaps. But it was the frustration of that enigmatic puzzle of words that had driven her to labor on a feast day, a holy day.

Pietro felled his third tree. Seven were now separated from the earth, from life, but wood never really died. Precious metal and jewels, though beautiful never really knew life. But wood, unless it went away through rot or fire, somehow retained the glow of the living. Like her father. His legacy lived on through Pietro. Did it live on through her, had she truly absorbed his heart into her innermost?

"How did you two both come to know that I am the daughter of Anselme, the man that you, Pietro, knew in Outremer?" It felt strange, almost a little frightening to hear the name of her *paire* pass over her lips, for she had not spoken it in years, perhaps since her mother had died. It was more than speaking his moniker. It was as if invoking his name would bring some unknown thing to life.

Her Painter responded first. He was beginning to load the trunks and larger limbs into her handcart. "I saw the bishop in Arles' *cathedrale* and talked with him. He asked of the painting first then the woodcarving. When I told him that I have someone else who does all my carving, his interest was arrested and he made inquiry about it. As a rule, as I have thus spoken, I do not reveal the name of my carver, but I felt safe in doing so with the bishop.

"When he learnt that my woodcarver, my carpenter, was a woman of twenty years of age who lived also in Orange, he started asking more of you, including your name and if your father was still alive. When I answered him, he became excited and said 'it is her, it must be her.' He kept making repetition of that phrase.

"As he talked of a man he had known in Outremer and to whom he had administered last rites, I realized, Eva, it matched with what you had told me of your *paire*. When he mentioned the letter, I knew it was providence."

"But I did not want another soul to have knowledge of my journey from Arles to Orange," broke in the bishop. "I left my personal guard and entourage in Arles. I told them I need make a pilgrimage, alone, and that I would be absent for some weeks. I did not say to where.

"I abandoned my vestments and miter and crosier for the tunic and sandals of a pilgrim. I journeyed first to Avignon, and then here. They will not question my journeying for they think me odd already." He smiled.

Eva laughed and the frustration lifted like a veil caught by the wind.

"I am a bishop, a so-called lord of the church, who would rather seek solitude or have holy conversations in the marketplace than carry out the ceremonial duties of my office." Pietro felled his fourth tree.

"Given the proximity of Arles to Saintes Maries de la Mer, and the fact that this is the very feast day of Maria Magdalen, they likely believe I have traveled south to the village of the three holy Marias of the sea to pay homage and fast and pray. Do you know of all three?"

Eva smiled. It was one of the first things taught to any child of Provence. "Maria Magdalen of course, and Maria of Bethany, the sister of Lazarus, and the virgin Maria, the mother of our Lord."

The bishop walked over and laid a hand on Eva's shoulder. "I did not make journey to Saintes Maries de la Mer but have found instead the true object of my pilgrimage. A young woman who gives to the work of Christ in this present age, one who holds lightly to her wealth, a Maria Magdalen, a Saintes Maria that is among the living, is of flesh and bone."

The praise felt embarrassing, all the more so because she knew its sincerity. "But I lack hair of red." Eva smiled and shook her head back and forth, swishing her blackish brown hair. Even as she made jest of her age's belief that the red hair of a woman signaled debauchery, she felt pride, affirmation at the words of the bishop, pride at being called Maria Magdalen. Eva thought for a second. "You put no stock, then, in the stories that she was a harlot, a wanton who possessed hair the color of bright flame?"

Pietro did not answer her directly at first. "I made pilgrimage to the village of Magdala when I was in the Holy Land. I wanted to see where our Lord drove the seven devils from the

Magdalen. I was indeed shown a dusty patch of street where, it is believed, blessed *Iesu* did battle and Maria Magdalen emerged cleansed of the enemy's hold.

"Amongst the Saracens in the village, even on that street, I saw some young Hebrew women in their *tallits*, their prayer shawls, with hair black as raven's feathers and dark eyes to match. I imagined anyone of them could have been the Magdalen. I do not believe she possessed hair of red nor was she a harlot. Her great name has been besmirched."

Eva lowered her axe. "What of this feast day? Will her name be further besmirched?"

CHAPTER 17

22 JULY 1209
THE FEAST DAY OF
SAN MARIA MAGDALEN

Andreas wiped the blood and sweat from his eyes.

He raised his shield as a club crashed down upon it and he thrust upward with his sword, pierced threadbare fabric, skin, muscle, and vital organ. The club fell into a puddle of blood, joined a second later by its wielder as Andreas kicked the chest of the next *rotier*, felling him and three others as they skittered on the crimson slick that was the street of the jewelers. Bertran came alongside and slit belly and throat before the blood soaked wretches could rise.

The knights held fast the streets that emptied into the plaza of the Church of the Magdalen. The bodies of the *rotiers* mounded ever higher. Their free flow joined the life that spilled from house and courtyard of the slain *Bitterois*. The wretches slipped, fell, and slid in the crimson stream of their own creation. Covered with a glossy purplish patina that baked quickly in the sun, left the *rotiers* smelling like a warm, meaty scab.

Andreas's weaponry was slathered, clotted from the gravy-like flow. There was no time for cleansing.

The sun, unrelenting in its intensity, heated the bodies of *rotier* and *Bitterois* alike, cooked the viscous liquid that flowed from the hewn corpses, generated a sweet sick smell that made the gorge rise to his throat.

Yet the stench was not only on the ground and splattered against the stone and timber merchant houses lining the street, it was soaked into the surcoats and boots of the knights themselves, garments smeared with blood, flecked with pieces of fat, and muscle, and bowel.

Vultures and kites were spiraling the city, seeming closer to the ground with each pass, their increasing ranks blotting out more of the sun. Andreas looked the opposite direction to the square as one of the archers aimed for the sky, loosed a cry of rage, and somehow felled one of the birds. The bowman likely would never release such a quarrel again, and never may he earn the chance.

As the scavengers flew overhead, the shadows they left seemed to change shape before his eyes into those of owls on the prey, but no owls soared in the skies above Beziers. He was reminded of hearing the screeching of owls four days past in the wood. The shadow of an owl swooped over him once more and he shivered.

What started as a dark impression in his soul, expanded like sodden grain to fill the whole of his very being, a mortal dread that caused him to believe that not only may thousands of *Bitterois* perish this day, but none of them who were of the Languedoc may make egress from the city among the living.

Would the French cavaliers have mercy?

Andreas ran through a *rotier* at the belly and collapsed the skull of yet another. Where were the knights from the North? Andreas believed Beziers may become his own stone sarcophagus.

Aimer rushed up to Andreas. "The rest of our archers have abandoned the wall and are encircling the church. They are piercing the *rotiers* as fast as they can loose arrows. The French knights scale the walls with ladders."

A brigade of archers, in leather armor covered by chain mail, reached them and took up positions around the church of San Maria Magdalen and at the head of each of the streets that emptied into the church plaza.

Andreas issued the order to retreat toward the safekeeping

of the Magdalen and moved toward the church. "Encircle the sanctuary!" The knights of the Languedoc moved to do so.

From his point at the main doors of the church, Andreas held a clear view down the approaching streets. The *rotiers* halted their advance and melted away into blood and stone. His mind proclaimed it good news because the Northern knights were likely chasing the demonic savages away, but something in his bowels countered the hope. It was a fear he could not put words to, that these cavaliers of the Parisian King may not be inclined to show mercy.

But what else could he do? At his leading, the Languedoc knights had packed the Magdalen church with perhaps as many as three thousand *Bitterois*. There was no other place to seek safe haven.

The last peeling away of the vagabonds gave way to the glinting of chain mail and swords.

A fair fight at last, thought Andreas.

He was forming a plan in his mind, looking to summon Bertran and Aimer, when they were attacked on all sides by foot soldiers who poured out of houses nearby, swiftly made charge into the plaza, caught Andreas's thinning troop unaware, tore into their ranks, killed the Languedoc knights and archers one by one, stabbed and slashed their way toward Trencavel's knights at the church doors.

They were overwhelmed on all sides.

Andreas prepared to face mortality.

"To me! To me!" Andreas roared above the din. The remainder of their company rallied to his side. They formed a human barrier in front of the doors of the church.

Their numbers had dwindled to twenty. They raised shields and stood shoulder to shoulder, like a Roman phalanx. A company of soldiers charged head on from across the plaza, swords and axes raised high. "Absorb their blows then thrust upward and gut these barbarians! Slay them!" Andreas took a blow from a tall, blonde soldier with an axe. Once the weapon was embedded in his shield, the *châtelain* thrust longsword between his and Bertran's shields and the Northerner died with eyes and mouth open wide.

Bertran blocked a cut from a sword and stabbed his foeman

under the ribs. All the soldiers were cut down. They repelled at least five more charges of the like until the French archers took positions in the upper floors of houses around the plaza. They smashed windows and nocked arrows. The broken glass made no sound at all when it landed, flowed away with the life blood of Beziers. Upon the order to "loose," the quarrels started to find their flanks and the phalanx crumbled one cavalier at a time.

At least two score of knights charged them and Andreas's troop could no longer hold formation. Their foemen were able to surround the church in total. Andreas, Bertran, and Aimer were pushed as if by a wave to the east, away from the doors of the church.

Andreas saw the Northern soldiers surrounding the church open their line, providing a way for the *rotiers* to violate the sacredness of Saint Maria Magdalen.

That was the point was it not?

The wretches, screeching like owls, streamed into the gap after helpless prey.

For a moment, all seemed to slow as silence erupted around the plaza. It eclipsed, overwhelmed all sound of battle. Andreas raised his sword to charge the French. A window of stained glass fragmented to shards that burst from the building as if belched from the mouth of a beast. There was no sound. He battled the beast. He battled the beast he had seen on the road to Montpellier, the beast that had violated his very bedchamber, his very slumber. A second window exploded noiselessly in the self-same way. It was the cries, both low pitch and high, of those that waged a precarious battle for life that restored Andreas's hearing. Like ants streaming from an anthill, they emerged from broken windows.

Blood pooled on the front steps of the church, flowing into the plaza.

The movement of swords, knives, and clubs flashed across broken windowpanes, slashing and beating those with hands raised toward heaven.

Andreas's rage returned, for he had seen enough rivers of blood this feast day to satiate any appetite for killing.

Only vulture and kite would consume a rich banquet. Is this how Maria Magdalen was to be honored? What saint would have such a taste for blood?

Andreas slay one knight, then another, and another, inched back toward the Church of the Magdalen.

Save even one.

A line of soldiers moved between Bertran and a young mother round with child and her little girl who had abandoned the church through a panic-smashed window.

As the Occitan cavalier slay one of the Northern soldiers and wounded another, two more French infantry grabbed the woman who was with child and slashed open her belly and slit the throats of mother and daughter in such a violent fashion they were nearly decapitated.

"No!" screamed Bertran in a wail of soulish agony. "*Kyrie eleison!*"

"The only mercy God can give now is if we all die here," said Andreas quietly. But in his spirit surrender was not found.

Raising his sword high, he brought full force crashing against the shield of a French soldier, who nearly tumbled over from the blow. In the instant the soldier lifted his arms to catch his balance while stumbling backward, Andreas pursued him and slashed him across the chest and kicked him to the ground.

He ran toward Aimer, who was attempting to fend off two more. Gripping the pommel of his sword and putting all his weight behind the thrust, Andreas forced it through the thin chain mail of one, while Aimer took advantage to slash the other across the face and bury a dagger in his side.

As the second soldier crumpled over, Andreas, Bertran, and Aimer took stock and saw they had been isolated from the other Languedoc cavaliers. More French knights stormed the plaza.

As they parried blows with the Northern knights who now surrounded them, Andreas saw that the three of them were being driven from the church and toward the city walls.

He saw the last of their comrades run through with French swords.

The only hands now raised in the church of Saint Maria Magdalen were French *rotiers* and cavaliers. The blood flow from the sanctuary was ankle-deep at the least, coating the plaza in an ever-growing purplish-brown sheen. Men were sliding and falling.

All that moved of the *Bitterois* was their still warm blood.

All Andreas, Bertran, and Aimer had to fight for was each other.

The street they were battling on led to a *tor* that anchored the curtain walls of the northwest quarter of the city.

For each French knight they felled, a replacement appeared. Andreas glanced toward the tower and knew an ambush awaited. "Fight through the trap."

"Beziers is lost." The words of Bertran lacked emotion.

The interior of the *tor* had an open staircase that circled around the circumference of the rounded structure, leading to the top of the walls. The *tor* was devoid of French when first they made entrance. "To the allure," urged Andreas.

As they climbed, they heard voices above and below yell but a single word in the tongue of the French, in *du Langued'oil*. "Assault!" French knights stormed the tower from both street and wall, advancing toward Andreas, Bertran, and Aimer.

"Keep climbing," said Andreas. The stairs had breadth enough for them to charge side by side. "False attack," said Andreas, the knights' code for starting with a low guard then striking from on high.

Keeping their broadswords in a defensive posture, they raised them as one when only steps from the descending French cavaliers. The simultaneous strike wounded two knights and knocked over a third and Andreas, Bertran, and Aimer shoved those knights off the stair, leaving them to plunge to the floor. They continued fighting their way up the stairs, determined to reach the allure before they had to engage the ascending knights behind them.

When they were within five yards of where the tower opened onto the wall, more French cavaliers flooded through the upper opening, halted the advance of the Languedoc knights enough for the pursuing French to reach their position. They were now battling on two very compact fronts. It was clear their opponents were trying to force them from the stair. All took blows from swords but their armor held.

A soldier wielding a pike swung the butt end hard into the legs of Aimer, robbed him of footing. As the strong cavalier stumbled backwards losing helmet and shield, the knights *de*

Fransa behind him moved aside until one with a clear strike slashed Aimer across the face, and another pierced his skull.

Aimer remained sprawled on the staircase as French reinforcements stepped over him, continued the upward charge.

Andreas and Bertran saw their comrade at arms, their friend, struck down and loosed a cry as one, raised their intensity. They were battling back to back now, Bertran facing down the stair and Andreas facing up. More than slashing and stabbing them, the Trencavel knights were seeking to push their adversaries from the stair.

Knock them off-balance and send them plunging below.

Bertran pierced a knight in the thigh with a downward sword thrust and brought his boot into the face of the knight, sending him reeling backwards, taking another six with him.

Bertran turned and fought side by side with Andreas as they pushed the remaining French cavaliers up the stair. They were nearing the exit from the tower onto the wall.

"What of the allure?" exhaled Bertran in rapid cadence as he clipped the legs of a Northern knight with his mace.

"The ladders *Frances*," replied Andreas as he pushed that same knight off the stair to the ground below. "Flee the city. Warn Carcassonne."

"If we survive," replied Bertran abruptly as he slashed another cavalier in the belly and struck him across the face, sending him plunging to the stone floor below. "You yourself need warning, Andreas"

"What warning?"

They had reached the top of the tower but found the allure, the ledge behind the crenellations, to be quiet and vacant, at least as far as sight could tell. All were down in the city.

Andreas heard a couplet of short wind bursts as Bertran slammed into his shoulder knocking him aside as his ears registered a fleshy thud. Hearing a gurgling sound, he turned to Bertran and looked in disbelief at the feathered shaft protruding from the neck of his friend.

Bertran grew wobbly as Andreas reached to halt his fall, as pain spiked in his torso and movement was constricted.

Two small bolts from a crossbow extruded from his chest.

The *châtelain* made sure they were both down out of sighting of the French archers. Bertran had absorbed the worst of it. He sought to bolster his sergeant at arms. "I will take you down a ladder." Each breath seemed to breed pain anew for Bertran, but the eyes of his friend were steadfast, calm.

"Andreas... hearken to me." His breathing was measured, but labored. "Take heed... of *l' orde.*"

"What are you saying?" Andreas wondered if Bertran was babbling, though his sound was coherent.

"You are... under their watching... an...oppressive watching." Bertran coughed and a red mist filled the air. "Everywhere *L'orde* is present. We are bested with the sword this day Andreas. Concede not... the battle of the spirit." Bertran swallowed and grimaced. "They would purloin your soul... unrelenting."

Bertran was wheezing now, fighting for every breath, the blood oozing from his throat in increased flow like a wine skin with a crack that did not cease to split.

"These things... are such a burden to know. The twelve of *l'orde* have laid claim upon your very spirit. You are seven jewels to them... twelve pearls of great price... three sevens. I vowed to Guilhabert to protect you from their wiles." More coughed up blood and gasps for air. "I have died defending you." Bertran clenched both hands into fists and shook them with feeble strength.

"You will yet live, Bertran. Who are they? How know you this?" asked Andreas tersely, but in a whisper, mindful of the charging French cavaliers several yards away who had just emerged into view.

Bertran struggled mightily to release the words of his response, gurgling and hacking up blood. "I heard them... speak of their plans for you. Guilhabert rescued me. Take heed... the coils of the serpent... be not struck but strike in the spirit...*memento mori...*"

Bertran's eyes remained open as his life drained away, as his soul quit his body and the look of his face was one of peace.

Andreas gently closed the eyes of Bertran. "Of what serpent do you speak? Why do you leave? Curse you Bertran! Why did you not tell me sooner, while you still drew unfaltering breath?"

The French were upon him once more.

Andreas raised his sword to parry a blow from a tall, powerful Northern Knight, as a well-placed kick in the belly sent another off the wall and into the city below.

When he turned to resume battle with the tall knight, that cavalier had disappeared. Seeing movement behind the diminutive mangonel that sat only yards away, Andreas raised sword to charge the elusive foe.

The *châtelain* felt pressure on his belly and found he was sliding toward the wall, unable to change course. He was looking at the crossbowmen in the city below as they recocked their weapons, then spun around, yet knew not how, and he was looking over the crenellations, across the river, into the forest.

He felt force applied to his backside and the forest inverted.

He was looking at the sky, then the exterior of the city walls, then the slope to the river, then the river, then the plains, then the forest another time, and then the cloudless heavens again, until his backside felt pressure once more and his vision was consumed by blackness.

⚜

When his eyes again received light, he was facing still an empty canvas of blue, marred only by the lazy circling of vultures and kites, whose numbers had seen increase.

Slowly he turned his head to take in his surroundings.

He was lying in a broad mound of hay, likely deep if its sponginess told anything. The pungent odors of pitch and oil permeated his nostrils. To his left towered the city walls so close he could almost touch the ochre stone with the reach of his arm. To his right, down a short slope and a sandy plain was the River Orb, perhaps two-hundred yards away.

But he dared not move his limbs yet. He knew not yet what was broken or who was keeping vigilance from above. The sun radiated its scorching heat and he could feel it exuding from his armor. The odor from his surcoat grew rancid, like fatty red meat left to rot.

He had been lying there some minutes at least. He was alive but how did he reach this place outside of the city? He must have tumbled over the wall in some fashion. Why did he yet draw breath? He could see a stout wooden beam, far above, extended

over the edge of the walls. The broken handle of a mangonel had
been used to dislodge him from the allure.

He felt moisture in his boots, his feet telling him they were
soaked. It was a strange sort of wetness, like one that would
never dry up, as if his toes had been lubricated.

Oil.

He had slipped on oil after the quarrels found their mark.
He had slipped, spun, and then been dislodged from the wall.

Arrows had pierced him. Out of his peripheral vision he
could see two *petit* wooden shafts, feathered at the top of each.
Then he heard repetitive sounds like staccato, concentrated
bursts of wind. He smelled smoke and felt swelling heat. The
pungent sweet smell of pitch and oil and hay aflame.

For an eternal moment he knew not whether to rise or lay
still.

The words he heard next seemed to echo from nowhere and
everywhere at once. "Andreas, cross the river."

Where did the voice originate? Was it in his own mind or
had he heard it aloud?

Again the same words: "Andreas, cross the river."

Was it his own thoughts or a voice from the ethos?

He could see this pile of hay that had been his salvation
would soon become his deathbed. As he rolled over to stand, a
sharp, stabbing pain ripped across his torso and down his legs.
As Andreas gained his footing he saw that he was trapped in a
half-circle of fire that started and ended at two points along the
walls.

A crescent of death.

This hay that the *Bitterois* had piled and soaked with flam-
mable liquids as a part of the defenses had been ignited by the
fiery darts of the French archers.

A yellowish-orange glint of metal led his eyes to his sword
only two yards away, point thrust into the hay, nearly buried to
the handle. His helmet had tumbled off during the fall and he
saw it only as it was engulfed by the spreading flames.

The fire lurched rapidly toward him now, greedily consuming the oil-soaked, combustible hay. Unbuckling and throwing
off his weapon belt, he pulled the arrows from his chest, their release coming surprisingly easy—and painlessly—from his flesh,

their slender bodkin tips proving that they were meant to pierce mail.

He tossed them aside.

Tearing off his blood-encrusted, fetid surcoat, he ran toward the edge of the flames nearest the river, arrows landing at his heels, the flow of blood increasing from the pierce marks, soaking through his armor padding. Sodden as it was, his surcoat would not quickly burn.

Grabbing his war sword in stride, he threw his surcoat over the flames to smother a small section and provide safe passage from the inferno. He could hear the hissing as the blood and fat that clung to the surcoat were licked by fire. He felt the heat as he leapt through the momentary gap in the wall of flame.

He kept running, down the green grassy slope, a step ahead of the missiles that kept raining from the walls, across the narrow sandy plain toward a small, whitewashed skiff with a protruding oar handle that lay beached on the east bank of the river. The cavaliers from the North must have used the craft in their haste to enter the breached city.

As he neared the river, he could see the speed of the current, and across the Orb, downstream, were horses tied to a wooden post. If he was judging the current right, and he paddled hard, he should be able to run aground within a few yards of the mounts.

Rapid fire thoughts popped into his mind: the open West Gate, *rotiers*, Bertran, Aimer, the Church of the Magdalen.

No time for mourning.

Carcassonne need hear his news. How long until the French break camp here and march on the stronghold of Trencavel lands?

Keep running.

He could hear the impact of arrows digging up ground where his feet were the second before. Reaching the riverbank, he dropped his sword into his means of escape.

The wooden skiff was light and he was able to push it into the river and jump in quickly. Grabbing the oar and dipping it in to the current on the right side of the craft, he paddled with long, deep pull strokes and kept his course aimed toward the horses on the other side. The quarrels launched from the walls were plunging harmlessly into the river downstream. He was out of range now.

With each stroke, painful fatigue reverberated in his arms and fiery sensations shot across his chest, but he kept paddling.

Reaching the opposite riverbank, about five yards downstream of the horses, he half-stepped, half-rolled out of the skiff, giving the boat a stiff shove back into the river.

The horses were unguarded and no one on the east bank seemed aware of his presence. Few cavaliers remained west of the river. All the French were in Beziers now, or nearly so, thought Andreas.

His focus instinctively went to the *caval* that evidenced the most power. It was an *arabit*, a black Arabian with muscular haunches and white fetlocks that sported also the most elaborate saddle and bridle.

Though lacking the crenellated blanket that signified nobility, it was likely the property of a Duke of Flanders. They seemed to have an eye for Arabians. Regardless, the current owner would lose all claim this day.

Yanking free the loose knot and testing the stirrup before swinging himself on, Andreas ascended the horse and spurred it off across the plain toward the forest, sword in one hand, reins in the other.

The *bòsc* was perhaps a league away. If he could reach that dense knot of trees he could make good his escape.

As he closed the space between himself and the edge of the *bòsc*, Andreas looked behind to see he had gained four mounted pursuers that were at best one-hundred fifty yards behind him, armored knights all, swords unsheathed, but no crossbows. Good.

He knew they would seek his death because he was now become a messenger. The French would not wish the news of this day to reach Carcassonne too quickly.

As he neared the forest it started to rain. Through the cloudburst, he saw the gap in the wood he sought, the trail that led to the Potter's Mound.

CHAPTER 18

22 JULY 1209
FEAST DAY OF
SAN MARIA MAGDALEN

Pietro and Eva worked together on the tenth tree, taking turns swinging their axes. When they had hacked a deep enough notch in the trunk, the bishop stepped aside and Eva pushed over the tree. Now all the trees were felled that she needed for the cathedral in Avignon.

Claris and the Painter had already stripped four of the fallen trees of small branches. They had filled the handcart with trunks and limbs and now pushed it down the hill toward the community. Eva watched them descend the gentle slope. The Painter pushed the load forward while Claris helped balance the cart to keep it from toppling. They work well together, Eva thought with mild surprise. She kept her gaze upon them until they reached the West Gate and entered the community.

The bishop watched as well. At length he turned and noticed the two large flaxen piles near cliff's edge. He raised the question for which she had been waiting. "What is the purpose of stacks of hay in an orchard of pears?"

"Come with me, I will show you," she said, beckoning him to follow. She was ready for a break from her labors. For the first time she felt a mild pang of guilt for her industry on a saint's day, though it quickly subsided.

Purposely approaching the side of the hay that faced toward the bluff, Eva reached her arm into the center of the stack and pulled out a long bundle wrapped tightly in oiled cloth. Untying the gray cords that bound it closed, she rolled open the olive green protective cover, revealing a slender bow four feet in length, varnished to a glossy sheen. It had an arrow plate of mother of pearl, and a handgrip of blackened leather.

The oiled cloth contained also a quiver of leather with five iron-tipped, black-feathered, lacquered arrows.

She noticed the surprise on the bishop's face, but only for a fleeting moment before astonishment gave way to a slight smile and a solemn nod, as if he had known something all along but had merely forgotten it for a moment.

"How does a woman who is not nobility obtain hold of such a weapon, Eva, especially one that is adorned with mother of pearl?" The bishop made his query in a tone both amused and impressed.

"Through much trial with a lathe and carving tools." Eva looked at the bishop and smiled. "Five good trees sacrificed themselves and became quarrels before I learned to carve a bow that did not snap in two."

"You made a bow out of *pera* wood?"

"I made the bow, though not the string. It is hemp, twisted and tied by a farmer. The arrow plate came from you, from Outremer. I had it made from a cracked portion of a box of mother of pearl. The bow, however, is a selfbow and is not constructed of *pera* wood. The wood in this *pera* orchard, and any *pera* wood I suppose, has not the straight grain, flexibility, and bending strength needed for a selfbow, which," she smiled shyly, aware she was lecturing a lord of the Church, "is a bow made from a single piece of wood.

"The wood from a *pera* tree would splinter and snap in half when you drew the string to loose an arrow. This bow is about four feet in length when at rest. The Welsh have the most powerful bows. Many of their warbows exceed six feet in length. Great is the strength and training required to use such a bow, but deadly the power and effectiveness. It is said the force of an arrow from a Welsh bow can pierce oakwood four inches thick or lift an armored knight off a horse at full gallop and pin him to a tree.

"There are yew trees aplenty in the river valley. That is the source of this bow."

Eva led the bishop back to the hay mounds. "There is more I hide here as well. Even the other women of the community would likely not approve of my little archery range." Reaching into the pile, she produced a rolled-up tan canvas, pockmarked with dozens of small holes, and draped it over the side of the hay.

"I come out here for target practice at least once a week. I think I shall take my practice this day if you will suffer to watch."

Pietro smiled, leaning his frame against a nearby tree. "I would gladly give you audience. Your father was the most skilled archer ever I have seen."

Eva straightened the canvas and secured it by pushing four long metal spikes through holes in the corners of the target deep into the hay. She hesitated. "Anselme was an archer..." Turning her back to the newly affixed cloth, she marked off her twenty paces carefully. Reaching the south edge of the orchard she halted and removed the bolts from her quiver, plunging each one point first into the dry earth in a straight line in front of her. She planted her feet shoulder width apart, perpendicular to the target. Snatching an arrow from the earth, she nocked it onto the string. Wrapping her left hand around the leather handgrip, she placed the shaft of the bolt on the mother of pearl arrow rest. Placing the fingers of her right hand on the string of hemp, with the shaft between the second and third fingers, she slid them along the string until they came to rest in the groove of the calloused joints nearest the tips. With fingers in place she focused on the target until it was all that lay in her vision. She drew back and tilted the warbow slightly until the arrow rested along her direct line of sight to the bullseye and the nock of the arrow touched the corner of her mouth. The best archers could pull the string back to their ear, but she worked hard to reach her mouth. Rolling the tips of her fingers off the string, she loosed the quarrel. It sliced the damp air with an angry, low whistle and buried itself a fingertip's width to the left of center of the target. She nocked a second arrow, drew and loosed, and fired the remaining three in quick succession. The first four arranged themselves neatly around the center and the final bolt found the bullseye.

"How did you learn to shoot?" The bishop looked duly impressed, though once more not surprised.

"Archery tournaments. I watched the winners and losers and what they did that was different. Much of it lies in the stance."

"Your father became an excellent bowman in the Holy Land." The bishop paused for a moment, looking across the orchard. "I see much of your father in you. He was not rebellious, but as fiery and spirited as one can be without crossing that line. I learned much from him about life and faith. Though I was a priest, it was he who taught me truly to believe. Because of him, I began to question if my life had purpose beyond the rigors of a dutiful cleric.

"The faith that led your father to the Holy Land was true. *Iesu* had called him there, I believe that. Unlike so many, he did not go simply to kill Saracens or Seljuk Turks, or whoever the infidel may be. Anselme went out of obedience, not understanding all reasons why."

"I have no memory of my father."

"I have remembrance that he talked often of you, of the spark of life he saw burning within you, even as an infant. He paid a price for his obedience as did you, Eva, as did Lydia, for you both were robbed of him. I personally went to see the infidel slain and God's justice restored in Jerusalem. I saw much of the former and none of the latter. I never even laid eyes on the holy city. It had already fallen to Salah ha-din and his hordes before ever your father and I arrived in Outremer. Even the Lionheart was unable to retake it.

"Some now say it is foolish to take the Cross and go on pilgrimage. I say it is foolish to go only to kill men of another faith, but also foolish to deny God's call, even if it leads you to Outremer."

"If not to kill the infidel, then what was the call of *Deum* for my father in Outremer?"

"I cannot tell all, for I have believed for a long time there is more than I know. But I will tell you I believe he was called to fight evil. But not in the way of the foolish, simpleminded man who thinks that wholesale slaughter of the infidel will bring God's justice."

"In what way then?"

Pietro shook his head. "That is what I hoped would be revealed in the palimpsest. I pray it will still be laid bare."

CHAPTER 19

22 JULY 1209
THE FEAST DAY OF
SAN MARIA MAGDALEN

H ie!" Andreas goaded the horse to fleeter speed. The tunnel formed by the foliage arched over the narrow trail, twisted and turned through the forest, shielded him from the sight of his pursuers, who had not yet reached the wood.

The driving rain suctioned his small-clothes to his skin. Double ring chain mail could absorb a blow from a mace, but gave little shield from a downpour. His tunic and under armor padding were drenched. He could feel the added weight on his shoulders.

Thankfully the rain was warm, and although it cooled him, it did not bring on a chill. Andreas knew that passing too quickly from hot to cold could be dangerous. In extreme fashion, it was one of the ways the *Bons Hommes* practiced leaving this evil world of matter for the pure realm of spirit.

An initiate would heat up his body in a nearly scalding hot bath, dive straight from liquid heat into a frigid river or lake, cause the heart to arrest, to burst open it was said, self-slaying at last one's evil flesh.

Which caused him remembrance of his own wounds. Though

he had given the piercings in his torso little thought since he had ripped out the quarrels on the run, he glanced briefly at his chest and was surprised that the bleeding seemed staunched, and the pain abated. Even with the thin-tipped bolts that had pierced him, his double ring hauberk appeared to have slowed their advance and kept them from plunging too deep. Even so, a shield buttressed with iron plates was the only defense against such arrows. The quarrels from the crossbows should have penetrated far between his ribs.

No time to examine the punctures now.

His chest ached from hurts far worse than an arrow could deliver. He would be the first rider to reach Carcassonne with the news. Andreas could not fathom another soul escaping the hellish cauldron of Beziers alive.

All the *Bitterois* they had led to slaughter in the Church of Saint Maria Magdalen, mostly families with children, little ones with eyes barely constrained by their eye pits, driven to silence or wailing by their terror. Why could he not save them? What other thing could he have done? Perhaps the rain was at least washing the blood from their riven bodies.

Turning a quick glance toward the city, he saw the clouds did not extend beyond the forest. The city was still dry. Their remains would quickly putrefy and burst in the heat, become carrion for vulture, raven, kite, and hawk. The stench by nightfall would be insufferable. Thousands of bodies that only this morning had been living and whole and safe.

Yet Andreas had not reached safety either. He could hear the pounding of galloping hooves behind him. It was time to lose his pursuers. Clutching black leather reins with locked fingers, he pulled the horse to the left then the right, weaving through the tightly packed, ever drenching forest.

As he buried his face in the horse's mane, he felt pain rip through him as an oaken limb roughly scraped the back of his neck. It was a stinging reminder his helmet had been claimed by the oily flames. Hot blood oozed down his back.

The height of the limb over the trail had been difficult to judge.

For a brief moment, Andreas looked up once more. Though enough light filtered through the tree canopy that he could see about fifty paces ahead, the foliage thickened and he was deprived of the view of the sky. He could not witness the origin of the downpour, the clouds that expended their wrath on the lands of his liege, Viscount Raimon Roger Trencavel I.

Relief, anger, guilt, and anguish all fought one another for the supremacy of his soul. As he tore through the forest on horseback, he knew somehow that anguish was at the moment victorious.

About one-hundred paces behind him he heard a muffled clank and the ripping crash of a limb torn from an ancient tree. He smiled that at least his own pain from the limb had proved the worse for his pursuer. But he knew there were more. Four knights had set after him, and now there were three. Though outnumbered, he knew he owned the advantage. He knew this forest, every hill and twist and turn. Many a time had he and Bertran practiced their horsemanship on this very trail.

Andreas reached the Potter's Mound, and knew if he could time his jump right, then at least one more of his pursuers would fall. As he crested the hill, he rejoiced that the fallen tree, stout and whole, lay still at the beginning of the down slope. As long as this horse can jump...

He pulled back on the reins and the *arabit* abandoned *terra*, flying over the thick, horizontal tree trunk, skillfully reengaging the rain-soaked earth, throwing clay in every direction.

He flew down the hill with nary a break in speed, pulled the reins to the right, directed the horse behind a craggy limestone outcropping, a giant fist of stone thrust through clay ground.

This was the place to make his stand.

After a few moments of near silence, the sound of the snorting of a horse and crack of tree limbs followed by a clanking, metallic thud reached his ears. Horse and rider had stumbled hard over the fallen tree trunk.

If events moved forward as he planned, the next knight would ride his mount into the horse and rider that had just crashed on the fallen tree and both would be unhorsed, leaving him but one mounted foe to battle.

As screams in the cadence of *du Langued'oil* penetrated the forest, Andreas heard more sounds of tumbling and cracking.

Now the chance lay before him.

Raising his sword high and digging his heels into the ribs of the Arabian, Andreas reemerged onto the path and charged up the hill.

The first knight to encounter the fallen tree was dead, eyes wide open, and head bloodied from the hooves of the horse of the second one. That second knight himself was alive, though he had just risen to his feet. By the time that knight looked upon Andreas, the blade of a slashing sword was inches from his face, and the final words he heard were Andreas's cry of "*Kyrie Eleison!*"

Andreas continued his assault up the hill. He knew his final pursuer would approach the potter's mound with greater caution after hearing the demise of his compatriots. His gut told him the last of the French would prove fiercest.

Leaping over the fallen tree trunk in an arc borne of power, the *arabit* rounded hill's crest, spurred on by Andreas. The final knight was nowhere in his vision or hearing. That one must have been riding farther behind the others than Andreas had reckoned.

The *châtelain* decided quickly he would continue to double-back on the path until he encountered the French cavalier. Then Andreas would confront him one-on-one. The cavalier would taste the bitterness of a fallen city, and a savage, senseless slaughter. Andreas would make him choke down whole the gall of this day.

As he drove the *arabit* down the slope, Andreas could see a thick rampart of billowing gray smoke rising in the distance.

Fire. Beziers.

The *rotiers* had likely put it to the torch, for knights and nobles would never scorch the plunder of so wealthy a city. With conditions dry and hot as they were, he knew the citadel, if indeed that was the source of the burning, would be devoured quickly by flame. Yet where was the fourth cavalier? Had he turned back? Andreas heard no sound of someone approaching or fleeing on horseback.

The *arabit* snorted and whinnied. He heard the sound of buzzing.

There was a rustling, a tearing of leaves, a scraping of stone on wood then pain emanating from the crown of his head, the impact of an object striking the top of his helmetless skull. His vision turned spotty and his muscles grew slack as sodden clay ground seemed to fly at him at frightening speed.

Crack! Pain reverberated in his lower left leg. He was unhorsed and his commandeered mount was charging off into the forest. He must focus his mind. No, it was not his *arabit* running off, it was another *caval* charging toward him.

He saw a faint shard of light, the silvery glint of a blade poised to strike. His felt his head bobbing sideways on his neck like a dead fish in the river.

Concentrate! It was the last of his pursuers.

Andreas knew he had to leave the path and avoid the charge or death would find him quickly.

His adversary was but yards away, closing the distance downhill at full gallop, dipping his upper body sideways, leaning, straining toward Andreas.

The *châtelain* wrapped his arms around the tree in a desperate embrace, pushed with his one undamaged leg, fought to stay conscious, willed his body to the other side of the broad trunk, and dragged his injured leg like the numb, useless appendage it had become.

The French cavalier flew past on his roan mare, clanged his blade sharply against the spot of the tree Andreas's head had vacated the second before, the muffled clang echoing through the drenched forest.

The momentum of the horsed knight carried him past the tree and down the hill.

Andreas had rammed his left shin against the tree when he fell, though the bone still seemed whole. Stand! The Northern knight will charge again.

He was seeing two of everything that should be one.

Gripping the tree so intensely that his fingernails bore into the rough, deep-grooved bark, producing bleeding at the tips of his fingers, groaning and wincing from the effort, Andreas planted his one undamaged leg in the thick, sloppy clay and pulled himself upright.

Though spots of light still danced amongst the raindrops, the danger of slipping to unconsciousness seemed to have ebbed, but his head throbbed and it was bleeding, though not sliced deep. It was a blunt object that had struck his head. Had the knight hurled a rock? Where lay his own sword?

He did not have to search far for the weapon. It lay prone on the ground in front of him, though slathered in chunky red mud. He must have kept his grip on it as he tumbled off the horse, at least until his shin struck the tree. He bent over carefully and picked it up by its water and clay greased leather bound handle.

The French cavalier was riding back up the hill, spurring the horse to a galloping charge.

Andreas hobbled around the tree, still clutched it with one hand as he did so, and stepped onto the path. Planting his feet squarely in the middle of the muddy trail and grasping his sword with both hands, the *châtelain* tested the strength of his injured leg, to see if he could push off on it. Andreas hopped on the leg, and although his shin protested severely enough to make his eyes water, the leg held. The pain was sharp and raw, but it seemed the appendage would bear up his full weight.

Brandishing his sword, Andreas waited for the knight to close the distance. He hoped that this French horseman would attempt to ride over him, making his counterattack all the simpler. Andreas kept his stand in the center of the path and the rider stayed his course there as well.

When the knight was within three yards of Andreas, he ran forward then dived to the left. He held his sword over the middle of the trail as his body flew to the side, pulled his outstretched arms back to him, slashed with his sword, slicing into the front legs of the horse, which buckled and lurched forward erratically, head plummeting to earth and hindquarters bucking skyward, as if tilting on a lance shaft pierced through the heart.

As his shoulder dug into wet ground and the rest of him followed, Andreas turned and looked in time to see the rider hurling in an arc to the top of the Potter's Mound, landing uphill of his crumpled mount.

As Andreas lay in the mud for a second, and again as he struggled to his feet, he tried to picture in his mind where this knight would have hidden before attacking him. On this slope of the Potter's Mound, there was really no place for mounted knight on horseback to seek cover.

Though this horseman had not a green surcoat, Andreas

thought of the words of the villager along the *Via Domitia*: *We had no knowledge of their presence until they were upon us.* He had experienced it near the road and in the wood by the stream-path. Was this one of those knights, one of a band of warriors that somehow veiled their presence? Did some sorcery mask their sight and sound or were they simply clever at concealing their appearance in some unknown way?

Regardless, he saw that his foeman had risen almost immediately to his feet after tumbling off the horse. The animal lay on its side, snorting and wheezing, its front legs broken and bleeding. Wielding his sword, the knight thrust it through the horse's skull behind the ear, relieving the mare of its misery and turning his controlled glare of cold rage on Andreas.

"Impressive," the French cavalier snarled in a voice deep but not sinister, one that bore a small note of admiration. "You have proven already a worthy adversary. All others would have slipped to eternity by now."

The knight raised his sword and whipped the blade right then left, checking for injuries that would hinder his movement. Andreas would have done the same.

"But if you will achieve wellbeing, your path still must come through me." The gray eyes of the cavalier shone with a cold light of the same hue, his features angular and unyielding, like the realities of this day.

"So be it," said Andreas,, tightening his hold on his long-sword, but otherwise unmoving.

The knight's desire to taunt was not yet quenched. "Where will you flee if you survive my hand? To spread declaration to the next city their destruction is also at hand? Occitan fool."

The warrior raised himself to his full stature. He exceeded two yards in height, solid in build, in appearance much as Andreas had imagined a Roman gladiator would look, only such a fighter would have borne not a cross sewn into his garment.

But fear leaked not into the soul of Andreas, it only filled further with resolve.

The tall knight did not appear injured from the fall.

Andreas knew he would have to draw the cavalier in close and best him with strength, for though he could walk at least, and run a little, he did not know at what speed he could move or how long his leg would hold out. Where was his pilfered mount, the *arabit*? Yet he could not concern himself with reaching Carcassonne as yet. He must first survive the battle of this Mound of the Potter.

The knight loosed a war cry and charged down the hill toward Andreas, who planted his feet firmly and waited. His foe was hurtling down the hill with abandon, skillfully keeping his footing sure in the suctioning mud. He was quick. Perhaps Andreas's match in that realm, but also aggressive, maybe overly so, which could be turned against him.

Instead of charging in kind, Andreas waited, kept his feet spaced about the width of his shoulders apart, gathered strength in standing still. He must negate the other knight's advantage of moving down the hill.

Keeping his warsword low and pointed at the drenched, maroon earth, Andreas tried to appear calm, almost uninterested, but he was studying every movement of his opponent, how he ran, how he held his sword, even how he kept shifting the weapon to the side opposite his lead foot, knowledge which could prove useful. The French cavalier kept making slight upward twitching movements with his arms, as if he was preparing to strike from on high.

Andreas let him advance to within two yards before moving.

In one deft movement, Andreas stepped to the side and brought up his sword, keeping it parallel to the sloped ground.

The tall cavalier did strike from on high, a quick movement that was hard to see. Andreas not only blocked the blow but pulled his sword back toward himself, turned the knight's sword and the knight with him as Andreas rotated on one foot and planted the other squarely on the torso of the knight, leaving a muddy footprint on the burgundy surcoat, , and sending the horseman sprawling backward onto the mushy trail.

Andreas charged the Northern cavalier, hoping to finish him. The knight flipped onto his side, pushed off with his free hand, and connected with a hard kick to Andreas's gut that knocked the *châtelain* on his back.

Andreas scarcely had time to react before his opponent was on his feet, bringing a downward blow from his sword, one that the Occitan knight had only time to raise his weapon and parry, then roll onto his knees, fend off another strike with the flat of his blade, then stand as his shin ached and swords again clashed, this time overhead.

Andreas now had the advantage of the uphill position and he intended to use it.

As he parried another blow, then went to cut on the offensive, intrusive thoughts of grotesque, deformed beasts with chiseled, greenish-red, leering faces rushed through his mind, like the one that seemed to leap out of the earth on the road to Montpellier, assaulting his own concentration. He jerked his head back instinctively at a silver line of light, and pain and blood were felt on his cheek. He had been slashed across the face, but the wound did not appear serious, only messy.

The next slashing motion of the French cavalier left his side vulnerable. Andreas swung and lunged, but before he could connect, stabbing images of children being tortured in a dungeon, crying out for mercy, slashed through his concentration and weakened the effect of his blow, which bounced off harmlessly. He heard the voice of Bertran yelling. *Focus your mind!* Yet he was unable to do so.

Andreas thought he had seen the tall knight's lips move ever so slightly as if muttering something. Did he speak some sort of incantation? He found himself being pushed back up the hill, for each time he went to strike a blow it fell useless, as he would lose control of his vision or thoughts.

He would see the knight, then a lion, then the knight, then an eagle with talons bared, then the knight, then a coiled serpent, then eyes of a human that transformed to those of a beast and back once more, then the knight, then bees swarming round a honeycomb. Though he was able to keep fending off the cutting and thrusting of the cavalier, he would not be able to do so time eternal.

He decided the only way he could gain victory was to slay the knight with his bare hands, to grip tight and hold unyielding, regardless of what invaded his mind.

Bending his knees and crouching slightly, Andreas waited until his thoughts settled once more and his adversary raised arms to strike again. Springing forward like a cougar, Andreas let fall his sword as empty hands reached out and joined together behind the nape of the knight's neck. Andreas yanked the knight toward him and brought his knee up hard into the gut of the cavalier, who groaned in spite of chain mail, flailing his sword about, the weapon useless in such a tight space. Keeping hands locked behind the neck of his foeman, Andreas yanked again and slammed his knee into the groin of the knight and once more into the knight's thigh and lifted him off the ground. He grasped the wrist of the sword wielding arm and slammed the hand against a tree and burnished steel met sodden clay. Andreas grabbed the shoulders of the Frenchman and threw the knight to the ground prostrate and jumped on him, hooking arm around the knight's throat.

Best him with strength.

He could hear the mutterings from the other's lips in words Andreas could not comprehend. Thoughts, images, some pleasant, like a pot of golden honey, some disturbing, like black robed prisoners being consumed by fire, continued to echo in his soul, but Andreas held on as the utterances compressed to sounds of gurgling and Andreas, refusing to let go at any cost, pressed the full weight of his body into the Northern knight, compressing the crook of his arm ever tighter.

Andreas rolled to the side, turned the knight to face the sky, pulled him on top, flexed his limb taut, pulled with all the fury and rage he could; muscle compressing flesh.

Never had he faced an opponent like this who could so toy with his mind. It was worse than the encounters on the road to Montpellier. The knight could not speak now but continued kicking his legs and thrashing his arms about uselessly until his movements convulsed to violent twitching and all motion drained away and his body went limp. Andreas shoved off the cavalier, picked up his warsword, drove it into the man's forehead, and slashed him across the throat.

He was dead.

But the intrusive thoughts did not cease, they only grew.

Like a kettle of lard left to linger too long over a fire, anger boiled to spewing rage.

A door in his soul gave way.

Gripping the pommel of his sword, Andreas thrust the point of the weapon through the dead knight's chain mail into his chest, and the blood spurted out like a fountain, entering Andreas's nose and eyes, yet the mental intrusion not only persisted, but grew, like a chorus in crescendo.

So Andreas stabbed with his sword, again and again, hacking at the body, yelling, though he knew not what was issuing from his mouth, but he kept screaming, trying to halt the images, drown them out, slash them to pieces, the thoughts, the voices, but they persisted. He saw *rotiers* and the Church of the Magdalen and rivers of blood.

The dead knight was soon dismembered and the blood continued to drain from limbs and torso, pooling in nearby muddy footprints, being diluted by rainwater.

Dizzy, his head aching, his body weary with an exhaustion he had never known, Andreas half sat, half-tumbled into the mud and lay on his side. The rain stopped and slanted rays of the sun poked through the trees. The angle of the beams of light meant it was late evening.

The sunlight did not halt the thoughts.

Finally, though his head ached along with the whole of his body, Andreas chose to ignore the noise in his mind. He needed to glean the identity of this knight and then take flight to Carcassonne, if indeed he had strength to travel that far.

Grasping the sword of the dead cavalier, an especially heavy one with a pommel set with a green stone, a true emerald by the looks of it, Andreas felt the intensity of the intrusion decrease. Searching the body, he found a thin gold chain sheathed in blood near the shoulders of the knight. It had somehow escaped damage at the beheading by his hand and bore a bejeweled geometric object that had the look of a talisman. He spat upon it and wiped it on his tunic. It was a square of gold with a circle within and a triangle within that, set with seven jewels like the dagger: four emeralds, a sapphire, and two rubies. The opposing side bore writing, five and ten words in Occitan, one on each side of the square, one on each side of the triangle and eight round the circumference of the circle: *quieria, dimartz, damnatge, hostals, heretier, trahida, glazier, guirensa, orguelh, onransas, soteiran, jusvert, jauzimen, unitat, uffrenda.* He spoke each one aloud in turn and the invasive thoughts ceased altogether.

The knight's surcoat was burgundy, or at least it had been

when it was pristine, before becoming sopped with wet earth and blood, the knight's own blood. Andreas knew most of it had been spilt after death by his very hand.

He held up his own sword as if the thing had acted on its own, purposelessly hacking apart the body of this cavalier. But he had wielded it, as if he could slay the chaos ripping through his head and obliterate the massacre of this day.

He knew not why the noise in his mind had halted now, but he was grateful. He shuddered at the carnage he had wrought, but did not dwell on it. The knight was exceedingly worthy of far worse. It mattered not since surely such a knight of sorcery was destined for hell, and would have no need of a body whole for heaven. Though he found himself wishing he had not severed head from shoulder, nor even limb from torso. The heart at least, Andreas had left in the body.

As he stooped to the task of searching further the remains of the knight, he remembered the muttering. He tried to force his brain to recall what the knight had said. He could tell it was not pointless babbling, but the words remained just beyond his grasp, something like.... 'Melimarpera'! It was the phrase given repetition by the villager whose distressed son Andreas had nearly trampled.

He resumed his corporeal search. Among the things he discovered was a small object with a hexagonal piece of soft, worn leather with two lengthy cords, each longer than his arms, tied to holes on either end of the hexagon. It had the look of a sling, but not like any Andreas had seen before. There was also a small red suede pouch with a white drawstring. In the bottom of the pouch was a small amount of rock dust. His head must have been struck with a stone from that very sling.

Andreas left the sword of the slain cavalier, but grabbed the talisman, sling, and suede pouch and stuffed them under his own tunic. Having abandoned his weaponry belt outside the city walls, he retrieved his warsword, not bothering to wipe off the day's carnage and mud, though knowing he would have to carry it.

A fiery blanket of foreboding seemed to drape round him and release its heat into every pore of his skin. His soul felt aflame and the hope of his world was burning to a charred stump of despair. God had cruelly denied them victory.

Stumbling erratically down the hill, Andreas wished fervent-
ly that like Bertran and Aimer he had been bestowed the honor
of perishing in battle along with the other valiant defenders of
Beziers.

Not knowing from whence the strength or the will sprung,
Andreas, finding the *arabit* feeding on ferns behind a boulder
at the base of the Potter's Mound, swung on and rode out of the
forest.

Andreas rode the horse on until twilight and sunset passed
and moonlight illumined the way, casting its pall upon the land.

He took his route cross-country, avoiding any paths or roads
and therefore any advance scouts, or pickets, or raiding parties
of the enemy, for he knew the land well. His sense of speed and
location told him that he could make Carcassonne before cockcrow. It was a strong destrier he was riding, and fast, and ought
be able to endure a hard night's journey across uneven ground.
If necessary, Andreas would kill the horse to reach Carcassonne
by first light. Raimon Roger would need all the time he could
muster to gather his forces to himself.

Andreas's thoughts returned to the Church of Saint Maria
Magdalen and lingered there. His grip on the reins grew tighter
as he imagined the assault on the church from every conceivable
angle. No matter what he had done, the French would have overrun the church, for their numbers were too many. Yet he could
not purge his mind of the faces of the *Bitterois*. They had been
so filled with hope, so grateful when Andreas, Bertran, Aimer,
and the other knights had given them safe passage to sanctuary,
to what they believed to be a haven in the Church of Saint Maria
Magdalen. But it was haven only for the host of hell. When had
Christians stormed a church, a church ancient and hallowed, to
slaughter fellow Christians?

Andreas did not pray to saints as many did, for he thought
it without purpose. He believed not that the spirits of the dead
lingered. Yet if he was one who petitioned the holy ones, then
the name of Maria Magdalen would have been accursed and
stricken from his prayers that day.

CHAPTER 20

22 JULY 1209
THE FEAST DAY OF
SAN MARIA MAGDALEN

Using the reading stone, a glass vial of oak gall ink, and a newly sharpened quill, Eva transcribed the original contents of the palimpsest onto vellum.

She liked writing on a surface that had a grain on one side, much like wood.

Made from whole animal skins stretched tight, vellum had such a grain. Parchment, made from split skins, did not. It was a small thing, but important to her.

The Painter used vellum for the few works he had created that were meant to be hung on a wall.

She liked the feel, the texture of it.

She obtained her vellum by bartering. There was a scribe in Avignon she kept supplied with pear wood for the covers of bound volumes. He gave her squares of vellum in return. Scribing on one of those pages, she took pains to match the letter size and spacing as found in the scarcely legible original.

Using a second sheet of vellum from her own stock and a dictionary to be sure of accuracy, she translated it also to Latin for the sake of the bishop.

As she went about the task, the only sound in the room the rhythmic scratching of the quill nib on unsplit sheepskin, she felt a deep, growing sadness she did not comprehend. It settled over her and seemed to invade body and soul, course through her veins still greater with each breath.

She looked round the room she used as a study. It lay across the hall from her bedchamber and was its equal in size. In the other row houses of the community such a room was utilized as a bedchamber also, since every other house was occupied by at least two or more Beghinas. This room had been the bedchamber of her mother. Claris had occupied it for a time during Eva's maternal grieving, after which Eva had been granted use of the house as her own by the Superior. Claris had taken residence with another supplicant who had been restored after violation of her vows of celibacy, and had since lived with others in need of mentoring. Ever did Claris seek restoration in others. The volumes arrayed on Eva's small shelf of poplar she had carved for Lydia not long before her passing, appeared as geometric shadows on the edge of candlelight.

There was *Against Heresies* by Irenaeus, one of the early church fathers and bishop of Lyon. Next to it a volume entitled *On the Origin and Timing of the Anticrist*. It was penned by a monk named Adso, who had written the treatise in the 900s in response to queries of the apocalypse that had issued from the French Queen. One in particular caught Eva's attention. Perhaps it would speak to her. Walking an oft trod path across the wooden floor, she grabbed her copy of St. Augustine's *Confessions* and began to flip carefully through the pages.

She'd had the book copied in the original Latin by the scribe in Avignon who had marked off places and drawn sketches for ornamentation. The Painter had then proceeded to fill the vellum pages of the book with color. In the three years she had possessed the volume, none of the paint had faded or smudged in the least. She had paid handsomely for it, but knew its worth far exceeded her investment. Manuscripts and books adorned by her Painter fetched a very high price in Provence and parts of the *Languedoc*.

It was a wonderfully written volume. Like David in the Psalms, Augustine had poured out his soul, his wrestling with temptation, sin, and God himself in living prose. Though he had mourned over his own transgressions, down to the theft of an apple, Augustine had cheered the spread of Christianity. Could he have imagined a day such as this, when Christian marched against Christian?

The world was changing once more. Yet an apple was like a pear. Would Augustine have mourned over the thieving of one of her pears? She felt it an odd, self-centered thought. Yet it demanded space in her mind nonetheless. Was the crop she raised and sold so worthy?

Thankfully, some things remained unaltered and festivals were a blessed reminder of such. The feast day of Saint Maria Magdalen was drawing to a close, and a joyous time it had been. The bishop had told great stories, and had been a source of delight.

But her sorrow did not seem to reflect the closing of the day. She returned to her scribing, and somehow, the more she wrote, the heavier her spirit grew, in spite of the simplicity of the words.

As the light of day faded, she lit more candles and arrayed them in half-circle round her writing desk. Looking at the clean burning beeswax candles, she was thankful to have means to afford those and not have need to purchase the less costly but smoky and oily burning candles of tallow.

She heard the bells of the high church, low and rumbling, peals strong as the muscled belly of a warhorse, tolling for compline. It was nine and yet edges of the day remained. Dropping to her knees on the pine floor, she crossed herself and thrice recited the *Paternoster*.

It was a phrase near the end that wedged itself in her mind during the final chanting. Though she had given that prayer of *Jhesu* hundreds, even thousands of recitations, when she said *libera nos a malo*, deliver us from evil, questions arose in her mind.

What does it mean to be delivered from evil? What does it look like? What is the experience of it?

She sensed it was the thing she would be pursuing in prayer on the morrow, for it was her time to go into hermitage.

All the Beguines were encouraged to take times to seek solitude and commune with *Deu*. Eva had chosen several years past to spend her time as a hermit on the eve immediately following the feast of the Magdalen.

Something about going from revelry to silence in so short a time span was a shock to the soul, like a rejuvenating splash of cold water, not always pleasant, but revitalizing nonetheless.

The hermitage was a cluster of small, austere wooden shacks on an isolated plot of ground in a depression surrounded by three small hills with no trees. The grassy mounds blocked out all sights and sounds of the world outside. Inside the tiny valley, there was no talking permitted, only meditative, prayerful silence.

Eva decided on a whim to go early and pass this night in hermitage as well.

Returning the letter to its wooden tube, Eva applied blotting paper to the newly scribed parchments. Setting aside her writing instruments, she flew down the stairs with the excitement of one on an unexpected and furtive mission. She blew air out of her nose in contentment and clenched her fists in joy. Possessing the freedom to determine one's own comings and goings was a gift with few rivals. Entering the pantry, she threw together a small basket of bread, soft cheese, pears, a water skin, candles, a sachet of fresh lavender, and a simple copy of the New Testament in Occitan.

She negotiated the common, her spirit heavy, glided toward the small hills as glowing purplish-orange twilight edged to darkness. The sorrow was consuming her still and she felt compelled to seek answers.

She would pass the night in prayer.

All three shacks appeared vacant. Following the delicious feeling of the dry, warm *Cers* wind blowing from the North, Eva chose the hermitage that was first reached by the peaceful breeze. It was as far north as ever she went. All her life had been to the south, for the north was cold. The north side of the structure, like so many buildings in Provence, bore no windows. Not because of the *Cers* wind but because of the violent, frigid *Mistral* that was visited upon them each winter. Eva also liked to think it was to block out the cold spirit of the North as well. Yet still the armies had come.

Chasing away the cobwebs, a few black-looking rats, and some luminescent beetles, Eva waved her candle around, checking carefully for scorpions. She had been stung on the ankle by one as a child, one of the small, foul things that crept in Provence. Her leg had bloated like an animal carcass in the sun, and she had been bed-ridden with a fever for days. Though she had been told that her illness was from the infection of the wound and not the poison of the scorpion, she had been loath to believe it.

Convinced at length that none of the black and yellow creatures had invaded the airy domicile, Eva consumed a couple bites of bread and cheese and plunged into prayer.

Almost instantly her sadness turned to foreboding. Again she knew not why. She stood motionless, circled the room, lay prone on the pallet, seeking any position, any cadence of action or inaction that could bring her closer to the presence of blessed *Jhesu*.

Her primary vision moved from her eyes to her mind, like a wash coming over sight, images in motion rising like otherworldly plants from fallow ground. Such things could not be cultivated or willed into being. One could only wait for them to ripen and harvest them at their maturity as with a scythe in a field of wheat or a basket under a pear tree. Silence and solitude merely provided clarity. This night she caught a glimpse of a stout-walled city on a hill. It was as if she were a hawk descending to the earth. She felt a deep sorrow open like a narrow gorge in her spirit and fill with water which was hot tears on her cheek. Her fists clenched and she gave vent to a weeping that rolled through her, first in small waves ever growing, flooding her, and carrying her off along a broad celestial waterway to a charred city by a river spanned by an arched bridge of stone, bringing a cramped ache to her belly at this revulsion of her Lord.

As she drew closer to the city, strange shapes leapt and protruded from buildings. It was a city ablaze. She heard the sharp crackling of flame and felt the pointed heat. The rumbling and crashing of timber and stone returning to earth sent tremors through the air. The smoke curling to the heavens like an offering, though not a fragrant one, and *Deu* was not pleased with the sacrifice for it lay smoldering on the bronze altar of another god. The words were spoken to her mind and heart. "The sacrifice of the wicked is an abomination to the LORD. The sacrifice of the wicked is an abomination to the LORD. Comprehend the meaning, for Abraham went and took the ram and offered him up for a burnt offering in the place of his son." The words reverberated in her mind. She knew they were from holy writ, but knew not where.

As the night passed, her spirit grew more fervent and the presence of *Jhesu* more encompassing. Her prayers turned to groans as she cried out for the burning citadel, seeking the meaning of the vision. Once more, the sight ascended in her mind and she could picture the city as the smoke continued to spiral from within its walls.

Shadows now swarmed and surrounded, and as one they swept into the city and toward a church that lay near its walls. The shadows were seeking to claim something, but she lacked clear sight to see what they sought. Entering the church through broken windows and a roof aflame, the wisps of darkness gave shouts in Latin proclaiming they had taken the ground and danced in jubilation. There was screeching that raised the goose-flesh on her skin and made her shudder violently, so disturbing was the sound. It was a terrible distortion of music, a massed hymn of the hellish host, as if an unholy choir sang a dirge of the demonic.

Was this the evil that required deliverance?

Night settled in and then light appeared. Eva was walking a dusty street in a crowded village. People were avoiding her, pulling back, moving in haste to the opposing side of the hardpan street. She looked down and she saw that her tunic was thread-bare and filthy. She was stumbling as she walked and could not concentrate on anything in her mind but for a moment until it vanished as if snatched away. There were words issuing from her lips she did not comprehend. She knew not even the language.

A soldier in armor stood guard nearby. The thought came quickly and violently. "Impale your belly upon his spear." She was unable to move.

The vision faded and the night air was still.

She walked outside the hermitage and looked to the heavens. It was the time of new moon. The sky was clear and stars shone brightly against their charcoal backdrop that was smudged with streaks of milky white. They always seemed closer in the dead of night, during the time of first waking, as if she could reach up and scoop them from the sky like specks of luminescent dust, but there was no waking for her for there was no first or second sleep that night.

She remained in the hermitage until the evening following, consuming bread and cheese amidst the material scent of lavender and spiritual odor of charred buildings, reading the epistles of St. Paul and praying.

But there were no more visions or weeping.

The sadness passed and resolve settled in its place, a determination to seek the meaning of the burning city and the shadowy spirits. Yet the last part of what she saw was more disturbing to her. Through whose eyes did she see?

Deliver us from evil.

The phrase continued to assert itself in her thoughts, reappearing with punishing repetition. What was God calling her to do?

CHAPTER 21

23 JULY 1209

The first beams of the rising sun hung bright colored threads of light upon the Narbonne Gate, draping it in a translucent mantle of orange and yellow. A garment of fire that gave illumination without desolation.

The sight of the eighty-foot round towers of sandstone that anchored the main portal into Carcassonne, clothed in the day's new radiance, was a glittering vision of untainted strength and glory, a celestial, heartening glimpse to Andreas, scarce removed from a precipitous plunge to hell.

Was it but yesterday morn he and Bertran were preparing defenses in Beziers and inhaling the aroma of feast food, of roast lamb and sweet meats?

Though the events of the day past echoed through his mind without ceasing, he scarcely had memory of the night's ride, only that he had seen things that were not there and had ridden with much fright through a tree that had planted itself before his very eyes, but lacked substance. Its branches had been filled with perched owls swooping at him and serpents, reddish even in moonlight, hanging from limbs, uncoiling, lunging to strike him. They were but projections of the ethereal, or of his own mind, of which he could not tell, yet still his shoulders and scalp felt ridden with bite marks unseen.

The dying words of Bertran. "Take heed the coils of the serpent."

Though no snake bites were visible, Andreas knew he looked terrible, bloodied, his tunic and *braguier* stiff with dried blood and sweat and the links of his hauberk filled with chunks of red clay, but he cared not.

During the moonlit ride, the pain had jumped between his torso, shin, fingers, neck, face, and scalp as his wounds had seemed to take turns dispensing torment.

He felt little sensation at all in his body now, except for the recurring chills, though his hands trembled from raw exhaustion. It was difficult even to keep tight grasp of the reins. A wave of nausea broke over him, the gorge rising high in his throat, burning, searing even his tongue, before slowly settling once more. Chilly sweat speckled his forehead.

Seeing the sandstone towers and walls of *la cite*, as the citadel of Carcassonne was known to those who made dwelling within, heartened Andreas and he cracked the reins of his wheezing, foaming mount and drove it faster up the hill.

As he approached the massive gate with its heavy, iron-clad wooden doors and two portcullises of iron—each flanked by murder holes, long narrow slits in the thick stonework—the sentry somehow made recognition and called to the guard to descend the drawbridge and raise both portcullises.

"Make way for the *châtelain!*"

Andreas did not have to check his speed as he rode through the Narbonne Gate and into *la cite* for the streets were quiet. The clicking and clacking of iron horseshoes on cobblestone streets echoed sharply through the city of honey-colored stone.

A few vendors and artisans fussed with their stalls of produce and cheese, jewelry and cloth, readied their wares for the day, but they ceased all activity when Andreas rode by and their hands loosed the objects they held and they stared at him slack-jawed. A bloody harbinger of battle in a pristine city of peace, however temporary that peace may be.

The *châtelain* knew it would be not hard for them to discern he was bringing news of war for he was well-recognized in Car-

cassonne and the people of *la cite* would have known Raimon
Roger had left him in charge of the defense of Beziers. They
would question why he had returned soon and bloodied.

Andreas hoped ardently a panic would not ensue and that
the defenses could be made ready before the fall of Beziers became common knowledge in *la cite*.

He must see his lord at once.

The *châtelain* prayed that Raimon Roger was indeed in Carcassonne and not off in the countryside exhorting his vassals to
arms. He need make sure that his lord send out riders for such
tasks. Raimon Roger could not simply deliver every message
from his own hand.

Going to Montpellier had been different, and the presence
of Raimon Roger necessary, though the result had been sour.
Yet Andreas was unsure that his lord understood the difference.
Few nobles were as personable or actually enjoyed meeting with
their subjects, knowing them. But such interactions must have
their limits.

Andreas rode into the *Plasa de Chateau*, the square fronting
the Trencavel castle, still at a full gallop. As he approached the
collapsible wooden bridge that spanned the grassy moat that
surrounded three sides of the *Chateau Comtal*, Andreas saw
that Robertz and Anfos were guarding the Oriental Gate, the
main entrance to the *Chateau*.

They were ever alert. Never once had he caught them asleep
at their post. Even at cockcrow they looked orderly, their mustard surcoats clean and armor and weapons burnished. They
were a welcome sight, a reminder to Andreas that order lingered
still in a few bright places of the world; all had not yet plunged
to chaos.

As their *châtelain* rode onto the oaken bridge, Robertz
and Anfos straightened to attention and quickly unlocked and
opened the gate and raised both portcullises. Andreas saw the
initial look of shock on their faces as they first gained recognition of him, but they recovered quickly and masked it well.

"Is the Viscount in residence?" called Andreas as he neared
the open gate.

"He is, my *châtelain*," replied Robertz, standing at attention
but eyeing Andreas, the befuddled look on his face had returned

and revealed his unspoken questions to be many. "Though he likely still slumbers in his bedchamber, my lord."

Andreas rode through the gate and looked back to the guards. "You must wake him at once, Robertz, he need meet me in council chambers immediately. Tell him I have returned from Beziers with the most urgent of news." His voice took a sharpened edge. "Now off with you, there is no time for delay."

Robertz efficiently closed and locked the gate, lowered the inner portcullis, and hastened into the *Chateau.*

Halting in the courtyard of the castle, Andreas called to the remaining guard. "Anfos, I need you to stable my *arabit.* Then return at once to your post." Anfos came running across the courtyard to Andreas and took the reins of the mount. "Tell no one I made this request, but help me dismount from this animal for I am exhausted. I battled through the day past and I rode through the night without halting."

Anfos braced Andreas as he swung his leg back over the pommel of the saddle and returned his feet to ground once more. The courtyard seemed to spin and Andreas's knees buckled and he winced from the pain in his shin. Anfos had to hold him under his arms to keep him upright.

"The *destrier* may remain here, at least momentarily" said Andreas, changing his mind. "Help me into council chambers, then return and stable the *arabit* and have the groom attend to him. It is a beautiful horse, no?" Andreas stared at naught and all. His voice grew quiet. "Our only spoils of war from Beziers I think."

Anfos looked at him, wordless. The guard draped Andreas's right arm over his shoulders and bore much of the *châtelain's* weight as they walked across the courtyard and up the stone steps to the hall where the assembly met. Andreas could tell that Anfos was having difficulty giving rein to his tongue. "You engaged with the enemy at Beziers, with the North. It must be so."

Andreas only nodded.

Anfos scratched his nose with his free hand. "I beg pardon, sir, but what became of your roan stallion and...?"

"My surcoat?" Andreas finished the sentence as Anfos nodded affirmatively.

Andreas stopped and looked the guard in the face. "Both

were consumed by the flames of the *Frances*." He spoke briskly, striving to hold back emotion from his voice, as if he could release the words in haste and then shutter the gate of his soul before a torrent burst forth. "Things went ill in Beziers. Truly, Anfos, you do not want to have knowledge of the rest. Though you will hear tell of it soon enough." He put his trembling hand to the face of Anfos and turned it roughly toward him. "I ask only this one thing you must do: Pray. Pray for Carcassonne, the Languedoc and for *Paratge* itself. I am unsure I possess any more prayers within."

Moments after Anfos had laid Andreas down on a soft couch of velvet and departed to stable the horse and regain his post, Raimon Roger entered the hall, still clad in his bedclothes, eyes reddened with the look of sleep, worry splayed like pale whitewash across his face.

"My friend, you have returned." It was a query as much as a statement. "Robertz said you had urgent need of me, but..." Raimon Roger finally gained a clear look at Andreas, and his voice grew soft. "But he did not speak the reason." He pulled a richly brocaded chair up to the couch and sat down. "By all that is holy...?" His voice did not trail off but disappeared in a sound not unlike a squeak, as if violently choked off.

Raimon Roger looked Andreas over, the distress growing on his face as he saw the blood covering Andreas's armor and tunic, each oozing wound, each lifeblood tinctured clunk of clay. "What of Bertran and Aimer and the remainder of the contingent I left at Beziers? What of the city itself?"

Andreas looked Raimon Roger in the eye and did not blink. How does one tell of things beyond comprehending? Lengthy speeches and gentle words would give neither solace nor clarity to his lord. Better to let it spill out like entrails. "They are all dead, my lord, every one."

Raimon Roger blinked. "All my cavaliers have been slain?"

"You do not understand, my lord." Andreas raised himself to a sitting position, his voice rising as well. "The *Frances* breached a gate and put the entire city to the sword, twenty-thousand slaughtered in one day, in mere hours, perhaps thirty, perhaps forty-thousand." He was shouting now. The anger and the intrusive thoughts had made vengeant return and the crown of his head was throbbing. He put his hands to his face and lowered his voice. His palms grew wet. "I alone have escaped to tell you."

Raimon Roger rose and looked round the hall at the banners of yellow, white, and black, the stained glass windows, the elaborately carved stonework and woodwork, the ceiling beams, the cut stone floor as if trying to draw strength, reassurance from something in the chamber, anything. His voice was soft. "Blessed *Jhesu* have mercy." When Raimon Roger looked again at Andreas, the Viscount's eyes were red and moist. *Los Frances* slew all in the city?"

Raimon Roger sat down and slumped back in his chair, the blood draining from his face like a pierced wine barrel, his widened eyes hollowed out, revealing a look of wild bewilderment Andreas had never seen visited upon the countenance of his lord before.

Andreas softened the tone of his voice. "To a person, my lord, my friend. *Los Frances* slew man, woman, and child, Catholic and heretic, clergy and lay. They drew no distinction between persons. None at all."

Andreas's voice and the pain in his head rose sharply as one. "Curse them and their Crusade! I witnessed a woman round with child have her belly sliced open and her and her little daughter slit at the throat. Bertran sought valiantly but in vain to halt that slaying. There were too many *Frances*, my lord Trencavel, there were too many." The tiredness throbbed in his body, pounded as if great rocks vibrated within him. He trembled, and the entire great hall seemed to quiver. "Too many."

Raimon Roger's reddened eyes and open mouth issued the query that did not find release from his lips: *How?*

The exhaustion that consumed Andreas felt painful. "The *Bitterois*, my lord. It was the foolishness of a few of the *Bitterois* that allowed first the *rotiers* through the West Gate. It was the *rotiers* that commenced the slaughter, but the Northern cavaliers did not halt it when given the chance. No, indeed, they joined it in the end, bathed their swords in blood and fat. It was *rotiers* and cavaliers both that slay the innocent in the Church of Saint Maria Magdalen."

"They massacred those who had taken sanctuary." Raimon Roger did not ask this time, but spoke, eyes fixed straight ahead, as if he was absorbing slowly the poison of what had been perpetrated in his own viscountcy, on his own lands, to his own people. *"Kyrie Eleison."*

Andreas lay back down on the couch as he saw the colors of the room bleed together and swirl. The dancing shards of light of the previous day returned. He could hear his own voice as he spoke, but it seemed hollow, distant, thin. "My lord, I was seen on the streets as I rode from the Narbonne Gate to the Oriental Gate. No doubt rumors and stories make circulation this moment throughout *la cite.* What will you tell the people?"

Before the *châtelain* slipped from consciousness, his last memory was of Raimon Roger straightening himself, setting his jaw, proclaiming, "Whether or not you were recognized, the people must know the truth unvarnished. They will be allowed at least a full day to mourn the *Bitterois* before *los Frances* are upon us. The bells of *San Nazare* will ring out a time for grieving."

CHAPTER 22

23 JULY 1209

The strong ringing of the high church bells for vespers prodded Eva out the door of the hermitage. One hand bore her supplies of solitude and the other shielded her eyes from the sun as it descended in the West. She recited the *Paternoster* as she ascended to the green grassy lip of the small valley of silence. The superior would have frowned upon Eva's insolence, not being on her knees. But St. Paul had instructed the recipients of one his letters to pray without ceasing so that had to mean when they walked and did all manner of things, not only when genuflecting.

After her time in hermitage, her heart was full to overflowing, like a deep well unable to hold any more rainwater. She need continue to exercise body and soul in prayer. "Blessed *Jhesu* it is scribed in holy writ that the peace that passes understanding shall guard our hearts and minds in *Crist Jhesu*. There is a man I have seen in my visions. I pray *Deu* reveal to your servant why I see him." She fixed her gaze upon the tower of the high church, the bells of which continued to ring out. The masculine sound of the ringing helped her focus upon this knight. "Armor guards his body, but I know not if he possesses a hauberk for his soul. He wields weapons in the natural with skill and abandon, but does he have mastery of the weaponry of the spirit? I sense a strong protection that was once upon him has vanished." She made entrance to the common. "Guard his heart and mind. Teach him to wield the sword of the spirit. He is in dan—" She had surprise that her voice halted at this moment. She shut her eyes tightly and breathed deeply. "He is in danger. I implore you to break his fall. In the strong name of blessed *Jhesu*, so be it."

Eva reached her row house, opened the door, dropped all she carried on the pine floor, and departed. She walked back across the common and made entrance to the high church for vespers. The Bishop of Siena presided over the service and performed the *sacrifici*, the offering of the elements to *Deu*, and they partook of the Eucharist. The *sacrifici* spoke eloquently of the holy offering of *Jhesu* the man upon the cross. The bishop placed the thin unleavened wafer on her tongue and she swallowed a generous portion of wine from the common silver goblet. As the elements reached her belly, the words from the night past made another appearing in her mind. "The sacrifice of the wicked is an abomination to the LORD." Yet she was not partaking of the sacrifice of the wicked but of the death of holy *Jhesu*.

The Beguines celebrated, delighted in the humanity of *Jhesu*. He was not spirit alone as the *Bons Hommes* believed, but a man of flesh and bone who felt pain and sorrow and joy as they did, who needed food and water, and who bled when pierced. A man who sweat drops of blood in his suffering and said, "Let this cup pass from me, but not my will but yours be done." Not a distant deity but a holy person of flesh and bone drawn near to them. It was why they partook of the Eucharist at a frequency that was unseemly to others.

In her vision of the night past, the abhorrent sacrifice had been laid upon the altar of another god. Like a hazy landscape brought into focus, her sight became clear at that moment: The sacrifice of the wicked was human lives, human souls offered up to another god. A sacrifice God abhorred. The sole human sacrifice He willed that of blessed *Jhesu* also raised from the dead. There was no need of another. "Abraham went and took the ram and offered him up for a burnt offering in the place of his son." All this ran through her mind before the taste of the rich red wine faded from her tongue and she regained her seat.

Pietro, as he officiated the Eucharist, noticed that Eva seemed consumed, troubled. He raised the query with the look of his eyes.

Claris approached Eva in the common after mass, a smile lighting her face. "I saw you return from hermitage. Your face was aglow. Your look radiant." Claris narrowed her eyes to a squint and peered probingly at Eva, studied her face. "Yes, a trace of it lingers still. The glory has not yet faded completely. You were in the manifested presence of blessed *Jhesu*. I bid you, tell me of it." Claris paused for a moment, allowing her excitement to subside somewhat. "That is, if you wish for me to hear."

Eva clasped her hands behind her back and looked toward the ground as she strolled across the common. Hooking her arm into Claris's, Eva led her friend across the courtyard, past the pear tree. "Let us retire to where Pietro has residence and I shall tell all to you both. What say you?"

"I think more shall be revealed than we expect."

Eva looked toward her mentor and scrunched her nose. "Perhaps you are right, for you seem to have a sense about these things."

Pietro opened his door before ever they arrived and strode out toward them. "When are the gates shuttered in Orange?"

Eva stopped and saw he intended to take his leave from the community. "They are shuttered at twilight. They remain so until cockcrow."

Claris had a look of intrigue. "What have you in mind, your grace?"

"We need learn more of Minerva and the Roman Trinity."

"We need learn more this night?"

"At first I thought so, yes." A long pause. Pietro had packed his canvas bag. Clearly he had done so before vespers. "Now I think not. We need wait, but soon we shall take our leave. I shall make journey to Orange and then to Avignon and I wish for you both to join me." He set down his bag inside the door. "Eva, I sense you need bring your bow and quarrels as well. Will your

Painter have us as boarders in Orange?"

Claris responded with eagerness and certainty. "He will give us lodging."

Eva looked upon Claris and furrowed her brow. She, who knew her Painter better than Claris, was not so certain, yet she kept her own council.

Pietro let them in and of a sudden seemed relieved they had come, as if their appearing enabled him to loose a giant weight. It was not the reaction or countenance Eva had expected. The color in the face of the bishop seemed to drain away before her eyes. He waved his arm at the couch in the front room for them to sit.

"Perhaps you ought to take a chair as well, my lord," replied Eva.

The bishop seemed only too happy to do so and settled into a stout wooden chair. She noticed that he was shivering and his forehead was damp. "Are you well, my lord? You seem ill."

"I feel cold. Help me to my bed for I fear I may faint."

Each taking an arm, Eva and Claris helped the bishop up the wooden stairs to the bedchamber. The layout of the row house was identical to hers and it was easy to negotiate the way. They gently laid him on the bed and he bid them remain. "I consider you as my family now," the bishop said as he looked upon Eva. "We have become as one in this quest." He looked toward the uncovered window. The awareness pierced her heart that he had shouldered this burden, carried the quest, as if he were her very father. "I do not believe you are yet in peril, but the current state of things may yet be altered. I was careful to be sure I was not followed here. I have ever been cautious, yet they were able to know that it was the scribe who had taken their document and made it a palimpsest. If they can know that, they can track it to you. They will track it to you. I would be surprised if someone in Siena does not know that you and your *maire* made journey here to Provence."

Eva shifted her position on the chair. "I would not know of that, and I do not know who would have knowledge. Perhaps there is nothing to lead them here."

"Perhaps. I pray you are correct." The bishop reached up and pulled her face toward him. "Hear me now, Eva. A time of trial approaches. You must be bold that day, be bold in that season, for that is the only way. If you are faint of heart, if you hesitate in the moment when you must act, they will crush you, they will crush us all." The bishop grimaced. "Can you bring me water and perhaps a little wine to settle my stomach? It roils inside of me like a wave of the sea."

Eva fetched a water cup and a flagon of mixed wine. After downing the water and a few sips of Provençal wine, his color seemed to strengthen and he sat up. "I just had a thought, and I am not sure why it did not occur to me before. The scribe, as I told you, had murder done to him in Siena as a sacrifice to Minerva, on a site that was once consecrated to her. Do you know anything of this supposed goddess?"

Eva merely shook her head. Never had she possessed a reason to learn of the pantheon of pagan gods, whether Roman or Greek.

"You are certain there is no mention of Minerva in the palimpsest?"

"No, unless it is very cryptic, and I am unskilled at deciphering."

"Ah, cryptic, yes. If there is a message deeply hidden, I lack the wits to uncover it. Apparently, I am unskilled at this also." He smiled. "Perhaps the mundane words in the palimpsest mean nothing for they only conceal the true message. I wager that is it, perhaps…"

"What know you of cryptic messages, your grace?" Claris had spoken.

"Rumors only. Stories that certain orders of knights in Outremer use all manner of codes and special inks to conceal the true messages of their documents. I put little stock in such stories before the scribe presented himself in my chambers five years past. As I said, he was in the service of the Knights Hospitaller in Outremer. Though, in truth, I know not if he remained still in the order when he came to call in Siena. Besides, it does not appear he wrote the words of the palimpsest."

Eva noticed the face of Pietro had whitened as he spoke and

drops of sweat flowed toward his brow. She leaned forward. "Your grace, do you need the services of a physician? We shall send for one if need be."

"I think not. Some more wine perhaps?" Eva refilled the small cup. The bishop took a sip and raised himself up to a sitting position. "I started to swoon after homily and felt weak. The burden of much travel and greater worry for you," said Pietro, looking at Eva with an expression of concern, "has left me weary indeed. I think a few days of rest will suit me, and then I must return to Arles, ere I will be missed."

"I think," said Claris, turning her glance toward Eva, "that now would be opportune to speak of your time in hermitage."

"Yes," replied the bishop, a look of anticipation rolling across his face. "I should like to hear of it."

"It will be raw and unrehearsed, but I shall tell you." Eva described the sadness that had enveloped her and the vision and how she wept over the sacrifice and demonic infiltration of a city, of a church. Pietro sat at rapt attention while Claris seemed to glow with approval, as if Eva was her progeny.

"Do you believe this vision to be rooted in time and place or simply in the realm of the spirit?" The bishop asked the question.

Eva scrunched her nose. "I am unsure. Perhaps both in some way. It seemed too stark not to have its roots in time and place as you say, though I know not."

"Was this vision the reason you were troubled after taking the Eucharist? I could see it on your face."

"No, but perhaps yes in another way. You spoke of the scribe being a sacrifice to Minerva on the feast day of the Magdalen. I think my vision was another such sacrifice on another such feast day, but consuming many more souls. I was troubled during Eucharist because I realized the sacrifice of the wicked at its base is human sacrifice to another god. I had a thought that it was the goddess Minerva.

Pietro sat up, his color strong once more. "There is another I know of who would very much like to hear of it as well, a man who has such visions himself. He travels even now to Provence from Toulouse, where he is a secular priest. There is a meet arranged with him in Avignon ten days hence for the evening meal. Will you come?"

Eva did not leave the matter to doubt. "I should be delighted to accompany you and to have a meet with this man. I need also to visit *la cathedrale Notre Dame de Doms* in Avignon."

"Perhaps Raphael will understand the full import of what you have seen."

Claris was looking at timber ceiling beams then at whitewashed walls and the unfettered window. "Perhaps. And yet with such things, often the full meaning is not evident until years later, if ever in our lifetimes."

CHAPTER 23

25 JULY 1209

The torso and severed head of the dismembered knight lay before heaven's gate. A burnished, fiery guard denied them entry. A host of angels made egress through the bronzed gate, descended through the skies, roamed to and fro across the earth, searched its uttermost lands for the limbs. Saints of old lamented how one who had received a Crusader's absolution from the pope should be barred from heaven, even lacking appendages. The knight possessed still his heart, they cried, though it was pierced through. His head had been unearthed. Perhaps in time he could cross heaven's threshold. But not before at least two of his limbs had been discovered.

Andreas arose and made pledge to join the search, said he had knowledge of the whereabouts. He rode to the Potter's Mound but the limbs had vanished. There was a rumbling and the clay ground of the hillside fissured in a great gash. He fell into darkness, plummeted through heated air, singed by the lick of flame. He landed in a church, struck hard against the stone floor. Rainaud, the Bishop of Beziers was saying homily, speaking of the resurrection of the dead, and how those who would rise in wholeness must be buried in wholeness. It was the church of the Magdalen.

Andreas stood and rushed down the center of the nave. "What of those who dismember, what penance, what absolution is there?"

The face of the bishop contorted to a scowl, and a raised finger pointed at Andreas. "There is none for you, apostate, for such is a mortal sin beyond redemption!" The floor split open beneath his feet and the air was cool, growing colder as he plunged in free fall, landing upon a smooth stone surface in a chamber lit only by candlelight.

Andreas awoke and he was lying on his back in his own soft bed in his own chamber. It was night, likely first waking. A few votive candles had been left to burn on wrought iron stands and gave unflinching orange radiance. Never had he dreamt with such vividness, if indeed it was a dream.

He stretched arms and legs and the pain and stiffness echoed from shin to scalp. Yet the fatigue of battle at least had drained away like dishwater into the sewer. His wounds had all been treated, wrapped in soft cotton cloths, his fetid tunic and breeches removed and replaced with clean bedclothes. Someone had been giving kind attention to him.

Yet it seemed he had been asleep for some time, days perhaps. How many sunsets had passed? His last memory was of losing consciousness in the Trencavel hall while Raimon Roger spoke of public mourning and of ringing the cathedral bells.

But no chimes sounded in the darkness at this hour.

The chamber itself was also quiet. The stillness bordered on the unnatural, as if the creaking and groaning of the ancient chateau was being somehow suppressed, as if the silence was palpable, as if it possessed vigor and substance.

Though still lying on his back, he was now alert, his senses finely attuned to the effort of comprehending the muffled nothingness. His soul shrank and wrinkled like picked grapes left in the midday sun.

He heard sounds, sharp and loud, cracks like the splintering of dry wood that issued from one dark corner of the room, then another, then from the roof beams overhead. He pulled a blanket over his head. He was six once more. There was a cold spiky prickling on the nape of his neck that moved to the top of his head and intermingled with the pain on his skull. It was as if thousands of fine sharp metal points were aimed at the crown of his head and each poked him rapidly in turn at a slightly different spot of his scalp. He shivered though it was warm in the room and he lay under several blankets.

There was something at hand in his bedchamber, though it had not physical form. He grew angry at himself and roared as he ripped the blanket off his head and sat upright on his sleeping pallet, vigilant, eyes darting about the chamber. The silence deepened and all he could hear was the ever-increasing pounding of his heart. The very air throbbed and pulsed, like the ground under a charge of mounted cavaliers. The imminence of the presence, with no veil, no rampart to shield him, drained his mouth of water. He felt as if this manifesting power could exercise but a little of its force and his very soul would shatter into a thousand pieces like brittle glass hurled upon stone.

He looked to the ceiling and saw nothing, less than nothing, for there was a void where even the darkness was absorbed and seemed bright by comparison, and the void seemed to be pulling in whatever light yet lingered in the room. There was a wind and one of the candles was extinguished, then another, then still another, until all radiance in the room was quenched, and all was cloaked in black.

But the darkness was not still. It was shifting and shaping itself into shadows that swirled rhythmically round the room in an intoxicating motion. Andreas looked around, unsure what action to take, what thoughts to think. He felt held in place, as if by an iron vice clamped down evenly over his entire bruised body. The amorphous shapes swirled round, brushed against him, and raised the gooseflesh on his skin. One of the shadows took the form of an owl, another of a female warrior clad in armor, another of a harp, and another of a sage. A train of numbers appeared in his mind that seemed to flow endlessly into the void of time past.

Looking up to the ceiling where the void had been moments before, he saw a pale blue light that radiated out from a center point, like a dim, ethereal torch, forming a perfect circle, casting a glow upon the stout ceiling timbers, causing them to appear lucent, like shafts of ghoulish light.

He heard the low voice of a woman in his ear, in his mind, as yet another of the shadows wrapped itself around him and all breath fled. "I am Minerva." The voice strong and seductive. "I am she who brings wisdom and music. I am she who wages war and numbers many things, including your very days. You have dismembered, Andreas, yet fear not, for there is penance. You have proven yourself valiant in battle. You have fought for many, and now I bid you fight for me. Prove yourself mighty warrior; ascend on high, blot out your sins. I will return for your answer. You will see me once more on the day that marks four and twenty years since your birth. Prepare yourself for my second coming."

"How do I prepare? What must I do?" He was surprised by the readiness of his response and his own ability to speak.

"I will send emissaries to aid you. Listen to them and be obedient. For if you obey, you will find life, and if not, only death awaits. No other choice lies before you. Journey to my house on the high place. Seek after the pure light, the spirit, for all that is of flesh and matter is meaningless, an evil in the sight of the Good."

The binding embrace of the shadow around him loosened and the pale light faded to nothing. The motion of the darkness ceased and the candles were burning once more.

Had he imagined the whole of it? He could almost bring himself to believe the entire ethereal experience had been the continuation of a dream. But if so, then much of his life had been as a wretched visitation in the night.

Thoughts of his natal day cascaded through his mind; Midsummer's Day.

Though it was nearly a year hence, he felt a foreboding simply thinking on that day. Always had he united it with warmth and lengthened bright light, as it was the day most abounding in radiance.

Yet a strangely light day it was to reckon with the darkness of dismemberment. Dualism. Indeed it was dualism of an odd sort. Odd like the equally weighted powers of good and evil propagated by the *Bons Hommes*.

CHAPTER 24

25 JULY 1209

After a long and sparse day of vending at Saturday market, Eva unloaded her cart and retired straightaway to her bedchamber. All this day she had known distraction thinking on her father, feeling her vague discomfort grow and knot itself deep and hard, bleed pain into her belly.

The presence of the bishop and her own visions notwithstanding, still she knew little of the mysteries that made intrusion upon her mind and soul. Always had she been aware somehow of such vagaries, but never even had knowledge of what queries to make, much less who to seek out for answers. The palimpsest had spoken to her only through a veil, perhaps the letter itself would speak clearly.

Removing the parchment cylinder from the trunk of cypress, she unrolled it and read aloud the letter penned by the bishop. Those words, at least, lacked obscurity.

Greetings Lydia and Eva.

In the Name of Blessed Iesu.

It is from a heart weary with sorrow that I write these words to you, feeble though I know they will be for the purpose to which they are meant.

That the fortress of Acre in Outremer has been reclaimed I fear will be of small consolation to you for the dear soul that has been lost.

Lydia, it was your husband that led the charge that very nearly breached the city and convinced the Muhammadan garrison to lay down their weaponry and throw open the gates.

Unhappily, Anselme was not among those who entered in triumph, for he was struck down by a hail of stones from a mangonel and his blood loss was too great to overcome. His heart was pierced and the pulsating flow gave reminder of the broken heart of our savior. By the grace of Deum was I able to administer the sacraments and hear the final confession of Anselme. His last words were of you and of Eva. Of his undying love for you Lydia and of his deep sorrow at not being able to see his little girl once more. He gave ardent thanks one last time that Eva possesses such a mother as you.

When I return home, I shall weep with you, but until then know that I have prayed for you and little Eva before even this letter arrives. A portion of the spoils of the conquered city will arrive also with this letter. Make wise use of them and have caution in selling them.

Anselme was an inspiration and friend to many. He gave reminder to us all of the true cause of our sojourn in Outremer. Anselme wasted no chance to speak with Saracen prisoners about the import of Christianity and of the resurrection of blessed Iesu. Some bowed the knee to the Savior and received the baptism before the claiming of the executor's sword.

Anselme was a fierce warrior also, and, because of him, the Latin Kingdom is being strengthened in Palestine. The Coeur de Leon, King Richard of England, marches on Haifa this very day. If he prevails, the retaking of Jerusalem will be within reach.

I charge you Eva, as you grow older, to remember always that your father was a strong, kind man who would not hesitate to lay down his life for another. Indeed, his perishing has saved many lives. May all of us have willingness to make this selfsame sacrifice, for greater love has no man.

In Christ and for His Glory,

Pietro

The bishop had returned as promised, but he had not wept with her. Time changes some things. A drop of water was loosed from gathered tears blurring her eyesight, falling next to a familiar watermark created some seventeen summers past. Her skin grew warm and she started to tremble. She cast aside the letter.

"Remember you as a kind man?" She laced her fingers together and held them against the back of her head as she looked to the ceiling beams. "A kind man. I possess no memory of you at all. *Paire?* Anselme? What am I to call you? All you did was battle in the desert and die and bequeath me Dead Things." She was speaking in quivering voice. "You have brought neither living comfort nor embrace."

She jumped to her feet, stomped across the floor, and threw open the trunk. She randomly thrust her hands into the Beautiful Things, grabbed hard what was at her fingertips, and yanked the object from the trunk as some other gold and silver baubles clattered and clinked at her feet. Hoisting aloft a square golden platter, ringed with bloodstones and set with four emeralds, two rubies, and a sapphire, her voice rose to match the release of anger from her soul.

"What am I to do with this cold, Beautiful Thing? I know the look of this object better than ever I knew the look of you, my *paire*. This ornamented thing can never embrace nor give warmth. Do you hear my words? Gold and jewels are cold things!" She shook the platter hard as tears flowed.

There was a muted rattling, as if something slid back and forth. Was it hollow? She drew it close to her ear and shook it once more. Something was moving inside the rounded handles of mother of pearl.

She sniffled and brushed away her tears with her sleeve hem.

Setting the platter gently on her mattress, she sat next to it and studied the handles. The *maire de perla*, green, blue, and purple, was adorned on each end by bright golden knobs in the shape of *seme fleurs de lis*.

She pulled on one then twisted it clockwise. Nothing. Then she turned it counterclockwise and there was a squeak, and movement. More firm rotations and more squeaks and it twisted loose. A half-dozen objects the size of over-ripe peas, yet metallic blue in color, rolled out of the handle and onto the bed, gathering in the small depression next to her hip.

In all these years, never had she examined closely any of the glittering items. Gingerly setting the platter down behind her, she scooped up the small bluish spheres in one hand, and with the other lifted a single one high. Its color flashed between blue and green. It was a dazzling effect. Never had she seen a stone like it. It was similar in sheen to the *maire de perla* that had encased it, but the color was deeper, richer, with the look of an inviolable mystery. As if it was from a place much farther away than even the Holy Land. The platter itself had bloodstones in abundance. She had heard those came from a place far to the east called India. Perhaps the bluish green stones hailed from that land as well.

Why had they been concealed in the handle? What of the other handle?

She took up the platter once more, and turning again counterclockwise a golden *seme fleur de lis* on the opposite cylinder of *maire de perla*, that adornment squeaked and came loose as well and another six Blue Peas, as she had started to think of the curious little stones, rolled into her cupped hand. She noticed one bore an etching. It was a letter, M. She rolled the others around and discovered each had but one letter inscribed in blue luminescence. The letters were A, E, L, R, L, M, I, A, M, E, P, R.

There were twelve. What of the number twelve? What of the twelve letters? She looked to the platter itself and noticed that it seemed to be perfectly square and that etched into the bright gold surface was a circle. The circle within?

Was her father speaking to her now? Not from the grave but across the years? Had he been seeking to tell her and her mother something? Were the Beautiful Things truly Dead Things?

Her eyes grew moist once more. "Forgive me, my *paire*, for I have lacked hearing. Speak now, I beg you Anselme, for your daughter now listens. What other things have you spoken to me from Outremer that I have not heard?" She went to her knees and looked heavenward. "Blessed *Jhesu*, I ask for ears of discernment to hear the living echoes of the past."

CHAPTER 25

25 JULY 1209

Andreas had to shove through the throng to advance even a step. "Never have I seen *la cite* so overrun."

The one next to Andreas, Raimon Roger, the Viscount of Carcassonne, Albi, and Beziers, issued no utterance, registered no sign he had heard. His look was sober and piercing, darkened eyes fixed straight ahead at the Narbonne Gate, as if he would stare down the approaching French, loose a torrent of flame from his eye pits, and scorch them to earth through sheer force of will. Raimon Roger, overwhelmed two days past, was now afire, though the blaze burned darkly and silently.

The *châtelain* was left to carry on the banter as they negotiated their way through Carcassonne. He had no desire for darkness or silence. "Not even Beziers was cramped in this way before siege. For battle preparation, this is madness."

Andreas halted his steps as a family with two cows, a bull, and a pig crossed the narrow street. The animals left a squalid trail on the cobblestone road. Knowing already the answer, Andreas still issued the query. "Is there nowhere else for these villagers to stable their livestock?"

Raimon Roger's eyes burned still upon the main gate, as if they would combust and ignite an inferno.

The gates of Carcassonne, a city that teemed with people in times of peace, had opened many a time over the two days past to allow the influx of thousands of villagers, merchants, overlords, and livestock. The collective stench the beasts left in their wake was already a trial to behold.

Yet it was trivial in comparison to the smell of sun-roasting, bloating human flesh.

Beziers.

He could not dwell on it for more than a few seconds, flashes invading consciousness. A family slain and hewn in their home, sanctuary seekers slaughtered in the Church of the Magdalen. Such things would flood his soul like the onrushing tide at Mont San Michel, abate just as quickly. He felt nothing and could not prod himself even to anger.

Leave the dead. Think on Carcassonne and battles to come.

This most urbane of cities had become as a fortified barn. Everywhere, inside and outside of buildings, were cattle and sheep, goats and pigs, some in makeshift pens, others wandering free.

A cow was helping itself to produce at a nearby stand, calmly feasting on cabbage and onions, while the proprietor waved his arms furiously and roared at the tan and white bovine. Andreas, feeling pity for the merchant, unsheathed his sword and struck the cow on the rump with the flat of his blade. The animal bellowed and sauntered up the street. So he could feel pity for a merchant over lost cabbage but not a woman with child slain while escaping the false sanctuary of the Magdalen?

"The fate of this city will not be as that of Beziers." Vision fixed still on the Narbonne Gate, Raimon Roger spoke at last, his words borne out in a tone of grim resolve, as one who attempts to transform belief to veracity through willforce alone. "Besides, if the *Frances* obtained hold of these animals, it would only prolong their ability to sustain a siege. No, these animals must remain within the walls of *la cite*.

"You missed much while you were asleep these two days past my *châtelain*." Raimon Roger's eyes brightened and he gave Andreas a hard jab in his chain mail covered arm that reignited the pain in his torso and forced water from his eyes. "I ordered every animal within two days march outside the city walls slaughtered, crops put to the torch, and every village emptied of people and provisions. The countryside will be barren, for the French will surely receive no welcome in my lands. I will leave them only with scorched earth and the hot sun of the South, to which they are most surely unaccustomed. Only pray that our own water supply holds."

"The cisterns will sustain, they must sustain us." The *châtelain* turned his head toward Raimon Roger. "And what of the position of the Northern army? Do they advance?"

Raimon Roger shook his head. "They remain. My scouts say *los Frances* still linger outside Beziers. Your ride through the night was not in vain. The morn you arrived I was to send letters to my vassals telling them to gather at a place to the west of Beziers. The letters were sealed, ready to be given to riders. After you told me of the *gran mazel*, I burnt those letters, tossed the lot of them into the fire at once. I issued new ones that selfsame morn summoning my barons here with all possible speed. They come even now. We shall mourn together, grow angry anew together, and prepare for battle. My scouts also report that the pickets and advance guards of the enemy move towards Narbonne."

Andreas held little respect for the people of Narbonne, the seat of the archbishop in the Languedoc, the ancient Roman capital; resided by cowards who had expelled the heretics from their midst. "The *Narbonnais* will not fight. They will wet their fine tunics at the sight of the army and capitulate, especially after the *gran mazel*. They will but swell further the size of the beast that will appear at our doorstep."

Raimon Roger nodded in affirmation. "Once Narbonne surrenders, Amaury will lead his rabble to Carcassonne." He looked Andreas in the eye and clenched his jaw. "We must break them here."

"Stand strong, my lord," called a merchant clothed in a fine tunic of blue, from under the lintel of a textile shop. "Do not accede to these beasts from the North. *Paratge!*"

The cry was absorbed and renewed by all within earshot. "*Paratge!*"

Raimon Roger unsheathed his sword and lifted it with out-stretched arm. "*Paratge! Paratge* will be held high!" he pro-claimed to the lusty cheers of the crowd.

Andreas, in spite of the mourning still being practiced openly by some and a palpable sense of angst in the ethereal undercurrents, thought the mood of the city strong, spirited, resolved, primed for battle. People were talking, laughing, and going about their business in spite of the lack of space in *la cite*. Such a spirit would prove useful if the hour grew dire.

He had to admit to himself, Raimon Roger had been pre-scient in his desire to allow the people to first grieve publicly *le gran mazel*.

Andreas had remembrance of another who had cause to mourn. "My lord, what of the troubled boy, Miquel, the son of the villager? Has he yet uttered a word?"

Raimon Roger looked upon the cobbles then upon the face of his *châtelain* as he shoved sword into hilt. "No Andreas, but the villager has proven false."

The *châtelain* thought of their encounter at the Inn of Guil-habert. "Did the fool conceal yet another thing?" The portcul-lises raised and the Narbonne Gate swung open as they took their egress from *la cite*.

Raimon Roger looked off toward the north. "It is better if you see for yourself. We will walk the battlements and then I will take you to where he has residence with the boy in *San Vicens*."

Andreas shuddered, though he was glad to be in the day-light, far from dark dreams.

He had dwelt little on Beziers and its aftermath this day, nor on his two days of sleep or of his rousing amidst the moving blackness at first waking, and much preferred it that way.

At least the unwelcome thoughts of beasts and torture had ceased.

His torso and shin also, though still very sore, did not hinder his movements, and his skull no longer throbbed. The stiffness of joint ebbed the more they walked. Yet still his shoulders felt punctured by bite wounds. Even the looking glass had not re-vealed them. Why had he hewn the body of the knight in the wood? He pushed the query from his mind.

Time to return to his duties and survey the battleground.

Their purpose was to walk the walls and check the fortifications. They turned first to the north and the *Tor Treseau*, and
next to the towers that dated from Roman times, including the
Tor Samson and the *Tor de la Carpentier*, both with round faces
of sandstone block interspersed with leveling rows of red brick.

These *tors*, roofed with terra cotta tiles of many hues that
contrasted with the honey-colored stone, anchored a crenellated
curtain wall that rose to nearly thirty feet in height. It was this
north side where the ground approaching the walls was most
level and thus most vulnerable to attack.

"If the fight comes to *la cite* itself, then we will have need of
the strongest garrison in these towers and along these walls."
Turning to Andreas, Raimon Roger said, "I would have you occupy the *Tor Samson*—if it comes to that—as its view is most
commanding of North, East, and West. You can anchor the
defenses from there." Raimon Roger stopped and was silent
for a moment. "You have belief twenty-thousand perished at
Beziers?" Andreas simply nodded and looked to the mountains.
Retreating to the High Languedoc held appeal at the moment.

"Carcassonne now holds at least twice that number." Raimon
Roger took him by the shoulders and turned him so they stood
face to face. "Andreas, hear me now. The city must not fall. I
shall do whatever is necessary; we must do whatever is necessary to ensure such a thing never happens. I will not allow another *gran mazel* on my lands. I will not." Raimon Roger turned
his look up the hill toward the graceful spires of *San Nazare*,
poking the cloudless, brilliant blue sky above the walls and red
tile roofs of *la cite*.

Andreas looked once more to the snow-clad peaks of the
Pyrenees. "We must simply keep shuttered the gates my lord."

Raimon Roger said nothing, but started walking, directing
his footfalls toward *San Vicens*, the low-walled suburb nearest
the River Aude.

Andreas called after him. "Where are the quarters of the villager and his boy, my lord?"

Raimon Roger motioned him forward without looking back.
"Come with me."

They joined the throng massed at the main gate of *San Vicens*. The ones making entrance to the vulnerable suburb seemed harried, tired, hollowed out with fear, and none took visible notice that the lord of the realm stood amongst them. Raimon Roger bore not a look of scorn but of pity, for whether Christian, Jew, or Saracen, they were his people.

The guards at the gate knew full well their Viscount and his *châtelain* approached and stood at attention. Upon entrance to the suburb, Andreas saw that the streets of *San Vicens* seemed cram-full.

"This way." Raimon Roger turned sharply left and led Andreas to a small, single-story, timber house near the north wall of *San Vicens*. Others were gathered there already and violent coughing issued from the bedchamber. Two priests and a physician attended to the stricken villager.

Andreas spied the thing out of the corner of his eye, cast upon a small wooden table. The table was near a sleeping pallet whereupon the villager lay pale and sweaty and out of his lips only groans issued forth. As the *châtelain* turned his head to look square upon the amulet, before he drew close enough to distinguish sapphire from ruby and emerald, he knew it identical to the one that lay under his own tunic, the very one that now cast strange warmth upon the skin of his chest. As if come to life in the presence of a twin talisman.

He blinked and the walls of the room seemed to bend and the very floorboards warp, and he felt changed himself, as if he were very large and thick and all was distorted in realms both seen and unseen. He heard the buzzing sound once more and rivulets of a viscous amber liquid flowed from ceiling to floor. Tricklings of honey faded as walls and floor straightened in an instant and all was restored.

The sole thing that had not distorted was the amulet itself. It was so near to what he already possessed, he was unsure whether he could distinguish between them. The one before him did not have the look of malevolence.

It was a square enclosing also a circle which in turn surrounded a triangle. Gold expertly crafted so each shape touched the others in fine points, marked by seven inlaid precious stones; four emeralds cut with facets that formed a shape of eight sides where square and circle joined, two rubies that possessed six sides where the two lower points of the triangle met the circle, and one sapphire, also cut with six sides where the apex of the triangle melded into circle and square.

The thin chain, also of gold, was looped through the circle.

Raimon Roger, eyes fixed upon the same, nudged Andreas and spoke in a low voice, though not a whisper. "An object of geomancy."

The *châtelain* had heard of the art of divining the future through the arrangement of geometric shapes. To him it seemed more pragmatic than tossing fish heads or pig entrails, and far less messy.

The priests also were looking upon the object. One spoke to the bedridden man. "I ask you once more, from where did you obtain such a thing?"

Andreas stepped toward the bed and his hand went instinctively to his sword. The scuffed and grayish floorboards protested violently as if they might succumb at any moment to such a burden. "Yes, fool, from where did you obtain such a thing?" The eyes of the villager grew large as he saw Andreas and Raimon Roger standing near the bed in the small, crowded chamber, and he recoiled to the opposing side of the pallet, trembling, all color drained from his face. "My lords... It fell from the knight when he hurled also the... the dagger in my village. I... I bore false witness unto you. It... it spoke to me and made promise of wealth and power. I beg of you, have mercy upon me... and upon my son."

"It spoke to you?" Andreas noticed for the first time little Miquel, sitting on a rickety wooden chair in the corner of the room, arms wrapped around his legs, nearly curled into a ball, straining to make himself as small, silent, and inconspicuous as lie within his very limited power. "Did it pilfer the voice of your son?"

"I fear it has done so," spoke the priest at bedside looking with compassion upon Miquel. "Your fate no longer lies in our hands, villager." The other cleric and the physician nodded in agreement. "Whatever hand of evil has wrought this sickness I fear has already apportioned your soul and will surely claim your body. Confess your many sins and receive the Eucharist.

Deu may yet have mercy."

The man clenched his body and fought and then yielded to a coughing spasm, spitting blood for the first time. His breathing grew labored. His eyes started to roll back. The skin ringing them grew dark. Miquel shut his own eyes. The priest by the bedside wiped the villager's brow and anointed his forehead with oil. "Tell us please your name."

"I... I will not. That is for *Deu* alone, for I... I am a fool. Know me by... by no other name." The villager, wild-eyed, looked in vain to find Raimon Roger. "Will you destroy it, my lord?"

Raimon Roger paused, looked to the priest at bedside, who nodded. "I shall destroy it. And, though you do not ask, I will make sure your son is well cared for. I will see to it myself."

"Bless you, my lord. My son... That thing promised to... to reveal secrets of life to me but... but has brought only torment and death." The villager made final confession in stunted, cough-riddled gasps, and the priest anointed his forehead with oil and administered the Eucharist wafer and wine. Thus the villager with unknown name who called himself a fool was shriven.

Andreas watched the boy remain curled while the soul of his father quit the body. Miquel did not go to his father, and the father did not bid him come.

As the body of the villager gave up the ghost and became spiritless, the eyes of the boy opened and he unwrapped arms from legs. For the first time since Andreas had seen him on the road to Montpellier, the boy had an intensity to his look and was alert. Andreas walked toward Miquel to comfort him, but the little one left the chair and met Andreas in the middle of the room, arms extended upward.

Andreas lifted the boy and embraced him and Miquel trembled and wept for some minutes. His chin on Andreas's shoulder, his cheek against Andreas's jaw. The *châtelain* tightened the embrace and the boy reciprocated and wept the louder. Father and brother dead in the span of a fortnight. No mother to speak of. So much loss for such a little one.

As the eyes of Miquel dried at length, the boy spoke. "My *paire* took that thing." He sniffled, wiped his nose with his sleeve, and pointed to the amulet. The voice was cracked and dry, but the words were those of Miquel. The only words any of them, other than the now deceased villager, had ever heard the boy utter, and he was not yet finished. "He took also a shiny knife off the ground as my brother, Jaufre, lay dying."

A pang of guilt rippled through Andreas, strong-armed and dark, and he shoved it with no small effort to some forgotten grotto of his soul. He winced as his gut was shot through with pain. "I am sorry he did so."

Miquel was not yet finished. "When we saw you on the road, my *paire* shoved me into your path. He told me to stay upon the road. He said if you heard our story, you would give us protection from the knights in green. Thus he could keep the treasures he found."

Tiredness and pity for the boy filled him, sharply checked the swift onrush of anger toward the fool who had justly met death. "Protection we gave you indeed. Come, Miquel." Andreas spoke gently in his ear. "There is no need for you to linger here."

Raimon Roger picked up the amulet. "This thing is evil and I shall have it destroyed." The priests and physician nodded in earnest agreement.

Andreas clutched at his chest to be sure his remained still under his tunic. Was it truly an inherent evil, or was it the deceit of the villager that robbed him of life? "Give me the object, and I shall see to its ruin. You have greater burdens to bear, my lord."

Raimon Roger handed over the object, sighed, and said simply "Thank you, Andreas."

As he grasped it, Andreas noticed the writing upon the back, fifteen more words in Occitan, differing words from the amulet he took off the dead knight in the wood: *Soldada, Flamier, Folpidor, Mostier, Mercadan, Valensa, Issartz, Ifernaus, Saumier, Sembelin, Noirisa, Autrier, Angoisos, Bendich, Benestan.*

As they returned to *la cite*, Miquel clinging still to Andreas, Raimon Roger steered the subject to Miquel's future. Andreas's lord spoke of a merchant family he trusted that wanted a son and would truly treat Miquel as their own. Raimon Roger spoke next of preparations for battle, and Andreas welcomed the change of topic. As he listened he gained also the realization his mind was set firmly as a mortared stone in a curtain wall; he had no intention of seeing to the ruin of either amulet.

A sentry reticently approached Andreas and Raimon Roger as they discussed strategies for the defense of *San Vicens*. "Pardon my lord, but two men in black cowled robes stand outside the Oriental Gate. They request to have audience with you." The guard shifted uncomfortably as Raimon Roger looked at him with questioning eyes. "They bid me tell you they are on pilgrimage to Rome to visit the Holy Apostles."

"*Valdenses*," said Andreas.

Raimon Roger returned his eyes to the document on the table. "Well show them in, and be quick about it."

"Yes, my lord." The sentry was already scurrying off toward the massive doors at the far end of the hall.

Those doors opened and closed and Andreas spoke. "Why would *Valdenses* request an audience with you, my lord?"

Raimon Roger did not look up. "I know not. Perhaps they seek further protection for their *orde*."

Momentarily, the heavy, carved oaken doors opened again and two men entered, one significantly taller than the other.

"I think we have seen them before, on the way to Montpellier," said Andreas quietly.

"My pilgrim friends," called Raimon Roger across the hall, bearing a look of amusement, "if you are truly seeking Rome, the Eternal City, you have been journeying the wrong direction."

"In truth, you are correct, my lord," spoke the taller one with loud voice, a low booming tone that reverberated off stone walls and floor. "Though it is not because we lack a compass."

Raimon Roger folded his hands and placed them on the table. "Your journey here from Montpellier has been through hostile lands. Tell me, how did you reach us?"

"With difficulty, my lord," continued the taller one as he and his shorter companion, both barefoot this time, briskly walked the distance of the hall. "I pray I am right in saying that you know who we are and the dangers faced by those in our *orde*. That is why our pilgrimage ruse is necessary and why also we have come to Carcassonne to seek an audience with the one of the few lords in Christendom to offer the *Valdenses* sanctuary unyielding."

"Perhaps I am one of the few to continue to offer such a protectorate, but you are not alone in seeking an audience, shall we say," Raimon Roger smiled. Andreas noted that his lord genuinely enjoyed the company of these men. "Quite a company of armed pilgrims comes behind you, at the behest of Rome, and I daresay their intentions are not as peaceful as yours. I trust you realize their impending arrival will soon mean there is no longer any exit from these walls and you are to be detained here in *la cite* with the *Carcassonnais*."

Waiting until his guests reached the table where he and Andreas were at work with maps and charts and scribes at their bidding, Raimon Roger rose to greet the mendicants and welcomed them warmly to his hall.

Andreas kept his seat and looked the men over. They smelled of the country and looked as if they had traveled through the wood, as if branch and bramble had clawed their faces and robes.

"I offer you the welcome cup." Raimon Roger nodded to a servant who came forward with two small silver cups on a golden platter and presented them to the *Valdenses*, who accepted them graciously. "This juice of the grape lacks ferment, I assure you. I keep it on hand for just such visitors as those before me. The leaders of the *Bons Hommes*, who often seek me out, do not imbibe wine either."

Raimon Roger motioned to a pair of oak chairs upholstered in velvet of emerald green. "Come sit and let us speak of the reasons for your presence here."

"We mean you no disrespect my lord, but we prefer to remain standing. We have been given a message—a noble lesson in our parlance—to present to the lord of this *chateau*."

Raimon Roger gestured to them with his hand as one beckons a companion to hurry along a trail. "Well then, out with it, my friends. But I shall listen only on one condition. You must first agree to sit at my board this eve and sup with me. It will be a sumptuous meal. You may possess all the spiritual food you require, but your faces look in want of corporeal nourishment."

The taller one smiled broadly. "We shall both accede to your request and give our thanks for it. Our steps here were arduous and furtive, but there is no denying the call of *Deu*, my lord. After we saw you on the road some days ago, we had planned on walking to Arles, to encourage the brethren there, and then on to Lyon. But as we slept that night in the house of a friend, a secret friend in Montpellier, we had both of us the same dream. Would you hear of it, my lord?"

Raimon Roger raised hands behind his head and laced his fingers together as he looked toward stained glass windows and loosed the air from his lungs. "I would hear of anything that would cast light in this time of shadow."

The speaker gave a deferential nod to his shorter companion but persisted in holding the floor. "We saw a city under siege whose ramparts crowned a hill and drew down to a river. All around the city, darkness lay in wait, stealing about in the shadows, crouching for an opportune time to strike. The darkness was as a serpent coiled round the city."

Andreas flinched, recalling the parting words of Bertran. He clutched at his chest, both amulets now draped round his neck. There was no warmth or distortion as he did so, only a calming of the mind.

"Within the city there was darkness also, even in the castle. We were told simply to come to this city of the dream and expel the darkness. The city was Carcassonne and the castle the *Chateau Comtal* my lord."

Raimon Roger clasped his hands together behind his back and broadened the stance of his feet. "I feel compelled to twice remind you that you have entered a city and a *chateau* soon to fall under the darkness of siege."

Andreas looked at his lord quizzically and was surprised that Raimon Roger had abandoned their maps and charts to parley with these men. In point of fact, all work at the table and throughout the hall had ceased. The *Valdenses* had garnered a rapt audience for their noble lesson and owned the moment. Even the scratch of the quills of the scribes on vellum had arrested.

"Nothing could please us more than to stand with you in this grave hour," said the taller one. "For we come not seeking protection but merely a chance to be heard. Your men gave freely of their lives at Beziers and fought gallantly," the *Valdense* paused, looking admirably at Andreas, "against the armies of the Whore of Babylon. I trust I will not be whipped or firebranded for speaking such in this hall." He smiled. "They fought gallantly to protect not only the *Valdenses,* our own brothers and sisters, but all *Bitterois*, whether pagan, Catholic, or *Bons Hommes*, all ones that our Lord *Jhesu* died for, blessed be his name."

"Blessed be his name," echoed the shorter one in loud voice.

Andreas felt an inky blackness course through him at the mention of the name, and he shivered. The ache returned to his skull and spread to his nape and his belly grew nauseous, and the pain was sharp. He quietly released a foul, gaseous belch. He found concentration difficult. His hands tremored.

"You offer also protection to Jews, to the chosen people of our Lord," continued the taller one. "Indeed our Lord *Jhesu*, blessed be his name, was himself of the stock of Abraham. The blessing of the Father be upon you for shielding his chosen ones."

"Not many who call upon the name of *Crist* believe as you," replied Raimon Roger with a note of admiration in his voice. "Officially the Jews are charlatans, whose very blood courses with greed, who, not content with having crucified blessed *Jhesu*, continue to separate Christians from their money through wicked usury to this very day. Even my uncle, the Count of Toulouse, has allowed the day of Strike the Jew to persist each year unabated."

"There are more than you might imagine that believe as we do and condemn such vile practices," continued the taller one, "but they are afraid of challenging Rome's hierarchy to suffer the branding of heretic, the ignominy of excommunication, or peril to life and limb. Many are the secret friends of *Vaudes*, the Poor Man of Lyons. Though the Church cannot seem to decide officially whether we are schismatics or true heretics."

Raimon Roger shook his head. "I think such a decision has already been reached. Armand Amaury called for me to surrender both the *Valdenses* and *Bons Hommes* of Beziers, at least the ones known of by Bishop Rainaud."

"Yes, the *Valdenses* are reviled in the same fashion as the *Bons Hommes* perfects. Though we have refuted vigorously the heterodoxy of the *Bons Hommes* for the thirty years past, our preaching is nonetheless perceived as a threat to the Roman church itself, which desires total control of the written and spoken word.

"I know of what I speak. You must understand that I and
my companion were once perfects, distinguished amongst the
Bons Hommes in Foix for our self-denial and devotion to the
God of Light. We debated in Foix against two *Valdenses*, one
of them a woman. We were by turns filled with condescension,
frustration, rage, peace, and then fire of the purest magnitude.
We became as the two travelers on the road to Emmaus with
our Lord, who said to one another, 'Were not our hearts burning within us while He was speaking to us on the road, while He
was explaining the Scriptures to us?' Those Valdenses stirred a
passion in us unlike anything we have ever known. Their gospel
was simple, not the complex rendering of the bishops with all of
their clauses and rejoinders."

"So have you made journey here to discuss the finer points of
doctrine?" remarked Raimon Roger dryly, seeming to grow tired
of talk in such a way as only nobility could.

"Not at all, my lord," said the shorter one earnestly. "You
have been generous in giving of shelter and protection and we
wish to give you what we have. It is what we seek to bring everywhere. For we believe not that the melioramentum or consolamentum of the *Bons Hommes* can make a man perfect, nor can
the venerated relics of the Church heal the soul of a man nor
even the sacraments, not even the Eucharist or baptism, for we
believe a man or woman should be baptized as a confession of
faith, not as a means of salvation." He looked up, as if beseech-
ing the heavens. "We would very much desire to see you, my
lord, baptized in such a way."

Raimon Roger shook his head and smiled. "You are far too
late, for I received already the baptism on my natal day."

"The baptism of a newborn has symbolic value only, but the
baptism of an adult, confessing simple penitence and belief in
blessed *Jhesu*, now that is a worthy thing. With such an act, *Deu*
is pleased. Many are those in your lands who have confessed,
in secret, belief for salvation in *Jhesu Crist* alone, not in relics
or dead saints or empty pronouncements of the pope. Many of
those furtive penitents, whom we call secret friends of *Vaudes*,
were slaughtered in Beziers in the *gran mazel*. We would bid
you join their ranks, Viscount Trencavel, as they were in life, for

salvation is to be found in no other name."

Raimon Roger walked and stood next to the *Valdenses* as one would an intimate friend. "Perhaps you can help me find words to my prayer, for not two days ago, I went to *la cathedrale*, seeking solace, seeking to pray, but I had not words to utter to the Almighty." Raimon Roger looked to the ceiling and round the hall. His voice cracked. "In these days of darkness, I know not how to reach him." The emotion rose in Raimon Roger's voice as bile climbed in Andreas's throat. "For the veil that had separated us from hell itself, that guarded *paratge*, has been rent and the heat singes us, but still a shroud remains before *Deu*. What can pierce such a veil?"

Andreas sprang to his feet, restless and disturbed. The trembling of his hands moved up his arms and his upper limbs shook. His head felt compressed in a vice and he wanted to cry out against this noble lesson that brought him torment, but his throat was parched, devoid of utterance.

"We *Valdenses* believe in simple prayers, for the Scriptures say that *Deu* looks upon the heart. This shroud you speak of exists because of the devil and the sin of man. That is why God sent the man *Crist Jhesu*. Our Lord *Jhesu* laid down his life for us, for greater love has no man than this. We bid you, my lord, make your prayer of confession here to *Crist* alone and be reconciled to *Deu*."

Andreas's nausea and agitation grew uncontrollable and he flew across the hall as one fleeing battle, sending his chair skittering across the stone floor and knocking a page and a squire into a carven table. As the great doors closed behind him, he heard the voice of Raimon Roger calling out to him. "Andreas, why flee you such a homily?"

But he did not answer nor slow his flight. Running down the steps into the courtyard, he sprinted across the paving stones to the wing of the apartments of the *Chateau Comtal*. He entered the hallway of the larger chambers, the acid determined in its rise and he gave way and vomited on the floor rushes.

But discomfort lingered and morphed into caustic pain in his belly. It flowed up his torso, his shoulders, and over his head, which throbbed with an ache he had never before known. The pain ringed his eyes and seared them as with a glowing branding iron. The very hallway seemed to throb, expanding and contracting before his eyes. Andreas dropped to his knees, rubbing his temples.

He felt a grip upon his shoulder and noticed a tall, thin man in a tunic of blue beside him. Andreas had heard not his approach. The hand pulled him to his feet, while the other hand went to his abdomen and rubbed it vigorously. Andreas could not issue utterance, but felt relief as the pain fled his belly. The man let his hand hover about an inch from Andreas's gut and moved it up over his chest, releasing him from the pain as it moved, up his torso, over his neck, across his face and over his eyes and skull. All torment fled.

Andreas's voice returned and he looked up. "How did you gain entrance to the *chateau*? How do you do such things? I know you not."

The man stood close to Andreas, yet the *châtelain* could scarce discern his face within the cowl, though his voice was clear, if somewhat disembodied. "There is much you do not yet know, or comprehend. I know you have dismembered and feel torment and seek answers, yet I watched you and you are right to flee the deception of the *Valdenses*."

Andreas shivered. "How knew you of dismemberment?"

The man remained without motion. "I am a healer and can absolve more than the pain of your mortal body, for the body is but a *gaol* from which you must be set free. The God of Light sees and knows all and speaks such to his servants as they have need to hear it. Fear not, Andreas, for you shall achieve your deliverance. There is a gathering in less than a fortnight in *la cite*. You need attend. Receive the laying on of hands and prayer and swear but a small vow and you shall receive the true light of knowledge."

CHAPTER 26

2 AUGUST 1209
SABBATH

Eva wrapped each of the little blue peas in a bit of cloth and bound the whole in a woolen scarf. Such padding should suffice to cushion the pearls from the jostling of the day's short journey on foot. Tying the ends of the square piece of knitted fabric, she placed the small light bundle in the tan leather satchel she used for her travels. Almost always did such treks involve business in the other cities of Provence, like Arles, Marseille, and Avignon, the latter being the destination most common and this day's journey's end.

Yet what concerned at the moment was not business, neither painting nor carving. The thing which never ceased to bring alarum unspoken was the very Beautiful Things themselves. After returning the platter to the wooden chest the week previous, Eva had wanted to pull out every other Beautiful Thing and shake it, pore over it. She had even walked back to the trunk and opened it, but still she found it difficult to even look upon the Things, much less remove them. They looked to her in the ethereal as always, as if coated in a black, viscous, steaming liquid that ever threatened to overflow the trunk, cover the floor of the bedchamber, and spill out down the stairs. She had long feared that if loosed from confinement, there would be no checking its spread. It was the hot flowing substance of death.

Somehow she knew.

She never witnessed it in the natural, yet her hands and even her arms would feel sticky after touching anything other than the letter or the parchment tube, as if she had dipped hand and arm in treacle up to her shoulder. Treacle was an antidote to poison derived from honey, but this treacle substance was somehow itself a honeyed poison. But unlike treacle, the gluey feeling was never removed by washing with soap and water. It would only fade after prayer, and not after rote recitation, but only through a prayer that issued from her spirit, then she would feel cleansed once more.

Yet never had she felt the hot burning until touching the reading stone upon the board of her kitchen. The letter. It was the relation of the Beautiful Things not to the words of the letter but to the palimpsest, the writing underneath. That was the thing that so exercised the host of hell. The reading stone had enabled Eva, Pietro, and Claris to read the faint scraped again script. What of the other Beautiful Things? Had they all been sent to shed light on the palimpsest somehow?

It was difficult to think of the golden items as anything other than death itself. Tempted as she had been many a day to remove the letter to another place, she had believed its presence in the trunk was a hedge against the rise of liquid death. What would occur if mortality itself was released? She allowed not her mind to dwell there. Was death truly held captive inside her trunk, constrained merely by boards of cypress? She knew the Beautiful Things were not life, but was not fully prepared to believe they were death either. Her grasp upon the platter from which the little blue peas had issued forth had not felt as treacle.

Even as she questioned why, still she refrained from looking at the items once more. She was afraid of being made to probe death itself. Yet the coming of the pilgrim army and the poking of Claris had prodded her to take up the task anyway. She feared not for her own mortality but for the unchecked spread of death to those around her.

So she had shut up the chest once more and then sat on it, as if death could be so contained. Not bearing to look inside, but reluctant to leave. It gnawed at her that she knew so little of why she saw the black liquid. At length, she had risen and decided she would start with the blue peas. Show those to the bishop. She would revisit all else upon returning from Avignon.

Deliver us from evil.

It was nearing last light and Eva joined Pietro and Claris in the common under the pear tree. Pale orange and yellow shades of sunset filtered downward from the rim of the world into the low edges of the sky. Yet her thoughts were on the color blue. She dare not show her travelling companions the little stones in this open place. But where?

The house of the Painter.

Eva and Claris took their leave as prearranged through the West Gate of the community as the guards of the prince stood at attention. The knights were fully armored with hauberk and helmet and shield and the glint of the setting sun off the polished chain mail was dazzling. It made Eva think of angels and she had a momentary sense such beings were their fore and rear guard. It was a potent, almost intoxicating assurance. She thought also of the knight she had seen in vision in the orchard. Her spirit issued the briefest of prayers that such beings would safeguard him as well.

They walked up the hill as if the orchard was their destination. They were then to circle back through the woods nearby and join with Pietro on the road to Orange. Yet the orchard was their destination, as Eva needed to retrieve her bow and quarrels. Pietro had not spoken of why he thought Eva need bring them, and she did not ask.

Her tools of archery in hand, Eva and Claris walked south into the forest. There was some risk in traversing the wood. The forest was daily searched and cleared as necessary by Prince Guillaume's men, so it was generally safe. Yet Eva had some trepidation as her and Claris entered the greenwood and emerged into the open beyond the sighting of the guard at the East Gate and joined with Pietro. They had weighed the risk of the forest against the risk of all three of them being seen leaving the community together, and the latter was perceived as the greater liability. Eva saw abandoned campsites and other evidence of habitation but no occupants in the wood.

The sun as it made descent in the west was still warm upon their backs as they walked the road to Orange. They encountered a few Beguines on the road making return to the community after a day of work in the city. Claris and Eva pulled their cowls forward and kept their heads down as they passed, but it mattered not since the tired Beguines they passed paid them no heed.

Pietro had expressed concern about the possibility of one of the Beguines in the community being an agent of *l'orde*.

The Bishop looked to the heavens and smiled. "It has been such a blessing to come here and know you at last, Eva." He lowered his voice. "The hand of *Deu* is upon you, and your adventure is but in its infancy."

Eva narrowed her eyes and looked at him askance. "Adventure?"

The bishop smiled but looked toward the orchard. "Many things are now in motion, and events will only rush faster."

Eva looked toward the disk of the sun as it descended toward the edge of the world, its fire flaming out as day began its slow summer bleed into night. "The pace is dizzying as it is, but so be it. I need show you something at the villa of the Painter this very eve."

"Can you not show us now?"

Eva shook her head. "Trust me. You will understand once we arrive."

Claris was sober, quiet, not speaking lessons of the setting sun heralding the coming of peaceful night.

The Painter was at work when they arrived.

Eva walked to the wooden table and opened her bag. She liked, at times, to have a certain flair in what she did. "I have brought something to show to all." She withdrew the scarf from the leather satchel and placed it on the broad table at the center of the studio, and untied it. One at a time, carefully, deliberately, she unbound each blue stone and laid them all out in a row. The room was silent. Twelve little spheres. "I have taken to calling these the blue peas. My guess is that they are some sort of bluish pearl, perhaps from India."

Claris had the look of surprise. "India? From where did you obtain them?"

Some of her hair was in her face, and Eva flicked her head backwards, throwing her dark brown strands over her shoulders. "From the Beautiful Things. From a golden platter with hollow handles of mother of pearl."

"You did not know of them before now?" Claris bore a look of bemused astonishment.

"I did not." Eva's attention was focused not on Claris, but on the Painter, who had remained silent but vigilant, and continued to look between her and the little stones. What of his thoughts? She wished him to speak. For the first time, she was excited about, felt connection to the Beautiful Things; there was no sticky black oil, no treacle-substance upon the bluish-green spheres. Yet the Painter remained silent. The man who never lacked for words, for wit, for a jest that provoked laughter and thought. Why did he not speak now?

The Painter kept his own council and remained wordless even when they departed for Avignon the following morn. Eva thought him pale, almost whitish about his face, a sight she had never beheld. No matter, she would charm from him the reason for his silence once he arrived in Avignon on the feast day of the Virgin Maria, nearly a fortnight hence.

They took their leave from Orange and trod the *Via Agrippa* until nearly midday, when they yielded to the heat and retreated to an inn for lunch. They were dining on roast pork and turnips when Pietro looked at Eva and said, "Why do you think there are twelve?"

"Twelve little blue peas? I cannot explain how I know, but I believe it a message from my *paire*." Eva recounted how she had shaken the platter out of anger at her father and heard the rattling of the bluish pearls.

Claris frowned. "Believe not that the dead speak, Eva. I know you long to know your *paire*, but seek not such contact."

Eva smiled and gently shook her head. "You are ever my

mentor and guide. I do not speak of channeling the dead or of geomancy nor any form of divination. I but wonder if my *paire*, many years past, wished to send a message to me before he met his end. What has lain dormant has now been awakened."

CHAPTER 27

2 AUGUST 1209
SABBATH

Andreas tarried in a darkened alcove of a hallway opposite a clear, leaded pane window. The moon, a bright full disc of light, illumined the courtyard of the *Chateau Comtal* beyond. He watched the Oriental Gate. It was safeguarded by a double portcullis. Robertz and Anfos stoically stood sentry, flanked each side like armored pillars.

The bells of *San Nazare, la cathedrale* of Carcassonne, began to ring out in clear, strong, defiant tones. The construction materials of the cathedral had been blessed by Pope Urban himself over a century past. It was only days after Urban had preached the first Crusade to conquer Jerusalem. Now a Crusade had come to Carcassonne, the first that had no pretext of going to the Holy Land.

The French had descended en masse upon the surround of Carcassonne the day previous. Another dramatic appearing that left him this time little moved. The enemy had refrained, albeit restlessly, from laying siege this day in deference to the Sabbath, but would not so refrain on the morrow, but a common Monday. At the moment Andreas cared not. For the past week, since his healing encounter with the man in blue, had he waited ardently for this night, the Sabbath gathering of the *Bons Hommes.*

It was compline. Robertz began to squirm as expected and then gyrate in his midsection like a small boy. He spoke a few words to Anfos, who frowned and waved him off as Robertz scurried from his post to relieve himself.

Loyal Anfos was now alone in guarding the Oriental Gate. Anfos, who when so bidden would refrain from ill-timed queries and words to others. Quite unlike Robertz, who would otherwise surely find means to inform Raimon Roger of Andreas taking his leave from the Chateau on the eve of battle, in the very hours before a midnight council of war.

It was forbidden for a sentinel to abandon his watch, ever more so in days of battle. Never had he seen Robertz do so unbidden. Yet the man in blue said it would be such this night. The God of Light would make a way. There were ways of avoiding the need to vacate one's post. There were precautions Robertz must have neglected entire this night. Now a way out of the Chateau was made. Wishing as he did to remain unseen, the breach of ancient protocol by Robertz was a thing for which Andreas was grateful. This night, as he sought to take his leave unawares, he had willed the quitting into being. Spirit had prevailed over flesh. There would be no reprimand for Robertz, for in his neglect he had done Andreas good service.

The *châtelain*, dressed only in the coarse robe of a penitent, barefoot, two amulets suspended from his neck, quietly left the Chateau. The air seemed aswirl with dark vapors. Andreas followed the hazy shadows close around the perimeter of the courtyard.

Anfos nearly became as a dead man when Andreas approached him from the side at the gate.

The *châtelain* put a hand to the shoulder of the guard, held him steady. "If you saw not my coming, vigilant as ever you are, than neither did another soul in the Chateau." Andreas breathed deeply. Being able to approach alert Anfos unawares imparted a thrilling, frightening sense of power, one that felt at once as soaring like an arrow in flight, yet free falling violently into the void. "Discretion is uttermost this night. I have a secret meet in *la cite,* a meet that may bring peace."

Andreas did not elaborate on which sort of peace he spoke. At the moment, he was more concerned about having the calm pervade his soul than seeing it temper the conflicts of men.

Anfos, eyes still wide, swallowed hard, nodded, and quickly unlocked the gate and raised both portcullises.

Andreas held up both hands, palms outward. "As far as you have concern, I did not pass through here this night."

Anfos' face was ashen, unusually so, even awash in the yellow of moonlight. He appeared to quake ever so slightly, like a leafy sapling of poplar quivering in late spring's breeze. "I saw only the approach of shifting shadows, my lord, and that is no lie." His voice cracked, as if sprung from a throat parched by hot desert wind and dust. "Even now I scarce discern your face within the cowl."

Andreas grasped firmly the shoulder of Anfos once more. "You are generous in your embellishment, my friend." The *châtelain* forced a smile, abruptly turned, and walked briskly through the open gate, gratified at the aid from Anfos, not wanting to look upon him anymore. Andreas knew the words of the guard echoed truth for he felt himself ever more as a shadow. The thought prickled and he abandoned it as if depositing a thing despised among a dense patch of thorns.

The portcullises were lowered slowly behind him. The subdued but rhythmic click clack of iron wheels and chains and bars echoed in his hearing, reminded Andreas of a *gaol*, the prison of the body from which he sought freedom. It was the evil urgings of the body that had caused him to dismember. He knew this now.

Andreas stole across the wooden moat bridge and through crowded streets toward the house. The one spoken of by the man in blue. Andreas knew it as the residence of the jeweler who was considered the most skilled in Carcassonne, perhaps in all the Languedoc.

There was no entering this night through the great gilded door fronting the house on the street of the jewelers. The man said the spies of the Bishop of Carcassonne and of Armand Amaury himself were everywhere present. Andreas need dress as a mendicant. He need use the entry for the servants in the alley to the rear of the house.

There was no living thing in the narrow backstreet. Not even cow or pig, perhaps the only place in Carcassonne thus vacant. It had been kept clear, of such there could be no doubting. Whether the feat was accomplished by hidden guard or sorcery he knew not, but it was no happenstance. The air seemed to thicken as he advanced, shrouded the center of the alley. A person standing at either end of the constricted way could not see the other end, nor even as far as the center. The wooden door was halfway down the alley on the right as he had been told, but he saw no one there. Instead, he heard his name spoken in low tones, but saw not the source of the voice. "Andreas, halt your steps."

He heard a sliding of stone and cobbles moved. In front of his feet a hole appeared in the very center of the alleyway, perhaps two feet square. Without the admonition his next footfall would have carried him tumbling unawares into the opening before him.

There was a scraping of wood on stone and the top of a ladder appeared just below street level. A single word in a voice guarded and raspy rose from below. "Enter."

He was to climb down the ladder. The ladder held more rungs than he had expected and took him farther than two stories beneath street level. The air grew cool and damp as he descended. He could not see beyond the ladder, but his nose caught the burning of beeswax. His bare feet went from the bottom rung to cool dry stone. Chilled air filled his lungs and momentarily robbed him of breath. His eyes watered and his body shivered a minor tremor.

While another slid back the cobbles above at street level and then descended and pulled down the ladder, the cowled silhouette of a man took his wrist and led Andreas down a stone-lined square passage, around a corner, then another turn and yet another still, until Andreas had lost all track of whence he had walked. He thought the tunnels slanted ever slightly downhill, but could not be sure. At length, tendrils of yellowish light flickered round a corner and he emerged into a chamber where others in the beast-colored robes of mendicants had gathered. They stood on what appeared a perfect unbroken circle etched in the honey-colored sandstone floor, facing outward.

One in a blue robe spoke. "The secrecy is necessary in these days when agents of the enemy are already among us in *la cite*. Welcome, Andreas. Long have we watched you from afar, knowing your soul would prosper amongst us."

Andreas squinted, allowed his eyes to amend themselves to the light of candles, which seemed vivid after traversing the long, dim passage. There were perhaps two dozen people in the chamber, men and women seeming equal among them in numbers. He shook his head and spoke without thought. "How shall my soul prosper among you? I have committed sacrilege. I dismembered a man, hewed limbs and head from body. Forever will my soul be barred from heaven. There is no peace in my innermost."

The chair in the center of the circle fell under his sighting.

The cowled one in blue motioned toward the only seating place in the chamber. "The chair is for you, Andreas. We bid you sit. We open all meetings with a simple prayer. Let us pray over you with the laying on of hands. Such will calm your troubled soul and draw you inside our circle."

He felt a sensation of warmth flow over him. Andreas relaxed his body and walked into the circle through the singular opening provided, as if those gathered awaited only his presence to be rendered whole. He sat down in the unadorned wooden chair that lacked paint or even varnish. He looked around and realized that twenty-four souls did indeed surround him, twelve men and twelve women. All stepped forward and closed in on him. As many as were able placed bare hands on his shoulders and cowled head and he grew warmer still. A light not of a candle became manifest and spread through the chamber. Somehow small shadows, geometric points of blackness—triangle, circle, and square—mingled with the luminescent glow. They merged together, separated, and merged once more.

The one in blue began the prayer. "God of Light, we gather here this night underground. Hidden away at risk of life and limb, for the agents of darkness are ever around us. Even as the armies of the god of this world surround this stronghold of the light, show us the pure way, the way of perfection. This supplicant, for whom we lift up our prayers, comes among us this night with a spirit in turmoil. A spirit trapped inside a body infernal. A spirit twice bound by the lies of the Catholic Church and of the

Valdenses. Let him abandon the vile of the sacraments. As if any are truly in need of the flesh and blood of the Eucharist or the water of baptism for salvation. For such things of the corporeal are but an illusion for the foolish, the weak of mind. They are a mere creation of the devil, the maker of all things seen. For you issued forth, *Jhesu*, from the God of Light as a spirit only. A spirit with no body who came to bring wholeness and light. Shine forth your light of the spirit then. Make this man before us whole. May his eye be single. Fill him with light. Cleanse him from all lies. Scour from him all things of the devil. May he ever dwell in the circle ethereal."

There was silence for some moments, then the sound of a long, slow, raspy intake of breath. The breath was released in a distinct, scratchy tenor of speech. The voice of an aged woman. Andreas thought of the ideal of the wise old hag. "I sense this man before us has made journey for many turns of the wheel, revolutions of life and migrations of the soul beyond counting." The sound of her voice swelled in anticipation like a rising great wave grasping for shore. "His spirit is aged and well-traveled. I see it. Yes. He has made residence in ancient Rome. There he walked the seven hills in the days of Augustus Caesar; there he sought the wisdom of Minerva. In Greece, he talked with sages and learnt still more of wisdom, partook of the richest mead in cups of gold. Yes, he drank the honeyed nectar of the gods, drank deeply of Ambrosia." Her hand gripped more tightly his shoulder. "Pythagoras he walked with, listened at his feet. This man knows the ethereal mysteries of numbers and shapes in his innermost, what is visible and what is unseen. Yet he can unlock them only if he looks within, deep within to the still small voices, the voices of Mary of Magdala and of Minerva, they of temperance and wisdom. He need join with them in spirit."

O God of Light, help this man, aid this warrior. May he abandon his killing and the warring ways of knights. Help him abandon the violence that would slay even animals, for even the beasts of the forest may be host to the tremoring souls of men. Souls in need of time for redemption, souls with desperate need for the animal to live long so the next body into which they will be imprisoned will be a higher form of life. Let him forsake the eating of meat and all things of the animal that men consume as food. If he abandons not such banal things, he may find his soul imprisoned in such an animal in the next life. Only if he lives purely, apart from such things, will he start to know freedom from the gaol of the body. May he be so purified. Blessed be the Lord, the God of Light."

The gathering spoke as one. "So be it."

Hands lifted from him and feet returned to the etched circle, faces now looking inward toward Andreas. Faces bearing the look of an austere peace, of sublime detachment from this evil world. The voice of the man in blue was raised once more. "Andreas, you are now a *credente,* a simple believer among us. Work to make preparation to receive the *consolamentum,* the vows of a perfect, if such is your desire."

Andreas felt at ease, all thoughts of torment and pain of the head faded. The Sabbath gathering of the *Bons Hommes* had proved worth the waiting. "Truly it is my desire to be perfect, to live in perfect peace. I find among you this night a place of rest. Show me the way and I shall walk in it."

The one in blue appeared to smile, though the effort turned down the corners of his mouth. "Very well then. Once the siege of Carcassonne has ended, you will begin a period of *abstinentia* in a place of isolation, like an extended season of Lent in which you will eat only what is harvested from the earth, will refrain from the use of all weaponry and the ways of war, imbibe not any fermented drink, and know not any woman, even through a kiss. Fight until the fight for Carcassonne has ended, then fight no more, do all these things no more. When that day is upon you will you so abstain?"

A calming presence fell upon Andreas. A feeling of peace. "I will so abstain."

The voices of those gathered all rose once more in unison. *So be it.*

Andreas arrived late to the midnight council of war. Raimon Roger and his barons and vassals were already atop the ramparts near the *Tor Samson.* If Raimon Roger had irritation at the tardiness of his *châtelain,* he betrayed it not. They watched

the campfires of the French gleam the darkened air and frame
their tents in flickering light. A sea of flame-lit canvas and wool
was spread before them to the North.

Raimon Roger turned to all assembled and made declaration. "To horse, my lords." Raimon Roger's eyes were burnished
and illumined the very air about his face. "Let us surprise these
Frances with a charge of four-hundred cavaliers at first light.
Ride into their ranks before they can mount a siege. By all that is
holy, all they have violated, we shall gain retribution for Beziers!"

Andreas could but stare at Raimon Roger. Had his lord
learnt nothing from the folly of the *Bitterois*? He remained silent, but his belly and thoughts roiled.

Andreas deferred to others and they raised strong arguments
against the charge. Yet it was another of his lord's barons, Guilhem of Minerve that seemed to speak most eloquently for them
all. "The host should not be attacked, my lord, when they are
newly arrived and fresh. Remember how Beziers was breached,
my liege. Remember the *gran mazel*. Let us wear them down,
draw out the siege. Perhaps the *Frances* will at that point prove
vulnerable to a sortie outside of the walls led by yourself and
your *châtelain*, Andreas, the lone survivor of Beziers. He above
all men should know of what I speak." The Baron of Minerve
gave the *châtelain* a respectful nod. "But we need choose time
and place wisely, my lord."

Raimon Roger turned and looked upon the French. "Perchance you speak truth, baron. Yet it grieves me to think on what
will transpire if *los Frances* are allowed time to deeply entrench.
I will not allow another *gran mazel*. I will not!"

Another of his vassals, the Baron of Bram, approached
Raimon Roger. "My lord, we will need every man in defense of
the ramparts."

Raimon Roger walked to a merlon on the wall. He placed
both hands upon it and looked upon what he could see of their
enemy, still at work setting up camp in the dark to the North of
Carcassonne. "Such abundance of good counsel." Raimon Roger
spoke to the night. He turned round to face them, a broad smile
on his face. That winsome smile. "Let us speak no more of this,
lest we dispel all wisdom on the eve of battle."

Wisdom. The lord of Minerve, of the citadel of Minerva, goddess of all wisdom. Was Minerve, that city perched on a plateau, the house of the goddess atop her high place, the destination to which Andreas was to journey, as the spirit had bidden?

When could he undertake such a journey? Did it mean he would survive the siege of Carcassonne as well? Had the migrations of his soul indeed taken him to ancient Rome and Greece? Andreas wondered if he could truly discern the mysteries.

Guilhem himself seemed imbued with the spirit of wisdom. Before the man in blue, the wise old hag, and now Guilhem, he had found no true sources of wisdom. Certainly not among priest and bishop.

Bertran seemed to have wisdom, but would not readily share it. Perhaps his friend had been only a poser speaking words with merely the ring of wisdom. The sum of the hints and riddles of Bertran had thus far amounted to naught.

After Raimon Roger and his barons had departed, Guilhem lingered. "Should the siege go ill, Andreas, and you need a place of refuge after battle's end, you would be a most welcome guest in my keep at Minerve. It was built over the ruins of a temple dedicated to Minerva. There is no better place to seek wisdom in these dark days."

CHAPTER 28

2 AUGUST 1209
SABBATH

T he locale the bishop had chosen for their meeting at
table was idyllic, thought Eva. A bastion of anonym-
ity.

The dining room was in a small inn tucked dis-
creetly into the terraced streets of Avignon, away from the merchant and trade guilds and the district of the clergy, though not
in a sordid quarter of the city. After journeys to Avignon beyond
counting, she was surprised to have no awareness of this estab-
lishment, for it was hidden in plain sighting. She had trod past it
many a time. There was no sign, only a small chrismon, the *Chi
Rho* cross, finely chiseled into limestone over the doorway. She
had seen the symbol once or twice before, but lacked knowledge
of the meaning. The Painter had mentioned it once, something
about the Romans and the Caesars and the martyrdom of the
saints.

The sign marked a place that seemed likely to shelter them
from unfriendly ears. No one else of consequence would likely
bear witness to their conversation, and the patrons of the inn
would probably care not if even they did overhear two priests
and two Beguines, all the more so with their banter being in

Latin.

As Eva and her mentor passed under the stout lintel of oak into the stone and timber frame building with tiled roof, the savory, spiced aroma of grilled lamb, duck, and venison taunted her rumbling belly and filled her mouth with water.

She and Claris, who had seemed far off and had spoken little during the day's travel, sat down at a round table that occupied the southwest corner of the room, as Pietro had bidden. Eva noted with some surprise that both table and chairs were hewn from the dark-grained wood of a pear tree. Some few other men and women, most in the colored wool and Egyptian cotton tunics of merchants, were consuming bread and soft cheese and *pate* at tables of ash wood, while others feasted on white bean stew, venison, and fowl. The stew looked and smelled delicious. *Cassoulet* she had heard it was called in the Languedoc. She would try some this night. Curious that their table was the singular one so fashioned from pear wood.

As Eva took in the oak-paneled room lit by notched beeswax candles, keepers of time which took an hour to burn between each mark, a man with red hair wearing both a brown smock stretched tightly over a rounded belly, and the concerned, slightly tired look of a proprietor, appeared. He offered his name, Renart, and a jug of hot, mixed wine to the Beguines.

Tasting it, Eva graciously declined and requested a bowl of vintage Toulousain burgundy, something more austere, not mixed, mulled, or spiced, and certainly not warmed over the fire. Claris spoke nothing.

Informing the younger Beguine that he would have to search the buttery in his cellar for the right oaken barrel to tap, but was happy to do so, Renart the proprietor scurried off.

As she relaxed in her stout chair at the small round table, Eva felt some of her weariness from the day's journey start to ebb, but the pulsating in her feet gave reminder she had gained blisters there.

Claris spoke first. Her eyes now sheathed in moisture. Why? "Eva, I am sure my lack of voice this day has not gone unnoticed. Much weighs upon my spirit. So much have we been through since the soul of your *maire* quit the body. Yet it seems even a surpassing amount has taken place in the fortnight past." Claris leaned forward, her green eyes bright, though reflecting only candle's flame. "I have a query and a challenge to issue and both are the selfsame thing: Have you made preparation, Eva, for what lies ahead? Truly, are you prepared?"

Eva, caught off her guard, had not made preparation for such a question. She sat up straight, as if a student at university. "What mean you? Speak of what lies ahead."

Claris noticed something in Eva's countenance, and her gaze upon her protégé was curious. "What is it, Eva?"

As Claris released the query, Eva's vision in the ethereal cleared around but one shadow swirling over her mentor, a demon of vacillating. The words may as well have been scribed onto the scales of the scratching, whispering little beast that looked upon Eva with glowering eyes. It endeavored to hold back Claris from a thing she must do. The message hung upon the air. Eva prayed *Deu* to remove the fiend, to vanquish whatever curse had drawn it there. She saw a sword flash and sparks and a burst of white light in the spirit and the foul thing shrieked one time and was vanished.

Eva focused once more on Claris, who seemed to lack any awareness of what raged around her. "What will you do next?"

"I know not, only that I possess an unshakable awareness change approaches," spoke her mentor. "I am unsure of my own preparation. I am also unsure I have knowledge to lead you farther, for I think you are fully weaned. You may not tarry much longer in our little community, and for that matter, I may not either." Claris reclined as much as the chair would allow, straightened her arms, and placed both hands on the table palms down. "Though I have been unsure what I shall do next. And yet, now, I know what I need do."

As Eva opened her mouth to give reply, Pietro entered the room engaged in animated conversation with a man in priestly vestments, hair and eyes black as night. A handsome man, with looks not unlike... not unlike whom? The man ceased conversing when he locked eyes with Eva. His gait saw increase, his gaze upon her unwavering. Eva's lips drew closed

When the two reached the table, Pietro spoke first. "Eva, here is the man I spoke of. You've seen him before, but not since you were weaned from your mother's breast." Eva rose instinctively. More weaning.

The new arrival's voice flushed with the breathless excitement of one who has journeyed a great distance to deliver a message of utmost import. "Your mother, Eva, was my sister, Lydia. My heart, I am your uncle, Raphael."

Eva was nonplussed. Raphael. The name held no meaning. "What else do I not know?" She loosed the words from her throat before thought. Eva stepped back and looked at him askance. Yet the shape of his mouth, the slender, straight cut of his nose, the spacing of his dark brown eyes was identical to her mother. "Forgive me." She spoke slowly, deliberately. "I knew not that Lydia had a brother, and I an uncle. I... do... see her look in you."

Raphael smiled and placed a firm hand on her shoulder, much the same way her mother had at unsure moments. "My sister would have concealed much from you, Eva, for your protection, to discover such things yourself when the time was full, for that was her way." He smiled, his look the fierce, certain gaze of the unhesitant. "Never have I known a woman as single-minded and unselfish as your mother. Our parents, your grandparents, were not so caring as she, and being several years my senior, Lydia watched over me, softened life's blow until I entered training for the priesthood. A compassionate woman she was, and she has done well by you, I see." He rubbed his hands across eye and cheek in a motion that bespoke weariness. "It grieves me to hear of her passing. I have heard nothing from her for these seventeen years past. As Pietro has sought you, so have I searched for Lydia and her daughter. And yet, in the brief time we have spoken this day, my friend the bishop could not stop his boasting of you, Eva. The life of my sister is renewed in you, and my heart is gladdened."

Eva knew not what to say. She smiled a brief smile, glanced at ceiling and floor.

Pietro looked pleased, but fidgeted with his hands. "Come, let us sit, ere we draw an excess of scrutiny upon ourselves."

Some of the patrons had sent only blank looks in their direction. No nods of recognition, and nary a sign anyone here has comprehension of proper Latin.

They all took their places at table, Raphael between Eva and Pietro. They commanded a view of the doorway and the whole of the room. Eva looked upon Raphael and shook her head. Who else lingers in other lands that knows of her and she not of them?

As they settled into their chairs, Renart, the proprietor, returned with a large flagon of Toulousain wine as promised, followed closely by three serving boys bearing a bowl of fruit, a small wheel of cheese, trenchers of roast lamb and venison, bowls of *cassoulet,* and fresh baked bread. Setting drink and nourishment skillfully and unobtrusively before the clergy and Beguines, the four left as quickly as they had come.

"Wonderful." Eva leaned back in her chair and reached for the ceiling. For the first time in a fortnight, she felt at ease. "I could not have dreamed up a finer choice for food."

Pietro broke bread and said grace. "I informed Renart in advance of our coming, and set the menu."

To the bishop, Raphael said, "We need to speak of Beziers."

Pietro nodded. "I hear tell the city comes under siege."

Raphael shook his head emphatically. "The siege began and ended on the selfsame day. The city was sacked."

Eva's stomach soured as she tasted her first bite of savory *cassoulet.* "What?" Had black liquid death already been loosed?

Raphael placed his hands palms down on the table of pear wood and leaned forward. "The people of the Languedoc speak of it already as the *gran mazel*, which in Occitan is *the great butchery*. Truly a great darkness moves through the South, this I know."

Pietro looked at Raphael. "Speak plainly of what you mean."

Eva spoke up. "So the *Frances* took the city and slaughtered many of the *Bitterois*? It is as I have feared then."

Raphael turned his matter-of-fact look upon Eva just as her mother had ever done. "I fear it is much worse, dear Eva. All in Beziers were slain and the city burnt."

Claris spoke a word, a name. "Catorna."

Raphael turned to Eva's mentor with a knowing look of care. "A friend that was of Beziers."

Claris nodded. "She was a *Valdenses*, and many of the *Bons Hommes* she led to become believers of the true *Jhesu* and secret friends of *Vaudes*."

Eva grasped hard the hand of her mentor.

Raphael paused for a moment. "I too, knew good ministers

of the gospel there. Good friends, good priests, good men who took seriously the care of souls. Who would not abandon the *Bitterois* as I hear their bishop so eagerly did. And truly abandoned the *Bitterois* were. After the butchery, the French abandoned the city itself, bothering not to leave even the semblance of a garrison there. It has become as the Scriptures say a *haunt for jackals.* I saw but one other living soul within the walls. A man who had made journey from Montpellier to bury the remains of his sister's family. I helped him carry the last of the charred skeletons outside the city walls for burial. He would not speak his name and let me help only when he found I spoke Occitan and was from Toulouse.

After the burial, I walked the city desolate and it has haunted my dreams and crowded my waking thoughts ever since. It was said that Armand Amaury, the papal legate leading the French army, requested that two-hundred twenty-two heretics be surrendered to the Crusaders. That very number has been lodged in my mind ever since. It causes me to have remembrance of six-hundred sixty-six in the Revelation of St. John the Divine. I cannot purge the thought that two-hundred twenty-two is one-third of six-hundred sixty-six."

Pietro watched Renart the proprietor bustling about as he served a meal. "Joachim di Fiore and his followers in Lombardy, whom I admire greatly, believe antichrist will come by the year 1260, but one and fifty years hence."

Raphael nodded. "Mayhap the immolation of Beziers is a sign of the coming of the man of sin." Her uncle was a prober, a problem solver like her mother and like Claris. Yet the coming of antichrist in this very century? A book on Eva's shelf: *On the Timing and Origin of the Antichrist* by Adso.

Raphael looked upon his niece. "I am sorry, Eva, to plunge so quickly into the matter before us." He took both her hands. "The daughter of Lydia lives. I had scarce held to hope. As radiant as your *maire,* and you a Beguine with choices to make of your future. A blessing. Yes, a great blessing." His face became drawn, as if pondering deep thoughts. He released her hands. "Have you the spiritual sight of your father?" Like her mother, Raphael drove hard to the foundation of the matter.

Eva smiled shyly and shifted her weight in her chair. "Well

Uncle, I seem to have been given what some call discernment and others call words of knowledge. I am unsure myself whether it be blessing or curse. Indeed, I had a vision after compline on the feast day of the Magdalen of a city aflame that was claimed by the darkness. I told it to Pietro and Claris, and we think it may have been Beziers." Claris smiled and nodded. Eva ever took heart from her mentor. "Is the city atop a hill, reached by an arched bridge of stone over a river that lies to the west?"

Raphael was clearly impressed. "Yes, the city is atop a hill up the bank from the River Orb, which is spanned by a bridge such as you describe. You hardly spoke even sentences when last I saw you, and now you speak of visions of the Spirit. You had the vision mere hours after the rout. The sack of Beziers was on the feast day of the Magdalen."

Pietro and Eva made eye contact at the mention of the feast day.

"I said all were killed in the city, but the story making the rounds of the inns and taverns is that one soul escaped massacre, the *châtelain* of the Viscount of Carcassonne, Albi, and Beziers. He has been called, strangely enough, the hero of Beziers, yet the name is true. It is said that after all was lost, he fought off a score of men to escape to Carcassonne and warn his Viscount days before the Northern army even withdrew from Beziers."

Eva saw a cavalier without surcoat wielding his sword in the wood against a single foe, then again with surcoat in a tent richly furnished as many more knights descended upon him. What would become of this man? It was the same cavalier she had seen in the ethereal while walking through her orchard a fortnight past. His surcoat bore a *seme fleur de lis*. Was this the *châtelain*, the hero of Beziers? She glimpsed him only from behind, seeing not his face.

Claris was astonished. "Truly my work here is finished, Eva."

Raphael reached into a pocket. "I do not believe the work of anyone here is finished. I have an item I am compelled to show."

Raphael removed a white, luminescent object, square in shape. As he turned it slowly so they could all examine it, it seemed to Eva to change color at every angle, from blue to green to purple to white and back to blue once more, like the handles of the platter or the arrow rest of her bow. It was *maire de per-*

la. The delicately carved symbols themselves seemed to change shape depending on the point of vantage.

Even illuminated only by beeswax candles, the carved piece held a polished luster that spoke as much of constant handling as fine craftsmanship.

It made Eva think of the little blue peas. "From where did you obtain such a piece?"

"I walked the abandoned city of Beziers, even through the ruins of the Church of the Magdalen. Though almost in a daze, I had felt compelled to search for some item, some personalized token that had survived the holocaust I saw all around me. I saw a few rings that had melted and fused to a finger bone, but nothing else that exuded even a hint of what I sought.

"Though I attempted not to disturb any corpses, I kicked by accident a blackened arm as I stepped over a body and, as I did so, a flash of light pierced my eye. I wondered what could remain in this funeral pyre I saw that would still give back the brilliance of the sun.

"Bending down, I locked eyes on this object. Why it was not melted or damaged in some way, I do not know.

"It has symbols I do not recognize and a script I cannot fully comprehend, twelve letters etched into spherical indentations. If a word it looks to be Occitan, but a strange vernacular, perhaps a dialect of the mountains of the High Languedoc."

Eva leaned in closer. "Twelve letters you say?" She reached into her satchel and removed the woolen scarf. Untying it she picked up one of the bits of cloth and unbound it. Raphael quieted his breathing when Eva lifted the little blue pearl. "Is one of the letters an M?"

Raphael did not speak but merely pointed at one of the spherical indentations which bore the selfsame letter at the bottom.

Eva placed the blue sphere at the spot and it fit snugly in place. "I have eleven more of these. They are from the spoils of war I have from the retaking of Acre. Pietro had them shipped to me. In truth, I have thought my Beautiful Things a poor substitute for a living *paire*, and have had little regard for them until now. I think my *paire* wished me to have these little blue peas as I call them, along with all else in my trunk. I think he has given me charge of discerning a mystery."

Eva untied another scrap of cloth. "This one is inscribed with a P." She set it in an indentation marked with such a letter. "I have a little blue pea with a letter that matches each letter on your square of *maire de perla*." She proceeded to unwrap each one until the little stones were arranged in corresponding indentations in the shape of the equilateral triangle. It caused her to think of Pythagoras. What has a Greek philosopher to do with triangles?

Raphael moved his finger in such a triangular shape round the little blue peas. "I call it Providence unbound. If the word starts at the top here and goes clockwise, which I believe it to do, ending here, it is *Melimarperla*."

Eva squinted, strained to read all the letters at once. "I see that it is *Melimarperla*. Yet when you speak it aloud, it sounds like *Melimarpera*, ending with pear the fruit."

Raphael shook his head. "No, not pear the fruit, but *perla* the jewel, *Melimarperla*."

"I comprehend, uncle." Eva smiled. "Yet could it be both? Perhaps *pera* is contained within *perla*."

CHAPTER 29

5 AUGUST 1209

The beast advanced. It rumbled toward the wall, dripping blood. It was broad and long yet moved as if it had no contact with the ground. A blackish-red trail coated the grass in its wake. The beast was made by the hands of men, but to Andreas it looked alive, as if it would at any moment snarl, exhale fire, and hurl itself across the field of battle.

"Flame your arrows!" Andreas dipped the pitch-coated tip of his bolt in the pot of fire at his feet, raised himself, and took aim. The cadre of archers, armored in leather, lining the allure of the stone wall, followed in turn. "Loose!" Streaks of orange and red rippled and pierced the already heated air, plunged themselves into the skin of the beast that drew ever nearer. The beast was a cat, clothed with the bleeding oozing skin of newly slain life.

"Destroy it! Loose at will!"

Quarrel after quarrel impaled the sodden hides. The skins were turned inside out so the beast was coated in the fat that lies just under the hide. The flames fizzled and released smoke and the redolence of charred meat. Little grayish-white clouds rose up, quickly dissipated like the defender's prospect of slaying the beast before it reached the ramparts. The hides were flayed from the carcasses of cloven-hoofed beasts, freshly slaughtered cow and bull, horse and donkey, mayhap even doe and stag. The singular purpose of the wet, bloody hides was to extinguish arrows aflame. They were nailed overlapping one another to the timber frame of the cat.

The siege machine lumbered ever closer.

Andreas flamed another bolt, drew, and loosed. The arrow struck the beast where its head should be, but the cat recoiled not. It was called a cat because such siege machines often had a mechanical arm with a metal-tipped claw that extended out the front and was used for scraping holes in fortifications.

This cat that rolled ever closer to *San Miquel*, the suburb nearest Carcassonne, lacked such an arm or even a battering ram or trebuchet affixed on top. Its purpose was likely to give protection to sappers who would seek to tunnel under and destroy some portion of the ramparts.

It seemed only to gather speed as it moved toward the wall of *San Miquel*. It was the last stronghold to contest before the siege turned to *la cite* itself.

The suburb nearest the River Aude, *San Vicens*, with its precious wells, had already fallen. It had only earthen ramparts and had been easily overrun by the French.

Andreas's recoiling at the violation of dead animal flesh brought surprise, shot through with a vague sense of guilt. He had watched the brutes being slain by the French, flayed for their pelts. Andreas had seen men enter the back of the rectangular beast and the thing had begun to move forward. The pushers and wheels were hidden within.

He felt his mind sliding into a bottomless mire and longed for Bertran and Aimer to stand at each side. Bertran to clear the confusion and Aimer to rally the battle cry.

The thought of migrating souls banished from the creatures slain for their fluid soaked hides, sentenced to dry wanderings in the void, left Andreas frozen with a nocked arrow for some moments. The guilt seeping through his own soul coalesced and gathered force like a murder of ravens adding numbers and noise as they flew. As if the blame of the slaughter of animals and the release of the souls bound therein could by all rights be laid squarely at his own feet, shod in boots of leather, the making of which had released another soul into the void. Archers to his right and left armored in leather from more slain beasts, more released souls. Would such souls now seek residence in a human host, to enter the womb only to be born once more, imprisoned in a higher form of life, but trapped in a *gaol* nonetheless? The thought plunged deep into his mind like a flaming brand: flaying is as dismemberment.

A hand on his shoulder, a voice in his ear. "Andreas, focus your mind! Loose your arrow, we are at war!" It was Raimon Roger. He grasped Andreas's jaw, turned his head, and looked him in the eye. Raimon Roger looked upon Andreas closely, probingly. He seemed to be unsure whom he saw. "My friend, your soul does not seem whole."

Restlessly Andreas left the released souls to their own fate. He loosed his flamed arrow upon the cat. Though the burning was quenched upon impact, one of the hides shifted, left bare wood exposed to sunlight and the sighting of the defenders.

Raimon Roger waved his arms and pointed. "There is a spot laid bare near its left hindquarters! Fire!"

Arrows arched and plunged and struck wood, burying burning iron tips deep in the bare plank. The cat rolled/floated across the filled section of the moat and slammed into the sandstone curtain wall of *San Miquel*, a shuddering of bloody hide-clad wood against stone, exposing further the bare spot as the pelts shifted. More quarrels aflame found their mark. The wood was wet and released steam in loud short bursts. Fire took hold, sodden wood burning, hides throwing out sounds of sizzling and popping, smoke rising, the wood aflame under the dripping pelts, the stink of charred hide and hair roughly overrunning the nostrils of those upon the ramparts. Eyes and noses watered from the stench. Sounds of crunching earth filled the ears, the bite of a shovel penetrating ground, the clinking of pickaxe on rock intensified.

The contest was on between flame and sapper.

The fire had gathered life and strength to the point where even the gore of the hides was evaporating before the hungry flames. A thick column of billowing gray smoke arose and broadened itself, partially blocking the view of the enemy massed across the field from *San Miquel*. More arrows flew from the walls to the cat lodged against sandstone below, more clinking of pick in soil and rock as fires burned wood that covered sappers, consuming hides, blackening the siege machine, but still it held.

Amidst the ascending plumes of smoke, Andreas thought he saw spirits of men and women writhing upon the air. As if each cloud of smoke split open and released a toga-clad body without substance, thousands of openings, thousands of smoke bursts clothed in whitish Greek raiment moaning. Their piteous cries drowned out all else. They were the spirits expelled into the void from the dead of Beziers. He could see it, but how? Their voices arose with but one word, besieging him, assaulting from all angles. "Andreas! Andreas!"

The ethereal beings assaulted the air wildly as if it had substance, heaving and clutching, seeking a thing to grasp onto. They loosed their lips and spoke in chorus. "We are released from our hosts. Guide us home Andreas, to where do we journey? Send us not into goat or pig, give us human bodies that we might become perfect. *Dismemberment.* Help us and you shall find redemption from your sacrilege of dismemberment."

A dull pain sharpening climbed rapidly the sides of his neck and ringed his temples and eye pits. He spoke out in loud voice. "What do you want of me?" Andreas's voice had erupted to a hoarse shout and drew a sharp glance from Raimon Roger.

The moaning upon the air sharpened to screams, discordant and high-pitched, like long slender needles piercing his ears and the whole of his skull. "Andreas! Andreas! Andreas!" None around him seemed to have any awareness of the chorus of shrill voices upon the air.

The *châtelain* shook his head, rubbed his eyes, nocked another quarrel, flamed it, and loosed. But the voices lingered, intensified, unrelenting. He knew at that moment that as long as he battled, as long as he consumed meat, drank wine, or sought after women, he would know only torment. Yet he had been bidden to fight until the Battle for Carcassonne was no more, so fight he would, though it anguish him.

In a great creaking, crunching sound, the cat below him seemed to quiver from fore to aft, and the rear heaved and collapsed, seeming to propel the flames forward to the front of the charred beast, advancing on the sappers throwing out sounds of digging ever increasing. Men fled from under the cat, some aflame, most who made egress from the deadly trap were pierced and set alight, if not already burning. One scrambled away and fell in retreat, as if with a broken ankle. A knight rushed forth from the French line, a lord, appearing to be the selfsame one Andreas had witnessed across the River Orb in Beziers seeking counsel from Armand Amaury as Beziers was overrun. De Montfort was his name. The Earl of Leicester. Andreas took aim and released the arrow and it whistled past the ear of the French cavalier. His foeman never once presented a stationary target, never ceased his zigging and zagging, but for a moment to hoist his comrade with broken ankle upon his shoulder and haul him away. Arrows fell at the feet of De Montfort, and he carried Andreas's admiration back to the French lines along with the wounded soldier. A foeman of worth.

A shower of sparks arose as the cat crackled and groaned and fell to the earth entire. Once the sound of falling wood ceased to rend the air, the scraping and pounding of digging tools rose once more. The sappers had hewn out their hole and placed themselves completely underneath the wall.

The rippling of the air seemed to reverse itself as all disembodied souls within sighting were drawn back into the slits upon the air and vanished. Andreas's torment diminished greatly, though it did not abate entire.

The *châtelain* returned his thoughts to the sappers below. If only Raimon Roger had obtained Greek Fire as Andreas had requested, a substance not quenched by water but ignited by it, then they would have had means to torch the cat unrelenting before ever it reached the ramparts.

"Andreas, to me!"

The *châtelain* looked down and saw Raimon Roger on horse with about three-hundred knights behind him, all on horse. Andreas shook his head, threw off his stupor, and descended the stair to his lord.

Raimon Roger listened to the sounds of digging for a moment. "The suburb has been cleared of all inhabitants. All of *San Vicens* is now in *la cite*. What of the sappers?"

"They have not yet completed their digging. We can hear the clinking of the pick axes from the top of the wall. We can attack them, my lord, and slay them all. The camp of *los Frances* is too far away to launch a counterattack."

Raimon Roger shook his head. "I had their full position scouted. They are massed in the woods near the river. If we open the gates, they can reach us in less than a minute. We know not how many French soldiers are under the wall with the sappers. No, we shall wait until the wall falls, let them charge over the rubble. The archers will loose, then we will sweep in and attack with a charge of cavaliers."

"Then we shall fall back to *la cite* as well?"

"Yes, we shall allow them *San Miquel*, but they will pay dearly for it."

⁂

The sounds of shovel and pick axe striking rock ceased, replaced by the sounds of nails being driven into wood. The sappers were building a wooden structure to support the weight of the walls above. The sound of nailing turned to digging once more. With the temporary structure in place, the sappers would dig until the full weight of the wall rested upon the wooden beams. Then there would be fire that would burn until both beams and stones collapsed. Raimon Roger charged his *châtelain* with guessing where the edges of the wall collapse would be and placing archers at both of those points. Andreas did so, stationing ten archers at each point, and then descending the wall to join Raimon Roger below as the smoke began to rise from beneath the wall.

The sappers fled. The archers upon the wall loosed. Andreas presumed some of the sappers were struck down while others escaped. He did not care to watch. Though the air had been cleansed of anguished souls, and the torment had lessened, a smoldering fire lingered in his brain.

Once the fighting ceased, Andreas could seek his solitude, for he was growing weary of warfare.

⁂

Sound preceded visible movement as the walls began to sag. Andreas, with one-hundred fifty mounted cavaliers behind him on a street hidden from the view of the wall, could see the ramparts through a gap between two houses. Stone rubbed then grinded against stone, beams snapped. The movement of the wall stopped but for a moment, then it dropped. A section some twenty feet wide seemed to be devoured by the earth. The archers on either side atop the walls loosed arrows, the French loosed their battle cries and charged across the jumble of stone. Through the gap Andreas could see them stop when they met no opposition. They started to fan out through the streets near the wall. Andreas heard one yell in *du Langue d'oil* that the cowards had fled the suburb.

Raimon Roger gave a shout, Andreas followed, and both wings of cavalry swept toward the enemy in a pincer movement. Hemmed in by horseflesh and houses, the French looked to retreat. But they were surrounded and all were cut down before French reinforcement could arrive. The *Carcassonais* had evened the odds for the assault to come on *la cite*.

CHAPTER 30

9 AUGUST 1209

An unformed thought had lain in the back of Eva's mind since the little blue peas were placed in the lid of *maire de perla* one week past. "My little *pera*." Eva pushed back her chair hewn of pear wood, jumped to her feet, swung her arms wide, nearly elbowing Pietro in the nose. "My little *pera*!"

Pietro, Raphael, and Claris gave only blank looks in return.

Eva calmed herself and pushed back the hair she had flung over her face. "Lydia, my *maire,* your sister, Raphael, called me her little *pera*. I thought it only a term of endearment, and indeed it was. But it was more, it *is* more. I know it to be so. She knew more than ever she told me in straightforward fashion. I know not how, but she knew. I must think on all else she spoke to me." She started to pace. The others followed her with their eyes, their faces a look of bemusement and bewilderment.

It was late afternoon. They were alone in the dining room of the Inn of Renart, Eva, Raphael, Pietro, and Claris. Renart and his serving boys were in the cellar and no other guests were in the Inn at the moment, even in the rooms upstairs. It was as if Renart had cleared the Inn on their behalf.

Eva leaned forward and spoke quickly. "How did my *maire* know to leave Siena with me so suddenly all those years past? Never did she speak of it." The questions had bobbed amongst the flotsam in the back of her mind these past weeks, but never found anchor until this day. "Why did my *maire* leave Siena, and why come to Orange? At the provoking of what? At the behest of whom? Had something in the letter or among the Beautiful Things caused her such alarum she departed without giving word even to her very brother? For I myself now know of the potency of the danger. But I know of it from the Bishop of Siena. I have a messenger."

Raphael shook his head and glanced heavenward. "Ah, now we come to it. Though we eventually heard from others returning from Outremer that Anselme perished in battle, many a night have I lain awake, wide eyes taking in the look of the timbers of my ceiling, wondering the same about my sister, wondering if I missed some hint, some clue as to where she had gone, unknowing if Lydia or my niece even tarried among the living." He clutched her shoulder in a grasp of warmth. "Though my sister is no longer among the living, my joy is renewed each time I look upon you, Eva. Whatever troubles await, there is hope." His voice grew soft. "There is ever hope."

Raphael picked up the pearl etched with the letter *P,* focused his intense hazel eyes upon it, held it between two fingers, and gave measured pressure. It was as if he intended to squeeze out the meaning, release all knowledge that eluded. As if he would have it flow blue and rich and shimmering like crushed lapis lazuli mixed with oils. Lapis lazuli, blue jewels come from Italy, from whence Eva had once come.

She thought of the Painter and the care he took in grinding the lapis lazuli to powder, in mixing and applying the precious blue paint, his satisfaction at seeing it perfectly adorn vellum or wood. The creator of such artistry would be making journey to Avignon but two days hence for the meet in *la cathedrale Notre Dame de Doms.* Though rarely did the Painter apply shimmering azure in such vaulted spaces. Brighter, bolder, more festive colors, like red from cinnabar, were called for to catch the echoes of stained glass at the hours of prime and vespers.

But her time since Sabbath past had been spent with the

uncle who had lived unawares and sought her unceasingly. The reality of having so many search for her, some seeking ardently her good, others craving fastidiously her peril, seeking to rob her of treasure and breath—while she lived in ignorance a much simpler life, at least in the natural, tending pears and carving wood, entered her mind like a cloud unbidden. It muddled her thoughts until she felt weak. Her skin tingled and nerves pulsed with a thrill she did not enjoy. Her senses quickened in a way that made the gorge rise high in her throat and burn, as if gaining realization one was already in the air in an unbreakable free fall, plummeting toward stone pavement and could not recall when the plunge began.

Pietro looked across the room, eyes probing for an answer. "I cannot tell either why she left or why she made sojourn in Provence, yet she was prudent to do so." He smiled. "Perhaps she was given warning in a dream as Joseph was admonished to flee Bethlehem for Egypt with blessed *Iesu* and Mary. All I know is that, like the holy family in Bethlehem, if you and your *maire* had lingered in Siena, you would have been slain. Perhaps even on the Feast Day of the Magdalen like the scribe, and left for dead in the Piazza."

Eva scrunched her nose. "So we do not know why she fled, but regardless, why go to Orange from Lombardy?"

"Again, perhaps a dream or vision. A sunrise of orange for the city where you have residence?" He smiled, as did Eva. "I know not." He shrugged his shoulders.

Eva scrunched her nose. "I shall fast and pray and seek of *Deu* the answer." She looked again upon the box of *maire de perla*. "You found this at the church of the Magdalen in Beziers?"

Raphael looked up. "Near the choir."

Eva put her hand on the nape of her neck and rubbed the gathering soreness. "The scribe is slain on the feast day of the Magdalen as a sacrifice to Minerva. Beziers, an entire city, is put to the sword and offered up in fiery sacrifice also on the day of the Magdalen..."

Raphael swung his face toward her. "Fiery sacrifice. Why do you call it such?"

"My vision. In my vision *Deu* was weeping over a sacrifice that was laid smoldering upon the altar of another god. What if the feast day of the Magdalen is also the day of Minerva or perchance some other god, even more hidden?"

A hole with tattered edges seemed to carve itself out of the door of the Inn, and Eva saw again the cavalier in surcoat with *seme fleur de lis*. He walked quickly at night through a city, the same city she had witnessed in her vision, though unburnt, following a man in dark cloak clutching an object that reflected moonlight in bluish brilliance. The cloaked one approached a building in a plaza. A church. The doors to the structure opened, the ragged hole upon the air billowed out to embrace her, and Eva herself entered the church, feeling hot sun burn her uncowled head and the sharp poking of gravel beneath her unshod feet. The odor of the unwashed rose up and laid harsh siege to her sense of smell and the stench was her own.

Unseen claws like sharpened flint raked her body unrelenting from without and her turbulent soul like a hot brand from within. All was as razor cuts and deep burns and blood unseen. Thoughts flew through her brain like a hail of arrows aflame. A crowd was ahead, massed like bees round a hive, clumped tightly between the market stalls lining each side of the dusty street. She had witnessed such before, in vision, and from a greater distance. In the center of the gathering, a man in simple woven tunic spoke to the crowd, healed the sick, and they were delighted, ever lingering. None left, only more came. The pain in her head grew and provoked a gaseous, poisoned nausea in her belly. A word in her mind, as seven words, manifesting in a million echoes of provocation. "Flee." The heat of the burning sharply raised. Yet she stumbled forward, pushing into the throng, people recoiling at her presence. Why? Never had a soul thus backed away from her. She entered his sighting. Giving voice to the words proved arduous, suffocating. "Heal me... *rabboni*." Then other words emerged and she knew not what issued forth from her lips. The *Rabboni* spoke, her appendages flailed, and her torso spun even as she felt the taut battle for her soul. She lost all track of herself, as if her mind was immersed in a great mass of shooting stars. Shards, fragments black as soot, devourers of light, seemed to break from her spirit. She was fissuring like a rock driven through with spike and hammer, as if her very essence was somehow being rent asunder and yet cast to a place of restoration.

Hard and razor-edged, like a double-edged steel blade newly sharpened, the words of the *Rabboni* sliced through to sinew and bone. The very joints of limb and torso seemed to pull apart as if the rack was admirably performing its cruel work. She cried out in sharp pain and suffocating terror. Darkness closed her eyes like woolen draperies pulled shut. The back of her head ground into the gravel of the market street, as if sharpened pebbles pierced her skull, her brain. The fire of the sun ignited and exploded in her mind like a shattering of bright stained glass...

"Eva." It was Pietro.

She was in the Inn of Renart in Avignon, in August 1209, not in a dusty village somewhere, sometime past. Was that blessed *Jhesu* the healer? If that was deliverance from evil, it was a painful, fierce deliverance from a great evil.

Pietro looked to the entrance and then back to her. "You focus so upon the door. Does the answer lie under the lintel?"

"Perchance it might." She smiled, and shuddered, blinking away the ragged hole and the pain convulsing. There was more she need see. This was but a continuation of the vision that first came to her on the Feast Day of the Magdalen, and more there was yet to be revealed, she knew it. Another time the remainder would be revealed to her. For now, she wished to see no more, feel no more.

Raphael continued. "Are you asking if 22 July is the feast day not only of the Magdalen, but the celebration day of a pagan god, one worshipped through fiery sacrifice? Do I discern correctly your intent?"

Eva leaned back in her chair, exhausted, throwing her arms aside as if a rag doll. She had more than just witnessed a continuation of her vision of Beziers, she had lived it somehow. Her joints felt stretched and sore. Her hands went to her knees and rubbed at the ebbing pain. "That is quite what I mean. Is 22 July a day of veneration not of Maria Magdalen but of some other god?"

CHAPTER 31

14 AUGUST 1209

As the siege ladder was raised, Andreas sheathed his
sword. He waited until the rails of the stout wooden
ladder clacked against the crenellation of the curtain
wall. Andreas planted his feet shoulder-width apart,
lifted hard, and yanked the bottom from ground. Rung by rung,
he gripped each in turn and lifted the siege ladder. The French
cavalier below, standing upon the lowest rung, was hurled away
from the wall in a backward diving arc, arms flapping wildly
like a mortally wounded bird, upended onto his back as Andreas
pulled the ladder up and over the north curtain wall of Carcassonne.

Hoisting the ladder over his head, the *châtelain* raised his
voice. "Hear me now, desecrators of Beziers, slayers of babes
and women great with child; you will not spatter Carcassonne
with blood!" He loosed a roar as he turned the ladder parallel
with the wall, scraped it wood on stone against the *Tor Samson*, hurled it towards an empty section of the street in *la cite*
below. Striking the cobbles, it cracked in two upon impact, and
the pieces bounced in different overlapping directions, forming
a *T* in the street, with the smaller piece falling upon the larger.

Andreas stared at it, immobilized, as the fight raged around him, as if the broken thing had ricocheted back and struck him a deep bruising blow in the cheek. The thought floated through his mind. *"Never mind that it formed a cross upon striking the cobbles, return to battle Andreas."*

The Northerners near the foot of the *Tor* were stricken motionless by the complete removal of their vertical route into the city. Siege ladders were generally pushed off the walls and not thieved by the besieged.

"Archers to me!" Andreas summoned four to his side and bid them loose at the *Frances* below. All who had once sought to climb the now broken ladder were pierced through. He saw Anfos push down another ladder and Andreas ran to him as a French cavalier made the allure of the wall from yet another climbing device left unguarded. Andreas blocked his blow while Anfos ran him through at the heart and sent him plunging and wailing to scorched earth below.

For over a week now had *la cite* itself been under siege. By day came attackers with ladders, and by night stones hurled against ancient walls by catapult and trebuchet. The ramparts had been unyielding, even as the garrison had repulsed every attempt to scale the walls. But the wells by the River Aude had been lost with the fall of *San Vicens* on the first day of the siege and the water within the cisterns of Carcassonne had fouled. Whether by pestilence or dark craft it was not known. Thirst had taken hold. Throats were not yet parched to the point where the swallowing of food was a bane without bearing. Some were already stricken with siege sickness and the bloody flux. The dead were hurled over the South Wall of *la cite* so the bodies would not bring more death.

Andreas looked down upon the French below and he saw everywhere the cross. As it was at Beziers, each man assaulting the walls had a scarlet cross sewn into his surcoat. The scorch marks of the burnt ground before him seemed to coalesce into the shape of a crucifix, then the silhouette of *Crist* faded until only the post and crossbeam remained.

Andreas blinked, squinted hard, shook his head to clear his mind, and grasped another ladder with three Frenchmen ascending the twenty-five foot high curtain wall. Taking the rails of the ladder, he shook it hard, but the French kept their grip, so he gave the ladder a kick and sent the cavaliers returning to scorched earth.

A rider on a white stallion emerged from the French encampment under banner of truce. Bearing no weaponry, he rode across the plain with all speed. Andreas admonished all upon the ramparts not to loose any bolts upon the lone rider. As he neared the wall he released his message. "Withdraw! There will be parley! Withdraw! There will be parley!" The French drew down the assault at once at the base of the ramparts of *la cite* and gathered ladders and weaponry and the Northern host peeled off its attack. They abandoned the assault and withdrew in good order for the sea of tents across the plain.

Andreas ordered those upon the wall, especially the archers, to draw down as well, to sheathe their war swords and stay their bows. As much as he wished to shoot the enemy in the back, it was against all training and rules of warfare. Andreas would hold to chivalrous codes even if the savage French would abandon their honor.

The battlefield was cleared of men in what seemed less than a minute, and for the first time in some days, it was quiet. The sun still shone in its wicked fierceness, the heat fouling the air, quickening the stench of siege. A voice in his mind. "It is almost over, Andreas. Soon you will leave this heat and make journey to the High Languedoc."

Andreas stood clutching his sword as he watched the retreat, wondering what would follow. Some defenders on the walls raised swords and a cry of hope, *"Paratge! Paratge!"* But Andreas remained silent, watching. Perchance the promise of parley was false and the French were preparing to unleash yet another siege machine like the cat they had used against *San Miquel*, or perhaps they had made preparation to offer terms. Perhaps. But only a fortnight had Carcassonne been under siege.

Some four centuries past, when Carcassonne had been held by the Saracens, Charlemagne had laid siege to the city for at least five years. Unable to take it, the great emperor had been forced to finally call off the attack. The story was legendary, like Charlemagne himself, and the French would have known of it, and known well how long Carcassonne, with even a skeleton of a garrison, could stave off the fiercest of assaults from thousands, even tens of thousands. Yet the French, from foot soldier to count, had pledged only quarantine, forty days of service, and the end line of their pledge drew nigh.

"Stay at your posts and at the ready." Andreas saw movement rising from between the pergolas. Pennons were raised and were moving toward them, rising and falling as if being held by horsed knights. The *châtelain* motioned for Anfos to draw near. The triangular flags drew closer for some moments until a cadre of some three dozen cavaliers emerged from the tents, increasing their pace to a gallop as they moved toward Carcassonne. They were approaching the Narbonne Gate. With neutral flags raised and led by a noblemen, they approached *la cite*. The troop halted at the bottom of the hill, while a single rider rode on to the gate.

Andreas beckoned to his new sergeant at arms. "Anfos, make haste for the gate I pray you, and see if the enemy truly has intent to parley with us."

Anfos nodded and descended the stair adjoining the interior of the wall. The *châtelain* grabbed another cavalier and bid him inform Trencavel of the riders at the gate. Andreas did not like the uncertain banner of peace he saw unfurling. He possessed doubt the French would extend any offer that did not leave them in control of Carcassonne. After Beziers and the slaughter wholesale and the desecration of sanctuary, could they be extended trust in any fashion? Yet clean water was scarce and hundreds had perished from siege sickness or writhed in its throes as they approached death's certain embrace. Parley might be their only hope.

The Oriental Gate opened and Raimon Roger rode out of the *Chateau Comtal* toward the Narbonne Gate. Raimon Roger approached the open gate, speaking with a Northern emissary through the portcullis for a very long minute. Raimon Roger gave a formal nod, wheeled his mount, and was met by Anfos, who bid him halt, and spoke with Raimon Roger, who kept gesturing toward the French encampment and in the direction of the *Chateau Comtal*. Anfos broke off from the Viscount, ran toward the curtain wall, and scrambled up the stair. The Viscount rode through the crowd toward the *Chateau Comtal*.

Andreas stood square upon the calmed battlements with arms folded across his breast. "Well. Out with it man."

Anfos halted to catch his breath. "Parley. Yes, it will be parley. They wish to treat with the lord of these lands." Anfos gulped in more air. "A relative of our Viscount awaits outside the city gate, down the hill. Of the *Frances* he is, a baron I think. Trencavel knows the man and has trust of him."

From atop the curtain wall, Andreas could see, down the hill, some fifty yards away, the unknown man who was known to Raimon Roger. The man noticed Andreas upon the wall and eyed him, a curious, knowing look. For but a moment, Andreas began to feel as if he were being pulled or pushed over the wall, much like Beziers when he had plunged off the ramparts into oil-soaked hay. With much effort, he righted himself. Though no good could spring from opposing his lord now, Andreas lacked Raimon Roger's trust of the man, mounted within a stone's throw of the *Tor Samson*. He wished he had on his person the sling he had removed from the dead knight in the wood, the knight he had dismembered.

Andreas frowned and his mouth puckered. "Is the man worthy of trust?" He knew when to question Raimon Roger and when to accept the judgment of his lord. At the moment, Andreas questioned.

Anfos shrugged. "I know not."

Andreas looked the unknown relative of his Viscount in the eye. "They offer hostages in return for the safe-conduct of our lord Viscount?"

Anfos nodded. "Yes, my *châtelain*. In addition to a grant of safe-conduct, hostages will be given. A son of a noblemen will be among them I am told. They are in the midst of the warband you see outside the walls. For his part, our lord pledges to organize one-hundred men on horse within the half-hour and commands your aid."

"It is given." Andreas began descending from the ramparts to the city below. "But vows of safe-conduct lessen not my concern about what awaits."

The cavalcade of five-score mounted knights gathered in the courtyard of the *Chateau Comtal*, a mass of weaponry, chain mail, horseflesh, and disquiet air. The men seemed not fearful but disturbed and unsure in a way in which they could not give voice, as if their spirits tremored slightly, but they knew not the reason. Andreas felt it keenly, spear points pressed against them all, though drawing no blood, piercing no flesh. It was as if Carcassonne would not suffer the fate of Beziers but another, the full manifesting of which lay beyond the realm of all sighting and hearing and knowing.

Robertz raised both portcullises of iron and opened the Oriental Gate as Andreas took his place beside Raimon Roger, who had donned his finest gilded surcoat and bore his ceremonial shield ringed in rock crystal. In but one half-hour, The Viscount of Carcassonne, Albi, and Beziers had raised a party fit to accompany any king or lord of the Church. Raimon Roger sat upon his *milsordor*, back straight and shoulders square. The fire no longer burned in his eyes. It had been quenched by a resolve much deeper; placid, bottomless pools of clear water that reflected peace without taint and a mind with but a single purpose. Never had Andreas seen his lord as dignified, as assured, with poise unwavering to rival any sovereign, any statesman, or field commander of old chiseled in marble or captured with colored oils on wood or parchment. Raimon Roger looked neither right nor left, but peered only through the open gate and nodded but once.

It was time.

Andreas unsheathed his sword and brandished it high. "Cavaliers of Trencavel, of Carcassonne, Albi, and Beziers, of the Languedoc, forward!"

Guilhem, the standard bearer, sallied forth, followed by Raimon Roger himself, then Andreas, then Anfos, trailed in single file by the remainder of the cadre. Once Guilhem and Raimon Roger crossed the wooden bridge and reached the *Plasa de Chateau*, it was as if they arrived at the shores of the Red Sea and there was a parting, not of water, but of a deluge of men, women, children, and beasts receding. Andreas needed to order no one aside. No child blocked their passage this day. A ripple moved through the thousands of *Carcassonais* and refugees gathered in the streets and a path opened to the Narbonne Gate as if all knew in their bowels the way of things.

The people were silent, but their lack of speech seemed more from a deep sense of wonder than trepidation. In this month of August, in the face of the *gran mazel* of Beziers and the besieging of his beloved Carcassonne, Raimon Roger had grown into the lord who now by his presence commanded every bit of respect and beyond that was demanded by his office. Whatever unknown battle was now to be waged, Raimon Roger would lead, firmly in command and with the admiration of all, a liege who was neither loathed nor lionized, but loved with a love that is of both silk and iron, of affection and will. As the standard bearer reached the Narbonne Gate and the cavalcade extended still to the *Chateau Comtal*, the keepers went to open the gate, and Raimon Roger halted them with a single gesture. Lifting high his jeweled sword, he loosed a word, not loudly at first, but with a firm, deep tone of voice. "*Paratge.*"

The tongues of Carcassonne lingered in silence even as looks of wonder softened to poignancy, the rich full coloring of the face that arises and tints flesh only from a deep stirring of the well of the heart.

Raimon Roger looked across the crowd as if seeking to lock eyes with all. He raised the sound of his voice. "*Paratge!*"

A few around him began to nod approvingly and look to others around them and mutter in agreement even as heads continued to nod, mutterings coalescing to the self-same word. That single expression of all that is free and good, all that is honorable, and that is full of true light, all that stands against oppression.

Raimon Roger filled his lungs to the full and emptied them to the whole of the city. "*Paratge!*"

The word broadened its path through the crowd and claimed more throats and tongues, ever moving, increasing its pace through the throngs flanking the cavalcade, reaching the *Plasa de Chateau*. "*Paratge!*" It seemed to shake the cavaliers from their silence that had remained as the crowd spoke the word. Reaching the rear of the formation it wheeled about and inhabited the throat of the lowliest knight among them, a bolt on a string pulled back with all tension in that sweet moment before release with all power. The word shot forward and inhabited the voices of the cavaliers who exhaled it in tones of thunder increasing. "*Paratge!*" Becoming one with the rumbling of the crowd. The city spoke with one voice of defiance, a voice that surely reached the French encampment and beyond. Hot and full of thirst as they were, their throats were hearty and strong as the word gave them voice. "*Paratge!*" It was an anthem, a hymn, a standard of defiance in seven letters. Seven! Completeness itself. What more dare one say? "*Paratge!*" The arrow shot through Andreas, drawing the word from his lips in spite of the pain that rushed his head and gut, a cry of all they held close.

In the exultant din, Andreas heard a whoosh that seemed released from the ethereal and loosed into the realm of matter. There was a light shone round Raimon Roger, and it was not of the sun, not the glinting of shield or armor. The lights swirled round the raised sword of the Viscount, a maddening, celestial dash, somehow amplifying the word, taking it into itself and releasing it with still more power. "*Paratge!*" Raimon Roger's voice rose above the crowd. His face took on a golden glow, the look in his eyes ever more peaceful. He uttered not *Paratge* again, there was no need. He had loosed the flame, the light, in the hearts of his people.

The swirling points of luminescence hurled themselves over the walls as if slung from David's sling. Lowering his warsword, Raimon Roger motioned for the gates to be opened and portcullises raised, and they were, with a smart, savage efficiency Andreas had never heretofore witnessed. The portcullises seemed to fly into the hollows of the massive double tower as if caught up to the heavens.

There was a moment when all seemed held in place without motion, as if *la cite* itself teetered on a fulcrum in perfect balance. All in Carcassonne seemed to strain toward the Narbonne Gate. Raimon Roger had mastered the rule of his people and he held fully their hearts to command. It was as if Raimon Roger had but to give the word, not "*Paratge!*" but "Attack!" and all within the ancient walls would have stormed the field of battle and charged with fury unbridled the French encampment.

Having grasped that true power, Raimon Roger dropped it lightly, as down feathers drifting toward ground, and he rode out through the open gate as Andreas followed, drawing the line of cavaliers behind him. They moved at a proud, solemn trot, horse's hooves clicking smartly on stone streets in precise, ceremonial rhythm.

The shouting of enlightened freedom gradually ceased as cheers issued forth. Cheers at first as in a tournament for the champion, then cheers as hailing the return of a conqueror. Raimon Roger was fully drawn to his people, and they knew he departed strong gates to wage a fight on their behalf.

CHAPTER 32

14 AUGUST 1209

Raphael and Pietro left the river's edge to return to the Inn of Renart to prepare for their journeys west to Toulouse and east to Siena. Each day in Avignon had they gone down to the River. Eva and Claris lingered by the great waterway of Provence. Eva loved the Rhône and Avignon was truly a city of the River. Where the bridge crossed they seemed as one, inseparable. So unlike people, who seemed ever parted or separating from one another. The unwalled city seemed to rise from the River with its shipping piers and graceful quay and splay up and over the eastern rise of the hillside. An orderly fleet of tall, sailless, rectangular boats ever at anchor upon an urban slope. It was as if the Rhône had purposefully spilled its spring floodwaters toward the rising sun and deposited not silt but a dense mass of buildings, and these in turn gave homage to and drew life from the river.

Like Avignon itself, the river was a gathering point for the lands around her, a gathering of water that had fallen upon the land, a gathering of rainwater into the streams and tributaries that fed the Rhône from much of the Languedoc and Provence. Eva thought of the words of King Solomon concerning the flow of a river:

All the rivers flow into the sea,
Yet the sea is not full.
To the place where the rivers flow,
There they flow again.

At times when she had felt scattered, in need of gathering together once more remnants of her inner life that flowed through a soul never completely full, she had ever looked upon the broad flow of the Rhône making its way to the Mediterranean Sea. As she gazed, her innermost would know restoration for a time.

But the River gave no succor this day, nor did Avignon, its inland port.

She looked up at the city from the quay of the river toward the *Notre Dame de Doms.* "Claris, walk with me to *la cathedrale.* I wish to see the choir and sacristy." The cathedral was another place that could bring revival of spirit and she felt troubled this day. Like Avignon, the city rising from the river, it also pointed east, toward the rising sun, toward light daily renewed.

Claris had been looking upon the high church of Avignon, not the flow of the river. "I shall be delighted. I have more to tell."

Eva turned away from the river so intricately woven into their lives, and they started up the hill. They trod alongside the arches of the bridge as it merged into the city slope, toward *la cathedrale Notre Dame de Doms.* Eva wanted to see anew the choir in *la cathedrale* that would be adorned by her carvings. They turned onto the street of the jewelers.

Eva noticed a particularly large house, a triple-story mansion on the left that rippled into her an involuntarily shudder. In the lintel over the door was carved a hammer, chisel, and saw. Within there were shadows, hidden, elusive, above and below ground, a deep rumbling evil. She could not discern the names. The stone and timber mansion outwardly had nothing to mark it as a haven of wickedness, yet dark potency lay inside, uncommon ethereal might. As if the Tarasque, the beast of the Rhône, made residence there after claiming its prey. As if the cellar was but an underground canal of the Rhône. Things hard to discern had occurred within to give place to such evil. The demon vanquished from Claris had been easy to see by comparison. It was also a house with façade under repair, the front crowded with wooden scaffolds and ropes and pulleys and piles of cut masonry. Some of it looked to be balanced precariously. Two masons stood upon the wooden scaffolds, setting the stones into place with a mortar of lime, sand, and water.

Eva turned back to her mentor. "You spoke of a thing you must do, a charge that you had felt hindered from fulfilling. I pray tell me more."

Claris stopped. "Did I say I was hindered?" The honest confusion on her face was endearing.

Eva hesitated. "No... no you did not. But I sensed you were hindered."

"Ever are you discerning." Claris smiled. "Regardless, I am hindered no more. Eva, as I told you, I think I might move residence to Orange itself, take my leave from the community. Yet there is more to tell."

Eva shot her a quizzical look as they approached a street corner and Claris stumbled into a short, stocky man with black hair, broad shoulders, and muscled arms. The face of the man expressed delight, while burly arms encircled Claris, who reciprocated the embrace. Why did Claris hug a stranger? Eva's brain seemed to freeze and the effort to comprehend brought sharp pain to her head, and she closed her eyes as something like a wailing scream curled painfully through her mind. Eva's first response was to grab Claris's arm and seek to draw her down the street. Eva, not gleaning a clear look at the face of the man, noticed his hands were splotched with embedded color. Red from cinnabar and blue from lapis lazuli.

It was the Painter.

Eva went to embrace him when she realized fully that the clasp of friends encountering one another unawares should have ceased by now. She saw that the Painter held Claris in a way that was a little too tender, in the way of courtly romance and not friends in common cause. Eva was the common cause. It was she that had brought them together. But at this moment, the Painter did not even see her. His eyes looked only upon Claris, in obvious surprise and delight. The Painter gave Claris a quick kiss on the lips. Eva looked upon them both and scrunched her nose. Why was he in Avignon on this day? "Painter I... I thought you would arrive on the morrow."

"Eva." The Painter had noticed her for the first time. He looked awkward in his stance. "I completed my work a day early and sought to surprise you both."

Eva looked askance at them, stood apart from them. "Surely you have succeeded in that endeavor." For the first time, she started to feel separate. The circle that had encompassed them all now seemed reduced to a line drawn between only two. The Painter had encountered both her and Claris and had seen only Claris. She knew her eyes betrayed her thoughts.

Eva stepped back. All felt unbalanced and her ears echoed voices beyond counting. Words of betrayal. She turned to Claris. "You spoke of changes. Of leaving the community for Orange. I did not think you intended to enter the marriage bed." The words emerged before she thought on what she was saying. She had spoken too much, not given filter to the tempest in her heart. The Painter and Claris simply stood there in the street. They made no attempt to further conceal what had obviously been hidden for some time, at least from Eva. The fondness that had grown between them was not the sort of bond forged only in a day. Was that why the Painter had been so distant in Orange ere they left for Avignon?

Claris and the Painter. The two people she cared for most would surely abandon her for each other. It would be Claris, not Eva, plopped in the overstuffed chair in the studio. Claris, not Eva, in the wicker chair in the room of light. She knew it was wicked but could not help herself. The thoughts demanded center space in her mind, crowded all else out. She felt hurt, angry, lost.

Vaguely, the opposing thought echoed in her brain that such an idea was but a seed planted by malevolent hands. Perhaps the barren kernel had indeed taken root and she no longer cared. Her father had abandoned, her mother fled to eternity also. Raphael departed for Toulouse on the morrow, to the Languedoc, a land of war. Pietro would soon take his leave for Siena, and the towering Alps would be between them once more. Yet Eva realized that losing the Painter, even more than Claris, Raphael, or Pietro would be the thing she could not bear. She had known her mother until majority, but since her fourth summer the Painter had ever stood in the stead of her father.

"Eva. Eva." Claris had severed embrace and stepped away from the Painter. "That is what I was going to tell you. The Painter and I plan to be wed. Yes, yes. I do plan to enter the marriage bed. I wanted to tell you before he joined us in Avignon. We wish for you to carve a misericord for our wedding."

Eva shot Claris a questioning look.

The Painter held up color-etched palms in conciliation. It had ever calmed her spirit, but it would fail this day. "Eva, we will not..." But she cut him off, never gave him the chance to finish.

"Abandon me? Is that what you will not do?" She turned to Claris as a surge of anger unknown rose in her innermost. She felt a dark presence growing but cared not. "Have you... have you made violation of your vows as a Beguine? Have your penitents to which you give counsel led you astray?"

Claris, with a look of shock, was silent, too aghast to speak.

Eva continued, unabated. "It matters not. You will leave me alone in the community. Move residence to Marseille, Milan, Rome. Perhaps you will abandon me to live in the shadow of the Lateran Palace. I hear tell that Innocent III is ever searching for great painters to mural the halls and chambers. Surely there you would have no need of a woodcarver!"

Eva started stepping back toward the house on the street of the jewelers. Claris and the Painter followed.

"Eva!" The voice of a man called her name, but she saw him not. "Eva!"

The Painter sprang forward in alarm as Claris called out "Eva!" in turn. Claris was closer to her than the Painter. There was a rumbling, a sliding of stone upon stone. A sound of grunting. Eva saw quivering shadows. Claris lunged against her and pushed Eva into the street as a pile of masonry gave way, burying Claris in a cloud of limestone and dust as a stone struck Eva in the shoulder, knocking her to ground.

Eva heard a growl of disgust then the voice of the man again. "Remember this day, Eva." But she saw no one occupy the space from whence the stones had just fallen.

The Painter had already dived into the pile and was heaving masonry in every direction. Eva, her brain cleared enough to realize what had just happened, ran forward, and started removing what stones she could. Claris's chest and legs were bleeding and battered, her breathing uneven, shallow, but still she lived.

The masons, with expressions of horror, frozen momentarily, flew down the scaffolding and assisted the Painter and Eva in the removal of the stones.

Eva cradled the face of Claris in her hands. "I am sorry. I am so sorry. The blame for this is mine, solely mine."

The Painter removed the last of the stones. His strong hands were trembling, his voice soft and weak. "Let us take her to the Inn of Renart." The masons offered their assistance, but the Painter refused them, his words strengthened. "If you wish to help, search out who did this."

The source of the voice disappeared and spoke no more. Eva had heard the voice before. The masons, angry and bewildered, began in vain a frantic search for the toppler of their stones.

Claris groaned in pain.

The Painter lifted her in his stout arms and carried her gently. The Inn was not far. Claris did not bleed heavily, but drifted in and out of consciousness. Eva was amazed she remained among the living. Many stones had fallen on her, but Claris had been far enough away that none of it had come down upon her head. Surely this extraordinary woman still possessed a chance at life. She could not perish now.

Eva was a selfish girl who had only the look of a woman. The fault was hers alone. If Claris died and the Painter lost his love, never could she forgive herself.

Eva looked around for the man as they moved through alleyways and came to the Inn of Renart. She heard not the voice again. The proprietor stood under the lintel, holding open the door, as if he already knew of what had befallen Claris. "Bring her to my chamber. She can have my bed. I will send for my physician and for a priest."

"No! She is not dying. You shall do no such thing." Eva was ignored. The Painter disappeared into another room.

The priest and physician both arrived within a quarter-hour. The physician said she bled on the inside and that neither bleeding her vessels to the outside nor using leaches nor poultice of pear would avail Claris. She was in the hands of God. Only He could bind up her inner wounds and restore the humors in her body and make her whole. The priest, whom Eva recognized from the cathedral, hung back, as if he sensed that Claris's time would come shortly but had not yet come.

Both the priest and the physician would have had much exposure to death and gained recognition of its approach. Yet Eva refused to allow such belief. Claris could not be dying. Eva came to the bedside, forced herself there, and took the hand of Claris. Eva willed herself to smile. "I have complained of you poking and wounding my soul to bring healing, but now it is you who are truly wounded. I am so sorry, Claris. If I had not been so selfish, if we had just kept walking, none of this would have taken place."

Claris spoke with eyes still shut. "Eva, you do not know that." She groaned. "Do not torment yourself."

Eva looked up and the priest stood on the opposing side of the bed. She was tired. Veracity flowed into her mind through many small, newly opened inlets. She turned to the priest. "It is time?"

The priest only nodded, his face sober.

The Painter entered the room, eyes red and swollen and face red as well. He did not express sorrow well in front of others. His expression transformed back and forth between rage and tenderness like a rapid changing of the guard. He did not look upon Eva. He took the hand of Claris. "My heart, how you have gladdened my soul." Eva moved back. "You will live, do not lose hope."

Claris's eyes opened and her words were breathy, forced, and faint, her eyes seeing only the Painter. "Painter, you gave me hope I dared not imagine before. I dreamt of a family. It was a sweet dream. You must watch over Eva. Do not be bitter towards her. We all have a calling and mine ends here. Eva, come to me. I wish to speak a blessing over you." Eva slowly approached Claris and the Painter, who looked upon her for the first time since they brought Claris to the Inn. His look held wariness but not anger.

"Dearest Eva, you must not blame yourself. I am truly sorry we did not tell you sooner of our plans for marriage. I had planned to tell you when the Painter was to arrive on the morrow. We did not want you to think we were abandoning you, which was the very reason why we were hesitant to let you know of us."

The Painter took the hand of Eva. "We were wrong, I see that now, and have paid a grievous price." Eva had never seen tears upon his face before.

"No, my Painter, Claris will yet live."

Claris shook her head. "Eva, hearken to me. Fear not. You must have courage. *Deu* has given you a mighty calling, to see those in heavy shackles unbound from dark chains. May His peace ever guard your mind and heart. May you see His light shine out clear and strong, even in dark places. May you never be without a companion to lift you up when you stumble. May you never forget that I loved you. Never forget all that I have spoken to you these many years. I see now that you are the reason I became a Beguine."

Eva leaned forward. "I shall draw upon all your words. You are a sage, a fount of wisdom. I have ever needed to you to prod my soul. I need you still. We shall meet again."

Claris smiled. "I know. Farewell, Eva."

Eva embraced Claris then withdrew out of deference to the Painter.

"Now come to me, my Painter. Kiss me once more." The Painter cradled Claris's head in his hands and tenderly brought his lips against hers. Eva felt herself an interloper but could not flee the scene. She had never before witnessed such passion between two people. It was a holy moment.

Once the Painter released the kiss, Claris's breath began to fade. The priest sat at the bedside. He administered the sacraments, anointed Claris's head with oil, and heard final confession. The priest was heartfelt in word and deed, and neither rote nor ignorant.

The Painter grasped one hand and Eva the other.

Like soft rain falling to earth, Claris breathed her last and died.

CHAPTER 33

AUGUST 14, 1209

R aimon Roger bid them halt some thirty yards beyond the Narbonne Gate. The cheers and shouts of *"Paratge!"* could be heard soaring above the walls. The company waited under the hot sun as the remainder of the cavalcade made egress from the city. Once completely outside the ramparts, the formation compacted from a single file line to twenty rows of cavaliers, each row five abreast. Raimon Roger was foremost, in the center of the first row, Andreas on his right, and Anfos his left, with the other sergeants at arms flanking them. Many in *la cite* had already clambered upon the ramparts to see for themselves the parley. The curtain walls between ancient Roman towers were packed with a garrison armed with their tongues, and of these they did not cease to make use. *"Paratge!"* The cries grew louder as more and more reached the allure on either side of the *Tor Samson. "Paratge!"* If no other thing, the French would know this day that the spirit of the *Carcassonais*, indeed of the Languedoc itself, was undimmed.

The unknown relative of Raimon Roger bore a kindly smile. His cadre of one and one-half score cavaliers had faces of stone.

Their leader exercised no effort to rouse his troop to meet Raimon Roger, but remained near the base of the hill. The smile remained affixed in place as well.

Raimon Roger moved to the fore, next to Guilhem the *gon-fanonier*, and hailed his relative as they drew close, calling him *my lord* and *my uncle*. Though he did so in such a way as one refers to either a true blood uncle or merely an intimate of the family, and Andreas could not tell which the nobleman was. Since Raimon Roger was related through blood or marriage to much of the nobility in the Languedoc, as well as Iberia, England, the Holy Roman Empire, and France, including the king in Paris, Philippe himself, it was lacking in surprise that Raimon Roger should be a relative of this particular baron before them.

The Unknown did not refer to Raimon Roger as *nephew* or any other term endearing, but simply called out to *my lord Viscount*. The man raised sword, blade thrust skyward, brought the weapon to his face, cross guard momentarily parallel with his deep green eyes. The noise of the *Carcassonais* dimmed. It was an odd gesture at such a time, for it was not a symbol of peace.

Raimon Roger withdrew his longsword and did likewise. Raimon Roger accepted the challenge. All upon the walls ceased utterance. Though it was hot summer, Raimon Roger spoke with an air crisp as late autumn, with very loud voice. "Do you have terms to offer, or must we ride to the meet?" Andreas could tell by the tone of the query that Raimon Roger knew already the answer. It was his way of informing his people gathered by the hundreds, perhaps thousands, atop the walls, watching in new silence, what fate awaited them all. The meet for parley would be but a singular sort of battle.

The Unknown did not move or alter his expression. Aware of his role in the unfolding drama, the baron replied with booming speech. "The meet for parley will be held in the pergola of the Count of Nevers, Herve de Donzy, in the tent of green rising in the center above all others." The baron gestured toward the expansive pavilion. "Nevers has given the pledge of his youngest son, Philippe, as a hostage in guarantee of safe-conduct."

The Unknown looked back and nodded his head but once. A rift appeared in the warparty and a knight rode forward with a boy clinging around his waist. Dressed in a fine tunic of green and gold, the lad, who appeared no more than four, looked around wide-eyed at the Trencavel knights before him and the people gathered atop the walls. Though seeking to appear brave, he clearly was scared. A vulnerable child among men at arms. Protected only by the promises of his father. Andreas thought such a coin not worth its weight in lead, much less in silver or gold.

Raimon Roger appraised the boy. "Are there others?"

"There are no others, only him. Nevers dotes on the boy. The Count is the most powerful lord amongst us. As Nevers goes so goes the army. He will not lay siege to the city with the lad inside. Philippe is a strong guarantor of peace."

Raimon Roger looked over the sea of tents and focused on the pergola of the Count of Nevers. "I have heard Herve does indeed dote on his son. Very well." Raimon Roger motioned and two knights withdrew from the ranks and moved forward. "Take the boy straightaway to the *Chateau Comtal*. See to it that he is well protected and well cared for, given every comfort." The lead knight of the two took the boy from the cavalier of the Unknown, and they rode toward the Narbonne Gate.

"We go to the pergola of the Count of Nevers." As he wheeled his horse about, a black *arabit*, tall and densely muscled, the Northern Baron who spoke Occitan fluently, the Unknown relative of Raimon Roger, turned his piercing, pale blue eyes and wide, noble brow toward Andreas for but a moment, giving a look that was both knowing and curious, imploring but asking nothing, pointed but falling short of giving recognition. Andreas sought to understand such. The Unknown spurred his mount toward the sea of tents and both companies followed. As the *châtelain* set out for the encampment of the enemy, one thought rose above all others. He need make journey to Montsegur in the lower reaches of the Pyrenees after siege, and there have solitary sojourn. That thought again. Why think on such now?

They rode across the plain of burnt grass and scorched earth at a pace beyond a trot but short of a gallop, a canter, the tempo at which one moves to attend to pressing but not urgent business. The Unknown directed his *arabit* this way and that through the tents of the French, as if tracing a geometric pattern, like the labyrinth etched in the floor of the cathedral of

Chartres. Andreas had went there once as a boy with his father on a journey to Paris.

Only himself and his father.

It was the sole time he had felt close to his father since the commencing of the cruel dreams, and the more cruel spurning of his torment of the night. They had both walked the maze in the cathedral of Chartres as many others did, in lieu of making actual pilgrimage to the Holy Land. His father had spoken kindly to him, saying *Deu* looks at the heart. "If never you make journey to Outremer, to the Holy Land in the natural, Andreas, have sojourn there in your heart and that is enough for him." It occurred to Andreas now, as they rode between tents, that it was the only time ever that he felt safe, unchallenged as a child, and lacked the need to battle any unseen thing.

His father had continued to instruct him as they journeyed to Paris and back to Chartres, but once they passed south of Orleans, he grew cold and distant once more. Whatever light and warmth his father had surprisingly exuded for several days in the North, had sprung from a place now slammed shut, never to be pried open again. His father had scorned Andreas on the final night of their return journey for crying aloud in his sleep.

A noise ripped his brain, a shriek, and the pain concentrated at the crown of his head and spread like a web round his skull. All thoughts of labyrinths and pilgrimage and Outremer seemed swept from his mind, and he saw only a barren wall of sheer rock he must climb and there remain. "You shall achieve your deliverance."

The Unknown stopped within sighting of the expansive green pergola adorned with bright gold cord at the edges, but still some yards distant. He held out his arm, palm vertical and to the fore. The countenance of the man grew even sterner, if such a thing was possible. "Your company need halt here my Lord Viscount. You and your *châtelain* must come alone." The man not only spoke Occitan, but was fluent with a strong Provençal accent, like speakers of the language Andreas had conversed with from Avignon, Arles, and Orange.

Raimon Roger looked the baron in the eye, his own eyes remaining deep wells of peace. "I bring eight men and my *châtelain* into the pergola, else I return to Carcassonne." The fire flickered in the depths for but a moment. "Think not that I cannot fight my way back to my city. My *châtelain* is the hero of Beziers. The lone hero of an evil battle. " Raimon Roger paused, unblinking eyes met those of the Unknown. "It is because of him, his early warning, and our preparation you are compelled to make parley. Do not think it otherwise."

The Unknown raised an eyebrow and his look was shot through with the briefest flash of surprise, a ripple moving at speed, easily missed if Andreas had not been studying the man. Here was the scene of the pitched battle, the ground where it was to be fought. His young, naïve lord, Viscount Raimon Roger Trencavel, knew the ground upon which he trod, knew it well.

The Unknown faltered but for a moment more, in the quick but awkward way of those unaccustomed to challenge or obstacle, proving that Raimon Roger could indeed fight his way back to *la cite*. "Bring the eight others you choose and follow me." With that he dismounted, turned on his heel and strode briskly toward the tent as green, gilded edge cloth gave way from the inside, revealed the opulence within.

Raimon Roger turned to Andreas. "Choose seven others to accompany us besides Anfos, and choose well I pray you for your very lives and all those within Carcassonne may hinge on the choice. We shall dismount while the rest remain on horse and at the ready. I desire you to be a witness to what is to come. Only I ask you do not deter me from the road I must walk. Will you accede to my request?"

Andreas spoke nothing, but merely looked Raimon Roger in the eye, even as his hand grasped his sword. He wanted to charge the company of thirty Frenchmen, slay them all, including the Unknown, and return to Carcassonne. He had no wish to linger among foreign tents outside the walls.

Raimon Roger laid his palm on Andreas's chest. "My friend, you will live to fight another day. Do not deter me from my course. I know you, Andreas. I knew you before ever you practiced swordplay with a *pels*. I know now what thoughts fill your mind." Raimon Roger lowered his voice and the words were terse. "But you must hold."

Andreas dismounted without making a reply and motioned to Anfos and the other seven he wanted with him and they unhorsed themselves and fell in step behind his lord, even as Andreas shot a look to the others to remain at the ready. The walk to the pavilion seemed as a slow march into an ever darkening cave. The grassy alley between pergolas steadily seemed to shrink and the doorway to the tent grew larger and all else faded. The Unknown stopped at the entrance and welcomed in Raimon Roger. Then he allowed the flaps to fall down partway, reducing the opening to only the width of a man, as if he were merely tolerating the entry of the rest.

The lords and knights of France gathered in the tent were many. Andreas thought that nearly all the nobles of King Philippe Augustus, the sum of the rulers of the North, must be assembled in this palatial canopy. Only the king himself was not present. The floor was laid with fine carpets of many colors, some of which appeared Oriental, as if Turkish or Egyptian, with bright geometric patterns. The furniture was of dark woods and brocaded in rich-colored cottons and silks. Tapestries of crests and standards and scenes of the hunt and of battle, most of knitted wool, ringed the cavernous tent, itself over half the size of the Trencavel great hall. Below the wall hangings, all about the pergola were knights in mail with longswords held against their breasts. In the center was a long, finely carved trestle table, some twenty feet from end to end. Though it appeared as if more than a score could comfortably dine upon the heavy, dark, gilded edge spread, only three chairs were on the opposing side. Those were occupied on the left by a lord Andreas had seen before but whose name he could not recall. On the right, there was the man whose surcoat matched the regalia arrayed about the pergola, the Count of Nevers himself, Herve de Donzy. In the center, in a large chair covered in silk brocades and gilded and set with sapphire and emerald, sat the abbot of Citeaux, Armand Amaury, the living papal legate of the Languedoc, who had benefited immensely from the death the year past of his counterpart, Pierre de Castelnau. Amaury bore the barest foundation of a smile, and seemed greatly pleased at the spectacle around him. Dressed in spotless white vestments and mitre, bearing a golden scepter, and multiple bejeweled rings, he was the lord of lords of this assembly, of this crusade, and was clearly enjoying holding court with such a prize as the Viscount of Carcassonne,

Albi, and Beziers before him. An intrepid hunter whose hounds
had trapped a mighty stag.

The Count of Nevers, for his part, furrowed his dark, thick
brow and studied cautiously Raimon Roger as one would accord
proper respect to a worthy enemy. He seemed apprehensive and
not overjoyed to be hosting parley. Andreas sensed that underneath it all, the man was merely a worried father who wished to
return home with his son. Did he presume too much? The Count
had come to do quarantine, his forty days of service to Pope and
Church for the absolution of his own sins, and cared not if the
people of the South were allotted either destruction or salvation.
A curious thing to see such in a man Andreas had never heretofore laid eyes upon.

The man in the left seat had sharp, active blue eyes that
seemed ever alert and prepared for battle. He would not sit still,
but kept leaving his chair or summoning his knights or squires
to him and issuing orders which were hastily carried out. He was
the one who had made charge to save a comrade escaped from
the burning cat outside *San Miquel*. A man of courage. Why is
he at table? The memory of the name returned to Andreas. The
man was Simon de Montfort, the Earl of Leicester in England,
but a lord in name only for his claim to the title was not recognized by King John. Such a dispossessed noble would be on
pilgrimage seeking more than the remission of sins. Simon was
the one Andreas had seen talking with Armand Amaury outside
Beziers as the *rotiers* streamed into the city. Andreas had also
heard tell of their conversation.

The papal legate, ever at the center of it all, cleared his throat
even as he focused on Raimon Roger, ignoring all others.

Raimon Roger took the bold step of approaching the table
ere he was bidden to do so. He stopped only a yard from the
lengthy table, opposite Armand Amaury, and spoke first. "I
know not your terms, my lord, though I may guess." He paused
as eyes all around him grew wide in surprise. "Here are mine."

Amaury held up his hand, palm outward. "Before you speak,
my lord Viscount, I think it prudent if you hear first our terms."
Andreas saw movement in the direction of Simon de Montfort,
and he drew his sword ere they were surrounded by a score of
knights bearing the de Montfort crest.

Amaury's lips curled into a thin smile.

The Count of Nevers rose to his feet. "I was not thus in-formed." He pointed in the direction of Carcassonne. "My son is hostage behind those walls."

Amaury laid a hand on the shoulder of Nevers to calm him. "No harm will come to your son, Herve. That I will promise you. The Viscount and his men will not return to the city. They're to be our hostages guaranteeing the return of your son, and..." The papal legate paused, a look of triumph on his face, "and the sur-render of Carcassonne."

"You will burn in hell you whoreson of a priest." Andreas spat on a fine carpet. "You are naught but a little pope, preening and pretentious. Your word is worth as little to you as the lives of the *Bitterois*." Andreas's rage burned hot. There was no longer any benefit in pretense. "I saw you outside of Beziers, convers-ing with de Montfort." Andreas pointed at the dispossessed lord. "Word has spread that the Earl of Leicester asked you how they would know heretic from Christian in Beziers. You said to 'slay them all, God will know his own.'" Andreas was shouting, vent-ing his full fury on the papal legate. "Do you deny it, hellspawn? Do you have so little regard for the flock you have been given charge to oversee? Is your word as worthless to you as the lives of the *Bitterois*? For that is the worth of your life to me."

Amaury flinched and his face flushed red. Andreas's fiery missiles had pierced that coiffed exterior. "I am not the one on trial here." The voice of the papal legate was husky, thick, barely controlled. "There was a trial by combat over Beziers and the right prevailed. The Cross and righteous justice itself were our standard."

Andreas tightened his grip on his sword. He could have slit the throat of the papal legate before any knight could intervene. The blade quivered as if it would do the deed on its own. "You prevailed because of fools who could not close a gate. Or was it treachery? How much did you pay the gatekeepers? Perhaps they are to be found amongst us here with new wealth." Andreas looked around as if certain to spot them in some corner of the tent. "If you seek to put Carcassonne to the sword, the son of Herve de Donzy will die as well." Andreas pointed at the Count of Nevers, who was on his feet.

The *châtelain* saw something else. A reddish light, small at first, appeared on the ceiling of the pergola and grew as if it possessed life, filling the air above the table. A single ray projected from the whole, reached low, condescended to earth and illumined the surcoat of Raimon Roger with a crimson light that sharpened into the shape of a Latin cross, crisp and alive.

It was as the sight Andreas had witnessed in San Peire in Montpellier the previous time they stood in the presence of the papal legate, yet there was no window this time, no point of entry in the natural for the light of the sun.

No other soul in the assembly seemed cognizant of the light, the rose cross, or any sense of the miraculous. He looked around the tent at the lords and knights assembled there, all with crosses of cloth sewn to their surcoats. His eyes returned to his lord and the crimson cross of light.

Andreas wanted to cry out in proclamation, but stifled the urge.

Amaury, his composure regained, smiled his wide smile as his eyes gleamed a wily glint. "All shall be allowed their leave from the city, but only with their shirts and sins still upon them. All other worldly wealth must be abandoned within Carcassonne." The papal legate looked to Andreas, and the *châtelain* knew with certitude what was to come, all he had feared. Safe passage would indeed be given, but Raimon Roger, the Viscount of Carcassonne, Albi, and Beziers himself, would be the price of such a grant. That was the request to which his lord had asked Andreas to accede. In spite of the words of Raimon Roger, Andreas was not prepared to yield his Viscount to the French, either as prisoner or sacrifice.

Raimon Roger withdrew his sword.

Andreas's first excitement drew quickly to anger as the cross of light seemed not a blessed sign but a cruel trick, a prank of a wanton deity who seemed to find enjoyment in the slaughter of innocents.

Was *Deu* taunting him?

Was not the act of taking the Cross a divine assurance of triumph?

It was assuredly not a sign of victory but of rank humiliation, of abject shame. Would yet another city be put to the sword at

the behest of Innocent's faithless envoy? Raimon Roger turned
the sword horizontal and bore it upon his open palms to the
papal legate. Armand Amaury gave a solemn nod and extended
his own hands and accepted the weapon. The little pope handed
it to Simon de Montfort, the Earl of Leicester.

Andreas motioned to the company to linger near the entrance of the pergola at the ready, they knew all of them the
signals well, and he nodded almost imperceptibly for Anfos to
follow him quickly. As all others in the pergola were focused
upon Raimon Roger, Andreas and Anfos flanked their lord at
the table. The others appeared hardly to notice, as if he and Anfos had ever been at the side of their lord. The Unknown was
nowhere within sighting. Throwing a rapid glance of warning
to his compatriots at the entrance, Andreas looked forward and
spoke to Raimon Roger without turning his head. "My lord, we
are taking you from here. I will not yield you."

The papal legate turned his eyes in surprise to Andreas. The
perceptive and ever alert Abbot had heard. "It is a pity, Raimon
Roger, that your considerable abilities have been wasted shielding heretics and their concealers. But you prove quite valuable
now as the condition of the surrender of Carcassonne and of the
freedom of your people. As I spoke truly unto you in the church
of San Peire in Montpellier, we keep no faith with those who
keep faith with heretics."

Raimon Roger spoke without turning his head and with
scarce movement of his lips. "Andreas, take your leave while you
may, this is no longer your fight."

The Count of Nevers heard as well but did nothing except to
look even more as if he wished to return to his own lands with
his son and be rid of the politics of the Church and of the South.

Simon de Montfort, already gesturing, issuing orders to others, leapt to his feet and some dozen additional knights began
approaching the table from the outer reaches of the pergola.

Andreas hooked an arm around that of Raimon Roger. "We
leave now, my lord."

With astonishingly quick movement, Raimon Roger deftly withdrew his arm before Andreas could tighten his hold,
and placing hands on the waist of the *châtelain*, the Viscount
wheeled Andreas round and gave both he and Anfos a stiff shove

toward their company and the doorway. "This is my path. Do not deter me. Lead my people to safe passage. Now go!"

Andreas brandished his sword high. "No, my lord! I will not yield!"

The cavaliers filled the gap between Andreas and Raimon Roger and surrounded the *châtelain* and his sergeant at arms. "If you would take my lord, then these fine carpets will bleed red with your lifeblood before ever you lay a hand on him."

The voice of Raimon Roger was no longer whisper. "All will be given safe passage to leave my lands. Farewell, my friend." Andreas looked upon Raimon Roger, studied him for briefest moment. Firmer resolve, though quiet it was, never had he witnessed before.

Two lines of knights were behind and one was in front. Their adversary moved slowly, warily as if hoping for surrender. The knights between them looked to Andreas then back to Raimon Roger, as if unsure whom to secure first. More cavaliers approached from the entrance and formed a half-circle around Andreas, separating him from Anfos.

"*Memento mori!*" Raimon Roger loosed the cry. "*Paratge!*"

Andreas whistled the song of the thrush. Anfos loosed a battle cry and charged, flanked by the other Trencavel knights. Andreas raised sword and charged the knights who ringed him, sought to break through to Anfos. The circle collapsed round them, but he knocked over the cavalier in front of him and broke through.

"Point of the spear!" Andreas joined up with Anfos, who was turning his small troop toward the door of the tent. Andreas moved in front and became the point of the formation as they broke through the outer ring of knights and barreled over a grouping of pages and squires, knocking them to ground but drawing no blood. The pursuit closed in from the side in a pincer movement and the four Trencavel knights in the rear were cut down. Andreas pressed forward, only ten feet from sunlight. He slay one knight, then another, then a bowman before he could loose any bolts. He and Anfos stumbled through the tent opening into daylight and called for their horses.

The Trencavel knight left in oversight outside had wisely moved the cavalcade close to the pergola. The mounted knights of the Viscount of Carcassonne, Albi, and Beziers swung around and formed a rear guard, slaying any French who emerged from the tent until Andreas and Anfos and the other two survivors were horsed and on the move at full gallop.

The French gave no more pursuit. The cavalcade zigzagged back through the labyrinth and emerged onto the abandoned battlefield. Carcassonne dominated the sight before them, but all Andreas had in his vision was the mountains beyond, the High Languedoc. Like a burst of sulfur from the abyss, it occurred to Andreas that Raimon Roger was no longer the Viscount of Carcassonne, Albi, and Beziers. He was likely already in fetters.

As *châtelain*, Andreas was now the de facto leader of these lands. In truth, there was an abeyance, for though Carcassonne was his to command he wished to have none of it. He would surrender the city for the safekeeping of its people, even if all could only leave with but their shirts and their sins upon them. At last, he lowered his sights and looked upon the city he so loved. The merlons of the ancient sandstone walls gleamed in the sun. The ramparts still swarmed with those waiting in expectation. Those walls would not come down, would not be breached, but Carcassonne had in fact already fallen. Without their Viscount, the people would be lost, sheep robbed of their shepherd.

The shepherd would perish that the sheep may have life. This was the final quest of Raimon Roger, why his lord had made agreement to parley. Raimon Roger had known full well what awaited him.

The *châtelain* knew it also. Andreas would spend one last night in his own bedchamber, if he slept at all. Tomorrow the city would empty. Only the frightened little boy of the Count of Nevers would be left behind. By all rules of warfare, Andreas had the right, some would even say the duty, to slay the child, to have him hanged atop the ramparts, for such was deemed to be the fate of the token of a broken pledge of safe-conduct. Yet to do so would be self-murder en masse. Andreas knew he could never issue such an order.

It startled him to realize that pity for the lad was also pity for himself. Never had he felt like such a lost little boy as at this moment. It was a terrifying free fall and his belly knotted hard. Robbed of all who had loved him, the few who truly knew him, Andreas himself felt alone. His calling was to lead in support of a greater leader. Raimon Roger had been—still was, Andreas admonished himself—such a leader.

Raimon Roger had spoken truly when he said he would not allow another *gran mazel* on his lands, would do anything to prevent it. "Greater love has no man than this…" Raimon Roger would perish and a Frenchman would take his place.

Armand Amaury had placed the sword of Raimon Roger in the hands of Simon de Montfort.

It was an abomination to their feudal laws, and an alien thought to Andreas. But nothing was true and right in this Crusade. The old laws, the time-honored customs were no longer in force.

He would return to Carcassonne one last time, but it was no longer his home.

CHAPTER 34

15 AUGUST 1209
THE FEAST DAY OF THE VIRGIN MARIA

At cockcrow there was a sharp pounding upon Eva's door. She had not bothered to dress for bed and had slept atop the blankets in her gray woolen robe. She arose slowly to answer the knocking. Her nose and throat burned as if she had the cough. She opened the door.

The Painter stood before her. He bore an axe and his brown eyes were gray, cold, inscrutable. "The slayer of Claris has been found. Grab your warbow and take your leave. We go to take our retribution."

Eva blinked hard, rubbed her eyes. Never had she felt as tired as at this moment. Her spirit was many heavy rocks piled within her. "In Avignon?"

"Near that accursed house."

Eva felt herself in a stupor, noticed as if an observer that the pace of her movement saw increase. She snatched up both bow and quarrels. "How know you this?"

"There is no time to speak of it. We have only minutes to act."

Eva left her room and the Inn itself behind the Painter and Renart. She followed close, bow in her right hand, quarrels in her left. The streets were not yet fully suffused with the day's first light. Her thoughts informed her that her feet ran through alleys and rats scattered at their approach. They moved in the direction of the dwelling with façade under repair. The city still slumbered.

They reached the place where the alley opened into the street of the jewelers. The Painter halted and Renart and Eva behind him. His face was red, his voice terse but a whisper. "The man wears a tunic of green. He stands in an alley behind that house opposite." The Painter nodded toward a residence on the opposing side of the street three houses up the hill from where they crouched in the alley. "One by one we cross the street and take up positions at each point where the man might escape.

Eva was fully awake now, her senses alert, attuned to every sound and movement.

The Painter motioned toward the other side of the street. "I will go straight across the street. Eva, you walk up the street and turn down the alley past the third house. Renart will approach from another direction. We will keep the man from fleeing while you loose upon him."

Eva's eyes grew wide and her breath shallow. "I have only loosed upon my target of canvas before."

"You can do this, Eva. The daughter of Anselme must do this."

She looked upon the Painter and saw her father.

"It is preferred to slay him by arrow from a distance. It is far better if none of us reveal ourselves this day." He grasped her hand. "This man means to see you dead. It was you he sought to slay. He will not halt his murderous endeavors. Now we take the fight to him."

Eva fingered the hemp string on her bow. "How do you know it is the man?"

Renart put his hand on Eva's shoulder. "You must have trust of us."

She looked him in the eye. "I do have trust of you both. But you need tell me when to loose."

"Once we have crossed the street and taken refuge behind the houses we will be able to see one another. If the man looks toward you, Eva, he will see only light from the rising sun. Aim for his heart. If he remains standing after the first bolt, pierce him once more. Do you comprehend?"

Eva nodded, her mouth devoid of spittle, her spirit resolved. The slaying of Claris had changed many things. Another thought told her that the Painter had led men into battle before. Eva knew she must be bold. This day the Painter led her into battle. She hunted a restless evil that must be tracked down and defeated.

Without another word, the Painter clutched his axe, rose, and walked across the street. Eva stood up. Once he disappeared behind the dwellings opposite, Eva turned onto the street of the jewelers and walked toward *la cathedrale de Notre Dame de Doms*. She attempted to carry bow and quarrels casually, as if one could do such a thing on a city street. She turned to the left into the perpendicular alleyway past the third house. She heard Renart moving across the street behind her but did not look back. The alleyway she walked met another behind the houses that ran parallel on the opposing side of the street of the jewelers. There was a niche that allowed her a view of the alleyway without being seen.

Two men stood behind a house, one in tunic of green looking impatient, the other in the coarse beast-colored tunic of a pilgrim. Both had cowls raised. Eva had hers raised as well. She had expected only one man to be present. She noticed also one of the serving boys from the Inn of Renart across the alley, his face visible above a stack of wooden barrels. She knew at that moment the serving boys were in fact the sons of Renart. The one opposite her was the scout. Renart was also more than the proprietor of an inn.

She saw the Painter and Renart, both in position.

At this time yesterday morn, Claris had slumbered in the room next to hers.

The moment of retribution was before her.

Eva nocked an arrow and drew back the bow, kept it pointed at the cobbles. Her cheeks and forehead were hot, her heart pounded in her head as if her very earlobes would vibrate off her skull. The Painter nodded. An alley cat ran noisily past her in pursuit of a spectacularly plump rat. The man in green looked up, shielded his eyes against the breaking dawn. Then he drew back, grasped a door handle. Eva raised her bow. The man turned. Eva loosed. The arrow shot down the alley with a low, angry whistle, plunged itself into his shoulder. The man in green released a yelp of pain. A bright hurling arc flew toward her. She drew back as a silver dagger struck the corner of the house, inches from her face. The owner of the dagger in pilgrim tunic flew toward her as well. She froze. When he drew within two yards of her he was slammed against the back of the house and thrown to ground. Renart grasped the thrown silver dagger and slit his throat. The dagger had jewels upon the handle; emerald, ruby, and sapphire.

The man in green opened the door and disappeared.

The Painter ran up. "Abandon the body, we need take our leave."

"What of the one in green. He is wounded." Eva was prepared to change in after him. All fear had departed.

The Painter grabbed them both and pulled them down the alley back toward the street of the jewelers.

They took a roundabout route in their return to the Inn of Renart. The Painter produced another robe from under his tunic and inside it they wrapped all their weaponry to conceal sight and sound of it. When they reached the back door of the Inn, Raphael opened it and Pietro beckoned them in.

Eva's spirit within no longer rocks but fire.

Her only thought that she wished she had arrow-shot the man in green through the heart.

CHAPTER 35

15 AUGUST 1209
THE FEAST DAY OF THE VIRGIN MARIA

nfos unlocked the Aude Gate at daybreak. One by one the *Carcassonais* took their leave from *la cite*. The Aude Gate was little more than a doorway. All were searched by the knights of the Count of Nevers. All were thus taunted: "You leave only with your shirts and your sins still upon you." A few merchants foolish enough to wear their finery had their buttons of mother of pearl ripped from their shirts, but were otherwise unmolested.

Andreas observed from the ramparts. It was dawn on the feast day of the Virgin Maria. Another feast day without a feast. He stood with Philippe, the son of Herve de Donzy, at the place where the walls of the *Chateau Comtal* were also the outer walls of Carcassonne itself. Andreas wore chain mail, his new surcoat, and his belt of weaponry. He wished to make it clear that the battle was not ended until all had safely departed Carcassonne.

The egress of some forty-thousand souls through a narrow portal was not a short-lived endeavor, even with the abandonment of all their worldly goods. The sun rose to its apex and started to make descent. The Count of Nevers enforced the strictures of the agreement. All were allowed safe conduct to go where they would. The *Carcassonais* went mostly to the south towards Foix and to the West towards Toulouse. A few turned to the east or to the north, presumably to leave the Languedoc altogether.

When fewer than one-hundred remained in the city, Andreas led the boy down from the ramparts, and back inside the *Chateau*. He returned to his bedchamber and stripped off his belt of weaponry, his surcoat, his armor, and his fine tunic. All that remained upon him was a thin inner tunic; the two amulets, the sling, and the empty pouch concealed beneath.

He would take that chance.

He left the *Chateau,* walked through the courtyard, out the open Oriental Gate, past the palace of the Bishop of Carcassonne, and joined the line. Only armorless, weaponless knights of Trencavel remained to take their leave.

When Andreas reached the Aude Gate, he released Philippe, who ran to his father. The Count of Nevers nodded his thanks to Andreas, picked up his son, and rode off. Yet four of his knights lingered. One spoke. "My lord has commanded us to escort you where you wish to go. We will take you as far as Toulouse."

Andreas did not wish to tell them that he would make journey to Montsegur in the Pyrenees. "I go to the mountains. If you will take me as far as the foothills, that is enough for me."

The *châtelain* turned to his sergeant at arms. "Anfos, to where will you go?"

"I have many relations in Toulouse. The count of Toulouse will need more knights I think. It will not be long until he is excommunicated once more."

Andreas smiled. "No, I think not. Godspeed my friend. *Paratge.*"

"And to you as well. Thousands of living souls owe you this day their very lives." Anfos set his face toward Toulouse and commenced his journey.

Andreas called out after him. "It is not I to whom their debt is due!"

The lead knight of Raimon Roger Trencavel I, Viscount of Carcassonne, Albi, and Beziers went to horse along with the four knights of Nevers and they began the ride south.

The *châtelain* glanced back to see Armand Amaury and Simon de Montfort enter Carcassonne through the Aude Gate.

Andreas turned his head away and forced himself to look upon the Pyrenees Mountains.

AUTHOR'S NOTE

When I was in college, I came across a book entitled *The Occult and the Third Reich*. This book discussed not only the general interest of the Nazis in the occult, but Hitler's particular fascination with the Albigensians (or Cathars) as potential possessors of the Holy Grail. A fascination so great that he sent individuals into the Languedoc in the 1930s and 1940s in search of the much coveted relic.

Much of *The Occult and the Third Reich* is devoted to the Albigensian Crusade. It was the first time I read about the Crusade against heresy. One of the individuals sent by Hitler in pursuit of the Grail, Otto Rahn, wrote of the Albigensian Crusade as the *Crusade Against the Grail*. The grail relic he sought, and believed the Cathars to have borne, was not the cup of Christ.

I was surprised I had never heard anything about this crusade before, and I read whatever I could get my hands on about the Languedoc, Provence, Albigensians, Waldensians, the Trencavels, the Occitan language. I learned of the Beguines and the many movements toward freedom that were birthed during this age. Tyranny is found here as well, as the Inquisition began after the Crusade, around the year 1230, as a concerted effort to round up the remaining Cathars not ensnared in the net of the Crusaders.

The question that arose for me as I read more books and articles about the Crusade against heresy was this: In such a confusing age, when Christians were battling Christians, what does it look like to be a true Christian, live like a true Christian? It's a question that provokes me still. *Taking the Cross* grew out of my attempts to answer it.

One of the unique aspects of the Albigensian Crusade from a historical perspective is that there are three surviving contemporary accounts. This is extremely uncommon for events that took place before the invention of the printing press in the fifteenth century. Two of the accounts were written by chroniclers in favor of the Crusade. While the third account, the *Chanson de la Croisade Albigeoise* (Song of the Albigensian Crusade), by far the best known of the three, was written by two different natives of the Languedoc, the first half written by one very much in favor of the Crusade, and the second half by one very strongly opposed to it. The *Chanson* is an epic poem written in Occitan, the language of the troubadours. It was meant to be sung at the courts of nobility. The oldest surviving copy of the *Chanson* dates from the year 1275, and is at the *Bibliotheque Nationale* in Paris.

One of the prominent Occitan words in the *Chanson* is *paratge*. This word was to the Languedoc of 1209 what the word freedom is to Americans today. It captured the heart of what they held most dear. *Paratge* is often rendered in English as nobility, but is essentially an untranslatable word. It speaks to an entire way of living and thinking about life, an entire code of ethics about how one should treat others. Embodied within it, among other things, are concepts of grace, forgiveness, right living, balance, tolerance for others, honor, excellence, and nobility of soul. It was written of the Crusader Simon de Montfort in the *Chanson* that he besmirched *paratge*.

Most historical accounts of the Crusade written in recent years, including *The Perfect Heresy* by Stephen O'Shea, focus completely on the Catholic – Albigensian/Cathar dynamic of the Crusade. Most recent works of fiction set in the Languedoc in the early thirteenth century do the same, such as *Daughters of the Grail* by Elizabeth Chadwick, and *Labyrinth* by Kate Mosse, and essentially distilled to a message of Good Cathars – Bad Catholics. However, the spiritual dynamics of the Languedoc in 1209 were far more complex.

There was a document compiled by Rainaud, the Bishop of Beziers that listed the names of two hundred and twenty two heretics in Beziers. While the majority of names on the list are Cathar Perfects, a handful of the names have the letters *val* next to them, indicating *valdenses*. However, there were likely more than a dozen *valdenses* or secret friends of Vaudes – or Peter Waldo – in Beziers, because they tended to be more covert and less prominent in society, being called as they were the Poor of Lyon. While the highborn of the Languedoc tended to be drawn toward the Cathars, many of the so-called lowborn were *valdenses*.

The sack of Beziers did occur on 22 July 1209, the feast day of Mary Magdalen. There is no historical evidence I found that any of the *Bitterois* survived until sunset that day. Perhaps there was an individual or two, like Andreas, that somehow escaped to warn Viscount Trencavel. While there are some differing perspectives among historians about whether or not the Crusaders arrived at Beziers on 21 July or 22 July, there is nearly universal agreement that the massacre of the city happened on 22 July. The churches of the city, including the Church of St. Mary Magdalen, were packed full by those seeking sanctuary where there was none. The *rotiers* did burn the city upon having their plunder stripped from them by the crusading knights. Beziers was deemed to be cursed and sat vacant for years afterward, a ravaged, urban, fallow field. To put the scale of the Medieval slaughter of twenty thousand *Bitterois* in perspective, Rome and London both had around twenty five thousand residents at this time. In 1209, Beziers was one of the more populated, and wealthier, cities in Europe.

The Beguines had their beginning in the second half of the twelfth century in what is now Belgium. The movement spread throughout Christendom during the thirteenth century until they too were eventually branded heretics and persecuted by the Inquisition. Part of the reason that I chose the city of Orange as the setting of the beguinage that is Eva's home is because of the subsequent ties that the Principality of Orange would have with the Low Countries, the Netherlands in particular. Though what we know now as the color orange was called red-yellow during the Middle Ages, this color came later to be called orange and to be associated with the city of Orange, France. It is where the Dutch Royal House of Orange derives both its color and its name.

The initial acceptance of the Beguines is an example of what would typically happen before the Albigensian Crusade, where a new religious movement would be absorbed into the Catholic Church rather than repulsed by it. The treatment of the Waldensians was atypical of previous centuries, but would become for several centuries the new normal. In 1209, by contrast, the same year that the Waldensians were being hunted by the Crusade against heresy, a new order led by a budding monk named Francis from the city of Assisi was recognized by Pope Innocent III, and the Franciscans came into being.

Viscount Raimon Roger Trencavel was taken hostage by the Crusaders outside Carcassonne after being granted safe-conduct. There is much debate as to what actually happened in the pergola of the Count of Nevers. Some, such as O'Shea, argue that in no wise would Trencavel have surrendered himself. The chronicler of the *Chanson* says Trencavel made himself a prisoner. There is widespread assumption but less evidence that Trencavel was at the least a Cathar *credente*. This is based primarily on the fact that Trencavel's tutor, Bertran de Saissac (mentioned in chapter 11) was a Cathar Perfect. Yet there were many spiritual influences in the Languedoc, and Trencavel could have chosen any number of routes before his death in the fall of 1209.

The *Carcassonais* indeed took their leave from *la cite* on the Feast Day of the Virgin Mary, 15 August 1209, with naught but their shirts upon them.

Whether all left with their sins still upon them as well is another matter.

Thankfully, no church official truly has the authority to condemn a person for or absolve a person from their sins. Perhaps here is where we begin to answer the question of where the true Christians were during the Albigensian Crusade. The true church is unseen and is composed of those, whether Catholic, Protestant, Orthodox, or none of the above, who have surrendered their lives to blessed *Jhesu* and no other man, whether that man be president or bishop, king or pope. *Jhesu* alone has authority to forgive sins. For He said "behold the Kingdom of Heaven is within you." It is found not in the Holy Land, the Languedoc, Rome, or any other earthly place. *Jhesu*, born of the Virgin Mary, born of flesh and Spirit, calls for surrender of body, soul, and spirit still today. May you know this sweet surrender and choose to have the King of the unseen church and his kingdom come to reside within you as well.

ACKNOWLEDGMENTS

As I have researched, written, and rewritten Taking the Cross over the past eight years, I have been continually humbled by the literally dozens of people that have provided help in some form. The people of Bridgewood Community Church have supported me in so many ways. I would not even try to list everyone here, but know that if you have provided ideas, feedback, encouragement, inspiration, and/or prayer, I am truly grateful. I can't say how much it meant to have people still asking "how's the book going?" three, four, and five years in. Jim Olson, I will always be grateful to you for "calling me out" and encouraging me to follow my calling. Diane Stores and Janet Nelson, I could not have written this novel without the freedom you have helped bring to my life. Julie Hawkinson, who read several drafts and greatly helped improve the flow of the story, and who kept saying she was waiting for the next installment. Allison Bottke, who first asked me eight years ago "when are you going to write a novel?" and opened up her extensive network of literary contacts to me. Kyle Duncan, who encouraged me to keep going and finish a complete novel. Keith Wall, who gave invaluable feedback for my first draft, including encouraging me to continue alternating the chapters between Andreas and Eva. My publisher, John Koehler, for seeing the possibilities in Taking the Cross and taking a chance on a first-time novelist. My editor, Joe Coccaro, who worked hard not only to help me keep the thirteenth century voice I was striving for but to improve on it. Extended family members who provided feedback, encouragement, and prayer, particularly Shara Anderson, Stacy Olson, and Heidi Gnadke. An extra thanks to Heidi for her excellent photography. My wife, Tricia, who helped me develop the characters, especially Andreas and Eva, and did so many of things needed to keep a household running while I worked two full time jobs (the second job being this novel). God has used you to help raise me up from the miry clay and set my feet on the rock. We have walked through so much together. I love you. Trenton and Logan your cheerful encouragement is always inspirational to me. I am truly blessed.

CPSIA information can be obtained at www.ICGtesting.com
Printed in the USA
BVOW04s1721210714

359747BV00003B/30/P